I0769340

Sweet TALK

a novel

RENA SAPON-WHITE AND ELLA SCHAEFER

For Leah and Rodrigo, who demonstrate just how sweet love can be.

CONTENT WARNING

This is an adult story with adult themes, language, and spice. We'd say it's a four chili pepper read (out of five). If that's cool with you, grab a pint of your favorite ice cream and dive in!

FOR IMMEDIATE RELEASE

Acclaimed Comedian Aarti Nair Named New Host of *Up Late!*

Network Taps Rising Star Following Guy Morrison's Departure

LA, CA June 2025 – CBT Studios announced that Aarti Nair will take the helm of the late-night talk show *Up Late!* effective in the fall. Nair, a versatile performer known for her sharp wit and compelling screen presence, succeeds Guy Morrison, who recently departed the show.

"Aarti brings an incredible combination of comedy chops, hosting experience, and fresh perspective that makes her the perfect fit for *Up Late!*" said Gretchen Gordon, CBT Studios President. "Her natural ability to connect with audiences and create pure entertainment is exactly what this show needs as we refocus on fun and laughter."

Nair brings extensive television experience to the role, having spent six seasons as a main cast member on the hit late-night program *Midnight Live*, where she rapidly advanced through the ranks to host the popular segment "Now News!" Her physical comedy, recurring characters, and incisive impressions made her a fan favorite and media darling.

Beyond television, Nair has established herself as a dynamic force in film and stand-up. She has appeared in acclaimed independent films, including the critically praised superheroine action comedy *The Red Dot*, showcasing her range as a performer. Nair has toured her stand-up across the country, where she has built a devoted following with her unique voice and perspective.

"I'm thrilled to bring my own style to *Up Late!* while honoring the show's legacy," said Nair. "Late-night television has always been about creating a space where we can laugh together while making sense of our world. I can't wait to invite viewers into that conversation every night."

The transition marks an exciting new chapter for *Up Late!* as the show pivots toward lighter entertainment. Nair's first episode as host will air Monday, September 29th 2025 on CBT.

Media Contact:

Diane Warnock

PR, CBT

dwarnock@cbt.com

CHAPTER 1
AARTI

ERRR! *Errr! Errr!*

My eyes fly open as the emergency distress signal that is my four-thirty a.m. wakeup call blares. The lithe, tan body of super-model Brigitte Blanchette jolts awake next to me. She falls off the bed with a thunk before struggling to untangle her Barbie limbs on the floor. It's physical comedy at its best–up there with my Shakira Does Mundane Tasks impression–except the panic swirling in my gut supersedes any possible humor I might find in the current situation.

You've done it now, Nair.

In the year-ish that Brigitte and I have been hooking up, the cardinal rules of our arrangement have been set in stone: no sleepovers, no PDA, just dinners in shadowy booths where wandering hands could caress a thigh beneath the table without an audience. This situationship isn't my first rodeo, nor will it be my last, and these are simply the guidelines that protect my heart and career from abject peril.

"Why would you get up at this ungodly hour?" Brigitte groans, voice muffled by the pillow she pulled off the bed with her.

"You said you were gonna drive home after a 'power nap' last night," I remind her brusquely, stalking to the kitchen for my morning matcha.

"*You* tired me out!" she protests.

I want to gloat at the orgasm-laden compliment beneath her complaint, but I'm too frustrated with myself to relish being the Casanova equivalent of a sleeping pill.

Brigitte has far less at stake in our clandestine relationship. Supermodels are allowed to be queer, or at the very least engage in public displays of sexual fluidity. Her personal brand thrives on a little edge. Mine depends on being relatable and safe—especially right now, with just one month until it's my turn to host the crown jewel of late night television.

Hosting *Up Late* is every comedian's pinnacle of success—the Beychella of career highs, if you will—and there was a collective hush of anticipation across the entertainment world after Guy Morrison was forced out. The network blamed budget cuts, but everyone knows the truth: he was too politically outspoken, and they needed someone who'd be hungry enough for the opportunity to play ball while offering plausible deniability to the accusations of an anti-woke agenda.

Ding ding ding. That's me.

Indian *and* a woman. The first of either demographic to host *Up Late* and a clear attempt to appease the backlash to Morrison's firing. The CBT president implied as much the day she offered me the gig. To the network, I'm two big checkmarks on a diversity spreadsheet. But to the brown girls who will be watching from their living rooms, I'm something else entirely. Dare I get cocky and proclaim myself an inspiration? Maybe I would have last week, but after being gifted another mile-high stack of rewrites with the note to "tone it down," I'm just holding out hope that I'll make it to TV, period.

Do I love being muzzled when fascism's on the rise? Hell no. Is the network exploiting the pressure I feel from my own communities to puppeteer me into the apolitical, brand-safe late-night host they prefer? Duh. But how could I walk away from this opportunity, strings be damned, knowing what it would've meant to young Aarti to see someone like her behind that iconic oak desk, knowing her own biggest dream wasn't totally impossible?

I know it's naïve to hold onto hope that despite the superficial reasons the network hired me, I might still find a way to create change from the inside. But hope mixed with stubborn faith has carried me this far, so I may as well carry that torch a little further.

Brigitte yawns her way into the kitchen, taking an uninvited sip of my searing hot matcha. She wrinkles her nose in annoyance.

"You need to leave through the service elevator," I tell her.

"Ew. Don't they use that for literal garbage?"

I shoot her a mocking smile and steal back my matcha. "Something like that."

"You're cranky in the morning," she sighs, tapping away on her phone.

"And you're not supposed to be here in the morning."

"You came too many times last night to still be stressed." Brigitte pouts her famously plush lips. "And to take it out on me of all people."

"You've got one job: look hot. I've got ten: look hot but not *that* hot, be funny but inoffensive, appear smart but not threateningly so, and somehow turn all of that into a show that won't get canceled before the wheatpaste on my posters has dried."

"This is true, I am unfairly hot-privileged." She slips on her flats by the door. "But it can't be that hard to make your show good. You're, like, the most naturally funny person on the planet."

"Is *that* why you frequent my bed?"

"Pretty much," she shrugs. "You're like if a lesbian ate Pete Davidson."

"I'll have to remember that one for when I never, ever come out."

She puts her hand on my shoulder and gives it a squeeze. "If only you were hot enough to be a supermodel, then you wouldn't have to worry so much about the whole being gay thing." She gives me a wink, then annoyingly pecks each of my cheeks before sashaying off. "Bye, bitch."

My sassy overnight guest represents the one demographic in my veritable grab-bag of diversity that I can–and do–conceal. If the network knew the *lesbian* part, I would've had a less than zero percent chance of landing this job. So for now, aside from a teensy corner of the internet who call themselves Gaartis (Gay Aartis, of course) and who are widely written off as fan-fic-obsessed wishful thinkers, that part of me is locked away tighter than Brigitte's legs around my shoulders last night.

I gulp down the rest of my scalding drink and head out the door to 68411 Hollywood Boulevard, where, in a few short weeks, my wildest dreams could finally come true... or collapse in spectacular ruin.

Midnight Live audition ideas

Hi I'm Aarti Nair and this is Tilda
Swinton being totally normal

this is Michael Cera selling a
used car

this is my mom talking about my
comedy career

Hi I'm Aarti Nair and this is Shakira
shopping for new furniture:

IKEA, IKEA ♪ ♫

CHAPTER 2
NOA

IT'S four-thirty a.m. and I'm dangling upside down from my Thinking Rod, eyes darting fiendishly around my inverted spice rack, when inspiration finally strikes. Basil. Saffron. *Bingo*.

The rusty pull-up bar came pre-installed in the doorframe of my cramped East Hollywood kitchen, the remnant of a former tenant who probably figured out Muscle Beach was too far in traffic for a daily commute. Despite carrying around nature's own kettlebells on my chest, my upper body strength is nothing to write home about, so for years I just used the bar as a spare towel rack. Until one night, very stoned, I realized I had enough strength to flip myself up and around to hang from the bar with my legs. Sometimes you need to stare down your ingredients from a new angle to get the recipe juices flowing. If that seems highly unusual, I don't care to hear it. I live alone and it is my flying-spaghetti-monster-given right to monkey around my apartment as I please. It's called being an adult.

I right myself, muttering calculations aloud as I swipe jars and sieves and scales out of crammed cupboards.

"Milk fat at 14%... no, 15%. Balance the acidity of the freeze-dried mango..." I unload my overfull arms so I can scribble in my trusty pocket notepad.

Experience has taught me that my mind, academic brilliance aside, cannot hold even the most important information for much longer than an Italian ice can survive a hot summer sidewalk. The daily life of one Dr. Noa Hart, PhD (Ice Cream Sciences), is a carefully crafted Hansel and Gretel trail of sticky notes, phone alerts, and mnemonic breadcrumbs sprinkled across various checkpoints to keep me on track.

The palest glint of sunrise through my bay window rudely taps me on the shoulder to remind me that I am, at this moment, very much *not* on track. I really shouldn't be awake right now, but a car alarm jolted me out of my slumber. Before I could count a single sheep, my brain bolted out of the gate, obsessively trying to crack the code of my latest frozen concoction.

Not that there's some urgent deadline for perfecting my mango crunch gelato with the ideal acidic bite. Come nine a.m., my ice cream engineering prowess belongs to my boss-slash-mentor, Stella Wexler, the legendary Chief Flavor Officer of Jen & Mary's Creamery. She's an undeniable visionary, but said vision leaves no room for mine... yet. My intrusive four a.m. thoughts drive me to my kitchen during the few hours when my time belongs solely to me, in the hopes that if I can perfect my wild ideas, one day Stella will take one of my inventions to the top floor to pitch to Jen and Mary themselves.

Ssssssszzzt. My Moka pot whistles its battlecry for the sleep-deprived from the stovetop. Time for a me-espresso or three. I spend so much of my workday sneaking bites in the ice cream lab that I don't have the best routine when it comes to actual meals. Coffee, on the other hand... that intoxicating goddess of fortitude and cognition is the fuel that keeps my tastebuds firing and my mind steady as I chase the perfect scoop.

By the time my don't-forget-you-have-an-office-to-commute-to alarm blares (Cyndi Lauper's *Goonies* song), I'm four espressos deep, a new record. With overcaffeinated shaky hands,

I spoon my latest frozen creation into a steel pint container, then stow it in the borderline-garish rainbow ice cream pint holder crocheted for me by my twin brother, Aiden. It's one of the more useful creations he's gifted me, compared to the Brat-green rearview mirror koozie that greets me as I slide into my very (very) old VW Bug, Ringo Carr. I've had him since I was in high school, and in spite of being on his third battery, he's proven as steady of a beater as his namesake. He's got as many bumper stickers as years he's been on this planet, a collection I've amassed over time that spectacularly represents me over the years–from *Books Made Me Gay* (my *Twilight* teen era where I realized I was not Team Edward or Team Jacob but a secret third team where Bella and I ended up together) to *Sappho Fucks* (my I-Have-A-Crush-On-My-Lesbian-Lit-Prof era immortalized by my brother's artwork) all the way to *What If We Kissed At the ADHD/Depression Wellness Camp* (present-day Noa's coping with the absolutely bananas world we live in). I get honked at a lot, and whether it's because of the freaking rad sticker collection on my car's butt, or some other unknown reason totally not at all related to my driving abilities… it's one of the little things that brings me great joy in life.

The two-mile drive to Silver Lake takes thirty minutes, during which I conclude that a fifth coffee at the office wouldn't be a crime, given the anomalously early hour of my rude awakening. I park Ringo and step into the headquarters of *Bon Appétit*'s reigning Most Delicious Workplace, six years and counting.

For the country's most successful independent ice cream brand, Jen & Mary's Creamery has managed to stay true to its activist hippie roots. Most small businesses that scale to this level get picked apart by hungry investors and venture capitalists along the way, pounding out every last drop of personality in their pursuit of the bottom line. Luckily for me–and for the future of full-fat ice cream–Jen and Mary aren't just names on pints; they're the wives who've been steering this company since it was an ice cream cart in Seattle. Those two badasses have never taken advice from anyone but each other, and for good reason.

Their independent spirit seeps into practically every inch of headquarters, from the mismatched diner mugs at the coffee bar to the tie-dye beanbag chairs that dot the space–remnants of a well-intentioned office chair purge that did not last. Sunlight floods through floor-to-ceiling windows, highlighting shelves crammed with dog-eared cookbooks and vintage dairy ephemera. The walls tell the founders' story in photographs: Jen and Mary at countless protests, arms linked, faces electric with purpose. Jen and Mary licking ice cream cones in front of their first truck, with *Scoop the Revolution* emblazoned on the side. Jen and Mary offering free scoops to petitioners during the AIDS epidemic. Like sweet-toothed Zeligs, the duo have seemingly been present, waffle cones in hand, at every major civil rights event of the last sixty years.

Peppered amongst these jubilant moments are their collection of mugshots, each one featuring their signature defiant smirks. But it's the massive painting above the communal snack area that best captures their particular blend of conviction and whimsy: an anthropomorphized ice cream cone, cherry-covered fist raised in resistance, crowned with a take on Woody Guthrie's famous quote: THIS ICE CREAM FIGHTS FASCISTS. "It's aspirational," Jen likes to say with a wink, before Mary chimes in, "I'm pretty sure the only thing our ice cream has fought is a few New Year's resolutions."

I stride through the corporate living room toward an innocuous oak door. Remember when I said that Jen and Mary's independent spirit seeped into *practically* every inch of headquarters? Welcome to the BFI. Not to be confused with the FBI, this is the Bureau of Flavor Investigation–although Stella, not normally punny, once tipsily referred to it as the Brain Freeze

Institute, which stuck–and it is a stark contrast in aesthetic *and* temperature to the cozy kitsch of the rest of headquarters.

As I descend the stairs into the basement, the scent of caramelized sugar and vanilla bean is the only welcoming aspect of the otherwise sterile corporate laboratory. Fluorescent lights hum softly overhead, casting a clinical glow over rows of industrial freezers, steel worktables, and neatly labeled jars of extracts and emulsifiers. At the far end of the room sits my workstation, cluttered with tasting spoons, a logbook filled with my scribbles, and a melted pint from yesterday's trial batch. *Oops.*

Standing ramrod-straight between me and my workstation is Stella herself, scrutinizing five test tubes of some ambiguous, glossy red liquid. Her signature black bob skims an uncannily clean line exactly one inch above the collar of her pristine white lab coat.

Stella has been my boss for three years now, including the summer I spent as her Flavor Fellow fresh out of grad school. On paper, there's ample evidence that she values me–believes in me, even. I wouldn't be here otherwise. But she also happens to be about as warm as an Excel spreadsheet, and just as compartmentalized.

In three years, the most intimate thing she has ever said to me was *I hope you get to celebrate*, a parting remark as she left me alone in the BFI late at night to finish an emulsification on my 30th birthday.

"Noa." She greets me without looking up.

"Stella!" I chirp back. Our vibes couldn't be more different, but I've never been one to dampen my sparkle to blend in. To her credit, Stella has never once suggested I should.

I unpack my latest creation from Aiden's crocheted pint holder and set it down beside the test tubes she's studying so intently.

"Maraschino cherry ribbons," she states. "If none of these

five iterations cool at the target rate, I am going to scream like a banshee."

Stella expresses her emotions exclusively through hyperbole, in monotone, and thankfully never through action. I have never heard her raise her voice a single decibel, but she often describes, in great detail, what she would do if she were the type.

"Maybe a watched cherry ribbon never... cools?" I offer. "What are these for again?"

I watch in horror as my boss attempts a bizarre impersonation, puffing up her cheeks and letting her jaw hang open before exclaiming in a terrible French accent, "Zees ees not blood! Zees ees m-m-maraschino cherries!"

Oh no no no. Just the mention of the b-word has me light-headed, gripping the table's edge. Stella's face rearranges into normalcy and now she's taking in my woozy expression with concern.

"Not actual bl–not that," she assures me, knowing intimately my phobia of said scarlet substance. Two Halloweens ago, we designed a signature ice cream for the Broadway premiere of Dracula. Despite my desperate pitch for garlic gelato, Stella decided to pursue a more... crimson creation. After one brainstorming session, I was relegated to taste-testing charcoal varieties in the other room due to the massive hematoma I received from a head-to-table collision.

"It's a reference. *Midnight Live?*" she tries again.

I stare blankly.

"'The Time-Traveling Dentist?'"

I shake my head.

"Noa, I know you didn't have the most traditional upbringing but that is *some* rock you're still living under."

Stella may not get deep and personal with me, but I'm a yapper to my core, so she knows a lot more about me than I do about her. Including the fact that my hippie-dippie family didn't have TV when I was growing up, which admittedly carried over into my adult life. It's not a moral stance, just what's normal to me.

But I have a feeling this may have some bearing on my career, which I do care about, so I ask, "What does the orthodontic Doctor Who have to do with us?"

"Well, technically King Louis. It's our next collaboration. I'm pitching her tomorrow." Stella handles all of Jen & Mary's celebrity pitches, a process I'm frankly relieved not to engage in. I prefer the power I wield in my own domain, the lab, to navigating big personalities and putting on airs of servitude.

"You're pitching King Louis? And he's a she?" I ask, confused as ever.

"Don't worry about it." Stella rubs her temples. "I'm certain maraschino cherry ribbons are the answer, but if I can't get them to cool down I'm going to–"

"Scream like a banshee, right." I nudge the steel pint I brought toward her. "Palate cleanser?"

Stella sighs, tearing her gaze away from the test tubes. She pulls a tasting spoon from her lab coat, unscrews the lid, and dips in with the expert precision of a jeweler inspecting a gem.

"Hm." Her eyes go distant, the telltale sign that she's sifting through the vast flavor archive in her brain, cross-referencing each note against a lifetime of taste. "It's... good."

I should know better than to take that initial approval at face value, but because it's me, and I am a hopeless optimist, I prod. "Good as in pitchable-to-Jen-and-Mary good?"

Stella tucks a runaway lock of black hair behind her ear. "Good as in, you always want to reinvent the wheel, but the wheel doesn't always want to be reinvented."

"And the metaphorical wheel is... ice cream?"

Stella looks at me like I just asked to confirm that $1+1=2$. "The wheel is wheel-shaped for a reason."

Now it's my turn to sigh.

Stella considers my orange concoction. "It's got a nice textural contrast. The basil is confidently incorporated."

But.

"We can be the brand that pushes boundaries with flavor, or we can be the brand that pushes boundaries in the world. But we can't do both–not at the same time."

"I know we've had this discussion before, but just because we're good at what we do doesn't mean we couldn't expand and be good at that, too!" I protest, but she's already locked into her defense.

"Sticking to classic but delicious ice cream gives Jen and Mary the foundation to drive real social change. When we veer into the experimental, we risk losing consumer trust. People come to us because they know we won't pull a Salt & Straw on them." Stella levels me with a look. "Noa, the last time I was at their flagship in Portland, I ate pig's... *b-word...* ice cream. Solely because I refused to let those hipster sellouts see me sweat."

In one fell swoop, I've gone from trying to defend the boldness of my mango confection to devoting 100% of my mental energy to not picturing porcine parfaits.

"Anything I can do that's not... cherry-related?" I ask weakly.

Stella beams. "You're on candy tooth duty!"

My lucky day.

mango crunch gelato notes:

2 cups whole milk

1 cup heavy cream

3/4 cup granulated sugar, divided

6 large egg yolks

2 cups ripe mango, peeled and cubed

1/4 teaspoon vanilla extract

Pinch of salt

crunch: toasted pistachios, candied ginger? coconut flakes

zero sanity???

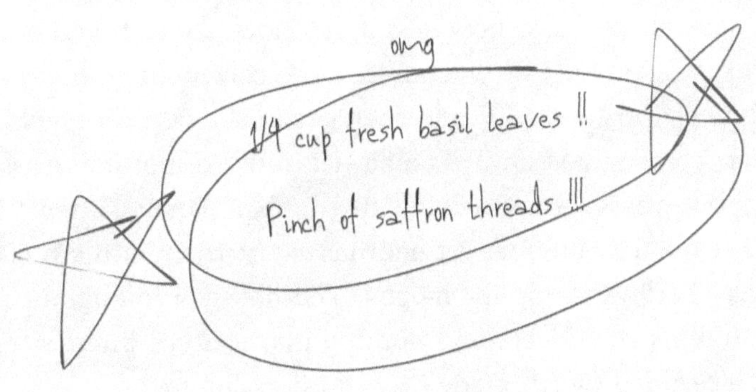

omg

1/4 cup fresh basil leaves !!

Pinch of saffron threads !!!

CHAPTER 3
AARTI

I ZIP down the 101 and take my exit to Hollywood. Even as someone who grew up in LA, I still feel a moment of awe when I catch a glimpse of the Hollywood sign out my passenger window, the morning light hitting it with an almost supernatural sparkle. Beneath that sign, I performed at every comedy show in town, breezed my way through the levels of every major improv studio, got on a house team, did some small headliners, then miraculously made it onto the biggest late night sketch show of all time... on my first audition.

Unlike most people who come here to achieve their dreams, Hollywood is my *homie.*

People always ask how I did it. How did I become the funniest woman on TV? Of course, I first correct them that I am the funniest *person* on TV, and then get to the part no one likes to hear: comedy has always come naturally to me. It's gross, I know, but years of mimicking my Indian parents after they yelled at me for bombing yet another extracurricular math class basically hardwired me for laughs. The first-gen immigrant kid math trauma runs deep, and nothing makes a girl funnier than being a certified fourth-grade Desi division dummy.

My phone rings through my Audi's speakers. *Incoming call*

from Maa. Perhaps my childhood fear that my overbearing mother could hear my thoughts wasn't so far-fetched.

I sigh and answer. "Whaddup, Maa?"

"You're up early, beta," my mom shouts through the phone.

I turn the volume down before my ear drums shatter. "You know I've got the show to get ready for."

"Show this, show that! Always the show! When are you going to settle down with a nice accountant or maybe a podiatrist? Both are very useful for you!" she yells. "I Googled yesterday and all of the boys who host the late nights have families! You can be like this!"

I know she means well. Both of my parents do. Although they've begrudgingly accepted at this point that comedy is my actual career, they still cling to whatever scraps remain of the life they once pictured for me.

"Maa, I have an accountant, I don't need to marry one. Plus, Diti's got the doctor thing covered for us both."

"Oh, Diti, how is she? Is she getting enough sleep? Are you feeding her?"

I don't bother with the truth, which is that my sister Diti didn't even come home last night.

"Of course. She gets all the crafty scraps from set."

"Beta! Your sister needs real meals, not that *tatti* from–"

"Maa! I'm kidding." Even after all these years as a comedian, my toughest audience is my own parents.

"You know I don't like it when you kid!" The speaker pops and I turn it down again as Maa rambles on about monitoring my sister's diet, which is ironic, considering I have zero control over the UCLA med student squatting in my spare bedroom. Diti doesn't get any shit from our parents despite being broke and jobless, but that's the perk of being the baby of the family. Of course, my parents don't know about the throwing-up-in-Ubers-and-crawling-to-bed-after-a-night-of-binge-drinking-with-future-doctors of it all. As long as she gets As, she's golden.

"…just because *you* live off of Maggi at 2AM does not mean a *doctor* can," she continues.

"All right, Maa, I'll be sure to relay the message. Gotta go."

I pull into my official parking spot–still labeled Guy Morrison–and steel myself for yet another day of trying to fill his shoes without doing exactly what got him ousted.

As a kid, I'd sneak out of my room past bedtime to watch any late night comedy I could get my eyes on. I'd tiptoe downstairs, my mom's favorite woven rug dampening my footsteps, and turn our modest little TV to the lowest possible volume. Guy Morrison and the early-aughts *Midnight Live* cast taught me about timing, punchlines, how to play to the top of my intelligence–concepts I couldn't name back then but which lodged themselves deep in my psyche nevertheless. Morrison in particular demonstrated that if you dig deep enough into the truth–about a guest, society, yourself–the best comedy would be unearthed.

Which is why I really wish they'd take his name off the parking spot already. Comparing myself on the daily to my childhood idol, the man I'm replacing, while hiding the very parts of myself he taught me to mine? Let's just say… it's not *not* taking a toll on the ol' mental health.

Also taking a toll on my psychological stability? The past six weeks of prep, which have been a masterclass in death by a thousand line notes. Every sketch my killer team of former *Midnight Live* writers has pitched has been dissected line by line by the least funny execs alive, each demanding to know, without a hint of irony, "But what's the joke here?" Gretchen, the network head, has turned guest booking into a forensic investigation, sending her minions to comb through internet archives for anything that might ruffle a sponsor. It's been a month and a half of constant rewrites, rejected segments, and terrible monologue notes sanding down every possible edge until what was once comedy feels more like assembling Ikea furniture.

No one else is in the office yet, allowing me to center myself ahead of the day. I take in our storyboards pinned to the writer's room wall and meditate. Well, my version of meditation, at least.

I am hilarious.

We're nailing it.

These jokes rule.

This is all I've ever wanted.

Seriously, I've never loved anything but comedy. This has to work or my career is over.

Wow, Aarti. Get a grip–

"This is bad, ohhhh god, this is *bad.*"

Ripping me from my zen is Magenta, my producer, as she bursts through the office door. Most people assume Magenta chose her name, but in reality, her bohemian Santa Fe artist parents pulled it out of thin air only to end up perfectly matching her colorful personality (and eventual hair).

Madge and I met when I first joined *Midnight Live.* She was a hungry upstart in the page program, and I was a wee television infant, thrust headfirst into the most competitive, high-stakes comedy environment imaginable. Where, just like in math class, I floundered.

My pitches bombed spectacularly. I barely got screen time. Nobody seemed to find me funny, least of all myself, which was a drastic change from always being so effortlessly good at what I did. I had no clue how to sell my humor among some of the best comedians in the country, and I lived in constant dread that soon, the network pages–the only people left who might still look up to me–would realize my fallibility, too.

So naturally, my rock bottom involved a page.

One afternoon, whimpering quietly in a bathroom stall, mere inches from losing my job, I heard a gentle knock.

"I saw your audition tape," Madge stated through the door, not bothering to introduce herself.

I peered helplessly through the crack, waiting to be punched while I was down. What she didn't know was that my confidence wasn't exactly the main issue right then–it was the questionable street meat I'd scarfed down thirty minutes earlier.

"You're like a hyper-caffeinated wolverine," she said earnestly.

"Like… the superhero?"

"Oh, god no, it's like a ferret. Found in the Arctic tundra. Freaky little thing."

I scoffed.

"What I'm saying is, you're funny, in this unhinged vaudevillian banana-peel way, and I don't think it's a mistake that you're here."

I groaned. "People think it's a mistake that I'm here?"

"They didn't cast you to be like everyone else. Stop trying to be."

My bowels spoke up in my defense, loud and mortifying.

I gasped, but Madge laughed, unfazed.

"See? Comedic timing's perfect. Even your gastrointestinal tract has it."

We've been a team ever since.

As I found my footing at *Midnight Live*, rising the ranks from wildcard impressionist all the way to the 'Now News!' desk, Madge was right there with me, from page to assistant to contributing producer. Now, she's the lead producer of my very own talk show, and I couldn't be prouder to have someone so sharp, so unflappable, so ruthlessly competent on my team. Although, seeing as how she is currently flitting around the office in a frenzy as her own version of a caffeinated ferret, 'unflappable' might be a premature assessment.

Madge flicks through a pile of scripts atop the long boardroom table.

"Ahem?" I offer.

She whirls, papers fluttering to the ground. "Jesus!"

"Call me Aarti," I quip. But Madge doesn't bite, the panic only rising on her face.

"They hate it. They hate it all. Oh, fuck. Our careers! Our bank accounts!" She collapses onto the script pages strewn across the floor.

I stand over her. "Words, Madge. Who hates what?"

"'Bus Boys.'" Her voice wobbles. "The network hates it. Gretchen called me gleefully at four a.m."

I blink. "'Bus Boys'? But that was already our ultimate compromise. No politics, no controversy, just a couple of sassy bus drivers bantering about the weather and reality TV. We gutted half the sketch packet to make room for it because Gretchen *loved* it."

"In a shocking turn of events, Gretchen changed her mind. Again."

"Fine," I sigh. "Note taken. We'll pivot. Again."

She throws her head back and laughs wildly. "'Bus Boys' is but the tip of the network executive iceberg of bullshit, my friend!"

I take a seat on the floor beside her. "Hit me."

Madge clears her throat and emulates Gretchen's demonic debutante drawl. "'We have immense faith in Aarti's brilliance as an interviewer, and the celebrity guests are fine–'"

"I'm sure they're *fine*. They've been cavity-searched by Legal more thoroughly than a drug mule at LAX." By sheer dumb luck, I never made having an internet presence a big part of my comedy career prior to *Midnight Live*. Otherwise, any number of my early impressions would have barred me from getting this gig.

"'–but the segments are feelin' awful generic,'" she finishes.

Now it's my turn to laugh hysterically. "Of course they're generic! They've spent the past six weeks neutering every authentic, funny field piece we've pitched. Down to rejecting the least authentic, least funny field piece *Gretchen herself* pitched, formerly known as 'Bus Boys.' RIP."

"Well," Madge winces, "they did float a solution."

"Me in a padded room reading aloud the phonebook?"

"A sidekick."

I stare at her. "A what now?"

"You know, like other late night hosts. Someone to riff with, do bits with, digital shorts–think Conan and Sona."

"Absolutely not." I'm up now, pacing. "First of all, I don't do sidekicks. I'm not Batman. Second, we have one month until air. Given that they've been vetting our celebrity guests like they're Supreme Court nominees, where exactly am I supposed to find a sidekick who I magically have chemistry with but who's also lived under a rock since birth and has never publicly expressed a single opinion?"

Madge grabs script pages off the floor and buries her face in them.

"Don't tell me there's more."

She peeks through the papers to deliver the final blow: "Advertiser-quarterly-is-Monday-and-if-we-don't-restore-their-faith-before-then-they're-swapping-our-slot-for-*Bedtime-with-Brady*."

"The show where the retired quarterback does ASMR sports trivia? That's not even a talk show!"

"Technically, it is."

"You're telling me that for the first time in eighty years, this show would have a female host *and* the shittiest time slot in its history?" I climb up off the floor, fueled by indignation.

She nods.

"Well," I say, offering her my hand and pulling her upright. "We can't let that happen, can we?"

"LATE!" Aiden declares when I arrive at his Los Feliz backhouse, wrapping me in one of his classic bear hugs.

"I know, I know. Stella–"

His hand flies up, silk tie-dye robe swishing with fervor. "Nope, no, don't want to hear your excuses about the flavor fascist, just want to rag on you for not being on time."

He ushers me inside, into his space filled with colorful paintings of psychedelic landscapes, papier mache cross-bred animal masks, and shadow boxes containing vintage trinkets and anal beads alike. I may seem like someone who marches to the beat of their own drum, ice cream PhD and all, but once you meet Aiden, any illusion of *me* being the free-spirited twin goes away.

For most of our lives, Aiden has had one and three-quarter inches on me in height, and about a hundred inches on me in gumption. We both inherited our dad's Jew-fro, but while mine's a dense, dark brown cloud, his is a riotous mass of fiery orange curls that refuse to be tamed. When he started testosterone in college, he grew a ginger beard to match, which is currently groomed into a hip stache.

An artist down to the very fibers of his being, Aiden has never shied away from being bold and outspoken when it comes to the singular vision of his creative work. I shudder to think of how he would have taken Stella's dismissal of the mango ice cream had he been in my shoes.

"So what's for dinner?" I ask, collapsing onto his vintage velvet couch. "Please tell me you actually cooked something this time."

Aiden fixes me with that look, the one that means trouble is brewing behind the hazel eyes we both got from Mom.

"I was thinking..." he drawls, twirling the tail of his mustache around his finger, "we could grab Leo's Tacos instead?"

"Aiden, nooooo..." I groan, already knowing where this is going. Leo's Tacos isn't just about the amazing al pastor–it's code for hitting up The Velvet Tongue afterward, one of the only full-time lesbian bars in LA. Usually, I'm all for sipping Old Fashioneds and admiring the walls covered in sapphic artwork, some of which Aiden contributed, but tonight? "I'm exhausted. Stella demolished my latest version of the mango flavor, and I've been on my feet since–"

Aiden flops down on the couch beside me, bouncing on the overstuffed cushions. "We haven't been out in forever! *And* Septum Piercing Danya is DJing tonight, *and–*" he pauses for dramatic effect, "I heard through the grapevine that your friend Casey might stop by."

I shoot him a glare. "Casey's not my friend, she's my ex. And that's exactly why I don't want to–"

"But you're still following each other on Gramsta," he interrupts, already reaching for his phone. "And she liked your post about the lavender honeycomb ice cream last week. That's practically a marriage proposal in lesbian terms."

"Just because I haven't blocked her on everything doesn't mean I want to run into her on purpose!"

He ignores me, continuing to scroll. "Oh look, she just

posted a story from Bar Lo-Fi. That's, what, five minutes from The Velvet Tongue?"

I press my face into one of his throw pillows–this one with an anatomically correct heart embroidered in trans flag colors– and groan.

The problem with Aiden is that once he gets like this, all frenetic energy and persuasive charm, resistance is futile. He's been this way since we were kids. I still remember him convincing me to climb onto the roof of our childhood home to test if umbrellas really work like parachutes (they do not).

He's deploying his signature move now: batting those ridiculous lashes that he somehow got blessed with while I ended up with Dad's stubby ones. "Just for a little bit?" he wheedles. "One drink? I promise to trip Casey if she dares show her face."

I peek out from behind the pillow. "You don't have to trip Casey."

He grins, knowing he's won.

"We're only staying for *one* drink," I tell him.

Aiden's already shrugging off his robe, revealing a perfectly coordinated outfit. Of course he was dressed and ready this whole time.

"Whatever you say, sis. Whatever you say."

I FLOP FACE FIRST onto my bed, the day a blur of scrapped sketches and inadequate pitches, desperately searching for any possible alternative to scouting a goddamn *sidekick* in a matter of days. I'm relieved that I have the place to myself tonight. Sex with models is great and all, but my brain is mush and the stress is compounding into an aching migraine.

"Tea?" Diti appears, pushing my cracked door open, steaming mugs in hand. *Guess I don't have the place to myself.*

"Ungh," I moan, rolling over to accept the drink from her. I take a sip and burn the shit out of my mouth, but it's worth it.

"Almost as good as Mom's." I fall back onto my pillow.

"Tough day?" Diti asks, sitting on the edge of the bed.

"How'd you know?" I say, dryly.

"No supermodel supercar in the guest spot."

"I need my space tonight."

Diti gives me a sly, knowing smile. "Oh, is that it, fuckgirl?"

I shake my head. My sister has always had my number, and it's both a joy and a nuisance to be seen this deeply. "This isn't about the supermodel or her supercar, D. It's the show. They want to send us to the midnight graveyard."

"Now why would they do a goofy thing like that?" She gets

in bed next to me, shoving me halfway off my own pillow to make a spot for herself.

"They called it *generic.*"

Diti fixes me with a look. "Well, you're not generic. And I think we both know how you could show them that."

I roll my tired eyes. "Sure, and then my entire career can end up dead just like my predecessor's."

"Mmmmk…" she shrugs. "But roasting the president is different than owning your sexuality."

"It's not different; it might even be worse. Are you living on the same planet as me?"

"I'm living on the planet where you're just too chickenshit to take a stand."

I hit her with my decorative 'You're the problem, it's you' pillow. "Shut up, ya straight."

"You'd think the best comedian in the world would have a better comeback."

"Get out," I groan. "I must wallow myself to sleep."

She stands, turning off my lamp. "You could come out with me and forget all your woes instead…"

"Begone!"

"Love ya, sis," she says as she closes the door behind her.

I stare at my dark ceiling and trill my lips. I have some of the best comedy writers in the world on my team. I know we'll get there. We *have* to get there. I've never been one to be patient, but I remind myself some of the best ideas come at the last minute, in the comedy pressure cooker. I'm just waiting for that spark, that *something* that takes my show from good to great. I *will* find it.

Just as I'm finally about to drift to sleep, my phone buzzes on my nightstand.

BRIGITTE

Come out with me tonight.

I turn over with a sigh. Not even the world's hottest supermodel could get me out of bed.

BRIGITTE

Pleeeeeease

BRIGITTE

Seriously, this is like the last time you'll be able to go out without everyone recognizing you!

She's not wrong. Sure, my golden years on *Midnight Live* made me a face that gets inquisitive double-takes, but I've also mastered the art of being incognito enough to pass unrecognized in most places I go. That's about to end. The billboards and building-side advertisements for the host changeover of the longest-running late night show of all time make it that way. I won't just be someone they know from somewhere, I'll be the brown lady in the suit who peers down at them when they're stopped at the endless red light at Virgil and Sunset.

BRIGITTE

I know you're seeing this your read receipts are on dumbass

As if by some miracle, my headache fades. I slide out of bed and pull my pants back on.

Did I say the world's hottest supermodel couldn't get me out of bed tonight? Well, I never claimed to be a reliable narrator. I live to entertain.

I arrive at the bar and valet my car in the packed lot. I walk in, searching for Brigitte's bombshell blonde locks, when I notice the art on the walls. A classic Georgia O'Keeffe. A portrait that proclaims *Sappho Fucks*. An intricate and anatomically correct 3D-printed labia.

I spot Brigitte amongst a school of women at the bar and pull her off of a stool.

"What the heck, Aart!"

I tug her into the empty All Gender bathroom and grab her shoulders.

"You brought me to a *lesbian bar?!*"

4G
4:08 PM
54%
Messages
Casey
Details
Sep 16, 2023 at 10:36 PM
you up?
come over sweet thang
>:)
home safe! when might i see you next :)
?
Oct 11, 2023 at 11:43 PM
went outta town for a min on a job, qt! you around tonight?
right now?

CHAPTER 6
NOA

FROM THE FIRST moment I laid eyes on Casey at lesbian book club two years ago, I was cooked. Perched on a leather armchair at Herstory Books, she commanded the room with an easy confidence, leading a heated discussion about the metaphor of time travel in Octavia Butler's work. Her pink-tinted wolf cut caught the late afternoon light, and I found myself mesmerized by her hands and arms, covered in fine line tattoos of constellations and botanical illustrations. I sat in the back, clutching my dog-eared copy of *Kindred* and praying I wouldn't have to speak.

Casey was a fashion photographer who knew every hipster lesbian east of Cahuenga, greeting them all with inside jokes and casual intimacy. She had strong opinions about magical realism and could quote Deleuze on demand, which should have been insufferable... But I was all in.

I had dated my share of women and men and enbies in my teens and early twenties, but I hadn't dated anyone since grad school and I was majorly out of practice. The isolation of my Flavor Fellowship with stoic Stella had set me back. When met with Casey's cool-girl ease, my brain and mouth seemed to disconnect in spectacular fashion every time I got within a few feet of her.

But Casey seemed to find my verbal stumbles charming. She'd laugh, not unkindly, and draw me out with gentler questions until we finally broke through that barrier of comfort where I could form complete sentences and she could get to know me. We bonded over our love of musical theater and experimental cooking (though her idea of 'experimental' usually involved something unintentionally fermenting on her windowsill).

The first time we kissed, I felt our entire future together flash through my mind. I saw Sunday mornings making mochi pancakes, road trips to exclusive desert art installations, growing old surrounded by rescue cats and floor-to-ceiling bookshelves…

Then she pulled back. "We can keep this low-key, right?"

I nodded dumbly, and we were off to the races for eighteen months of inconsistent texting and missed hangs, punctuated by handwritten poems slipped into my bag. Candlelit dinners followed by being ignored at parties. Sweet nothings undermined by stinging caveats.

I wish I had the self-worth to have ended things for good, but it was Casey who called it. She met some tarot reader who does non-competitive gymnastics *as an adult*, and fell in high-key love like she never did with me.

It's been six months since the breakup. The rejection still stings, but what's worse is knowing I had so little self-respect that I would've accepted her scraps forever.

Now I'm hiding out in the bathroom stall at The Velvet Tongue, stress-scrolling my favorite food chemistry blog about the crystallization patterns in chocolate tempering, all because Casey's disruptive pink hair materialized at the other end of the bar as I was closing out my tab. Aiden didn't notice my exit because he was, as per usual, surrounded by a gaggle of gays and theys, the perpetual life of the party.

The restroom door bursts open with such force that it bangs

against the wall. Two sets of footsteps click across the tile floor, accompanied by heated whispers that quickly escalate.

"You brought me to a *lesbian bar?!*"

I can hear the panic in the woman's voice.

"For one of your last nights on the town! You might not get to come here again, unless… you know." The second woman trails off.

I can see the panicking woman pace through the crack in the stall door. "You had no right to put me in this situation."

"These are the safest people you could ever be yourself around. No one is trying to tattle on each other, they just want to have a relaxed, gay time."

There's a long silence and I realize I'm holding my breath, I'm so invested in these two strangers' sudden drama.

The pacing woman stills. "This is not working."

"Oh, we're doing this again?"

I can't tell what's happening beyond the confines of my little eavesdropping booth, but I hear more footsteps then the door swinging open again, followed by silence.

At least someone's having a worse night than me.

I'm not surprised that closeted lady freaked out about being here. Even the sinks at The Velvet Tongue are gay. The faucet is a tongue emerging from between two fingers in a peace sign. Which is aspirational to me, but I get that not everyone will be on the same page.

I finish my article on chocolate tempering before leaving the stall, because why rush? It's not like Aiden is missing me. No one is. I wash my hands and something clatters in the supply closet to my left. Probably just a mop falling over, but in my current state, I'll take any excuse to linger in this bathroom. I dry my hands and head over to investigate.

I turn the door handle.

"JEEPERS!" The scream tears out of me.

There's a woman wedged halfway through what has to be

the tiniest window I've ever seen, her legs kicking in the air like an overturned beetle. The window is a good seven feet up the wall, a stack of paper towel boxes arranged below her into a makeshift stepladder.

"Do you need–"

"Shit." One leg stops kicking long enough to wave at me emphatically. "Don't call anyone!"

"Are you… stuck?" It's a stupid question, she's very obviously stuck, but my brain is still trying to process the scene in front of me.

"No, I often like to hang out of small windows," comes the muffled response.

"Right, well I'll leave you to it, I guess–"

"Yes, of course I'm stuck," she snaps. "And if you could maybe help instead of just standing there; this is taking every last bit of ab strength I have."

I square my shoulders. "Right. We're gonna get you down, no problemo."

The woman groans. "No, I need you to help me get the rest of the way *out*. I'm *leaving*."

"Right. Yes, one sec," I tell the maniac, not wanting to upset her delusion. I step into the messy closet with zero plan on how to help. "Any suggestions as to how I can assist?"

The woman manages to twist her body to the side just enough to look at me. *Maybe she's an adult hobby gymnast, too.*

Well, if she is, she's an adult hobby gymnast with a face that could convince me to start doing gymnastics as a hobby. She's got Pantene-commercial thick black hair, and dark lashes to match, with two arched, perfectly manicured eyebrows currently raised accusingly at me.

"Sorry, I zone out sometimes. Did you say something?" I scramble my way out of the embarrassment of being caught checking her out.

"I need you to lift my knee–cup it–and push me up so I can swing my leg over the ledge."

I do as I'm told. "You're very spatially aware for someone who got stuck in a window."

She snorts so softly I can tell she didn't intend to laugh but couldn't help herself.

"Okay, that's good, now push," she instructs.

At first I'm not sure I'll be strong enough to give her the boost she needs, but then her weight is off of me and she's climbing through the window... and landing with a metallic crash.

Now it's my turn to scale the tower of boxes. I poke my head out to find her face-down in a dumpster.

"Are you–?!"

She gives me a thumbs-up from her prone position.

"I've never met someone so desperate to get inside a dumpster."

"I do it for the thrill," she mumbles into the sticky plastic.

"Do you need me to call someone? Mom? 3-1-1? Therapist?"

She attempts to right herself atop the mountain of trash bags, but her arms just sink into the mushy, shifting heap of crumpled poetry-reading flyers and expired dental dams.

"Does it look like I have a therapist?" Her balance betrays her every time she nears stability. It's a slow-motion disaster until she finally ends up right back where she started.

"There's a straw on your head."

She fishes it out of her locks. "Better me than a sea turtle."

Finding a foothold on a nearby trash hill, she hoists herself up with frankly impressive upper body strength. Like an Olympian on the planet's nastiest pommel horse, she swings her leg over the rim before landing with an offensively gentle thud on solid ground. Maybe if I used my Thinking Rod for its intended purpose, I could one day climb out of a dumpster with such effortless grace.

Her head pops back up over the metal wall. "I look forward to never seeing you again."

"Same," I wave.

And with a small tilt of her head and a tight smile, she spins on her heel and disappears into the night.

CYNDI LAUPER'S *Goonies* song yanks me out of REM sleep, and I jolt upright on Aiden's plush couch, disoriented and embarrassingly hungover from a single cocktail. The blackout curtains in his backhouse, no doubt a necessity for the bizarre hours he keeps, make it impossible to tell the time of day.

My eyes fumble through the darkness, locking onto the cuckoo clock above his TV.

Eight fifteen a.m.

Panic seizes me for three chilling seconds before I remember... *Wait, it's Saturday? Why the hell is my commute alarm going off?*

The panic I momentarily assuaged rises back up as I pick up my phone and realize Cyndi is belting out her ode to the *Goonies* because I'm getting a *call*. From my boss. On the weekend.

"Stella? Is everything okay?" I croak.

Spoiler alert: everything was *not* okay. My pint-sized flavor genius of a boss had driven to the lab overnight after an epiphany about the cherry ribbons. She'd cooled them to the perfect temperature, only to spill the viscous red liquid in front of her designer loafer, slip, and wipe out spectacularly. The end result? A sprained ankle, a mild concussion, and me, careening

Ringo Carr down the 101 in a panic so that I can fill in for my injured boss at our biggest meeting of the year with an apparently huge celebrity I've never heard of. *This oughta be good.*

In the frantic five minutes I had to collect myself in Aiden's backhouse, I ransacked his kitchen for every ice cream tool I'd ever passed down after upgrading my own equipment. I stuffed spice sachets, food coloring, and a nitrogen sprayer into a beat-up rolling suitcase from the back of his coat closet–no real plan, just blind hope that a Mary Poppins bag of food science props might help me channel my expertise and calm my nerves during my first-ever celebrity pitch.

I know this is a chance to prove myself. To show that when sage collides with poached pear and my brain lights up like the Fourth of July, it isn't just neurons misfiring–it's because I'm creating something others can actually taste, too. Still, there's a safety in clocking every working hour in the BFI basement rather than out in the world.

Aiden loves to remind me that a lifetime under Stella's exacting eye will never pave the way for me to make my own name in the ice cream industry. But for all the hours I've spent dangling from my Thinking Rod, refereeing pre-dawn flavor tournaments with my spice rack, and daydreaming about pitching my original creations to Jen and Mary, the truth is this: I'm terrified that stepping out from Stella's shadow won't illuminate my talent, only my flaws.

As I merge onto the 101, a familiar voice slithers in: *You didn't earn this opportunity today. Stella had to face-plant in maraschino juice for you to even get a shot.*

Meet Jerky McGee: my therapist's idea of creating separation between me and the part of my brain that's convinced I'm one mistake away from everyone realizing I'm a fraud. Except Jerky McGee isn't some external demon. He's just me at three in the morning, replaying every fumbled social interaction, every promise I've broken to myself, every ounce of blame I've ever siphoned from other people's pain. *People pleaser* sounds so much tamer and sweeter than the reality.

Someone honks at me for refusing to turn left into a pedestrian. I wave an apology in my rearview mirror. Even road ragers in traffic awaken my desperation to please.

I circle the brutal congestion around Hollywood and Highland for the third time, hunting for the studio entrance like it's the wardrobe to Narnia. When I finally spot the CBT Studios sign, I nearly clip a tour bus making my hasty turn.

After I explain the Stella situation, a wary security guard waves me through with directions to Studio 3B. I hurry across the bumpy concrete lot, Aiden's rolling suitcase clinking and clanging. I crouch down and unzip the bag, donning the large gloves necessary to handle the nitrogen canister before tucking it under one arm. Probably best not to be responsible for an explosion this early in the morning.

Passing through the double-wide brass doors of 3B, I've never seen anything like it, despite my decade of living in LA. Gigantic black-and-white photos of late-night hosts line the walls, interspersed with sleek display cases filled with fancy-looking trophies. I'm sure the space would impress me more if I'd grown up watching TV, but even without context, the air of legacy and importance is thick in this place.

A harried-looking green-haired woman with a headset barks something about meal penalties while four guys hurry past carrying half a living room set with a disgruntled-looking extra dressed as a banana trailing behind them. I look around for someone to direct me, but everyone here seems to be marching to their own orders. I decide to do the same.

I follow the flow of traffic down a corridor, past dressing rooms and offices, catching glimpses of the machine behind late-night TV as I stroll: bulletin boards plastered with index cards, producers hunched over laptops, racks of clothes being wheeled about.

Then I spot *her*.

The crazy woman who crawled out of the bar window last night is holding court in a conference room, that same silky hair pulled back into a high pony, effortless flyaways framing her captivating face. Even under fluorescent lights, she radiates a compelling magnetic energy, like she knows a secret, and if you can catch her off guard for a moment, maybe you'll be privy to it, too.

On second thought, I suppose I *did* catch her off guard and *do* know one of her secrets.

Our eyes lock through the glass, and her face goes white as a freshly churned *helado de coco*. She stands up so quickly her chair rolls backward and crashes into a whiteboard, sending dry-erase markers scattering. She speed-walks toward me with the kind of practiced smile a flight attendant gives just before informing you that you and the ghosts you're seeing are no longer welcome on this flight.

Then she's standing in front of me, so close that I can smell her perfume, a nutty gourmand that would pair super well with a Madagascar vanilla bean.

"You're here, too?!" I ask her incredulously. "Thought we'd sworn to never see each other again."

Her brows raise as she glances at the metal canister under my arm and my other hand gripping the handle of the suitcase.

"I'll be right with you," she tells me, before promptly clicking the door shut in my face. And locking it.

I stand there, baffled, as she turns back to the room. Through the glass, I can see the other people looking curiously in my direction while she grabs her phone and speaks rapidly into it, shooting glances my way that make me feel like I'm some kind of dangerous animal at the zoo.

Which is when two pairs of burly hands grasp my shoulders.

Security. She called *security* on me.

"Ma'am, you'll need to come with us."

"What? No, there's been a misunderstanding–"

Dumpster Lady emerges from the locked room and stares me down coldly.

"I'm not sure how you got in here, but it is completely inappropriate and frankly pathetic that someone would go to such lengths to stalk me."

"Stalk you? I don't even–I'm here for a meeting! About ice cream!" I try twisting around to face her as the guards steer me, my canister, and the rolling suitcase toward the exit. She's trailing behind by a few feet, but she glances up at my latest outcry.

She smirks, then speaks like she's talking to a child. "Okay, well, if you go with these nice men out to the Boulevard, you can have your ice cream meeting there."

I look at my captors, who honestly do seem like pretty nice men, their faces apologetic as they do this crazed parkour princess's bidding. "Aarti Nair. Aarti Nair! That's who I'm looking for! *She* knows we have a meeting!"

There's a snort behind me. "She most certainly does not."

The record scratch in my brain is so loud I'm convinced everyone can hear it.

Oh my God.

Oh my God!

Dumpster Lady and Aarti Nair are one and the same.

Wait.

Oh.

Everything about this interaction comes into focus in one fell swoop.

Remember how I said my brain and mouth short circuit sometimes around a pretty girl? It turns out they do that even if she's about to call the cops on me, because I don't have the cognitive ability at this moment to try and explain any of this mess articulately. So I just shout:

"This isn't blood, this is maraschino cherries?!"

We're right by the front doors. Aarti walks around to face me. *"What?"*

"Zis isn't blood, zis is maraschino... ch-ch-cherries," I say, suddenly less confident in my secondhand impression.

"Have you ever actually seen that sketch?"

I groan. "No. But in my defense, I didn't grow up with a TV!"

Aarti gives me a withering look. "That's a new low, a stalker that's too lazy to do their research."

And just as the guards are pushing me out to the Boulevard to have my ice cream meeting, I give one final battle cry, because I have nothing left to lose.

"Stella Wexler! Jen & Mary's! The FBI! I mean the BFI!"

The double doors slam shut in my face. Aarti turns on her heel and strides away without a second glance, while the guards eye me through the glass.

I'm frozen in place, hugging my nitrogen sprayer like a security blanket, unwilling to accept defeat but equally uncertain of my next move.

I'm weighing the consequences of laying down in front of the doors amongst the Hollywood stars and seeing what the gods have in store for me when the door whips back open. The green-haired woman I saw earlier stands in front of me, headset askew, looking between me and her tablet.

"Stella Wexler?"

Oh, sweet relief. I fish out my Jen & Mary's corporate badge from my suitcase.

"That's my boss, I'm here in her stead. She had a... cherry-related incident."

The woman shakes her head sympathetically, as if cherry-related incidents are commonplace atrocities.

"Come on in, sorry about the confusion. A few weeks 'til air is not a great headspace for most of us." She leads me inside by the elbow, shooting a pointed look at one of the now-sheepish guards. "I'm Magenta, by the way. Lead producer."

"Noa–" I start, but she's pressing a button on her headset and muttering something about an eagle and the lobby.

Seconds later, I watch with muted smugness as Aarti Nair reemerges from that treacherous hallway and stomps up to us, glowering.

"Madge." Aarti greets her producer curtly, not even offering me a glance. "Explain."

Magenta appears unfazed by Aarti's simmering annoyance. "I forgot to mention this meeting yesterday amidst the... *sidekick spiral*." Aarti opens her mouth to speak but Magenta cuts her off. "And that'll be seven Hail Marys and a life sentence of being relegated to the transpo bathroom."

I can't help my snort of laughter. I'm starting to vibe with Magenta's fearless shtick but Aarti is not. She folds her arms. "What meeting, exactly?"

"You get to collaborate with Noa on your very own ice cream flavor!" Magenta pitches, like a mom cajoling her two-year-old into eating broccoli.

"Oh!" Aarti mimics Magenta's tone. "No, thank you! I have bigger fish to fry, like, I dunno, making sure our show doesn't get cancelled before it even airs!"

She turns on her heel and walks away. Magenta scurries to follow, jerking her head at me to come with.

"This is coming from the biggest fish." Magenta catches up to her boss, giving Aarti a loaded look. "A signature ice cream can establish who you are. It's another way to keep your brand from feeling..." she stage-whispers, "'*generic*.'"

Even with her back to us, I can feel the disdain radiating off Aarti. "Silly me. I didn't realize scrapping the segments we've been workshopping for months and feigning enthusiasm about the impossible task of finding a mini-me over the weekend weren't adequate displays of fealty for the C-suite."

She pivots, pushing open a heavy door with her back, then lands her gaze on me. I wish she'd go back to pretending I didn't exist.

"So what do you need from me? My astrological chart? Social security number?"

"I mean, if those are important to you, maybe not so much the social–"

The rest of the sentence dies on my lips as I take in the vast room we enter. We've stepped into the bustling soundstage of *Up Late*. Crew members hurry past, muttering into headsets and looking like they belong–more than I can say for myself in this moment, clutching my nitrogen canister, trying to convince a terrifying and gorgeous woman with her name in massive neon lights into giving me something to work with so I don't lose my job.

Even half-built, the space is undeniably *hers*. The glow of her name and the *Up Late* logo hover above the stage. A sleek wooden desk sits opposite plush guest chairs. The backdrop is nearly complete, and at its center stands a sprawling 3D diorama of a city. Instead of the buildings drawing focus, it's the glowing pathways that dominate–thin golden lines weaving through the landscape, intersecting and converging like a circuit board. Telephone wires? Rivers? Something about the pattern tugs at my brain, familiar but just out of reach.

"Wait," I squint. "Is that… the LA public transit system?"

Magenta nudges her boss. "Hey, someone finally got it!"

Something flickers across Aarti's face–annoyance? vulnerability?–before she schools it back to neutral.

"Soundbooth, Madge?"

Magenta scurries off with a mock salute, leaving us alone with my tiny moment of triumph. I, Noa Hart, professional ice cream hermit, first-time celebrity pitcher, just understood something about America's next late-night darling that apparently nobody else did.

"Don't look so pleased with yourself," Aarti says. "It's a bus map. Not the Rosetta Stone."

"That's exactly the kind of detail I need for your ice cream!" I blurt, clutching my canister tighter. "Your history, what matters to you, what shaped your comedic voice–"

"My comedic voice?" She arches an eyebrow. "The one you picked up from the Time-Traveling Dentist sketch you've never seen?"

Heat floods my cheeks. "Okay, I'm not an Aarti Nair expert. Yet! But I *am* an ice cream expert." I pause. "Enthusiast? Aspiring authority? The point is–"

"Great." She cuts me off with a fake smile. "Sounds like you're a real self-starter. Why don't you take a few minutes to sniff around my set, collect some insights–invent them for all I care. Madge loves ice cream, she'll be your contact."

She's already turning away, but sheer panic at screwing up this job emboldens me and I reach out to grab her toned upper arm. "Wait!"

Aarti whips around, glaring at my hand on her bicep until I sheepishly remove it.

"I need to know *you*, not Magenta." The words tumble out faster than I can organize them. "Even though she seems super cool and I love the green hair and standing up to her boss situation. But here's the thing–I've seen my boss Stella do enough collabs to know that even when celebrities claim they don't care, they *will* hate the final product if they don't see themselves in it."

She scoffs. "You and everybody else wants to 'know me', but only in a way that fits neatly on a poster." Her voice goes sharp. "This show is dangling off a cliff because I'm told it's 'bland' when I play it safe, and 'too much' when I try to make it mine. Every time I put more of myself into it, the network slaps my hand away. Too divisive, too inconsistent, too bold–pick your critique. So yeah, maybe it's better for you to just whip up a crowd-pleaser sundae than pretend you're bottling my soul."

She pivots on her designer heel.

"But that's what makes this opportunity exciting!" I chase after her. "You can show people you're all those things at once. Contradictions don't cancel each other out, they create flavors. That's the beauty of ice cream!"

Aarti looks momentarily amused, then catches herself, and I watch it transform into a smirk. "Noa, was it?"

I nod.

"Noa, that's very poetic and all, but I'm gonna level with you. I'm happy you're passionate about what you do. So am I." She gestures at her bustling domain. "Hopefully you can empathize that I have a lot more pressing things to do than weigh in on old-fashioned versus French vanilla."

This is why I've always known that celebrity collaborations would not be for me. I may not be comfortable in the spotlight, nor particularly outspoken in most situations, but there's one scenario that never fails to fling me to the far opposite end of the spectrum, and that's being condescended to. Maybe it stems from defending Aiden from bullies and transphobes when we were growing up. Even though I was shy, I knew my twin needed me more than I needed my dignity.

I set the nitrogen canister on the ground before standing back up. My spine straightens like someone's pulled a string through the top of my head.

"Aarti, was it?" I begin. Her eyebrows shoot up in surprise.

"Yeah, name's right there in *neon*."

"Aarti, I *am* passionate about what I do. And there's a lot more to it than waiting around for some diva to choose between two of the most basic ice cream flavors in the world." I'm on a roll now and I can't stop. "You're not the only one whose job is on the line here. The sooner we actually get started, the sooner we can be done with this and go back to our regularly scheduled programming or whatever you TV people say." I pull the notebook from my back pocket and give my pen a pointed click.

For the first time, Aarti looks nonplussed, like she's unaccustomed to being spoken to so bluntly. When she finally speaks, her nostrils flare like she's just taken a putrid whiff of Hollywood Boulevard.

"A *diva?*"

Of course she got stuck on that.

And of course, I immediately apologize.

"I'm so sorry, I didn't–"

"Seems like you think you know me pretty well. A diva TV person with the most basic taste in the world?"

I throw my hands up and my pen goes flying off my notebook. "I don't know you, okay? That's the point! I just need you to answer a few questions. I'm sorry for the name-calling, this is quite literally my first time filling in for my boss and also my first time being woman-handled by security guards and also my first time–"

Aarti takes a step toward me, her head tilts just so... *Is she going to kiss me?*

Before my brain can catch up to what's happening, she's bending down and grabbing my pen off the floor. She holds it out to me.

"Fine. You have five minutes."

She walks over to the oak desk and points to the armchair beside it. I take a seat. It's surprisingly cushy and I tuck my legs beneath myself, no energy to care that I'm doing what Aiden lovingly calls the bisexual perch.

Behind the desk, I can see why the network cast her as a host. She's tall, so even sitting down, she has an impressive stature that makes her seem larger than life. The stage lights bathe her dark hair, highlighting the ethereal bluish undertone of her silky black locks. Her eyes are deep brown, so I haven't been able to differentiate her pupils until this moment, noticing flecks of gold dotting the coffee-colored swirl of her irises.

She blinks, and I jolt, realizing I've been totally and utterly staring. Again.

"First time on TV?" she asks.

"Just here to promote my new show, Noa Hart, PhD, Totally Bombs Gigantic Career Opportunity As Expected." I pretend to take a sip from an invisible mug. I may not have grown up watching late-night but its tropes have still seeped into my knowledge base by osmosis.

Aarti's lips twitch like she's holding back a smile. "Nice space work."

I grin. *Maybe this won't be so torturous after all.*

"Enough about me." I nod at her desk. "Seems like I should be in that seat today, seeing as I'm interviewing you."

I was trying to quip my way into easing us toward the whole ice cream flavor pitch, but as soon as I say it, I see her bristle all over again.

"Right," she says tersely.

I flip to a fresh page in my notebook, attempting to glide past the awkwardness. Luckily, everyone around us is busy, not paying attention to this unintentionally twisted interrogation.

"So what makes you… *you?*"

I know I could start by asking what she thinks of Stella's *Midnight Live*-referential cherry ribbons, but just alluding to the b-word right now would nauseate me even more than I already am.

Aarti rolls her eyes. "I can see why this is my job and not yours."

Ticket for one right back on the saucy train.

I try to regain my composure. *What did Stella say in my crash course this morning?* Don't go straight for preferences, that's amateur hour. Start with their home turf, where you're meeting them. The framed photo on the desk, the scent of their oil diffuser. Get them comfortable talking about the objects around them so they don't feel like the subject of a scientific study.

"The bus map." I point behind us. "That's proof there's more than what we're seeing on the surface of Aarti."

She glances at the map and back at me, her eyes pitch black again.

"Yes, I have utilized the LA transit system. Next question."

I jot down her answer, even though it's useless–I just need to busy my hands.

"So does it mean something more to you? Like, do you care about the environment or…?"

She exchanges a look with Magenta who I can barely make out in the soundbooth. The producer gives a quick shake of her head, and I realize the entire stage is mic'd.

"Next question," Aarti repeats.

"What's the point of having it there if you can't even talk about *why?*" I mumble to myself, but Aarti's eyes narrow.

"I grew up in an immigrant family who ran a restaurant. We didn't have a lot of money, hence public transport." She somehow sits even taller as I write that down. "Next. Question."

Ooookay. I flip through pages of half-questions I scribbled on my steering wheel at stoplights, but *why do you love your job?* and *what are you most excited to share with audiences?* feel aggressively glib at this moment.

I rack my brain for Stella's next morsel of advice: bypass media training with specificity. Don't just ask what they like to eat, ask what they like to eat when something *specific* has happened.

"Um. What's a comfort food for you? Like, what do you eat after…" I try to come up with a compelling scenario, but improv was never my specialty, so I just blurt out the first thing that pops into my dumb, curly head, "…you've just had a breakup?"

The speed at which Aarti's face goes ashen is equivalent to

the speed at which I realize just how poor of a choice that scenario was.

She thinks I'm trying to allude to last night at Velvet Tongue.

"No! I didn't–I would never–" *Out someone*, I want to say. But despite my chronic foot-in-mouth disease, I have the wherewithal to hold that part in.

Yet I'm still met with a death glare icier than the industrial freezer in the BFI.

I avert my eyes, furiously studying my notepad, like the terrible questions I brainstormed will magically transform into brilliant, probing-yet-tactful interrogations. Aarti's short, manicured nails land at the top of one of the pages, and I reluctantly look up.

"What are you–"

She snatches the notebook from my hands and leafs through it. "You're asking questions that aren't even in here. Why?"

I go to grab the pad but she holds it out of my reach.

"Answer. The question."

"I'm improvising! I'm sorry! I've never done this before and you're not exactly being the most forthcoming! Can I please have that back?"

She snorts. "Leave the improv to the pros. You don't need this poor attempt at a dossier on me. Like you said, I'm not giving you much to work with anyway."

I reach for it again and she yanks it away, looming above me like a schoolyard bully.

"There's a lot in there other than our non-interview, okay? My brain can't really hold onto a thought for longer than three seconds. You're holding all of my thought soup right now!"

She flicks through more. "This page just says 'camomeal pudding' and *chamomile* is heinously misspelled."

"I'm an ice cream scientist, not a literary genius!"

If only Stella had prepared me for what to do when a deranged celebrity is playing keepaway with the physical manifestation of the humiliating contents of my brain. I decide to switch gears–what would my brother do at this moment? We played our fair share of tug-o-war with twin birthday presents over the years.

I stop trying to snatch the notepad and settle back into my chair, folding my arms. Aarti sits, too, mirroring me aside from the journal tucked against her side. I watch as her eyes dart back over to Magenta, who's giving Aarti a disapproving look.

"Magenta thinks you should give it back."

"Luckily Madge works for me, not the other way around. But," she scoots her chair out from the desk and stands, "I'm glad you feel some kinship there because she will be your point person going forward. I think we've fully established that this will go a lot smoother without us having to liaise any further."

I hold up my hands in surrender. "Fine. I'll probably get more out of her than I ever would from you."

I know we're throwing barbs, but Aarti looks genuinely relieved at my acquiescence. She walks around the desk and heads toward the soundbooth, giving Madge a twinkly wave. I get out of my cushy seat and pick up my nitrogen canister from the floor before following Aarti across the stage.

When we're about halfway there, a crew member stops Aarti to show her something on a clipboard, and the demon in my head gives me the signal: *now*.

With her distracted, I take the quietest steps I can manage to sneak up behind her. I can see my notebook peeking out between her torso and toned arm. With my free hand, I grip the corner of the pad and yank with all my might.

Remember when I said her arm was *toned*? Would that I had realized just *how* toned. Yanking the notebook does nothing for my retrieval mission except alert its captor to my intentions.

Aarti turns on her heel, and in a flash, I'm nothing more than a twelve-year-old again, trying vehemently to stake my claim to the singular Gameboy gifted to Aiden and I on our shared birthday, similarly poorly matched to the strength of my opponent.

I go to grab the notebook from the front this time, and in spectacularly blustering Noa Hart fashion, manage to swipe her left boob instead. The crew member takes a horrified step back as Aarti's eyes widen in shock.

"Seriously?!" she spits.

The crushing defeat should have me sprinting out of the studio at this point, probably fleeing the country, but instead, I get tunnel vision, perhaps because I have nothing left to lose.

Famous last words.

She's gripping the notepad with both hands now as I attempt to brute force it away from her. Suddenly, the golden flecks in her eyes are twinkling again, and in slow motion, *she lets go.*

I fly backward into the elaborate LA transit diorama, crashing with all of my body weight into Beverly Hills, my precious journal clutched to my chest. I hear crew members heave a collective gasp.

Then I hear the hiss.

Through my daze, I turn my throbbing head to the side and spot my canister–now resting directly on a blazing stage light.

"Oh no, no–"

The valve hisses open. Nitrogen erupts in ghostly tendrils, creeping through the destroyed cityscape like fog in a disaster movie. The vapor engulfs Aarti, who towers over me like Godzilla's extremely well-dressed nemesis.

True to Murphy's Law, which should maybe get renamed after me, the nitrogen triggers the fire alarm, and at the exact moment my eyes meet hers, the studio sprinklers pour down upon us.

I look up at Aarti through the thick mist and torrential monsoon to give her two shaky thumbs up. But her expression is pure horror, and not just because I've destroyed 90210.

Something thicker than water runs into my eye. I swipe at it. Red streaks across my fingers.

Have I mentioned I'm very not good with blood?

"Hey..." I wave hazily at Magenta, the gathering crowd of crew members, and my definitely-now-sworn-enemy Aarti Nair. "This isn't blood! This is marasch–"

I promptly pass out atop the ruins of Los Angeles and my own dreams.

"...me Traveling Dentist"

KING LOUIS

Magnifique! My mouth does hurt terribly. Must be from all ze... smiling. Yes, smiling at my subjects!

HE BRINGS A HEAPING SPOONFUL OF ICE CREAM TO HIS MOUTH, WHEN A POLICE BOX POOFS ONSTAGE. DR. CHRONOS STEPS OUT.

DR. CHRONOS

Your Majesty, you're experiencing severe periodontal disease from anachronistic dairy consumption!

KING LOUIS

What sorcery is zis?

DR. CHRONOS

I'm a dentist--

KING LOUIS
(taking a bite)
I know not what zis means.

DR. CHRONOS

Your teeth are literally rotting from eating ice cream 200 years before dental hygiene exists!

KING LOUIS

Nonsense! My teeth are perfect!

A TOOTH FALLS OUT OF HIS MOUTH.

KING LOUIS (CONT'D)

Zat was supposed to happen.

CHAPTER 8
AARTI

THE DRIVE HOME from the studio is a blur of red lights and self-loathing. I keep replaying the moment that nitrogen-wielding psycho crash-landed on my seven-hundred-thousand-dollar set piece, but what really stings is how I handled it. The great Aarti Nair, comedy genius, interviewer extraordinaire, reduced to shrieking like a marmot over a chemical spill.

My condo greets me with its usual bachelorette-pad charm, which is to say, yesterday's takeout containers from dinner with Brigitte are still on the coffee table and my laundry has achieved sentience on the bedroom floor. But right now, I need only one thing: my emergency stash.

I dig through the kitchen cabinet behind the protein powder I've never used and extract the family-sized bag of chakli and a jar of mango pickle my mom smuggled to me during her last visit. "For emergencies only, beta," she'd said, knowing there would be nothing family-sized about the single person consuming that entire bag.

If her very presence–and her very annoying, probing ques-tions–hadn't immediately set me off, I probably would have told Noa earlier that this was my comfort food for every situation. Bombed the Improv 101 show? Mango pickle and chakli. Period came a day early? Mango pickle and chakli. Crawled out of a dumpster at a lesbian bar in front of a maddeningly gorgeous woman? Make haste to take your trashy self home and dig into mango pickle and chakli.

I settle onto my couch, spreading my feast before me like a sadness buffet. The first bite of pickle-loaded chakli hits different when you're questioning your entire career trajectory. The tangy, spicy crunch is basically a time machine to my childhood kitchen, where failure meant getting a B+ in chemistry, not potentially tanking my own talk show before it airs.

Am I even meant to do this?

The thought arrives uninvited as I crunch through another handful. The people in my corner keep telling me I'm breaking barriers–first woman, first Indian, youngest host in *Up Late* history. But what if I'm just the first to fail this spectacularly? What if I'm simply not capable of molding myself into everything the network needs me to be? What if I'm just becoming totally flavorless in my attempt to be palatable to everyone? Even Noa was scornful of vanilla.

I dip another piece of chakli directly into the pickle jar, no longer bothering with a spoon. The crispy spiral breaks apart in the oil, and I fish out the pieces with my fingers. Rock bottom tastes like fermented mango and gram flour on a Saturday afternoon.

Maybe Mom was right. Maybe I should have taken supplemental math more seriously, pursued a stable career, married a nice Indian podiatrist from Santa Barbara.

But even as I think it, I know it's not true. I was born to perform, to make people laugh, to turn my body into a vehicle for joy, to disarm my guests for seven short minutes, long enough to demonstrate how beautiful human connection can be if you just listen.

The afternoon sun slants through my windows as I work my way through the bag, each bite a small act of defiance against the glossy image I'm supposed to maintain. By the time I reach the bottom, my fingers are stained yellow from turmeric and my stomach is protesting the sheer volume of fried dough I've consumed.

I should probably eat something real. Maybe order a salad. Do some yoga. Process my emotions in a healthy way like Madge keeps suggesting.

Instead, I grab a throw pillow, curl up on my side, and let the food coma take over.

BANG BANG BANG.

I jolt awake, disoriented and dry-mouthed. The room is dark—*how long was I out?*

BANG BANG BANG.

"AARTI! I KNOW YOU'RE IN THERE!"

Magenta. Of course. I stumble to the door, still half-asleep and fully annoyed.

"Do you know what time it is?" I ask as I yank open the door.

"Ten forty-seven," she says, pushing past me. Her usually perfect green hair is frizzed, her production binder clutched to her chest like armor. "And before you say anything in response to what I'm about to tell you, remember *I'm* the one who pulled you out of that bathroom stall in your darkest hour at *Midnight Live.*"

"What did you do?" The food coma fog clears instantly. I know that look on her face—it's the same one she had when she accidentally switched my lines with our celebrity host on a *Midnight Live* 'Now News!' segment.

"I think I solved our problems," she says, but her voice wavers. "Like... all of them."

"Did you wave a magic wand and reassemble the most expensive diorama in a century of late-night?"

She takes a deep breath. "No, but… think about how great I must be at my job if Gretchen doesn't want to can our entire show after today's disaster."

"Madge. What. Did. You. Do?"

She takes a deep breath. "I may have told her we found your sidekick."

"What do you mean? Who?"

Madge looks at me with guilty eyes.

"Madge. *Who?*"

She still doesn't say anything. And yet, her lack of response speaks volumes to my rapidly increasing heart rate.

"Madge. Please tell me you did not pitch the ice cream demon as my *sidekick*."

She tilts her head to the side. "Would that I could."

I pinch my forearm. *Dammit*, I'm not dreaming–or nightmaring, rather.

"The ice cream demon who destroyed our set? Who *attacked* me on my own stage? Whose emotional attachment to her Moleskine is pathological?"

Madge sighs. "I pitched the ice cream demon whose very presence goaded you into a full-scale vaudevillian two-hander and with whom you have undeniable, electrifying banter. And may I emphasize to you, while you've been sleeping off said altercation, I've been in Gretchen's terrifying corner office, explaining the security footage from today and doing my own song-and-dance routine to keep *Up Late* from being purged from *TV Guide* for having one of the most expensive insurance claims in the history of shows that haven't aired yet."

I sink onto my couch, head in my hands. "Please tell me you're joking."

"She loved the tape. She said, and I quote, 'Aarti finally looks alive.'"

"That girl didn't even know who I was!"

"Exactly!" Magenta sits beside me, her energy desperate.

"That's why it works. You've already got a built-in segment together figuring out your ice cream flavor, and it's not a gimmick like 'Bus Boys'. She treats you like a real person. She brings out a different side of you."

"The only side she brought out was my litigious one."

"It also doesn't hurt that, according to Gretch's interns, she's seemingly never heard of Twitter, much less X."

"Shocker."

Madge folds her arms. "Aarti, please. I cracked a door open with Gretchen, but you'll still hafta do the legwork to make it come together. You and..." She pauses. "I called Jen & Mary's."

I stare at her. "Without asking me?"

She grabs my shoulders. "Gretchen opened our meeting with proposed severance packages. This isn't just a chance to save ourselves from some shitty one a.m. slot after that sportsball man reads bedtime stories. This is our chance to have a show. Period."

I stare into her hopeful gaze, reality sinking in.

"Gretchen wants you and Noa at the studio Monday morning," Madge continues. "She liked my pitch, but she said she needed to see the chemistry firsthand before the advertiser quarterly."

"Together."

Magenta studies my face. "Think about it, Aart. A series about creating your signature ice cream with someone who, for whatever reason, gets your guard down–it can show audiences the real you, in a cute, harmless context that's as uncontroversial as can be."

Uncontroversial. Ha. I think about how Noa's hazel eyes widened when her hand brushed my boob.

"The real me," I mutter.

I look around my place–the empty chakli bag, the pickle jar leaving a ring on my coffee table, the general disaster of my real life. *The real me?* Madge has no idea. The mess she can see is nothing compared to the parts I keep hidden.

"Yes. Because that's what I saw today." Her voice drops, losing its producer polish. "You forgot to perform. You were just... reacting. Unscripted. Alive. That's the Aarti they need to see."

I want to stay angry, but the fight drains out of me. I'm too full of chakli and self-pity, too aware that Madge–who's never steered me wrong before–might be the only person willing to tell me the truth I don't want to hear.

CHAPTER 9
NOA

I'VE BEEN VIBRATING at a frequency only dogs can hear since Saturday's CBT Studios fiasco. It's Monday morning now, and I'm convinced every footstep above the BFI is Jen and Mary themselves coming downstairs to personally fire me for humiliating them in front of such an important client.

"The emulsion is separating," Stella's voice pierces through the lab. "Are we making ice cream or conducting a fifth grade science experiment?"

Stella hasn't mentioned my Aarti pitch yet, which is either a miracle or she's playing some kind of psychological long game. Whichever it is, I'm certainly not going to be the one to bring it up first. And anyway, I haven't had a spare moment to question it, because she's been on one since I arrived this morning. Being on crutches has transformed my control-freak boss from a precision instrument into a medieval torture device.

I rush over to rescue the batch. "Sorry, I'll re-whip it–"

"With what technique? The one where you flail around like an uncoordinated cephalopod?" She's balancing on one crutch while using the other to point accusingly at my whisk. "Thirty-degree angle, Noa. We've discussed this."

We've discussed everything. Six times. Since seven a.m. She

made me recalibrate the thermometers twice, reorganize the extract shelf by molecular weight, and explain the difference between Tahitian and Madagascar vanilla until I considered chugging the freshly steeped extracts to end my suffering.

The thing is, I can't even complain. Not when I'm waiting for the other shoe to drop. Or crutch.

"Better," she concedes as the emulsion comes together. "Though I don't understand why you need constant supervision after three years."

Because I'm pretty sure I gave myself a concussion this weekend and haven't slept since, I don't say.

"Now, the cacao levels in batch six were–" Her phone buzzes. She glances at it and her expression shifts. "I need to take this. Do *not* touch the centrifuge. Or the blast chiller. Or anything more complex than a spoon."

She hobbles to her office with surprising agility. Through the window, I watch her on the phone, gesturing with her free hand like she's conducting an orchestra or performing an exorcism.

I stand there, pretending to study our flavor development chart while actually spiraling. Maybe Aarti Nair's people finally called. Maybe they're suing. Maybe I'll have to sell Ringo Carr to pay legal fees and take the bus everywhere.

"Get your things." Stella's suddenly beside me, moving silent as a ninja despite the mobility aids. "You're coming with me."

"Like… *all* my things?" I ask, voice trembling.

Stella curtly shakes her head no. *Phew.*

"Okay. Where are we–"

"Meeting. Across town."

A meeting. Sounds totally normal and non-threatening.

Or she's taking you somewhere nice and private to fire slash murder you! Big ups to Jerky McGee, who never fails to catastrophize. I mentally flip him off and slide into the backseat of the rideshare Stella ordered, trying to become one with the upholstery.

I sneak a glance at Stella. Her hands are folded over her

crutches like she's sitting for a Victorian portrait. She's never been overly pleasant toward me, but my god, she'd give a speck of dust on the dashboard more warmth right now.

We're halfway down Sunset when I realize we're heading toward Hollywood. Toward a very familiar part of Hollywood.

"Stella–"

"So," she says, staring straight ahead. "Saturday."

My soul exits my body. "I can explain–"

"You bled during a celebrity client pitch?"

"A little?! From my face! And I cleaned it up–well, actually I passed out, but I'm sure someone cleaned it–"

"And destroyed property worth more than your annual salary."

"I'll fix it, I'll fix everything! I can apologize, or build them a new one, or–" We're pulling up to CBT Studios. "Oh god, are they pressing charges?"

"Get out."

"Stella, please, I love my job–"

"Noa." She turns to look at me with an expression I've never seen before. Is that... *amusement?* "Do you know what happened during my first celebrity collaboration?"

I shake my head, still clutching my seatbelt like a lifeline.

"Food & Wine Festival 2008. I accidentally triggered a champagne sorbet explosion that coated three Michelin-starred chefs and a very, *very* prominent Food Network host. You know the one. There were photos. So many photos..."

"But–"

"The point is, we all have our disasters. Yours just happened to be captured on security footage." She gestures toward the studio entrance with her crutch. "Now get out. You have a meeting."

"A meeting? About what?"

"You'll find out, I suppose." A sneaky smile flickers across her face. "Try not to bleed on anyone important this time."

"But I don't–"

Before *'even know if I'm allowed within one hundred feet of Aarti Nair'* can leave my lips, the door slams in my face. Stella–and any hope of not confronting my colossal failures–screeches off into the morning Hollywood haze.

CHAPTER 10
AARTI

I SLIP into the studio like a teenager sneaking in past curfew, except instead of avoiding my parents, I'm dodging my own writers' room. Through the glass, I can see Madge with our three segment writers, their heads bent in deep concentration. I duck past before anyone can see and barricade myself in my office.

My hands are actually shaking as I lock the door and grab an emergency kombucha from my mini fridge. *What the hell is wrong with me?* I've pitched to studio executives before. I've performed for millions. I've literally hung from a helicopter for a *Midnight Live* cold open. So why does the thought of sitting across from Gretchen Gordon make my palms sweat like I'm back in middle school math class?

The answer: because Noa Hart will be sitting beside me.

Noa makes me antsy, and I have to admit, it has very little to do with her destroying the diorama. It's because Noa doesn't look at me like everyone else does. She doesn't see "Aarti Nair, Comedy Genius" or "Aarti Nair, Diversity Hire" or even "Aarti Nair, That Woman from That Thing." She just sees some unhinged lady who falls into dumpsters and calls security on (aggravatingly insistent, curly-haired) business associates.

Which is equal parts refreshing and mortifying.

I slump into my desk chair and spin, staring at the ceiling. The truth is, once this show launches–really launches–I'll be so deep in the closet I'll be finding Christmas presents from 1987. Every relationship, every moment of intimacy, every honest expression of who I am will have to be delicately managed, hidden, danced around, more than ever before.

I'm tired already.

My phone buzzes. *Brigitte98 just posted a new carousel to Gramsta.* Brigitte on the runway, Brigitte with a SpongeBob Band-Aid on her alarmingly flawless tan skin, Brigitte in a blurry selfie in the back of some black car with… that starlet, whom she told me was just a friend, planting a sexy kiss on her neck. Can I even blame her for the soft launch? I freaked out at The Velvet Tongue. We always had an end date anyway.

I met Brigitte eighteen months ago at a Chateau Marmont party that I was only attending because Madge threatened to submit my headshot to *The Bachelor* if I didn't get out more. She was by the pool, impossibly long legs crossed, making everyone around her look like Cabbage Patch kids. When our eyes met, she blushed, and I knew it was a done deal.

We went back to her place that night. And most nights since.

Before Brigitte, there was Samira, the burgeoning sapphic pop star who wrote songs about me that she performed in dive bars while I sat in the back, hood up, pretending I didn't know all the words. Before Samira was Chloe, a slightly older method actress from my first indie film *The Red Dot*, where I played a superhero who gets her powers on her period. Chloe insisted on staying in character even in bed, which was hot until she was prepping for a biopic about a doomsday cult leader. Before Chloe was… well, a rotating cast of women. Some of them were out, some were not, but all of them understood the rules: be discreet, be cool, be gone before morning.

The only other people who know the truth about me are my

sister and favorite uncle, Arjun. I haven't even told Madge, although I'm sure she has her suspicions. She'd accept me, I know that. She'd make spreadsheets about optimal coming-out strategies and roll out Pride merch for the show. But I can't put that burden on her. It's not fair to make her keep a secret that could tank everything we've built.

My phone buzzes again. This time it's a photo from Madge—a selfie with our writers, all of them making exaggerated suspicious faces.

MADGE

We saw you walk by earlier.

I drag myself out of my office and shuffle down the hall like I'm walking to the guillotine.

"There she is!" Sydney Remsho, our head segment writer, spins her office chair around, revealing her Burger King employee shirt with the original name crossed out and *Syd* scrawled in Sharpie over it. "Savior of our livelihoods! Restorer of frozen dessert diplomacy!"

I nod at Madge. "Credit where it's due, all I did was let my festering annoyance bubble over. She's the one who somehow convinced our network overlords it was comedy gold."

Rohan doesn't even look up from the origami giraffe he's meticulously folding. "Also, nothing's been greenlit yet, Syd."

"Don't be a downer, Ro!" Freya, a young staff writer we poached from *Midnight Live*, lobs a crumpled notebook paper at Rohan. He bats it back.

Madge claps her hands. "Settle down, Musketeers. Aarti's gonna do great. She's good on her feet–"

"–but even better on her face," I finish for her. It was the tagline for my first standup tour while *Midnight Live* was off-season.

"Look," Madge says, switching into producer mode. "The meeting is going to be fine. Gretch the Wretch is gonna love it because it's exactly the kind of authentic chemistry the network felt was missing."

"Authentic chemistry," I repeat. "With someone who brought a weapon to our first meeting."

"Nitrogen isn't technically a weapon," Rohan points out. "It's more of an industrial hazard."

"I have to go," I announce, standing abruptly. "Can't keep Gretchen waiting."

"You're fifteen minutes early," Madge points out.

"Even better." I head for the door before they can psych me out more. "If this goes badly, it's on all of you."

"If it goes well, we're taking all the credit!" Syd calls after me.

The elevator ride to the executive floor goes so fast my ears pop. Gretchen Gordon's wing takes up almost the entire top floor, and everything in the space is combatively grey.

Her receptionist, a terrifyingly polite older woman named Diane, looks up from her computer. "Ms. Nair, thank you for being here. Ms. Gordon is expecting you. You can wait just down the hall."

I follow her directions, the hallway seeming to stretch forever, lined with photos of *Up Late* hosts through the decades— a visual reminder of the legacy I'm about to either uphold or destroy.

God, I hope my new sidekick is more prepared for this meeting than she was two days ago.

I round the corner and immediately abandon all hope.

Noa is standing, even though empty chairs abound, looking like she might vomit or faint or possibly both. She's clutching a weird little crochet bag like it's the only thing keeping her tethered to Earth.

"So... like... what's–?" Noa chokes out, radiating utter panic.

Great.

My pitching partner is not prepared at all.

EXT. HOLLYWOOD STREET - CONTINUOUS

Paparazzi swarm. Odette cuts through the crowd.

                    PAPARAZZO 1
          There's our girl!

                    PAPARAZZO 2
          Is it true you're dating Toxic
          Masculinity of the Toxic Twins?

                    PAPARAZZO 3
          What's life like as the world's
          favorite superhero, sweetheart?

We finally see her wearing a bright red super suit with her
TAMPON NUNCHUCKS and PAD MASK.

                    ODETTE
          It's The Red Dot to you. No time
          for questions, pap smears. I've got
          a feminist event to save.

END

She whips out two super sticky MENSTRUAL CUPS and scales the
building.

EXT. CAPITAL RECORDS BUILDING ROOF - CONTINUOUS

The Toxic Twins take hostages as the fire spreads.

                    HOSTAGE
          The Red Dot will save us!

                    TOXIC MASCULINITY
          Not today lady, her period is
          over.

                    TOXIC SHOCK
          We looked it up on the Internet. No
          period, no powers.

                    ODETTE (O.C.)
          Why does everyone believe
          everything they hear on the
          Internet?!

Odette appears behind them. Toxic M rushes her and she RAMS
into him with an uppercut. He flies backward.

An EAR PIECE RINGS in her ear. She taps it.

CHAPTER 11
NOA

AARTI TAKES a seat across from me in the reception area, swinging one lanky leg over the other. "You look ill."

"I *feel* ill! I just found out what's happening here about... seven minutes ago?" My voice ratchets higher than my blood pressure.

Aarti's eyes widen. "Seven–what do you mean seven minutes ago? You didn't know about this meeting?"

I shake my head. Seven minutes ago, I was standing in a janitor's closet with a hyperactive PA named Claire, learning that the woman I was about to meet could destroy careers with a single raised eyebrow.

"Gretchen Gordon *is* late-night television," Claire told me emphatically. "She took *Up Late* from nothing to everything. She eats executives for breakfast. She once made a showrunner cry just by sighing."

Claire deposited me in this waiting area with a peppy "godspeed!" which felt about as reassuring as being pushed out of a plane without a parachute.

"Okay," Aarti says, recalculating. "Okay. We have maybe three minutes. Just breathe. Follow my lead in there. You know the cardinal rule of improv? 'Yes and'?"

"No, but–"

"Right. So do the opposite of that." She's talking faster now. "Go with whatever I say, but don't expand too much. Actually, don't expand at all. But also don't just sit there. Support but don't embellish. Actually, maybe embellish a little if–"

"Ladies."

We both jump. Gretchen's receptionist materializes in front of us.

"Ms. Gordon is ready for you."

She marches us to Gretchen's office. The door opens to reveal a space so aggressively minimalist it makes me nostalgic for the janitor's closet.

Gretchen Gordon stands behind her desk, pouring amber liquid into a crystal glass. She's smaller than I expected, but her sharp gaze makes me feel two inches tall.

"Sit," she commands.

We sit.

"Relax."

We become even more rigid. Gretchen's Southern drawl sounds like she's about to offer us mint juleps before burying our bodies in her garden.

"When Morrison imploded, your name ticked every box," Gretchen tells Aarti. "Headline gold: 'Late-night finally hands the desk to a woman of color.' The board loved the optics, advertisers loved the novelty, and I assumed you'd keep things breezy enough for the heartland. Instead, we polished the you-turd so smooth there's nothin' left to hold on to. That's not gonna cut it."

Gretchen circles us like a shark as she continues. "*Up Late* viewers need more from you than the impressions that rocketed you to stardom on *Midnight Live*. Even behind their 'Now News!' desk, you played a facsimile of a talk show host. This new audience needs to know who the real Aarti Nair is. Without alienatin' anyone, of course."

Gretchen returns to stand behind the desk. "I said as much to your green-haired lackey last week, and she was… less than receptive to my solution. Said you were gonna need convincin' to accept a sidekick to draw out your authenticity."

Her gray eyes needle in on Aarti. "But that was before Saturday."

I feel sweat pooling in places I didn't know could sweat.

"You see, ladies, when a show hemorrhages money before it even airs, when the insurance claims start pilin' up, when the board asks pointed questions about cuttin' our losses…" She trails off. "Producers get a lot more receptive to the laughable notions of a network president."

Gretchen swirls her drink and the clinking sounds like a jail cell door. "Suddenly, I'm hearin' that you two have unprecedented chemistry. I'm hearin' that your rapport with this ice cream scientist–" *Oh god, she's shifted her penetrating gaze in my direction.* "–is gonna save our show."

If it were possible to shrink smaller in my seat, I would. I feel Aarti's eyes pinging to me in my periphery, but I'm not prepared to glance back, lest I call even an ounce more attention to myself.

"So." Gretchen finally takes a sip of her drink and grimaces. "I'm not convinced this isn't just a desperate act to distract me from cancelin' the show after your soundstage antics this weekend."

She sticks a finger in her glass and stirs the steel whiskey cube. "Convince me."

I swear our hearts collectively stop beating.

"Well," Aarti starts, and I can hear the scramble in her voice, "our thing is–"

"We met in a bathroom," I blurt.

"Not like that," Aarti says quickly.

"She was climbing out a window–"

"Escaping. Through. Strategically exiting–"

"And she was stuck–"

"Temporarily delayed–"

"So I pushed her–"

"Assisted me–"

"Into a dumpster."

We both stop. Gretchen hasn't blinked.

"And then," Aarti rallies, "the next day–"

"I brought nitrogen–"

"*Nitrogen*–"

"To a meeting–"

"That I didn't know was happening–"

"And there was that incident with the backdrop–"

"Which I was *so* grateful the network approved–"

"And which I'm totally gonna repair–"

Aarti cuts me off with a glare. "She crushed it–"

"Then I passed out–"

"–because she realized there was bl–"

"–maraschino cherries–"

"That was blood–"

I shudder. "Right, but I was pretending it was–"

"...cherries," we finish in unison.

Gretchen's expression hasn't changed. We're breathing like we just ran a marathon, but her silence stretches. And stretches. And stretches.

I can hear the thrum of my heartbeat in my skull.

"You're tellin' me that your revolutionary chemistry is based on..." She savors her pause like it's a Michelin starred meal. "...mutual incompetence?"

"Yes," we say. Then, horrified: "No!"

"I mean–" Aarti says.

"We're very competent–" I try.

"It's more like–"

"Controlled chaos?"

"Nothing about it is controlled."

The silence this time is infinite. Geological. Pangea rearranges itself in the time it takes Gretchen to respond.

Finally, she shakes her head.

"There is somethin'…" She searches for the words. "A frenetic energy between you two that I don't entirely know what to do with."

My stomach is attempting to exit through my throat.

"This has been one of the worst pitches I've ever witnessed." She continues like she's not delivering scathing professional insults. "I've never seen Aarti more off-balance. I've never met you before, Noa, but your performance has been equally underwhelmin'."

Even Jerky McGee is rendered speechless in the presence of Gretchen.

"And yet." She sets down her whiskey. "There is something here. Buried under all that…" she waves a red manicured hand, "…whatever that was."

I realize I'm holding my breath.

"Field segments are crucial for any late-night host. Audiences want to watch you out in the world, interacting with the same reality they navigate every day. When a host comes across too polished…" She shakes her head. "Our reality is, we can't afford to be edgy. Can't ruffle feathers, can't alienate advertisers, can't give the board a reason to pull the plug."

She turns her gaze on me again. "A sidekick is someone who can draw out those genuine moments, the unguarded reactions that make a host feel real without needin' to court controversy."

Her eyes bounce between us. "I'm not convinced you two even know what you have. But perhaps that's the point. Your chemistry isn't manufactured. It's chaotic but it's authentic."

She shrugs, a movement that probably costs more than my car. "Stranger things have saved shows."

"So we're…" Aarti ventures.

"Not dead yet," Gretchen finishes. She turns to her window, dismissing us.

Aarti and I scramble toward the door like freed prisoners.

In the elevator back down, Aarti turns to me, a look of amazement softening her sharp features. "Holy shit. We did it. I still have a show. You–" She points at me. "You are going to be on national fucking television with me."

It hits me like a nitrogen canister to the face. *Me. Noa. On TV.* Actual millions-of-eyeballs, every-bad-hair-day-immortalized-forever TV. My mouth opens. Closes. My brain short-circuits.

"I'm gonna–" I whisper.

"Be on TV! With me," she gleefully repeats.

I slap a hand over my mouth. "–throw up," I manage to croak, then bolt as soon as the elevator doors ding open, sprinting for the exit with Olympian speed.

IT'S BEEN, oh, ten hours and thirty-seven minutes since Noa ran out of our meeting faster than Sha'Carri Richardson, and I haven't heard a peep from her since. Neither has Madge, even after contacting her boss, Stella.

I can't entirely blame Noa for ghosting. Is professional ghosting a thing? I wish I'd known sooner. There have been plenty of times in the buildup to this show where I, too, wanted to run for the hills.

I knew being the face of *Up Late* would be a fresh challenge, but being unable to find my schtick, even with a team of the most brilliant comedy writers in the business, is embarrassing. What's even more embarrassing is the fact that the success of this career-defining moment I've worked toward my whole life is being held hostage in the sweaty palms of a neurotic ice cream scientist who has zero interest in saving my ass, let alone appearing on national television with me. Why would she? She met me at rock bottom, and ever since, I've dragged her through one nightmare scenario after another. The common denominator in all this chaos? Me.

Welcome to my brain at midnight: the time where, if I'm not asleep, bad things begin to happen. My mind splits open and becomes a dark, never-ending vortex of stress and (sometimes good, but mostly bad) ideas. A haunting remnant of *Midnight Live,* you'd think, but no. My subconscious has been primed for all things late-night since my days of falling asleep to audiobooks on cassette tapes as a child.

"Do not flip the tape, beta, you will be up late and too tired for school," my mom would tell me. Some nights, I'd listen. But other nights, like tonight, I'd flip the tape. And grab the next. And flip it. And grab the next and flip and flip and flip until I made it to the end of whichever fantasy novel I was listening to for the thirtieth time. I'd lay there under the Kantha quilt my grandmother made me, hands folded across my stomach, listening, thinking.

One of those nights, it was as if my dad could hear my thoughts spiraling from the other room. He crept in and placed something on my nightstand.

"Here, Aarti," he said, giving me my first ever night notebook. "To rid yourself of the Chinta."

My dad had always been somewhat of a lowkey yogi, meditating in his chair after dinner or hitting a downward dog between his classes as a professor. I thought he must be doing it all to deal with the stresses of Maa. And then I grew up and realized it was probably to deal with me, too.

I scribble "professional ghosting" into the current notebook on my bedside table. I've lost count of how many I've been through at this point. At least a hundred during *Midnight Live* alone.

I roll onto my back. Turn on my right side. Then my left. I wriggle onto my stomach, so much more restless than I even was as a kid. *That's me—always regressing!*

I scream into my pillow so that Diti doesn't wake up. If she's even home. Who's to say? She's probably out enjoying her life, performing emergency CPR at a college rave, doing what our parents told us to do. *Be a doctor, a lawyer, anything but a comedian.*

I reach for my pen and haphazardly scrawl "rave CPR" in my notebook.

I should have listened to my parents.

Nope. No. I would have been miserable as anything but a comedian.

Although... I am currently miserable... as a comedian.

Fuck.

I trudge into the office after a nearly sleepless night and am greeted by Madge and a god-tier-sized matcha.

"I spoke with Stella at the crack of dawn," she says as we walk down the hallway. My tired ears perk up. "She and Gretch the Wretch exist in the same maniacal time zone, apparently."

My half-functioning brain interprets the rest of the words coming out of her mouth: *Something something five thirty a.m. Really crazy. Noa will come around. Don't worry.*

"Wait," I laugh, "Don't worry? Noa's been MIA for nearly twenty-four hours. And that Stella woman also made it sound like Noa had a heads-up about the meeting yesterday. Breaking news: she did not."

Madge pats me on the back a little too hard. Droplets of my precious matcha spill through the spout.

"I can tell you're not at peak Aarti functions this morning, so follow me on this. We have to pretend like everything is okay, because, my dear, we have no other option."

She charges ahead into the writers' room, leaving me in the wake of her truth bomb.

"Hello everyone, everything is fine," I begin our pitch meeting. Madge tries to hide her facepalm. "Let's talk about ice cream, unfortunately."

We spend the next several hours throwing around ideas

about how my segments with Noa could be structured, and it's a struggle.

"Truth or Dairy?" Rohan pitches. "Aarti has to answer a personal question or eat a weird flavor Noa whipped up."

"We're trying to play to ice cream's strengths, not gross out the audience about frozen desserts," Madge points out, much to my relief.

Syd rips out a page from her journal and crumples it up. "There goes Brain Freeze Roulette."

"Wheel of Portions!" Freya reads from her notes. "Spin a wheel, add whatever it lands on to the sundae. It can have a bunch of different ice cream flavors, toppings, syrups, yadda yadda!"

"Could still wind up eating something pretty off-putting like watermelon chocolate with caramel drizzle," I point out. Freya wrinkles her nose, deflated.

"Okay, okay," Rohan leans forward. "Ice cream speed dating. Noa brings out different bases, Aarti has thirty seconds with each to find 'the one.'"

"I don't hate it," Madge offers, which everyone present knows means it's not good enough.

"What if Noa teaches Aarti to make ice cream, like a cooking show?" Freya suggests.

"How does that move the needle on flavor development?" I ask. "Plus I'll give our audience the ick with how bad I am at measuring stuff."

Madge groans, a canary in the coal mine for the low morale in our writers' room.

"Just waterboard me in gelato and call it a day with whatever flavor I pass out on."

Don't worry, no one else laughs at my joke either. I lower my head to the table face-first.

We are quickly on our way to nowhere.

· · ·

I slide into my car at the end of the day, a puddle of exhausted, human-adjacent goo. We landed on the most mundane segment imaginable for tomorrow's shoot, and it took everything in me not to spill the beans to my writers that one half of our talent wasn't even confirmed yet.

Somehow I manage to drive all the way home even though I don't remember a single traffic jam or stoplight. I trudge up the stairs to my condo, missing the elevator entirely, and walk in on Diti making pakora. Gram flour covers every surface and oil sputters out of a pan that's on way-too-high heat. She has unfortunately never been any good at cooking.

"Make sure to clean up after yourself," I say tersely.

"Hello to you, too," she replies. "Good day, I presume?"

"Just swell."

I crash onto the couch and close my eyes. I hear Diti place the fritters in the pan with an oily pop.

"Put it on medium."

"Whatever," she grumbles. "Want to talk about it?"

Several more mini explosions erupt from the pan.

"You forgot to chop up–"

"The beans, I know, Aarti. Geez. I was just trying to make you feel better."

I muster the strength to open one eye at her.

She shrugs. "You walked out of here like you were on your deathbed this morning. You didn't even hear me say hi." She goes to flip the pakoras.

"Leave them," I command. She rolls her eyes and puts down the slotted spoon. "For two minutes, at least." The last thing I wanted was to come home and give my sister a culinary lesson.

"Can't you just let me handle it?"

"They're going to come out all wrong. I'm just trying to–"

"Help. Sure."

We stare at each other in a classic sister standoff.

She tucks her lips. "Has it been two minutes yet?"

I sigh and stand. "I think I'm gonna–" I point to my room and then walk into it.

"Let me know if you want–"

I close the door. I love my sister, I do, but simultaneously being the responsible one and the most disappointing one is a double whammy I cannot bear right now.

I throw myself into my bed and scroll through Gramsta. Along with the rest of my life as of late, my algorithm loves to punish me. The same photo of Brigitte and the starlet, Mila, appears, now with over a million likes. I heart it. Might as well join the masses in throwing her my support. Or jealousy. Whatever it is.

Ding! My phone lights up with a text.

BRIGITTE

Finally falling prey to my little thirst trap?

I nearly correct her that *that* is less thirst trap and more relationship announcement, when she pings me again.

BRIGITTE

It's nothing serious, my little Aart-nigma ;)

BRIGITTE

So are you going to invite me over or what?

I groan.

Did I mention there's one thing that can keep me out of my endless nighttime spirals? Unfortunately for me, it starts with O and rhymes with shmorgasm.

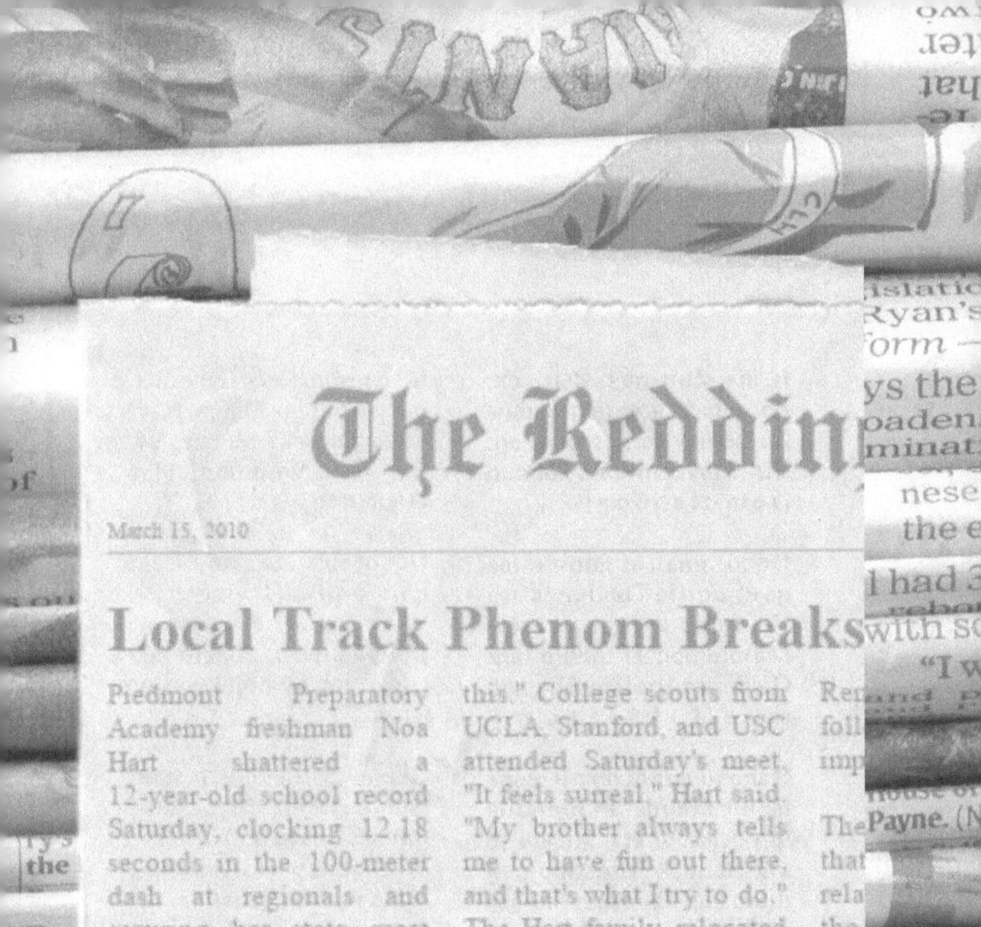

The Reddin[g]

March 15, 2010

Local Track Phenom Breaks

Piedmont Preparatory Academy freshman Noa Hart shattered a 12-year-old school record Saturday, clocking 12.18 seconds in the 100-meter dash at regionals and securing her state meet spot. Hart, 14, transferred from Washington this fall and has turned heads since September. Her time broke Jennifer Walsh's 1998 record of 12.31 seconds and places her second among California freshmen this season. "Noa is something special," said coach Maria Santos. "In 18 years of coaching, I've never seen raw talent like this." College scouts from UCLA, Stanford, and USC attended Saturday's meet. "It feels surreal," Hart said. "My brother always tells me to have fun out there, and that's what I try to do." The Hart family relocated to Redding in August when Noa received a full athletic scholarship to Piedmont's elite sports program. Her father David will begin teaching English at Shasta College this fall, while twin brother Aiden is also a Piedmont freshman. Coach Santos believes Olympic development programs could be on the

GROWING UP, my dad loved to tell anyone who would listen that I learned to run before I could walk.

"This one," he'd say, pointing at me like a prize heifer at the county fair, "came out sprinting."

Which, gross. But also kind of true.

By sixth grade, I was the girl who had other kids faking asthma attacks to avoid racing me during PE. Coach Martinez actually cried when she clocked my hundred-meter time. Happy tears, she clarified, while shoving a track & field permission slip at my father through the driver's window of our Subaru in the pickup line.

"Your daughter could get a full ride," she said. "The Olympics aren't off the table."

Sitting in the backseat, Aiden cooed, "Noa's gonna be famous. Better practice your autograph, diva."

"Shut up, buttface."

But secretly? I was already dreaming up how nice *Noa Hart, Olympic Gold Medalist* would look on a cereal box.

The thing about track was, it was mine. Just mine. Being twins, Aiden and I did basically everything together–same classes, same friends, same cavernous hole in our heart left by the passing of our mom when we were toddlers. Aiden would cheer me on from the stands at every meet, but when I ran, it was the only time I wasn't part of a matched set. I was just Noa. Singular. Flying. When I was running, I didn't owe anything to anyone but myself.

Maybe that's why it was so easy to give up.

By eighth grade, I wasn't just good–I was untouchable. College scouts were showing up to my meets, timing me with professional equipment, whispering to each other behind clipboards. When Piedmont Prep in Redding, California offered me a full ride to join their elite athletic program, it felt like destiny calling.

"This is it," Dad had said, eyes shining as he read the scholarship letter. "This is your ticket, kiddo."

We sold everything, although we didn't have much to begin with. Packed our whole lives into a U-Haul and drove south to move in with Dad's sister and chase down my future.

Aiden had officially become Aiden the year before, and being trans in rural Washington had not been easy. Even though technically he was born three minutes before me, I've always felt like the elder twin, protecting his softness from the world's sharp edges. Defending my sweet, creative sibling felt as inherent to me as breathing.

We hoped that California would be different for him. Progressive. Accepting.

We hoped wrong.

Piedmont was paradise for athletes. Olympic-sized track, professional coaches, a nutrition program that actually understood carb-loading. The varsity team welcomed me like I was their missing link, their secret weapon for nationals. But while I was doing two-a-days and getting fitted for my uniform, Aiden was navigating his own special hell.

He didn't tell me, and I was too high on my own glory, too

drunk on the new social echelon I'd been ushered into, to notice my twin was drowning.

One afternoon in early spring, I was in the locker room, lacing up my spikes for our first big meet, when Coach pulled me aside.

"Your brother's been suspended," she said. "Fighting. He broke another kid's nose."

The world tilted. Aiden didn't fight. Aiden made art and cracked terrible puns and cried at dog food commercials.

"The kid called me a freak," he'd tell me later. "Said worse things. I just snapped."

The suspension meant he couldn't attend school events. Including my meet.

"It's fine," he'd insisted as Dad drove us to the track. "I'll wait in the car. Read or something. Better than watching other kids sweat anyway."

"This is bullshit," Dad muttered.

I warmed up, trying to focus. This meet was important. Scouts would be there.

They called us to the starting line. I crouched into position, fingers pressing into the rubberized track. The official raised his gun.

That's when I looked up, past the stands full of strangers, to the parking lot, where I could see our beat-up Subaru just outside the gate. Dad and Aiden leaned against the car, arms folded identically. The two people in the world who mattered most to me.

"Runners, set!"

I rose into position.

But all I could think about was my brother. Punished for defending himself. Banished because yet another place had decided he didn't belong.

The gun fired.

Everyone exploded forward. Except for me.

I stood up, stepped off the track, and walked away.

Coach was screaming. Officials were blowing whistles. I didn't care. I strode right through the chaos, across the field, past the gawking spectators, to that goddamn parking lot.

Dad saw me coming. His face went through about seventeen emotions in three seconds.

"Noa, what–"

"We're getting our GEDs," I announced, yanking open the back door. "Both of us. Together."

"Noa, no," Aiden protested. His eye was still swollen from the fight. "This is your dream–"

"Dreams change," I said. "We're done here."

Dad tried to argue. Aiden begged me to go back. The coach jogged over, promising we could work something out.

I didn't budge.

That night, I took my shoebox of medals and buried them in Aunt Susie's hall closet behind musty board games and Hanukkah decorations from the Carter administration. We were looking up GED programs by morning and I never ran competitively again.

The rest of that spring, I was climbing the walls. Track season was happening somewhere without me, and I needed something, anything, to fill the Olympic-sized hole I'd punched in my own life. Dad had started teaching English at the community college, and I'd wander campus between GED classes, restless and untethered.

That was how I wound up at the chemistry department's open house one sunny afternoon. Colorful neon balloons summoned me into the lab, where a small crowd gathered around a woman in a tie-dye lab coat as she poured cream into a bowl smoking with nitrogen, turning it from liquid to solid in seconds. It was magic. It lit up my brain like a starting gun.

Forgetting anyone else was even in the room, I looked her in the eyes and asked, "Can I try?"

I didn't know it yet, but that sorceress in front of me was Professor Celia Kersey, and she would become my mentor in all things ice cream for the next three years.

The precision of it hooked me immediately. Ice cream was all about timing: knowing exactly when to add the stabilizers, how fast to churn, the ideal moment to stop before ice crystals formed. It required the same obsessive attention to split seconds that track had demanded, except instead of shaving milliseconds off my time, I was chasing the perfect texture, the ideal melt, that fleeting moment of transformation.

Best of all, it was safe. No crowds watching. No scouts judging. No stakes except whether the lavender honey I brought home for Aiden tasted like frozen soap or actual dessert. I could pour all my intensity into something that wouldn't leave anyone behind, wouldn't force impossible choices.

But today reminded me that sometimes even a life devoted to ice cream can't protect me from myself.

Sprinting out the doors of the CBT building is the fastest I've run in years. I don't make it far, doubling over just around the corner, adrenaline burning through my veins. Those fast-twitch muscles still know what to do... my lungs, not so much.

I call a ride to Aiden's, knowing he won't be home for hours. Better the colorful chaos of his maximalist backhouse than the unhip ADHD tornado waiting at mine. I curl up among his throw pillows, turn off my phone, and fall asleep way too early, thankful for his blackout curtains and the half-smoked joint I find (and finish) in his vintage ashtray.

I'm awoken by blinding light and a bloodcurdling scream. Aiden, in an offensively sparkly poncho, stands by the lamp, hands clutched to his chest.

"Noa Jacqueline Hart! You just scared the living glitter out of me!"

I sit up groggily as everything I fell asleep to escape rushes back in. He must clock my overwhelm because he rushes over beside me and wraps me in his sequined arms.

"Talk to me, Nono. Why're you here?"

"Spooey," I mumble into his shoulder.

Like a drill sergeant, he repeats back, "Spooey, sir yes sir!" and hops up off the couch to grab the two most important ingredients to ever grace a kitchen pantry: pretzels and frosting.

Mouth full of my favorite snack, I finally tell Aiden everything that's been going on, from Stella's injury to destroying the city of Los Angeles with my butt to the horror of potentially being on national television followed by the horror of potentially *not* being on national television. The hot talk show host of it all…

Aiden listens without interrupting–truly, a spiritual feat for him. He sits cross-legged on the rug in his poncho, swirling a pretzel through the frosting tub while I talk myself hoarse.

When I finally run out of humiliating details, he crunches down on his pretzel and gives me a head tilt. "You done?"

"Pretty much."

"Cool. Here's what's not gonna happen." He sets the frosting down, climbs up onto the couch, and wedges himself next to me so our knees knock. "You're not gonna run away again. We don't do that anymore."

"I wasn't–I didn't–" I sputter.

He flicks my forehead. "Yes you did. You bolted. And you've used up your lifetime supply of bolt credits, okay? You walked off the track for me. You've been stepping off tracks for years. You don't get to do it again."

My eyes sting. I lean my head against his shoulder, ignoring the sharp bite of sequins. "But what if I screw it up even worse? What if I'm not good enough for this?"

"Then you screw it up." He shrugs like it's obvious. "Big

whoop. You're still doing it. You're not allowed to run away from yourself anymore. Not on my watch."

"Coming from someone who calls watches 'time shackles for the unimaginative.'"

"A gay can metaphor, okay?"

"It's just... not that simple."

"But it is." He tugs me closer and drops a kiss on my hair. "Run *toward* something for once. Even if you trip over your own feet. Even if you demolish multiple fancy LA neighborhoods again. The world deserves to see what Noa Hart is capable of."

I nod.

"Great," he says. "Now that little fit is over, we're going to get you prepared."

"What do you–?"

"It is so *utterly* embarrassing that you showed up without doing your homework, so we're not gonna let that happen again."

Aiden pulls out his laptop and we spend the rest of the night watching clips of Aarti on *Midnight Live*. Even when she's a brand new cast member with bit parts, she's a star. Her timing is flawless. Her characters are unhinged and wide-ranging, from Wanda the Witness Protection Bridesmaid to Woman Who Got Neanderthal Results On 23andMe. When she takes over the 'Now News!' desk for the first time and interviews the Pompeii Volcano, we both have tears in our eyes from laughing so hard.

I wish I wasn't so genuinely impressed with her, but it's pointless to deny it.

"This show rules," I yawn to Aiden as I drift off on his shoulder.

I sleep another few hours, then text Stella when I wake up.

Tell Madge I'll be there tomorrow.

I'm just drained enough that not even Jerky McGee can bully me into dressing up my exhaustion for someone else's comfort.

                    ANGIE
          I think we're gonna be white people
          finding out we're white people.
                    CHARLOTTE
          Let's open and see!
THEY TAP THE RESULTS ON THEIR PHONES.
                    ANGIE
          British. French. Nonspecific Northern
          European. It's official, I'm white.
                    LUNA
          I have 2% Middle Eastern in there
          somewhere. What about you Bekah?
BEKAH LOOKS UP SLOWLY.

                    BEKAH
          I am Neanderthal.

                    CHARLOTTE
          Weird, but okay.

                    ANGIE
          I'm glad someone got some cool
          results! Let's move on to the health
          portion. It looks like I--
BEKAH DIPS HER FINGERS IN THE HUMMUS.
                    CHARLOTTE
          Bekah what are you doing?
                    BEKAH
          Oh, um, sorry.

"23 and Me-anderthal"

                    CHARLOTTE
          Anyway, this says I'm less likely to
          consume caffeine. So true. I'm
          naturally energetic.
                    ANGIE
          I'm likely to flush from alcohol. Like
          I didn't already know that.
                    LUNA
          I'm--
BEKAH DROPS A GIANT ROCK ON THE COFFEE TABLE AND CHISELS.
                    CHARLOTTE
          Bekah, what the hell?
                    BEKAH
          Make tools to hunt!
                    LUNA
          Just because there's Neanderthal in
          your DNA doesn't mean you're actually
          a Neanderthal.
                    CHARLOTTE
          And you're fucking up my coffee table.
                    BEKAH
          Sorry, learning my genetic history has
          been a lot. If you'll excuse me--
BEKAH EXITS. SHRIEKING NOISES COME FROM THE KITCHEN.
                    CHARLOTTE
          Bekah, what is going on?!
          ...S DRESSED IN BLOODY FURS.

CHAPTER 14
AARTI

WAKING up with a leggy supermodel in my bed should feel like winning the lottery, but I'm so fucked up that all it does is tie my stomach into knots. Not only is this the second time Brigitte has broken our gone-by-morning agreement, but last night it wasn't even for a sexy reason.

For the life of me, I could not get it up, so to speak. Even with Brigitte trying her damnedest to help matters along, I kept getting distracted by intrusive thoughts about nitrogen canisters and wild curls and whether Noa was okay after she bolted from the Gretchen meeting.

"You hearted my story," Brigitte finally said flatly, rolling off of me to stare at the ceiling.

"I heart a lot of things," I mumbled, cringing in the dark at my own casual cruelty.

The silence that followed was excruciating. Eventually, she just went to sleep, leaving me to doomscroll my overactive mind into submission. I didn't have it in me to wake her back up and ask her to leave.

Now, in the harsh light of morning, I walk a stone-faced Brigitte to the door. From the kitchen, Diti watches the whole exchange over her coffee mug, smirking like the Cheshire Cat.

"Don't," I warn as I trudge back.

"As long as you get tested," she shrugs.

"You know I do, *doctor*."

I grab my keys and flee before I have to hear any more of it.

The moment I arrive on set, Madge rushes over to me.

"Noa's in hair and makeup," she says breathlessly.

My heart does a weird flippy thing that's definitely just anxiety about the show.

"She's worried you're upset," Madge continues.

"I am upset."

"Don't act like it."

I'm about to elaborate on all the reasons Noa Hart has every right to be worried that I'm mad when the hair and makeup door swings open.

A woman emerges with glossy, pin-straight amber-colored locks cascading over... overalls? She's in full glam–smoky eyes, nude lip, the works–but the candy-striper attire makes her look like a 1950s ice cream parlor employee who got lost on her way to the general store.

Oh my god. It's *Noa*.

My admiration snaps to outrage. They straightened those wild curls? That seems so... *not* Noa.

I shake my head internally. I don't know her. Maybe she chose this. Maybe she likes looking like a Stepford Wife.

My annoyance only feeds Madge's worry about me looking angry, and I don't realize I'm full-on glaring until I catch Noa's already-wide eyes widening even more. Well, let her think I'm pissed about the other stuff. Probably best not to voice my anguish over her curls, lest it be... misconstrued.

"Look who decided to sprint back to CBT."

"I'm here, okay?" Noa is defensive. "Let's just do this."

We position ourselves at the retro ice cream counter they've constructed on the soundstage. Production has set up a blind taste test for Noa to administer in order to determine my *flavor profile*. The array of items is hidden beneath a tarp, which Noa immediately peeks under, clucking her tongue.

"I'm the one who has to eat whatever that is," I remind her.

She pops up, nose wrinkled. "These are flavor extracts, not actual fruit reductions. The molecular structure of artificial strawberry is completely different from–"

"Maybe you could've had some input if you'd shown up yesterday."

Noa's jaw tightens and she returns to her inspection like I'm not even here.

Madge claps her hands. "Okay, places! Let's get loosened up. Just run through the taste test, find Aarti's preferences. Nothing fancy."

Her tone tells me she's white-knuckling her way through trying to sound unstressed. *Bless her heart*, Gretchen would say.

Madge hands me a black silk blindfold.

"Fifty Shades of Dairy!" I quip, and Marcus, our sound guy, chuckles in more of an appeasing way than a sincere one. *Off to a great start, Nair.*

"Noa will bring you the samples," Madge explains. "See what your favorites are."

"I can put it on myself," I snip when Noa reaches for the blindfold.

"I wasn't–" She pulls her hand back. "Fine."

I tie the blindfold, plunging myself into darkness.

"Rolling!" someone yells.

"And... action!" Madge calls.

Dead silence.

"Ahem," I venture into the darkness. "I'm Aarti Nair, and today I'm being subjected to a taste test so that middle America can relate to me. And this is my... *sidekick*, Noa Hart."

I can practically hear her eyes roll. "Just… here." Noa's voice is strained. "First sample."

I open my mouth like a baby bird. The spoon hits my bottom teeth.

"Ow."

"Sorry." She doesn't sound sorry.

I gag. "It's vanilla extract?"

"Brilliant analysis," she mutters.

"What else do you want me to say?"

"Maybe something more than naming the flavor?" Magenta interjects. "Like, I don't know, how it makes you feel? What it reminds you of? Whether you'd want it to represent your entire brand?"

"It's a lot. Reminds me of you. Next."

I hear some of the crew snicker.

"Cut!" Madge calls. I push up my blindfold.

"Noa, maybe guide her more?" Madge tries. "This is supposed to be fun!"

Noa tosses her WASPy mane over one shoulder and feeds Madge a bright smile.

"Rolling again!"

Blindfold back down. Take two.

"Aarti Nair, America's taste bud, reporting to you live from Narnia–"

Noa brings another spoon to my mouth and a glob of delicious strawberry compote lands on my tongue.

Mouth semi-full, I manage, "More of that please."

I can *feel* Noa shake her head. "The point of the taste test is to taste, not to consume."

I scoff. "You like this, don't you?"

"What mistakenly gave you that impression?" she snips back.

"While I love the heat, let's try something different," Madge suggests, desperate. "Noa, why don't you describe what you're giving Aarti?"

"Doesn't that defeat the 'blind' part?" I pipe up.

Noa has the audacity to *shush* me as she clatters around under the tarp of terrors for my next mouth delivery.

"This one is… a simple syrup." Her voice takes on a particular tone I'm starting to notice she employs when she's about to be insufferably educational. "Which, for the record, is a terrible way to evaluate this specific flavor profile. The syrup destroys the textural contrast that makes mint chip work. Oops, said the flavor. Can you cut that part out?"

She feeds me a spoonful anyway and I gag again.

"It's like someone decided chocolate needed to be punished."

"Exactly!" Noa exclaims, then seems to catch herself agreeing with me too easily and dives back under the tarp.

By taste test five, I can no longer recall if I've ever enjoyed a flavor at all. My stomach is gurgly, a sloshy smoothie of extracts and flavorings at which Noa can barely contain her disgust when feeding me. Just when the nausea threatens to escalate to something no one wants on camera, Madge yells:

"CUT! Meet back in the writers' room in one hour."

I rip off my blindfold. Noa and I bolt for the exit like salmon desperate to reach their spawning grounds, which is to say, we find ourselves in a literal jam with one another as we try to get out through the stage door simultaneously. We're living out a hacky physical comedy sketch that would've been binned immediately in the *Midnight Live* Monday pitch meeting. I give up thrashing like a pregnant fish and Noa manages to brush past me.

Before I can weigh the pros and cons in my tiny salmon brain, my mouth asks dumbly: "Where are you going?"

She whips around. "Lunch. Legally I'm allowed to get away from all of this for one hour."

I hold up my hands. "Me personally? Big fan of legality."

She doesn't crack a smile.

"Come with me." The words tumble out before I can stop them. "I mean, if you want. Legally speaking."

She looks at me as if I've suggested we go commit arson. "I'm *hungry*," she says, like that's supposed to be a deterrent.

A laugh escapes me in spite of myself. "Then you're in luck."

CHAPTER 15
NOA

AARTI DRIVES FAST. Her Audi tears down the 101 with such velocity that I'm pressed back into the buttery leather seats that smell faintly of new car and financial stability. I wonder if there was ever a moment she felt impressed by this car, or if luxury immediately became mundane for her, just another Tuesday in the life of a TV star. Growing up the way we did made me weirdly uncomfortable with nice things. Even now, in this rocketship of German engineering, part of me wants to apologize to the seat for sitting in it.

We exit at Sunset and wind up into the hills. The roads get narrower, the houses get bigger, and my anxiety about wherever we're going increases proportionally. Finally, Aarti pulls off a parallel parking job made possible by the aforementioned German engineering. I get out, following her to an unassuming arched wooden door covered in creeping ivy.

She pushes the door open, revealing a charming periwinkle-blue stucco bungalow surrounded by an enchanting garden patio carved into the cliffside. Twinkling lights are strung between orange trees, and the view of the city below is so perfect it looks fake. *ARJUN'S* is painted on the side of the house in burnt umber script.

As I follow Aarti, I notice waiters and patrons alike giving her warm smiles and nods. To my surprise, she doesn't brush them off, instead offering back equally warm smiles and nods. We seat ourselves at a corner table surrounded by jasmine and just a single inhale of the scent has me calmer than I've felt in days.

"What is this place?" I breathe.

Before she can answer, a handsome middle-aged Indian man emerges from a door swinging out of the kitchen. He's covered in tattoos and wearing chef's whites, arms spread wide.

"Beta!" he calls out, approaching our table.

Aarti launches herself at him. They share a hug so genuine and full of uncomplicated joy that I have to look away.

"Uncle, this is Noa," she introduces us. "Noa, my Uncle Arjun."

"Arjun as in...?" I gesture at our surroundings.

"At your service!" His eyes twinkle. "Any friend of Aarti's gets the royal treatment."

I'm not sure she'd go as far as to call me a friend, so I just tell him, "Your restaurant is really lovely."

He hands us menus, which I eagerly reach for, but Aarti waves them away.

"Restrictions? Allergies?" she asks me.

"Nope."

She winks at her uncle. "Do your thing."

"You got it." He disappears inside.

"Your uncle started this place?" I ask in awe, taking in the herbs growing in planters, the mismatched vintage plates on neighboring tables, the feeling that we've stumbled into a secret garden.

"It used to be my grandparents' restaurant. They opened it when they first immigrated–named for their newborn son," she nods her head toward Arjun's kitchen. "The first of their children to be born in America. When they retired, Arjun took over."

"His namesake," I ponder.

Aarti nods. "My mom is three years older, born in India, but she was raised in that kitchen, too. Same with me and my sister."

I raise my eyebrows. "You have a sister?"

Aarti laughs. "Why do you sound so surprised?"

"I'm cobbling together very sparse knowledge of who you are, every detail feels precious."

"And why exactly do you need the minutiae of my life?" she retorts.

"Don't laugh–" I warn her stupidly. "I'm an artist. Ice cream is my medium. You have to actually sit for the portrait if you want it to capture you."

She deflects with a smirk. "I'm sure you've already figured out plenty without my help."

"I've learned, like, three things about you in total."

"Oh?" She leans back, amused. "Do tell."

"One," I count on my fingers. "You have a sister."

"Groundbreaking detective work."

"Two, you're aggravatingly funny."

"Oh?"

"I watched all of your *Midnight Live* sketches and loved them. I don't want to talk about it. And three..." I pause, scrambling for something clever to cap this off, but improv is her department. So I default to honesty: "LA matters to you. Like, really matters."

I can tell I've caught her off guard.

"How do you figure?"

"The bus route diorama." I meet her gaze. "I didn't grow up with television and even *I* know late night backdrops are supposed to be generic city skylines."

"And what exactly does my public transit Rorschach test reveal about my psyche, Dr. Hart?"

I consider my words, careful not to make overt what she so clearly doesn't wish to acknowledge. "That you want to be known. The real you, not the TV you. But it feels safer to hide it in plain sight, in a backdrop that will never be fully in focus."

I can't tell if she's offended or amused, and I wonder if maybe she can't tell yet either.

Aarti runs her finger along the rim of her water glass. When she finally speaks, her voice is softer.

"I was thirteen when I figured out the bus system. Really figured it out, I mean, not just which one went to school, but how to get anywhere in the city." She looks out on the canyon below us. "My parents worked constantly. We had one car that barely ran."

I stay silent, afraid that any sound might break whatever spell is letting her tell me this.

"Comedy clubs don't run on a thirteen-year-old's schedule. Open mics start at nine, ten at night. My parents thought I was sleeping over at friends' houses." A smile plays on her lips. "I'd take the 720 down Wilshire, transfer to the 33 to get to Venice. Or the 4 to West Hollywood. I memorized every route, every connection. How long I'd need to get home before they woke up."

"That's..." I search for the right word. "Terrifying? Impressive? Both?"

"It was freedom," she says simply. "Those buses made the city mine. A pimply first-gen brown-skinned thirteen-year-old with a student pass and a notebook of terrible jokes could go anywhere, become a new person behind a mic. Drivers began to recognize me. Some of them would even wait if they saw me running."

She turns the glass in her hands, watching the light refract through the water. "I wrote my best material on those rides.

Watching people. Learning to read the comedy in someone's posture, their exhaustion, their phone arguments in languages I didn't understand."

"So the backdrop…"

"A love letter," she admits. "To the city that raised me. That taught me that comedy comes from contrast: wealth and poverty, hope and despair, foreign and familiar."

She gives me an expectant look, and I think maybe she wants further penance on my part for the destruction of her expensive diorama, but triumph is coursing through me too potently to override. I beam at her.

"I was right."

Aarti immediately bristles again, and I can't stifle my laugh. "Right about what?"

"You love LA. And I dug up all of *that* just by asking about your backdrop." I take a smug sip of water. "I'm pretty good at my job. As a doctor and all."

She scowls but I can tell she's fighting a smile.

"I appreciate you sharing that with me," I continue. "When I was a broke grad student in this city, I relied on the buses a lot at different times, although I don't think I've ever done anything more creative on the bus than down an entire sleeve of Ritz crackers over the box to avoid crumb-age."

"Cocktails!" Arjun appears, landing two glasses filled with something orange and frothy on our table. "My special lassi. With a kick."

We grab the drinks like lifelines and down them too quickly. The *kick* turns out to be a generous amount of gin.

"Oh, *wow*," I yelp.

"He doesn't mess around." Aarti sips the boozy lassi and smiles at her surroundings, like she's finally at home.

"This restaurant is important to you, too," I observe.

A wistfulness flickers across her face. "There aren't a lot of places that can override my usual frequency."

"Your usual frequency is...?"

She laughs a little sadly. "Buzzy and frenetic and running away from my problems."

"I'm tuned into that station as well, unfortunately."

Aarti looks sheepish. "That's why I brought you here. I kinda felt like the doorway traffic jam was a sign from the universe to stop fighting the current so hard. I figured maybe you and I could use a dose of–" she waves around us, "this."

"And this." I raise my glass to her and we cheers, eyes meeting without daggers for what feels like the first time. I sigh, but it triggers a look of worry from Aarti.

"That's actually a sigh of relief," I assure her. "I wasn't certain until just now that you didn't bring me here to poison me."

She cringes. "Have I been that villainous?"

I shake my head.

"I'm terrified," I admit. "Of being on TV. I barely know what I'm doing. Finding out about that meeting seven minutes before–I'm competitive, so of course I wanted to *win*, but the second I realized *what* I'd won..." I shake my head. "I just ran."

"I know the feeling. When you get what you thought you wanted and immediately want to throw it back."

Are we having a breakthrough? I don't have time to investigate it because my senses are abruptly bombarded with a wave of spice and aroma so complex and delightful, I lose all speech.

Arjun personally delivers a platter of golden-brown pastry parcels to our table, the early afternoon canyon sunlight glinting golden off the silver serving tray.

"Samosas!" Arjun announces proudly. He watches me bite into one. "We make the dough with ajwain–carom seeds–and the filling has pomegranate."

The shell shatters perfectly in my mouth, revealing spiced potatoes dotted with pomegranate tartness that sends me to high heaven. There's heat, but it's layered; it's not just capsaicin burn but something broader, earthier. I can't contain my blissful groan. Arjun does a delighted little jump before he strides away.

Next, a handsome server with a nose ring who waved at Aarti earlier approaches with a creamy yellow curry with cubes of white cheese floating like islands. He starts to walk back to the kitchen, but Aarti catches his sleeve and nods at me to take a bite in his presence.

The first spoonful makes me close my eyes involuntarily. It's rich without being heavy, singing with ginger and something else I can't place. The paneer is soft, fluffy, soaking up the sauce like a sponge.

"It's something else, eh? Shahi paneer," the waiter explains reverently. "Arjun's version anyway. He adds cashew paste and chars it."

Aarti takes a bite, and I can tell she gets sent to outer space for a moment just like I did.

"Mmm," she breathes. Her long dark lashes flutter as she closes her eyes. I look away.

The handsome waiter throws me a kindly wink before walking off. He passes Arjun, who's walking back toward us, and they share an intimate glance. I want to ask Aarti what their relationship is, but now doesn't feel like the time.

Arjun sets what Aarti tells me is a brass thali upon our table, its small bowls filled with jewel-toned preparations. Emerald spinach with cubes of paneer. Ruby-red tandoori cauliflower. A dal so transcendent I want to bathe in it.

"What's in *this*?" I ask between bites of dal.

Aarti gets a look on her face of pure mischief. She snags a clean cloth napkin from the next table.

"Tie this around your eyes."

"Excuse me?"

"Your turn. It's only fair."

I do it.

"Okay," Aarti says, and I can hear the smile in her voice. "Taste it again."

I feel the spoon touch my bottom lip, and she feeds me a bite of the creamy, rich sauce. "What flavors do you recognize, doctor?"

"Cumin," I identify, almost competitively.

"Yes," she says, bringing the spoon to my mouth, dropping her voice to a lower register. "And?"

Her tone soothes me, taking away my edge and allowing me to just... taste.

"Black mustard seed." I lick my lips. "But there's something else..."

"Curry leaves," she says. "From the garden. And a tiny bit of hing–asafoetida. It's what gives it that savory depth."

She leans in to give me another bite; this time her knee grazes mine beneath the table. I try to wrap my head around the taste–something cool and springy... Or is that my heart rate?

"Cardamom," I ponder. "Rose. Or..."

"Kewra water. Screwpine essence."

"Screwpine," I ponder the new word. The way she said it. How it makes my mouth water.

I push the blindfold up to find Aarti watching me with an expression I can't quite read. We're closer than I realized, her hand holding a piece of naan inches from my mouth. I take it between my teeth and her gaze doesn't move from my eyes.

"That's good," I say. She nods. Stares. I don't know how her guests are going to remember their own names with a stare like that.

"I have to say thank you," she says, and I remember to breathe. "For not saying anything about... you know. You could've easily taken that to the press."

"I–I could *never*. Out–" I lower my voice. "*Out* you?"

She shrugs and leans back with her drink, taking a long sip.

Her chic loafer touches my ankle, but she doesn't move it away. "You never know."

By the time the next course arrives–an eggplant dish that makes me reconsider my relationship with vegetables–we're halfway through our second round and I can feel my edges getting fuzzy.

"So," I start, noting how my tongue feels slightly too big for my mouth. Aarti shakes her head woefully.

"We're so screwed," she drops her head into her hands. "I have no idea how to make this segment work."

"I've never had to perform my job and make it entertaining," I lament. The word *entertaining* takes two tries.

"You're entertaining when you're not trying to perform," she tells me.

"That's like telling a worrywart to just stop worrying."

"Isn't that the solution though?" She flicks me that glowy gaze. "In this instance, at least. Don't try to tell me the same."

I groan, gesturing a bit too widely with my glass as I try to ignore her maybe-flirting. "I'm not made for television! I live in the sensory realm! I need to touch and taste and smell and see and hear…"

My god, did she just *lick her lips?* Either that or I'm more drunk than I realized.

"…the world around me." I try to finish the thought. I can hardly remember my point. "I can't just… exist in someone's TV box!"

Aarti strikes a sarcastically worried expression. "You know that's not how television works, right?"

I roll my eyes, her teasing making me slightly dizzy. "You know what I mean."

"Take it from me. Newbies navigate broadcast nerves every day. You don't have to reinvent the wheel–or should I say the banana split–in order to figure out how to be at ease on TV."

Like a sleeper cell awoken by a code phrase, my eyebrows jump halfway up my forehead.

Aarti looks confused. "What… just happened?"

"You were making a salient point, but you invoked my activation trigger," I inform her.

"You're an ice cream scientist *and* a secret agent?" She slips into a Mid-Atlantic drawl, like something out of a noir film. "You're full of surprises, sweetheart."

I blush. "Not quite a secret agent, but I *am* on a lifelong mission to reinvent banana splits, rendering your reassurance kinda moot."

Aarti snorts, shaking her head. "I should've known. Please, explain. I can tell you want to."

She's right, I do, and I'm just tipsy enough to give her my entire spiel about how there could be a whole world of fruits split open and piled high with ice cream and toppings, if only we would stop limiting ourselves to mere bananas.

She gives my rant her full attention, nodding along vehemently as I sell her on the myriad sundae splits I've dreamt up over the years. Only when I finally finish, a bit breathless, does she respond.

"You're worried about your ability to translate what you do through a TV, but just hearing you describe your sundaes, I need them. Like, now. And I'm very full."

Her compliment warms me from within, and my cheeks heat even more.

Something about what I just said seems to strike a chord with Aarti–her face takes on a wistful look.

"What?" I ask.

"My grandmother used to say, 'beta, you must romance food with your whole being, with every sense you've been given.'" She bites her bottom lip. "You do that. Obviously."

The idea hits me like a freight train. I jump up from the table, fork clattering to the ground. Aarti opens her mouth to say something, but I hold up my finger and frantically search my being for my idea notebook. I quickly remember where I last saw it: clutched in my hands, soaked in sprinkler-water, right before I passed out.

"You still have that terrible joke notepad???" I ask fervently. "You kinda owe me one."

"Not with me. Also you kinda owe me an entire backdrop?"

I wave my hand. "Forget I said anything."

I settle for the Notes app on my phone even though my fingers aren't quite cooperating with my brain anymore. "What was the thing you just said? Grandma said?"

She raises her brows at me. "You must romance the food with your whole being."

The letters on the screen swim as I furiously type, the plight of being a lightweight.

When I'm done, I hand her my opus.

- Ghee
- Aroma????
- Smell yum
- Memorees
- WHole beinfg
- Oh shit
- The fivresennsez !!!!

"Are you having a stroke?" Aarti grabs my phone, squinting at the screen. "What is a *fivresennsez*?" She says it like it's a French delicacy.

"SENSES!" I exclaim too loudly, spooking a nearby server. "Each segment explores a different sense as we develop your flavor!"

"'Memorees?'" She's trying not to laugh.

"You know I can't spell for shit! Memories! Like–" I take the phone back, nearly dropping it. "Like comfort foods when you're sad, or–" I'm typing frantically again, each word a small victory against my uncooperative thumbs.

"I can't believe I'm saying this about something that looks like a drunk text to your ex," Aarti says, "but this could actually work."

I look up from my phone, where I've written RMEMBER THIS TMRW WHEN SOBER, to find her watching me with something resembling hesitation. And... hope?

I must've mumbled the words aloud as I typed because she hits me with:

"Fortunately you don't even have to save this for tomorrow. Since we're going back to work right now."

Oops.

CHAPTER 16
AARTI

THE RIDE back to the studio is a blur of Noa frantically typing notes into her phone while I text Madge that she'll need to send a PA to fetch my car from Arjun's. *Just like the old days.* Uncle Arjun's mango lassi concoctions definitely got me, though not quite as hard as they hit Noa, whose enthusiasm has reached a fever pitch.

We burst through the writers' room door like we're being chased.

"You know how shitty that segment was this morning?" Noa announces, sweeping her hand out dramatically and knocking over Rohan's coffee. Dark liquid floods his origami collection. "Never again!"

Madge's eyes bulge with horror, darting between Noa's flushed face and my probably-not-much-better one.

"We figured it out," I jump in before Madge can intervene. "How to make this work."

Syd spins in her chair, waving her hand in front of her nose. "Are you two drunk?"

"Tipsy," Noa corrects, then hiccups. "But brilliant."

"The five senses," I say, pulling focus back. "We're going to explore LA through each of the five senses, one per segment."

Blank stares all around.

"I don't follow," Freya says slowly. "How does that relate to your ice cream?"

Noa sways, but there's a fervor in her eyes. "It's never been about the ice cream itself. Ice cream is just–it's the vessel."

She searches for the words. "When I'm brainstorming a flavor, I'm not just thinking about emulsifiers and fat content. I'm thinking about the person who's going to taste it. I'm imagining them at their kitchen table at midnight, or on a park bench after a breakup, or–" *hiccup*, "celebrating something they thought would never happen."

Her words gain momentum. "Every flavor I create is a translation. I take someone's sensory world: their memories, their longings, what makes them feel safe or wild or homesick, and I distill it into something you can taste. I'm not a food scientist. I'm a... a medium. Between people and flavor."

The room holds its breath. *Thank god LA people don't scoff at mediums.*

Then Rohan, still clutching paper towels to his coffee-soaked origami, ventures, "But how do we film that? The translation part?"

"We don't film the translation," I jump in. "We film the source material. My LA. The city that raised me. Noa..." I glance at her. "Noa does what she does. Takes all of that and alchemizes it into ice cream."

On *Midnight Live,* I was an idea machine. There was nothing like that propulsive motion of the lightbulb moment when I shared it with my writers, and how we could write all night, looking at the clock at six p.m. and then suddenly realizing it was four a.m., but knowing it was all going to be worth it come Saturday. The adrenaline and drive that a body delivers at the thought of something so pertinent, so human, so *vital* that the only thing one can do is execute... there's nothing like it.

And Noa is feeling it.

I'm feeling it.

Madge might not be feeling it *yet*, but she looks more curious than skeptical, which means the scales have begun to tilt. "Where is your LA, Aart?"

Noa looks at me. "You said you wrote your best material on the buses."

"But also in my car," I add, remembering. "Once I bought my first piece-of-shit Honda, I'd drive where the buses didn't go. Windows down, music loud. I'd pull off the road to write, of course."

Freya looks up from her laptop, interest piqued. "What kind of music?"

"Everything. Bollywood from my parents' cassettes. Alternative from KROQ. Hip-hop rattling the doors." I can feel myself back in that car, nineteen and invincible. "I'd drive these winding roads up in the hills, finding cul-de-sacs with views of the Hollywood sign. There's this spot in Beachwood where the mist rolls off the Santa Monica Mountains around five p.m., and I'd just sit there, writing."

"That's your sound segment!" Syd exclaims, already scribbling. "'Carpool Karaoke' but make it an LA mixtape roadtrip."

Within minutes, the whiteboard transforms into a sensory map of my LA. The one built from night drives and bus transfers, from my grandmother's jasmine to the morning marine layer.

I've grown accustomed to the rhythm of our writers' room. How Syd is always there to summarize, Freya to lend her analytical eye, Rohan to throw us curveballs. But Noa introduces a new element to our creative process. Maybe it's taught in ice cream school, but I suspect it has more to do with her special gift as a... what was it? ...flavor psychic?

She keeps asking things that catch me off guard: *Do certain sounds make you nostalgic or anxious? Is there a texture that feels like home? When you smell the ocean, what age are you?*

I humor her cerebral questions, though, because she's lit from within with a sense of purpose and a confidence I had yet to see in her until now.

"I haven't felt like this since my Shakespeare group project in ninth grade," Noa whispers to me during a brief lull, her eyes bright.

"You're killing it," I tell her, leaning back in my chair. "This should be *your* show."

She giggles. "Couldn't have gotten here without you by any stretch of the imagination. Or Arjun."

"Genuinely, the world would not spin without Uncle Arjun."

"He definitely made my world spin," Noa cackles adorably.

Madge pops the tab of her energy drink, breaking our moment. She looks at me with her tongue over her teeth, trying to hold back a grin. I shoot her a pinched brow. *What could you possibly be so smug about right now?* She shrugs, shooting a quick glance at Noa, and I glare, our nonverbal shorthand so quick and practiced that no one else clocks it.

By the time we wrap, we've mapped out our first segment for Friday's shoot and everyone's buzzing with possibility.

This feels different from the forced concepts we've been pushing.

This feels real.

Hours later, Madge and I are the last ones out. The parking lot is empty except our two cars under the harsh fluorescents. She's uncharacteristically quiet.

"I can hear you thinking," I say as we walk.

She shrugs a shoulder. "Doesn't matter what I think as long as the job gets done. And it's getting done." She shoots me a little smirk.

I roll my eyes. "You saw it first. Noa and I have creative chemistry."

She bites her bottom lip and nods. "Mhmm."

"That's all it is."

We've operated under this silent treaty for years. Madge is meticulously observant, a necessity in her line of work. So I've never doubted she was clocking every lingering glance I gave a woman, every pronoun I carefully edited out of a story. She's also too good a producer–and too loyal a friend–to name it out loud. Usually that discretion feels like a gift. But tonight, her knowing smile irritates me.

"I'm serious!" I say. "You should just be glad we came up with something better."

"I am. Very." She unlocks her car, but I can see the look in her eyes. The same look she had years ago, standing outside that bathroom stall at *Midnight Live*. Like she sees something I'm not ready to see yet.

SOUND NOTES:

SoCal exports: avocado, citrus fruits, cactus flowers

Base notes that arrive later on palate:
lingering apricot of aged white,
robust cocoa bitterness of dark chocolate.

holy shit, she can rap

??? lillith fair ??????

"MORNING!" Claire the PA pops up in my personal space like a caffeinated jack-in-the-box. I'm pretty sure this level of enthusiasm at five thirty a.m. violates the Geneva Convention. "Ready for your road trip?"

"I'm ready to file a labor complaint," I smile.

She laugh-shepherds me to hair and makeup. "Aarti nixed the straightening today, she said we gotta keep the curls."

I don't have time to ponder the meaning behind that directive because two women suddenly descend upon me with fluffy powder brushes. Claire disappears in their talcum smokescreen.

An hour later, Marcus the sound guy wires me up with practiced efficiency. "Rule numero uno: mic is always hot. Take it off before you deal with the aftermath of lunch."

Before I can unpack that horror, Aarti appears in ripped jeans and a Blondie tee, twirling keys like she's in a music video.

"Ready to cruise?"

She leads me to the parking lot which hosts a vintage cherry-red convertible fit for Guy Fieri.

"This is very bus route of you," I deadpan.

"I contain multitudes." She runs her hand along the hood. "V8 engine, rally pack gauges–"

"Are you seriously explaining car specs to me right now? You gonna show me your golf clubs next?"

She laughs. "Fine, I'm a walking late-night host cliché. Get in, hater."

The camera crew follows as we peel out. I keep a death-grip on my door handle because Aarti drives like she's fleeing a crime scene.

"So what's the angle here?" I ask as she rockets onto Los Feliz Boulevard, trying to ignore the microphone taped to my chest.

"We drive, we listen to music that shaped me, you ask your flavor psychic questions or whatever."

"My flavor psychic questions?"

"You know what I mean." She fiddles with the stereo. "Ready?"

Magenta's voice comes over the walkie in the cupholder. "Rolling!"

"Action," Aarti says, wiggling her eyebrows.

The opening beats of "Maahi Ve" fill the car. Aarti moves to the rhythm, one hand on the wheel, the other tapping her thigh.

"First stop, 2003," she says over the music. "This dance was everywhere after the movie *Kal Ho Naa Ho* came out. Every desi party, every cousin's wedding, every time my parents had friends over. Preity Zinta is... very talented." I swear she growls in gay.

"What were parties like?" I ask, reaching for the first question that can get my mind off of Aarti's queer childhood crush.

"Utter chaos," she grins. "Someone's mom would always end up grabbing the mic for karaoke to absolutely destroy a classic."

"Did your mom sing?"

"My mom?" Aarti laughs, taking a sharp right. "She would sooner let Auntie Priya win at Teen Patti—and hell would freeze over before that happens. She'd dance, though. After enough wine, she'd grab my dad and they'd do the numbers they learned for their wedding."

She turns up the volume during the instrumental break and pulls out some expressive hand gestures like a Bollywood starlet. I mimic her and she nods like I'm doing something right.

"What about you?" I ask. "Were you a performer then?"

"Always. I'd memorize comedy sketches from borrowed DVDs and perform them for literally anyone who would watch. My poor Nani... I think eventually she'd just turn her hearing aids off."

Aarti reaches for the dial, jumping to the next track. The opening of "California Love" explodes through the speakers.

"Oh, hell yes," she exclaims. "Whoever made this playlist rules." She winks to the camera and I remember it's there. She's rapping along with Tupac's opening verse and in the side mirror, I see the pass van keeping pace, but it feels distant, unimportant.

I watch, mesmerized, as she navigates the canyon curves while perfectly hitting every beat. She's completely unselfconscious, using her whole body to emphasize the lyrics.

"What?" she asks, catching me staring. "Everyone in LA knows this song."

"You're different in cars. Freer," I say without thinking. I'm sure they'll cut that. Not funny, too familiar.

The song fades and Aarti shoots me a look.

"You want to pick?" she asks.

I protest. "This is about *your* ice cream."

"And as my ice cream sidekick, I feel like we need to know you, too." She grins and hands me her phone to scroll through music. I select Fiona Apple's "Paper Bag."

Aarti snorts. "Of course you're a Fiona girl."

"What's that supposed to mean?"

"Nothing, nothing. Just very... Lilith Fair of you."

I scrunch my nose. "Lili–what?"

Aarti laughs a little too loudly and I can tell I've said something wrong, but I'm not sure what it is. "You really did grow up under a rock, huh? How'd you even find Fiona?"

"She was one of, like, ten CDs at our public library in Washington."

"Quaint." Aarti pushes a few buttons on the stereo and "California Love" disrupts Fiona's brooding.

"Wha–for real?" I object.

She seems to find it pretty amusing, her mouth twitching before she launches once more into Tupac's verse.

I gesture at her full-body commitment to the song. "Should you be operating heavy machinery while doing… that?"

"I'm multimedia. Deal with it."

We crest the canyon. Aarti lowers the volume fractionally as we stop at a red light.

"I used to drive this loop when insomnia won," she admits. "Three a.m., four a.m. Whenever my brain wouldn't shut up."

"Jerky McGee," I nod.

"Excuse me, *whomst?*"

"Just my inner critic. You know," I say.

"Do I." She sighs.

"Next time you have a thought like that, just name it. Jerky McGee, Bully O'Burden, Shitty McWeeniepie." I slap a hand to my mouth. "Can we bleep that?"

Aarti just laughs. "I like that. Shitty McWeeniepie. Fuck you, McWeeniepie!" She raises a fist in the air.

"EAT A DICK, SHITTY!" I yell into the echoing canyon, hands raised above my head.

The driver of a silver Volvo in the next lane shoots us a bewildered glare. The light changes and we lurch forward. I giggle like I'm in high school, on a joyride for the very first time.

"My therapist is going to be *thrilled.*"

. . .

Hours of filming later, I've learned so much about Aarti Nair's musical tastes that I'm itching to get to the BFI for an evening brainstorm. She loves the sounds of her hometown, from Brian Wilson to Nipsey Hussle.

SoCal exports: avocado, citrus fruits, cactus flowers.

She gets a cute, smug look on her face when she can tell she's usurped my expectations of her, transitioning from rapping along with *To Pimp A Butterfly* to belting Cher's "Believe" at the top of her lungs.

Base notes that arrive later on the palate: the lingering apricot of an aged white wine, the robust cocoa bitterness of dark chocolate.

Aarti whips the car around a sluggish Prius with visible disgust.

"Where did you learn to drive? The *Fast and Furious* franchise?"

"Twenty in the left lane? Death penalty."

"Note to self: never accept rides from comedians."

She parallel parks at Echo Park Lake as the sun goes down.

"One of my first real sets was here," she nods at the waterfront. "About being too ethnic for white kids, too assimilated for Indian kids, too female to be funny."

"A triple threat."

"Killed at that mic, ate shit everywhere else. But that one show..." She shrugs. "Gateway drug."

"And look where you ended up." I shake my head.

"This has been a PSA," Aarti tells the camera. "Comedy: all the highs of drugs with half the felonies... So far."

"And cut!" Madge says over the walkie. "Great job, you two. We've got lots to work with. That's a wrap on the Sound shoot everyone! Roll back to the studio."

Aarti unclips her mic pack with the ease of someone who's done it a thousand times. When she sees me struggling to do the same, she brushes my hands away. She detangles the wires, reaching around my back in a one-armed almost-hug to detach the battery pack. I hold my breath, as if inhaling the scent of her conditioner would be breaking some sort of rule.

She sits back. If she noticed me holding my breath, she doesn't acknowledge it.

"Shall we?" She starts the engine.

As she drives us back to the studio, I'm acutely aware of the sudden lack of recording devices. Somehow, it was simpler to feel at ease with her when we had a reason to perform amicability for the camera. She was right at Arjun's–getting over the nerves of being on TV isn't reinventing the wheel. But I didn't anticipate that the moment we were off-camera would be its own nerve-inducing spiral.

Desperate to fill the newfound silence, I blurt out the one thing I've been dying to get clarity on.

"What's Lilith Fair?"

Aarti lets out a surprised laugh. "That's been plaguing you, huh?"

I nod.

"It was a women's music festival in the late nineties. Sarah Maclachlan started it, and all the nineties icons played it–Jewel, Dido, Tracy Chapman." She darts her eyes at me. "Your fave, Fiona."

"That sounds… super gay," I observe, my filter completely fucked after our long day.

Aarti laughs again. "No shit."

"That's why you backpedaled earlier?"

She shrugs. "I shouldn't have brought it up in the first place."

It's not an answer, but it sort of is. I want to ask her fifty more questions about her lesbian pop culture knowledge, pick her brain on what else she's censored herself from acknowledging in her public persona. Sure, I've known I was bi since forever, but I have a feeling that, closeted or not, Aarti Nair's exposure to the queer zeitgeist growing up as a city kid was a lot more expansive than my sheltered upbringing allowed.

Instead, I pluck the phone off its mount and scroll through songs until I land on my other favorite track from *When the Pawn*, "Get Gone".

Aarti nods along as the drums kick in to Fiona Apple's growing indignation, and for a few perfect moments, we glide toward Hollywood listening to the soundtrack of my angsty teen years, like a couple regular people getting to know each other in any context more normal than the one we're in.

And then she says: "There's something I've been meaning to ask you."

I turn to her, my face burning before she's even asked the question.

"So you... watched all my sketches, huh? You think I'm... what was it? 'Aggravatingly funny?'" That triumphant smirk of hers makes my brain freeze.

"Don't let it go to your head," I mutter, but there's no bite to it. For the first time, neither of us is trying to draw bloo–*you-know-what*. And somehow, that feels more dangerous than any of our fights ever have.

AARTI YIELDS her Formula 1 driving fury only when the bumper-to-bumper rush hour traffic demands it. She pulls the convertible into the left turn lane at Hollywood and Highland.

"This area, at this hour..." I shake my head. "I avoid it like the plague."

She laughs. "But isn't there something so magical about Timothée Chalamet leering down at you from the world's biggest movie poster while an impassioned wannabe-priest audibly assaults you via megaphone about finding Jesus?"

"You do make a compelling case," I laugh. "I'll have to–"

Aarti's phone buzzes loudly in the console between us. She checks the number and answers.

"Hey, just getting off set, what's–"

Her eyes go wide with alarm.

"I'll be right there." She hangs up the phone. "Fuck."

Aarti looks over her right shoulder and does some Hollywood traffic voodoo, cutting her way into the far right lane.

"What's going on?" I twist around to glance at the driver of the pass van trailing us back to CBT.

"Diti," she says, making a hurried turn toward East Hollywood. "My sister."

She looks at me as if she's just remembered I'm there, then to this busiest corner of Hollywood, like she's finding somewhere, *anywhere* to dump me.

"DO YOU HEATHENS HAVE ROOM FOR THE LOVE OF JESUS IN YOUR HEARTS?" the megaphone man shouts at us.

"Not tonight, buddy," Aarti says, zipping us around the corner, nearly running him over.

We pull up to a familiar Silver Lake strip, a long line of extremely cool, extremely pierced patrons lined up in front of a cement facade. Aarti slams on the brakes, hardly putting the car in park before leaping over the door to storm the bar. All eyes are on her as she races to the front and demands entrance. Hipsters in line mutter amongst themselves–something about *C-list celebrities*–and sneak glances at me in the car. I can feel the heat of their gaze and shrink down into the convertible that now feels like a fishbowl.

Aarti must've made it in as I feel everyone in the line move on from their stares. *I hope that was my fifteen minutes.* As I scooch up in my seat, I see two young women several paces away from the line. One is doing what appears to be an interpretive dance as she attempts to waltz into traffic while the other, a tall blonde, frantically grabs her arm.

"Please just stop for a second!" the blonde pleads.

The dancing woman spins around dramatically. "I am a DOCTOR! Well, like, twenty percent. I diagnose *you* with being a buzzkill!" She points an accusatory finger, nearly poking her friend in the eye.

Without thinking, I stand and call out, "Diti?"

Both women turn toward me. The dancer waves and nearly collapses. I bolt out of the car and approach them.

"Who are you?" the blonde asks cagily.

"I'm Aarti's... friend. Noa. This is Diti?" I ask, but I don't need to. The precariously balanced girl is the spitting image of Aarti, but with a fuller, angelic face.

"NOA!" Diti shouts and tries to give me a high five but claps a passing stranger on the shoulder instead.

"I don't know what happened," Steph says, voice cracking. "She said she pregamed but she seemed fine before we got here." Tears well in her eyes. "I'm trying to be a friggin' doctor and I don't know what to do!"

"Home is where the heart is, and my heart is at the BAR!" Diti protests. "I haven't even shown them my signature dance move! It's called 'The Appenendo–nope–appdec–appendectomy!'"

Aarti darts out of the building and clocks us each holding onto one of Diti's elbows as she attempts to wriggle free.

"Where did you find them? Steph, what the hell is going on?"

The blonde looks at Aarti and the dam of tears breaks. I don't blame her–Aarti scares the shit out of me, too. "She won't listen to me. She kept trying to diagnose the bouncer with 'acute grumpiness' until he threatened to call the police. I didn't know what else to do except call you."

"AARTI!" Diti yells, even though she's inches away from her sister's face. "I'm being KIDNAPPED by responsible people! This is DISCRIMINATION against fun doctors!"

Aarti fixes her sister with a true death glare capable of penetrating even the thickest of tequila goggles. "Get. In. The car. NOW." She spits each word through clenched teeth. Diti balks but simultaneously relaxes from trying to wriggle out of our grasp as we steer her into the backseat of the convertible.

Aarti climbs in beside her sister, who immediately slumps against her and mutters, "Don't tell Maa I failed the fun test."

I hop into the driver's seat without hesitation.

"You drive stick?" Aarti asks. I can feel the worry emanating from her.

"I drive stick." I give her a reassuring smile in the rearview. Aarti gives me the address to her condo miles away, but

Diti's begun oscillating between catcalling passersby and clapping her hand over her mouth, gagging. I make an executive decision and yank the wheel toward my brother's backhouse just three blocks from where we are. I've barely thrown the picture car in park before Diti tumbles out and christens Aiden's lawn with vomit, narrowly sparing the convertible's interior.

"Where are we?" Aarti asks, rushing to Diti's side on the grass to hold her hair back.

"My brother's place is back here," I tell her. "Maybe we take a beat and clean her up in his bathroom?"

"Is he home?"

I shake my head and relief etches her face.

She checks her phone with her free hand. "Only eighty-three texts and twenty-seven missed calls from Madge, cool." She taps away. "I dropped a PIN, production can come pick up the car."

I help Aarti hoist Diti around my shoulder so she's mounted over both of us. She's a tiny thing, but she's gone from dancing queen to a pile of deadweight.

"I can walk!" Diti protests while her feet drag. "I have LEGS! Two of them! That's the normal amount!"

"Steph, I'll call you a ride home. And don't even think about texting our parents." Aarti attempts to shoot Steph a glare over Diti's head.

"Yeah, of course not," Steph says from where she's still seated in the backseat, giving Aarti a petrified half-thumbs-up, half-salute.

I manage to pull out my keys and open the door. Aarti and I make our way through the slight frame, counting to three to heave Diti over the threshold.

We plop her upright onto Aiden's velvet couch and I can hear him in my mind. *I am fully in support of you caring for a sick girl but Noa that is SALVAGED MILO BAUGHMAN.*

"Spinny spinspin," Diti mumbles, flopping face-first into the cushions. Aarti heaves her back up.

"I'll get the shower going for her. Aiden's got the best robes," I tell Aarti. "You can call Steph's ride?"

Aarti nods, not taking her eyes off Diti.

An hour later, Steph is gone and a stick-proficient PA has picked up the convertible. Aarti and I have managed to wrangle Diti into a shower that finally pushes her over the edge from belligerent to catatonic, and tuck her in.

We collapse on the floor of Aiden's living room, completely worn out.

"Do *you* need anything?" I ask from my splayed position on the wooden floorboards.

Aarti lets out a soft laugh. "No. Thank you."

We lie there in silence for a moment. The adrenaline from the evening is finally wearing off, leaving me feeling oddly floaty.

"I know we had a major detour at the end there," I venture, "but do you think the shoot went okay? Be honest."

I don't know what it is about Aarti Nair that keeps making me lay myself vulnerable in front of her intimidating brashness, but I do. Maybe it's like how dogs roll over in front of bigger dogs–some primal instinct to show I'm not a threat.

"I think it went well," Aarti says, rolling up onto her elbows to look at me. "Surprisingly well, actually."

"Yeah?" I prop myself up on my elbows too, mirroring her position. "Even though I'd never heard half the songs that were formative to young Aarti?"

Her smile crinkles her eyes. "Part of your charm."

"Oh, good." I'm glad the lights are dim so she can't see me flush.

"What's the story there, though?" she asks. "Growing up with no TV, ten CDs at your local library. Fundie kid? Raised in a fallout shelter?"

I grab a merman stuffed animal off the couch and toss it at her.

She blocks it with her elbow. "I'm just asking! I'm a renowned interviewer, you should be honored."

"Nothing that extreme," I laugh. "My mom died when my brother Aiden and I were two, and my dad didn't entirely know what to do with us. It was the '90s, there was lots of boogey-manning about letting TV raise your kids, so he just kinda veered to the extreme as a parent and told us we had three options to occupy our time: go outside, read a book, or make art."

Aarti's eyes dance around Aiden's menagerie of out-there sculptures and paintings. "I think I can guess what your brother chose to do." She looks at me. "What about you?"

"The great outdoors. My first love was running."

Her mouth quirks. "Ah. It's all coming together. You *did* sprint like a pro after that Gretchen meeting."

I duck my forehead to the floor in embarrassment, but pop back up when I hear Aarti scooting toward me.

"Hey! Truly impressed by your athleticism. I may have long limbs but they're better for tripping over myself to get laughs than taking majestic strides."

"For the record, I've never seen anyone crawl out of a window, or a dumpster for that matter, with such grace. That takes *skills*." Maybe I shouldn't be bringing it up again, but when she rolls her eyes at me, it's fond rather than annoyed.

"I have to say, your particular skill set came in pretty clutch tonight."

"My skill set of... having a brother with a nearby backhouse?"

"No," she says, and her voice goes quieter, more serious. "Your skill set of staying calm in a crisis. I pride myself on keeping a level head, but when it comes to my sister..."

She trails off. Her playful energy from moments ago shifts.

"Thank you," she says hesitantly. "For not asking questions or judging the situation too harshly or–"

"Aarti," I interrupt. "You don't have to thank me."

"I do." She sits back on her heels, facing me fully now. "I know I probably haven't made your life any easier since, I dunno, the moment we met?"

She's looking anywhere but at me. I wait until her eyes finally snag on mine, not in some show of dominance, but because I really, *really* want her to know I'm being genuine when I say: "You haven't made my life easier, but you've already made it better. I've been doing things on autopilot for a while. I'm totally freaked out about being on television and screwing all of this up for you and Gretchen hanging my severed head from a flagpole in front of CBT Studios, but... I'm happy to be here. I promise not to sprint away again."

I'm so intent on holding her gaze that I don't even bother to brush off the wayward ringlet that escapes my bun. Her brow furrows, and at first I think it's something I said, until she reaches out and tucks the curl behind my ear.

The brush of her fingers sends electricity through me. My pulse quickens. We're so close now I can see the exhaustion around her eyes, mixed with something new.

"Dr. Noa Hart saved the day," she says softly, her hand lingering by my cheek.

I catch the dart of her tongue grazing her lips, and my breath hitches audibly enough for her to hear. The volume of the rest of the world is suddenly muted as Aarti leans in ever-so-slowly, giving me every chance to pull away, but I don't.

I feel the warmth of her breath commingling with mine. I part my lips.

And then the front door opens.

CHAPTER 19
AARTI

GROWING UP, Maa always made chapati on Saturday mornings. Diti and I would sneak into the kitchen to steal the warm rounds from the griddle while her back was turned. The look on my face when she'd catch us red-handed, ghee dripping down our chins–that's exactly how I must look right now as the person who is unmistakably Noa Hart's brother bursts through his own front door.

"WELL, WELL, WELL!" Aiden announces, striking a pose in the doorway like he's auditioning for a Broadway revival of *Hair.* His rainbow-striped overalls are tucked into combat boots with teddy bears sewn onto them and glitter peppers his orange curls. "There's a party in my house and I wasn't invited?"

I don't remember moving, but Noa and I are suddenly standing, a not-at-all conspicuous space between us. My hands are thrust deep into my pockets like I'm *so freaking casual.*

"Aiden," Noa says, her voice pitched higher than usual. "This is–"

"Aarti fucking Nair!" Aiden claps his hands together with glee. "Oh my GOD, you're taller than I expected! But like, in a totally hot way. Very commanding hotness."

"Aarti's sister was ill, and your place was close by," Noa tells him.

I open my mouth to explain more, but no sound comes out. This is a nightmare. An actual, honest-to-god nightmare.

"Mmph." A small voice comes from the bedroom. Diti appears in the doorway, swaying slightly, wrapped in Aiden's vintage kimono. Her hair is sticking up at impossible angles, and she's squinting like a confused baby deer.

"Oh, hello, little fawn," Aiden coos, immediately switching into caretaker mode. "How are we feeling? Scale of one to something?"

"Seven?" Diti ventures. Her eyes land on me. "Aarti, where–? Steph–?" She looks around the room. "Is this Burning Man?"

"Sort of," Aiden replies, "but with better wi-fi."

I spring into action, partly because my sister needs tending to and partly because movement is better than standing here marinating in the mortification of what almost happened between Noa and me.

"We're going home," I announce, already looking for my phone to call a ride.

Diti seems to come into her lucidity for a moment. Her eyes widen as she looks at Noa across the room.

"Noa! Noa saved the day," Diti says dreamily, still swaying. "Noa's a hero."

"Yes, she is," I mutter, stabbing at my phone screen. Three minutes for pickup. *Can I survive three minutes?*

"A hero who was about to get very thoroughly thanked, from the looks of things," Aiden stage-whispers to Diti, loud enough for everyone in the room and probably the neighboring apartments to hear.

"*Aiden,*" Noa hisses.

"What? I'm just saying, the energy in here when I walked in was very–"

"The energy was *gratitude,*" I cut him off. "Professional gratitude. Between colleagues. Who work together. In a professional capacity."

Aiden raises his eyebrows so high they disappear into his glitter-crusted bangs. "Uh-*huh*."

My phone buzzes. The car is here early. Thank fuck.

"Come on, D," I say, wrapping my arm around my sister's shoulders. "Let's get out of here."

"But I like here!" Diti protests. "It's colorful. And that man called me a fawn."

"Maybe the nice man will let you visit again someday," I tell her, steering her toward the door.

I turn to look at Noa, and for a split second, our eyes meet. There's something there–concern, confusion, the ghost of whatever was happening before Aiden burst in. But I can't. I cannot go down that road. It's a *blessing* that Aiden interrupted that moment of temporary delusion.

"Thank you," I say stiffly. "For everything. Tonight."

"Anytime," she says quietly.

Aiden is watching this exchange like it's the season finale of the queer *Ultimatum*. At this point, I wouldn't be surprised if he pulled popcorn out of his prismatic pants.

Our ride honks outside.

"Gotta go," I say, already dragging Diti out the door. "See you at work. Tomorrow. For work."

"For work," Noa agrees, and I don't miss the slight deflation in her voice.

As we're getting into the car, I hear Aiden's voice drifting from the house: "Girl, you are *fuuuuuucked*."

I have no idea if he's talking about me or Noa. Likely both.

Diti nods in and out against my shoulder while I spend the ride home internally berating myself. Shitty McWhateverHis-NameWas can't save me now.

What the actual fuck was I thinking? One successful shoot day, one heroic act from Noa, and suddenly I'm cracked wide open, trying to kiss her while stone-cold sober with zero regard for the utter catastrophe that would create for my entire life.

This is exactly the kind of impulsive bullshit that got me grounded for half of sophomore year. The same reckless energy that had me sneaking out to open mics when I was thirteen, cutting class to audition for improv teams, declaring my future major to be "jokes" at the high school career fair.

The difference is, back then, the worst-case scenario was disappointing my parents. Now the worst-case scenario is not only disappointing my parents as an adult–which somehow might be worse–but also tanking my career, destroying the show, letting down my entire team, and becoming a cautionary tale about what happens when you mix business with... whatever desperate horny hell that was tonight.

Diti shifts against my shoulder, and I catch a whiff of whatever booze-heavy cocktail she'd been drinking before things went sideways. My sister, who spent our youth playing the golden child while I was our family's riotous rebel. Diti, the one who never missed curfew, never forgot to call, never made our parents wonder if they'd completely failed as human beings.

Somewhere along the way, we all stopped keeping track of Diti. She learned to hide her misbehavior so well that when she did get caught, it looked like an anomaly instead of a pattern. Meanwhile, I was the squeaky wheel, demanding attention through sheer volume and chaos.

At home, I tuck Diti into my own bed after making her drink two full glasses of water. She's asleep before her head hits the pillow, and I spend the rest of the night dozing in the armchair beside my bed, watching her breathe and trying to figure out how to unscramble my brain until my eyelids thrust me into sleep.

The morning sun wakes me to an empty bed by my side and the smell of breakfast sausage sizzling from the kitchen. Diti is pushing turkey links around in a pan, scrambled eggs already cooling on the counter. She whistles away like she didn't spend the previous evening semiconscious in a stranger's bathrobe.

"Morning, sunshine," she says brightly, not meeting my eyes. "Want some eggs?"

"You feeling okay?" I ask.

"Perfect," she lies. "Ready to seize the day."

Right. We're doing this. The Nair family pretend-everything-is-fine special.

I can work with that.

I arrive at the studio inspired to treat Noa exactly the same way Diti is treating me: with aggressively normal professionalism. A production van idles in the parking lot, and Claire bounds over.

"This is gonna be so cute!" she chirps. "Hometown visit! Kinda-sorta, right?!"

Nope. Nopenopenope. We will not be alluding to dating shows this morning or any morning ever, if I have my say. I give Claire the least passive-aggressive thumbs-up I can muster as I make my way to the van.

Madge sits in the front passenger seat with her tablet. "Glad to see you made it home after your joyride last night. You do know how much that car costs hourly, right?"

I shoot her an apologetic grimace and she moves on, rattling off logistics for today's Sight-themed shoot. Behind her sits an overly enthusiastic rep named Trevor from Scan-Do, the portable scanner company that's doing product placement for this episode.

"The XR-4000 is revolutionary," he's saying to no one in particular, patting a sleek device that looks like a lightsaber. "Click, glide, and you've got a perfect digital scan of any surface texture, color gradient, or dimensional object."

Noa climbs into the van, smiling at everyone, until she makes eye contact with me.

"Hi," she says.

"Hello," I respond with the same energy I'd use to greet an IRS auditor.

She retrains her expression into something politely neutral.

Great, at least we're in agreement: *last night did not happen.*

My childhood neighborhood in Alhambra hasn't changed much. The same bungalows with their postage-stamp lawns, the same grocery where my mom sent me for coriander and turmeric, the same red brick elementary school where I first performed a comedy routine for my third grade talent show–a move-for-move replication of Donald O'Connor's "Make 'Em Laugh" from *Singin' in the Rain*–and brought down the house.

And yet, everything feels different with cameras following us. Noa walks beside me, but we're maintaining maximum distance. When the sidewalk narrows near Mrs. Joshi's over-grown jasmine bush, we each attempt to let the other go first, resulting in an awkward dance that halts the entire crew.

"After you," Noa says.

"No, please, you–"

"I insist–"

We step forward at the same time, our shoulders colliding. Noa rebounds like she's been shot from a cannon, stumbling backward into the jasmine bush.

"Fu–*crap!*" I reach out to steady her, then think better of it and freeze with my hands hovering uselessly in the air.

"No problem!" Noa chirps, extracting herself from the foliage with leaves in her curls. "You know, jasmine has this almost crystalline structure up close, kind of like when we freeze dry vanilla pods in the lab. The moisture sublimates and leaves these tiny–"

"We should keep moving," I interrupt before she can launch into a full dissertation.

Scan-Do Trevor bounds ahead of us, vibrating with enthusiasm. "Aarti, your street has such amazing textural variety. The weathering patterns on the concrete, the rust on these fire hydrants–pure gold!"

"Pure gold!" I parrot, and the sarcasm in my tone is enough for Madge to shoot me a warning look.

"So... this is where you grew up," Noa says, gesturing vaguely at everything and nothing, her waving hand barely missing my face.

"Yep," I reply with award-winning conversational skill. "Houses. Sidewalks. Anti-dog-shit signage. The whole suburban package. Lived here until middle school."

We approach my family's old house, a cramped two-bedroom where Diti and I slept on a bunkbed from Goodwill.

Trevor demonstrates the XR-4000 on the picket fence post, narrating like he's hosting a QVC special. "See how it captures every grain of the wood? Every layer of paint?"

Noa is watching him with performatively rapt attention, so pronounced that Trevor notices and holds the scanner out to her. "Wanna give it a spin? Or should I say *glide*?"

She nervously darts her eyes to me. "I mean, it's Aarti's old house, maybe she should..."

I wave my hand. "Go for it."

When Trevor hands Noa the device, she holds it like it might explode.

"Just click and slide," Trevor encourages. "Get nice and close to the surface."

Noa leans toward the fence to scope out the texture. I lean in to confirm she's angling the scanner correctly and our heads collide. We jerk back so fast that Noa accidentally scans Trevor's face instead of the fence.

"Let me just–" I reach for the device at the same time she tries to hand it to me. Our fingers brush and we both jump. The scanner goes flying. Trevor catches it with the reflexes of someone who's definitely dropped expensive equipment before.

He hands the scanner back to Noa, and I don't miss the quick glance of annoyance he shoots at me before tasking Claire with grabbing his backup scanner from the pass van.

Once I have my own, I busy myself with scanning the blooming jacaranda tree I used to climb to get some privacy.

"Maybe we should move on to the next location!" Madge suggests cheerily as soon as I pull the scanner away.

Walking the perimeter of my elementary school, Noa and I maintain an invisible force field between us. When the DP asks us to stand closer for a two-shot, we shuffle together with the ease of repelling magnets.

"This is where my career as a performer began," I tell the camera, speaking into the lens even though Noa is standing right beside me. I explain how I practiced Donald O'Connor's moves for months in front of the television until I trail off, no further fodder to fill the silence.

"Speaking of performance," Noa jumps in, "Did you know that the presentation of ice cream actually affects its perceived taste? Like, the same exact formula can taste totally different depending on the vessel, the temperature of the spoon–sorry, I dunno if that's relevant to–"

"Very relevant!" I say too loudly. "Ice cream facts are always welcome! Please, tell us more about spoons!"

Noa blinks at me. "Well, the thermal conductivity of different metals can impact..."

I zone out as she embarks on another lecture, her wild curls bouncing as she speaks, eyes lighting up with passion. When I zone back in, Noa is quiet, staring at me expectantly along with the rest of the crew.

"Let's scan the playground!" I shout.

From opposite sides, we approach the parallel bars where I used to practice gymnastics, like we're flanking some dangerous animal. I scan the tall rung. She scans the short rung. When we need to switch sides, we orbit around each other in a wide arc that probably looks insane on camera.

"You guys okay?" Madge asks during a battery change. "You seem a little… spacey today."

"We're great!" we say in unison.

"I love scanning!" Noa adds. "So many textures! Like that rough bark over there, which reminds me of the praline crumble we use in our butter pecan."

"Should we get that on camera?" the DP asks.

"Yes!" I exclaim. "Let's definitely scan that tree. From different angles. Far apart angles."

We spend the next twenty minutes scanning everything in sight while maintaining physical distance.

"These basketball hoops have aged since I was a slam-dunking six year old," I remark to no one.

"The oxidation process is similar to how we age our bourbon extract!" Noa calls from the other end of the court. "The way the metal breaks down over time creates these unique flavors–I mean, visual compounds!"

Trevor, bless him, seems to think this is all very normal banter for our segment. "And the XR-4000 captures every detail of that oxidation! Every flake, every gradient!"

"That's fascinating!" I interrupt. "Hey, Trevor, could this thing scan a toaster in a bathtub?"

Trevor's eyes light up. "Actually–"

"Let's not find out!" Madge interjects. "Let's scan that bench instead. You probably sat there as a kid, right, Aart? Go scan it together. Standing next to each other. Like normal humans."

We approach the bench like it's a bomb that requires two people to defuse.

"I think I sat here?" I offer unhelpfully. "I'd venture to guess that I've probably sat in a lot of places."

"Cool!" Noa responds, for once not running with another barely-relevant ice cream science fact.

We're standing close enough that I can smell her shampoo–something citrusy that momentarily transports me to the night before, which I am desperately trying not to think about.

"Tilt yours a little left," I say, not looking at her. "We can each scan half the bench, but the angles should match up."

"Like this?" She tilts right.

"Other left."

"That's right."

"No, I mean–"

I reach for her scanner to adjust it and she immediately drops it on the ground. Trevor snatches it up.

Madge looks at us–Noa babbling about how the criss-crossed back of the bench has the same pattern as a waffle cone, Trevor practically making love to his product as he checks it for scratches. She sighs.

"That's a wrap on location," Madge announces, and I can hear the relief in her voice. "Great stuff, you two. Really... unique."

"The scanners performed beautifully!" Trevor adds, clutching them like a proud parent.

"The production van can take everyone back to the studio," Madge continues, but I'm already pulling out my phone.

"Actually, I'm going to grab a ride," I say. "Faster for me."

"But the van's right here," Madge starts.

"Already ordered," I lie, frantically tapping at the rideshare app. "Thanks, though! Great scanning today! Really captured those... textures!"

Noa opens her mouth, then closes it. Opens it again. "The wood aggregates were particularly interesting," she offers weakly.

"So interesting," I agree, backing away. "The most interesting aggregates."

"The XR-4000 really brought out their mineral complexity," Trevor says.

"My ride's here!" I announce, though the app says two minutes. I walk briskly toward the corner, then realize I'm going the wrong way and have to circle back, giving the entire crew a wide berth.

"I should probably help Trevor pack up the equipment," Noa says to no one in particular. "Make sure all the… scanning data is… secured."

"It auto-uploads to the cloud," Trevor says helpfully.

Noa falls in step with him anyway.

I finally spot my actual ride pulling up and practically dive into the backseat. As we pull away, I spot Noa in the side mirror beside the production van, pointedly staring anywhere but at me, despite facing in my direction.

Monday, I tell myself. I have one gloriously unbooked Sunday to get my shit together. Monday I'll have figured out how to work with her without feeling like I'm constantly trying not to step on a live wire.

Monday I'll remember how to be professional without improvising elaborate physical comedy routines to avoid accidental contact.

Monday I won't think about how her hair felt between my fingers or the way her breath hitched when I leaned in or the fact that for one perfect, terrifying moment, I wanted to kiss her more than I wanted my next breath.

Monday.

SIGHT NOTES:

Childhood home: cozy, cramped = brown butter base?
Warm but dense

Weathered fence posts = aged vanilla?
Something with character

Jacaranda blossoms = purple swirl?
Floral but not overpowering
like this TENSION

Elementary school playground = childhood nostalgia flavor?
BUT HOW CONCENTRATE WHEN SMELL LIKE THAT

Flavor direction: "Awkward Distance"
sweet but unreachable center, crunchy exterior
falls apart when touched
FML

THE BFI IS BLISSFULLY empty on Sunday morning, just me and the hum of the blast freezers. No cameras, no crew, no devastatingly attractive comedians treating me like I have the plague.

I've been here since seven a.m., telling myself I'm being productive, but really I'm hiding. Yesterday's Sight shoot was… well, "dumpster fire" seems too on-the-nose given how Aarti and I met, but that's what it was. We made scanning tree bark look like a competitive sport where maintaining maximum distance from your partner determines the winner.

I pull out my latest test batches, where I've attempted to synthesize our two sensory shoots into something coherent. Orange zest with bourbon extract. Black sesame and rose kewra. Crystallized ginger folded into a brown butter base.

They all taste incredible. None of them are right.

So much for being a flavor psychic, you charlatan, Jerky chirps in my brain.

I start over, measuring cream into the pasteurizer, watching it swirl. My phone buzzes. Aiden. I've been dodging his calls for two days. Every time his name lights up my phone screen, followed by increasingly dramatic selfies, I let it go to voicemail.

I know what he wants to talk about, and I'm not ready to dissect the disaster that was The Phantom Kiss.

Because that's what I'm calling it in my head. A phantom of a kiss, where the air between us knew exactly what was transpiring, where the particles rearranged themselves to better accommodate the magnetic rush pulling our lips together just before–

The cream scalds. *Shit.* I dump it and start over, forcing myself to focus.

But my hands are on autopilot while my brain replays the events of Friday. The Sense shoot went perfectly, our best day yet. When Diti needed help, jumping into action felt natural and kind of exhilarating. I could tell Aarti didn't often ask for help, which made being useful feel even more important. Later, on Aiden's floor, the adrenaline crackled between us like static electricity. Behind those blackout curtains, we were in our own private bubble.

Until Aiden burst in and she freaked the freak out.

It's not like I can't read the room. From the moment I overheard her lovers' spat from the stall at the Velvet Tongue, her stance on not being visibly queer was clear to me. *But then why did she try to kiss me?* It's more painful to have been so close to the real thing and then discarded than for me to continue finding her hot and unattainable, her desires enigmatic but also none of my beeswax.

During yesterday's shoot, she acted like making eye contact was a federal crime and touching me would give her hives. Which, yeah, has its own physical comedy to it, but her cold shoulder isn't exactly helping me learn enough about her to create an ice cream flavor.

Although... *Cold Shoulder?* Not a shabby name for a pint.

The thing is, for all her sharp edges–not in spite of them–I'm attracted to Aarti. Devastatingly, inconveniently, career-jeopardizingly attracted to her. I've always had a thing for confident women who could destroy me. Blame it on formative sleepover viewings of *Heathers* and *The Craft*. While those movies tried to paint powerful women as inherently dangerous, all they did was awaken something in me. And Aarti? She's brilliant and terrifying and takes no prisoners, and unfortunately, that combination short-circuits my brain.

But it's not just the intimidation factor. It's the moments when her armor cracks. Like when she told me about writing comedy on those late-night buses, or how fiercely she protected Diti. The way she lit up at her uncle's restaurant, her whole body relaxing into something softer, realer.

The new batch reaches temperature. I add my experimental blend—orange blossom for LA sunshine, cardamom for heritage, black pepper simple syrup for that sharp teasing wit. I churn it slowly, watching the mixture transform. When it's ready, I have a taste.

Wrong, wrong, wrong. The flavors are fighting each other—how apt.

My replacement notebook sits open on the counter, filled with barely legible observations from our shoots. I comb through, searching for something, anything, that will help me understand her.

The problem is, how can I translate Aarti into ice cream when she won't let me see who she really is? When she pulls me close only to shove me away?

I slam the freezer door harder than necessary. Three batches down, nothing to show for it.

The next morning, I climb into the production van and take a seat beside Claire with a pit of dread in my stomach. Today's segment is Touch and I can only imagine how we'll navigate a shoot about literal physical sensation.

When the driver pulls the vehicle to a stop. I peer out the window at a towering rock formation.

"Wait, I thought we were doing a Korean spa?"

Claire's perpetual enthusiasm doesn't waver. "Change of plans! Isn't this exciting?"

'Exciting' is not the word I'd use.

Aarti's already there, decked out in climbing gear and a harness that makes my mouth go dry. She's stretching against a boulder, her ponytail swishing this way and that across her shoulders as she switches positions. Her leg swings atop the rock and she leans forward across her toned quad. I definitely don't stare at the way the harness accentuates her–

"Noa!" Madge calls out. "Ready to get vertical?"

I blink back to reality. "I don't *love* heights," I tell her, trying not to sound as panicked as I feel.

"You won't need to go high," Madge assures me. "We can get what we need pretty close to the ground."

"*Pretty* close..."

Aarti approaches, acknowledging my existence with a smile so fake it could be sold at a dollar store. She turns to Madge. "I'm gonna clip in."

She walks away, but Madge calls after her. "Aarti, can you help Noa with her harness? Safety crew is still setting up the ropes."

I catch the flash of annoyance before Aarti's professional mask snaps back into place. She strides over with the determined energy of someone about to perform an unpleasant but necessary task, like a root canal.

"Step in," she instructs, holding the harness open.

"I can wait for the safety crew."

She raises her eyebrows. "And make this shoot even longer than it has to be?"

I roll my eyes and stick my feet in the harness. She hoists it up over the curve of my hips, snapping the buckles into place.

She squats down, eyes to my thighs, and grips my leg as she pulls the straps tighter with quick, forceful tugs.

"Does it–" *Snap. Snap.* "–need to be that tight?"

She peers up at me through those dark lashes, cool as ever.

Slowly–maddeningly slowly–she loosens the left strap first, her finger brushing my inner thigh. Then the right strap. Maintaining eye contact the whole time.

"Better, princess?"

My earlier pit of dread turns into an unwelcome thrum of heat in my core.

"Turn around." No *please*, no explanation. Just a command. I hate that it makes my pulse jump.

I do as I'm told. She tests the straps under my ass and I fall forward, pressed into the wall of rock in front of me.

"Looking good," murmurs the most audacious woman I've ever met.

Still flush against the rock, I sputter out, "Great, yeah, thanks so much." I'm aiming for biting and sarcastic but my voice comes out breathy and strained. Thankfully she's already striding away.

A few minutes later, the safety crew calls us over to clear our equipment and fit us into helmets. Charlotte, the woman checking my harness, shakes her head.

"Textbook. Aarti Nair, is there anything you can't do?" she asks. "Most folks can barely clip a carabiner."

"I'm a woman of many talents, Char," Aarti replies, flashing her self-satisfied grin at me for one fleeting, aggravating second.

By the time Marcus mics us up and the camera crew launches their drones, my annoyance and arousal are competing for top bunk. It's almost enough to distract me from the fact that I'm about to scale a mountain.

"And... action!"

I manage to get approximately six inches off the ground

before my brain helpfully reminds me that humans aren't meant to be vertical on rock faces. I drop back down.

"Not a lot of opportunities to boulder in your science lab?" Aarti observes dryly.

Just like that, my annoyance has won out over... that other thing. The upside of triggering my indignation is that nothing kicks me into athlete mode faster. I re-find my foothold and climb, this time far past those initial six inches.

Aarti matches my newfound pace, scrambling up the rocks, her long limbs allowing her to catch up to me with ease. "Alright, Hart. Look who found their confidence."

"Wouldn't want to make this shoot any longer than it has to be, right, Nair?" I throw back her earlier words.

She snorts and gestures to the mountain above. "Be my guest."

I scan the cliffside for my next handhold as she does the same. "So why are we dangling here today?"

"I started climbing a few years ago. I was constantly working in air-conditioned rooms, sitting on my ass, putting off me-time for a month, then another, then another." She swings her body up a foot and I follow. "I took a walk around the reservoir near here one day, trying to brute-force my brain into a solution for a routine I was writing and I saw these little specks on the rocks. I realized those were people, and it made me want to feel small like that."

"What's the appeal of feeling like a speck?"

She's a foot above me again, but waits until I catch up before answering. "I guess I needed to feel connected to the world in the context of something bigger than myself. Something ancient and tangible and eternal. I needed to touch grass, as the kids say. Though I actually needed to touch rocks."

She runs her hand along the rock face. "This is a good reminder. When you're climbing, you can't think about anything else. Just the next hold, the next move."

"Speaking of." I've mapped out my next three moves and I execute the first, swinging my right leg out to boost myself up to the next perfect handle.

"Are you challenging me to a race, Noa Hart?"

I shoot a quick glance down at her before I make my second maneuver.

"It's on." She expertly spiders her way up to my side. "Once a competitor, always a competitor, huh, trackstar?"

Even though my muscles are burning, the fact that she's referencing something I told her minutes before Friday's Phantom Kiss makes my heart race for reasons that have nothing to do with exertion. I shove the feeling down and remind myself I'm going for the gold.

"In it to win it," I say.

Before I even finish my sentence, she drives a knee up to her chest and uses a foothold to push off, instantly gaining three solid feet of height above me. Only then do I realize she's been holding back on my behalf. As I reach for my next handhold, she's already four moves ahead. But I'm determined not to give up. I wrap my hand around a little jut of rock, gripping tightly as I transfer my body weight to that arm.

In a flash, the cone of rock snaps loose and tumbles to the ground. I go flying backwards, limbs flailing in the open air, panic flaring in my chest, until I miraculously find purchase with my foot on a ledge. I wedge my fingers into a cranny, breath sawing in my throat, every nerve screaming as I cling to the wall.

I glance up at the speck that Aarti's become, still scaling the rockface high above me, blissfully unaware of my recent brush with death. Then I make my next mistake: I look down.

Holyfuckingshit the ground is so much further away than I expected.

My ears are ringing with adrenaline. My hands are sweating. The rock face feels like it's tilting away from me.

"Good save, Noa!" my belayer yells to me from below.

"I need to come down," I gasp, squeezing my eyes shut. "Now. Right now."

"Okay, no problem," he calls up. "Just lean back and–"

There's a mechanical grinding sound that definitely shouldn't happen. The rope system jerks, then stops. A piece of rock whizzes past my head.

"Hold on." I can hear controlled panic in his voice. "Small technical issue."

"*SMALL?*" I shriek.

"The runner's stuck," he shouts. "We're sending someone up from the top trail to free it. Ten minutes, tops."

Ten minutes. I'm going to die here. This is not how I pictured my demise. I always assumed it would be ice-cream-related in some poetic way, not during an activity I'd never willingly agree to.

I clamp my eyes shut and try to remember the box breathing Aiden taught me. *In for four, hold for four, out for–*

"Hey."

Aarti's voice is in my ear. Not from above. Right. In. My. Ear.

My eyes fly open. She's next to me on the rock face, having apparently ninjaed her way back down while I was hyperventilating.

She reaches toward me and for one insane second I think she's going for my butt, but then I realize she's switching off my mic pack. She turns off her own, too.

"They don't need to hear everything. Just us now," she says. "Look up."

"What? Why?"

"Look up instead of down. Trust me."

I tilt my head back. The sky is impossibly blue, with wisps of clouds drifting by.

"I look at clouds when I'm too high. Reminds me I'm much closer to earth than outer space. You can focus on your harness, too. Feel how secure it is? I strapped you in, after all." She wiggles her brow at me. "The runner being stuck doesn't mean you're in danger. It just means we get to hang out for a bit."

"Shocked you're good at this, too," I manage.

"What?"

"Being... comforting."

A smile plays on her lips. "Want to turn your mic back on and say that?"

I actually laugh, some of the tension easing. "Not a chance. I'm not moving a muscle until I am going *down*."

"Just think: at least you're not on *The Bachelor*. They make you jump off bridges for first dates on that set."

The mention of dates has us both glancing to the clouds again, looking for anything else to talk about. But it's not so bad; quiet, suspended together. The earlier panic is still there but manageable now, contained by her presence.

"We should probably–" I stammer.

"I wanted to–" she says simultaneously.

We both stop. Start again. Stop.

"Allow me," she says. "I'm sorry. About the other night. At your brother's."

"You mean... our almost-kiss?"

She looks away, studying the rock. "Yeah. That."

"Why are you sorry?"

She's silent for so long I think she won't answer. When she does, her voice is careful, measured. "I really like you, Noa. I wanted to kiss you. But this is all so much bigger than me. I can't afford to take risks."

I study her face. "Do you think you ever will?"

The question hangs between us. Before she can answer, there's a shout from above. The runner has been freed. We descend in silence, and when we reach the ground, Madge is in damage control mode.

"We can work with what we got, add some funny narration

in post," she's saying. "You really held your own up there, Noa. Let's call it for today."

The crew breaks down equipment while Claire herds us toward the production van. I slide into the middle row. Aarti climbs in after me, taking the seat by the window.

We've been driving for about ten minutes when she leans forward to the driver.

"Actually, can you drop me at the corner of Hillhurst and Franklin?" she asks.

"Sure thing," the driver says.

I stare out the window, trying not to wonder where she's going, trying not to care that after everything that just happened on the rock face–the almost-conversation about the almost-kiss–she's just going to disappear again.

The van slows to a stop. Through the window, I can see a small storefront with cartoon paw prints dotting the windows.

Aarti unbuckles her seatbelt, then turns to look at me. For a second, I think she's just going to say goodbye.

Instead, she tips her head toward the café.

"Come with me? Touch something better than rocks."

TOUCH NOTES:

How does one incorporate straps into ice cream
asking for a friend

THE KITTY COMPOUND is exactly what it sounds like: a sanctuary for cats and the humans desperate enough to pay fifteen dollars for the privilege of being ignored by them. The moment we walk in, Noa's eyes pop, the greenish flecks near her pupils catching some sun through the window. Something told me that she'd love this place, and when I see the smile spreading across her pink lips, my stomach flips in on itself.

"Two for the Catbana?" I ask the heavily tatted barista who's tapping away on their phone.

They don't even look up. "Twenty extra."

I fork over the cash and we're led through a gauntlet of wannabe influencers sprawled on bean bags, all desperately trying to coax apathetic felines into their laps for the perfect Gramsta story.

The Catbana is a small, private room painted electric blue with fake palm trees and seven cats in seven unique states of repose. One particularly rotund tabby is sprawled across a miniature beach chair.

"This is…" Noa starts, then sneezes. "Adorable."

I grin. "Cheaper than Soho House and way more private."

"Private is kinda rare in your world."

"Only gonna get rarer."

We settle onto the floor, and a black cat with one white paw makes a beeline for me, headbutting my knee with determination.

"Someone likes you," Noa says, reaching for an orange cat who promptly walks away. I scratch behind the black cat's ears, and we're quiet for a moment.

"So… up on those rocks earlier," she says.

"Up on those rocks," I agree, leaning back against the wall. The black cat claims my lap–most definitely a bad omen. "Do you know what the headlines were when they announced me as host?" I ask.

Noa shakes her head.

"'Diversity Hire.' '*Up Late* Goes Woke.' 'The Death of Comedy.'" I laugh bitterly. "One Gramsta account coined me 'Affirmative Action Aarti.'"

"Jesus."

I focus on the cat's purr, steady and grounding. "Last month, I wore a kurta to a network event. Just a simple kurta with jeans. The next day, there were think pieces about whether I was 'playing up my ethnicity for points' or 'finally embracing my heritage.' A fucking shirt, Noa, turned into a referendum on my authenticity."

Noa sneezes again, more violently this time. "That's–*achoo*–exhausting."

"If I came out? I wouldn't just lose the show for no longer being the uncontroversial, apolitical pawn the network needs me to be. I'd become the reason every queer woman after me doesn't get a shot." The words tumble out faster now. "I'm not just carrying my own dreams, I'm carrying theirs, too. And I don't know how to set that weight down without crushing everything underneath it."

A gray cat approaches Noa, who reaches out hopefully. He sniffs her hand and walks away.

"I get it," she says. "I mean, not the fame part, obviously. But the weight of representing something bigger than yourself."

"When did you know?" I ask. "About being…"

"Queer? Bi? Pan? I still don't have the perfect label." She shifts, and I notice her eyes are getting red. "But I knew in seventh grade when I had simultaneous crushes on both leads in the school play."

I snort. "What was it, *The Music Man? My Fair Lady?*"

"*Little Shop of Horrors.*" She grins, then sneezes so hard she startles the tabby in the beach chair. "Sorry, buddy."

"You okay?"

"Fine, just–*achoo*–cats are really–*achoo achoo*–fluffy."

I study her more closely. Her eyes are watering and her nose is red.

"Oh my god. You're allergic."

"No, I'm–*ACHOO*–fine."

"Noa Hart, are you seriously sitting in a room full of cats while being allergic to cats?"

"You seemed like you needed to be here. And I–*achoo*–wanted to keep talking."

Something in my chest does a complicated twist. "Come on. Let's get you some Benadryl."

We extract ourselves from the Catbana, Noa sneezing the entire way out. The bodega on the corner is blindingly fluorescent after the mood lighting of the café. I grab the antihistamine, a bottle of water, and throw in some candy because Noa looks pathetic.

"That's $12.47," the cashier says, then does a double-take. "Wait. Holy shit. You're Thing-a-ma-jig Cindy!"

I freeze. Thing-a-ma-jig Cindy was a recurring character I did on *Midnight Live,* a QVC host who could never remember product names but sold them through pure chaotic energy.

"Do the thing!" He's bouncing now. "Please? My girlfriend loves you. Say the thing about the whatchamacallit!"

I can feel Noa watching me. Can feel the moment sliding away from us, from Aarti and Noa having a real conversation to Aarti Nair, TV Personality, performing on demand.

"This dealy-bob right here?" I slip into character, holding up the Benadryl. "It's got those thingamawhos that make your whatsits stop doing that thing they do!"

The cashier loses it, pulling out his phone. "Can I get a selfie? She's gonna die."

"Sure," I say, the word automatic.

He leans over the counter, snapping several shots while I hold my smile like a hostage. Noa stands to the side, provisions in hand, watching.

"You're the best," he gushes. "We're definitely gonna catch your new show. *Up Late*, right?"

"Right." My smile is starting to hurt. "Two more weeks!"

Outside, the late afternoon sun feels too bright. Noa's already popping a Benadryl, washing it down with the water.

"That was…" she says.

"What my life is. What it's about to become times a thousand." I can't look at her. "Everyone thinks they own a piece of you. And maybe they do. Maybe that's the deal."

We stand there on the sidewalk, the moment from the Catbana officially dead. A woman walks by with her phone out, and I instinctively turn away.

"I should go," I say.

"Yeah." Noa's voice is small. "Me too."

"See you tomorrow?"

She nods. "Taste, right?"

"You're gonna love Don Chente's. Best tacos in LA." *I could use my emotional support chorizo right about now.*

She gives me a small smile and a nod, then we part ways.

I slip into my cab home. My phone buzzes–the cashier's already posted our selfie. The caption reads: THING-A-MA-JIG

CINDY BOUGHT WHATSITS FROM ME!!! #UpLate #CantWait #FunnierInPerson

"Can I change my dropoff?" I ask my driver.

I'm making myself wait to savor Don Chente's tomorrow with Noa, so there's just one other place to go where I can always eat–or drink–my feelings.

The dinner rush has already begun when the car drops me in front of the familiar ivy-covered doorway. I weave through the bustling patio, making my way to the dimly lit indoors. My shoulders drop several inches when I spot the person tending bar.

Benny, the emerald dangling from his nose ring twinkling just like his eyes, whirls around at the sound of me sitting down, face lighting up.

"Aart! Does Arj know you're here?"

"Nope, it's a surprise." I'm going for nonchalant, but Benny sees right through me. He's an empath through and through, and not in the narcissistic constantly-alludes-to-being-an-empath way. No, he's just intuitive and perceptive, with endless compassion and a heart of gold. Lord knows I adore my uncle, but he and Maa have their rough edges, necessary coping mech-anisms for the turbulence of their childhood. Benny smooths out Arjun's prickliness just enough; it's not hard to understand how they've made their relationship work for over a decade.

"Long day, huh, kid?"

I shrug. "Long life?"

He laughs, shaking his head. "Don't I know it. You want a hug?"

I snort. Our family has never been touchy-feely and Benny knows this, but it's never stopped him from offering hugs to any of us–at least any of us Nairs he really knows. Even though he and Arjun have been together for my entire adult life and then some, Benny's never been introduced to Maa and Dad as more than a colleague.

That's why Uncle Arjun and I have always understood each other–we both know what it's like to hide parts of ourselves. I've felt a kinship with him since I was little because he was so different from my parents. Where they sought to control my future to protect me from repeating their struggles, Arjun always celebrated my rebellious streak. He'd whisk me away to spend weekend afternoons at the restaurant when he first took it over from my grandparents, sneaking me contraband candy from his pockets, and swinging me by Amoeba Music to buy bootleg vintage *Midnight Live* tapings before he dropped me back home. He was the only adult in my family who seemed to understand that wildness wasn't something to be tamed.

When I was thirteen and found him kissing a man behind the restaurant, just months after my own secret first kiss with a girl, the reasons for our lifelong kinship suddenly made even more sense. He understood my need to escape, my urgency to have an identity beyond the one my parents predestined for me.

"Your Maa and Dad are good people, they're just so tradi-tional, beta," he'd said after he'd bid the 'friend' he was Frenching goodbye and ushered me to the same bar I'm sitting at now. "No need to bother them with something they won't understand. Not everything is meant to be shared with everyone."

I took his words to heart, promising his private life was safe with me. When I eventually told him my own secret, he showed me so much warmth and pride and acceptance that it almost counterbalanced the loneliness of never sharing that part of myself with my parents.

When Benny came to work at the restaurant, Arjun trans-formed. He was lighter, with an ease about him I'd never seen before. By the time I was sixteen, sobbing through my first real heartbreak, they were both there to counsel me through it. In their classic Good Cop/Bad Cop fashion, Benny rocked me back and forth in his arms while Arjun told me she was never good enough for me anyway. All these years later, they're still together, still a secret from my parents, still the safest place I have to fall apart.

"No hugs, fine, but then take a *liquid* hug, eh?" Benny pours two shots of whiskey, sliding one across the bar to me. We cheers, and I down the burning amber with a grimace.

"Traitors!" Arjun strides in from the kitchen, clapping a hand on my shoulder as he leans over the bar to kiss Benny. "Having all the fun without me?"

"If only, my love," Benny sighs, shooting his partner a loaded look. I have a theory that when no one is around, the two of them are capable of silently communicating entirely via eye telepathy.

"Uh-oh." Arjun takes a seat beside me. "What's troubling my favorite niece?"

I snort. "What about Diti?"

"Ah, Diti!" He hits his head in pretend frustration. "I do love that little imp. But unfortunately my favoritism is inversely proportional to my sister's approval and there's nothing I can do about it."

He's not wrong. His unwavering admiration for me has been a lifeline in my darkest moments, especially the ones I couldn't share with my parents.

"So," Arjun leans in. "Lay it on us."

I sigh. "Remember the woman I brought to lunch last week?"

"You mean the one you blindfolded *9 ½ Weeks*-style with one of my white linen napkins? That one?" Benny teases.

"Oh god. You saw?"

"If you think we don't have cameras all over this place, you're sorely mistaken, my darling," he says cheekily.

Arjun waves his hand at Benny. "Enough! We're lucky to get the hot goss. Now, what about Miss Curly Thang?"

I tell them about the dumpster and Gretchen and the

nitrogen incident and the sidekick ultimatum, all the way up to today's sneezy non-date in the Catbana.

"...why can't I just keep things simple?" I finish miserably. "Why do I have to fall for someone right when everything's at stake?"

Arjun and Benny exchange one of their telepathic looks.

"When sparks fly like that," Benny says gently, "it's hard to deny them. Trust me, we know."

Arjun reaches across the bar to squeeze Benny's hand. "When this one started working here, I thought I'd lose my mind. Having him so close to the family business, to everything I was trying to protect... It felt like playing with fire."

"But you found a way," I point out.

"We did," Arjun agrees, but something in his tone makes me look at Benny, who's intently studying the glass he's been polishing for several minutes.

"It's not perfect," Benny says. "Twelve years together and I'm still 'Arjun's business partner' at family events. If I even get invited."

The words hang in the air. I've never heard Benny sound bitter about it before.

"We make it work," Arjun adds quickly, though I catch the flash of guilt in his eyes. "Because the alternative–not being together..."

"That wasn't an option," Benny finishes for him, finally setting down the over-polished glass.

"None of this is easy or simple, beta," Arjun says, patting Benny's hand. "You're allowed to feel complicated about it. Hell, we feel complicated about it every day."

"So what do I do?"

"Right now?" Arjun gets up, heading toward the kitchen. "You focus on tomorrow's shoot. Do your job. One step at a time."

"Don't put the cart before the horse," Benny adds. "Or in your case, don't put the U-Haul before the second date."

"Technically… the first."

"Oh, you're screwed," Benny laughs, and despite it all, I laugh along with him.

"Thank you, Benny."

Arjun returns with a plate of sizzling pakoras.

"The answers will come with time." He sets the tray down on the bartop. "For now? We eat."

As the dinner rush swirls around us, we share food and laughter and the easy comfort that comes from being known. But I can't shake the image of Benny's sad smile, or the way Arjun keeps glancing at him with an apology in his eyes.

Maybe there's no perfect solution. Maybe there's just choosing what you can live with, and hoping the people who love you can live with it too.

WE'RE on our way to what should ostensibly be my favorite shoot day of all–Taste–but I find myself bending to the residual sadness emanating from Aarti, even though she's trying her darnedest to hide it. Her longing looks out the pass van window grip my heart. This recognition that her life is going to change in a mammoth way, for her to achieve her dreams but simultaneously be trapped in this box of her own making... It weighs on me.

And *maaaaaybe* a bit of that is my own disappointment. The moments where my thoughts slip out of their safeguards and I let myself imagine what that kiss would have felt like. What it could've become. How Aarti showed me a side of herself that she rarely shows anyone–her softness, her tenderly fierce alertness for someone she cares about when they're in trouble. She didn't even have to say it, but I know she cares about me.

I take to my own window and yearn, hoping no one–especially Aarti–notices. The love I so desperately hope for, a love like the one my parents shared, isn't even safe from the brutality of the world. They were so adoring of one another, a piece of each other's puzzle that could only come unhooked by something as clawing as death. I equally crave and fear feelings that big entering my life. When a love so deep and pure can be lost so easily... is it even worth it?

I am jolted from my melancholic thought-spiral as the pass van makes its way down the bumpy wooden trail of the Santa Monica Pier. The typically tourist-lined path is blocked off for our show and is instead filled with LA's finest food trucks, hand-picked by Aarti. I roll down my window to breathe in the mouthwatering aromas from each truck as we pass, which seems to improve both of our moods.

"Food trucks from all over the city, parked together for just one massively expensive, Gretch-the-wretch-had-to-approve-this-twice location shoot."

"All for us?"

"You and me, baby," she says, promptly flinching at her casual term of endearment.

After we're mic'd, Aarti leads me toward a faded orange truck with MUMBAI NIGHTS painted on the side.

She speaks in rapid Hindi, and the elderly man behind the window breaks into a grin.

"Aarti beta! Still doing the comedy, I see?"

"Always, Uncle." She switches to English. "This is Noa. She's helping with the new show."

He tsks. "You too skinny. Both of you." He disappears into the back.

Aarti smirks and shakes her head at his comment, and... *is that a once-over she gives me?*

Mr. Patel returns with a feast: pav bhaji, vada pav, and something wrapped in newspaper that smells like heaven.

"Bhel puri," Aarti unwraps it reverently. "Off-menu special."

"Eat, eat," he waves us away.

We find a spot by the railing, and Aarti demonstrates the proper way to eat bhel puri–quickly, before the sev gets soggy.

It's an explosion of textures and flavors: crispy, tangy, spicy, sweet.

"Every week after temple, my parents would bring us to his truck." She takes another bite. "Mr. Patel learned to make bhel puri exactly how my parents remembered it from Juhu Beach in Mumbai–the tamarind vendors, the sunset over the Arabian sea, how they'd share one plate between them when they were dating."

She gets that look again, the one where the armor cracks just a little.

We move to a truck with a mural of roses adorning the Filipino flag on the side. The woman running it breaks into a huge smile when she sees Aarti.

"Ay! Anak! Look at you, all grown up and fancy!"

"Rosa used to park up on Foothill Boulevard," Aarti tells me. "Right by the old comedy club that's a Starbucks now."

Rosa prepares two plates of lumpia and garlic rice with tocino. "Extra pineapple, no green onions. I remember."

"She'd save me food," Aarti recalls. "When I was a tween, sneaking out to open mics. I'd perform for seven minutes, bomb spectacularly, then cry into her ube halaya in the parking lot."

"Ube–what?"

Rosa holds up a finger, ducking down beneath the window. She pops back up, handing over two ice-cold frozen purple drinks. Aarti watches me take a sip. It hits like velvet cake through a straw–creamy, nutty, almost floral. I close my eyes in utter bliss and when I open them, Aarti wears a proud smile.

"Did you know she was thirteen?" I ask Rosa.

Rosa laughs. "Half the titas and taqueros in LA knew. We had a whole network. Someone would text that Aarti's at The Laugh Track and we'd make sure one of us was there to feed her, walk her to the bus stop."

"They just…" Aarti shrugs, her voice thick, "let me be. Fed me. Made sure I got home safe."

Rosa hands us our food, then pauses. "You know, I never told you this, but your papa came by one night."

Aarti freezes. "*What?*"

"Oo. You were asleep in my truck." Rosa looks at me. "I let her nap there sometimes when the bus was late. Two in the morning, this man walks up, and I'm ready to fight, you know? But then he asks if I seen his daughter."

"My dad?" Aarti's voice is barely a whisper.

"I think he is going to yell, drag you home. Instead, he looks through window at you sleeping, and his face..." Rosa shakes her head. "Like his heart break and fill up at the same time. He said, 'thank you for watching her. How much I owe you?'"

I can see Aarti processing this new information, rewriting her history.

"I tell him he owes me nothing, you are a good kid, and he say, 'I know. I know she can't stop. This thing inside her, this comedy, it's bigger than me. Bigger than be in bed at ten p.m.' Then he give me his number. Said, 'Call me if she ever doesn't make it to your truck.'"

"He knew?" Aarti's voice cracks. "The whole time?"

Rosa nods. "Every week. He drive by, make sure you get on the bus. Never let you see him."

Aarti turns away from the cameras, and I can see her struggling to keep it together. My hand twitches at my side, every instinct screaming to reach out, to offer comfort through touch. To tell her it's okay that she was a complicated kid with complicated dreams, that it's okay to not have known your parents could hold nuance when you were so young. But I know that crossing that line now, here, would only make things harder for her.

So I hold it in.

When she turns back, she's reassembled her TV smile. Only the slight redness around her eyes gives her away. I catch Madge's eye over Aarti's shoulder. She gives me the smallest nod—part acknowledgment, part thank you. At that moment, I understand that Madge has been doing this far longer than me: standing guard over Aarti's heart while she gives pieces of it away for public consumption.

"Shall we move to the next truck?" Madge suggests gently.

Aarti nods, grateful for the redirect. "Yeah. Yeah, let's keep going."

At the pupusa truck, Aarti orders before I can even read the menu. "Queso con loroco, and one revuelta," she tells the vendor, then turns to me. "This truck? Changed my life."

"How so?"

"The Hayworth. Pico-Union. Talent scouts were in the audience, but I didn't know." She accepts the hot pupusas. "I'd been surviving on coffee and anxiety for three days. Couldn't afford food, too proud to ask for help. Classic broke comic spiral."

She tears into the pupusa, and I watch the cheese stretch.

"So I'm backstage, dizzy from hunger, and Doña Carmen—" she gestures to the woman in the truck, who waves, "—shows up with a bag of pupusas for *her* daughter who was also performing that night. Just walks into the green room like she owns the place."

"You all needed to eat!" Doña Carmen calls out.

"I'm trying to be professional, right? Can't eat before my set. But my stomach growls so loud it would be actually rude to refuse her at that point. So fuck it. I grab a pupusa and walk on stage with it."

"You didn't."

"I did. Took a huge bite and said—" she switches into her stage voice, "—'my white friends' parents say 'I love you' but my parents say 'Did you eat?' Doña Carmen shows up to comedy shows with pupusas like other people's moms show up with flowers.'" She takes another bite, remembering. "I think I ended with: 'This pupusa is priceless. It's handmade by someone who'd cry at my funeral. Your Erewhon smoothie doesn't care if you live or die as long as you part with your life savings to pay for it.'"

"Brilliant."

"Scouts thought so, too. Came backstage after, but all I remember is being mortified that I met them with curtido on my shirt." She grins. "First meeting with an agent and I smelled like fermented cabbage."

Doña Carmen leans out of her truck. "I told you that night, when you're meant for something, it doesn't matter if you're perfect. It matters if you're real."

"Thank you, Doña," Aarti says, squeezing Carmen's hand.

I press my hand to my stomach. "I'm stuffed."

"Well, make room, cuz I saved the best for last! Don Chente's, the one I mentioned to you. The one truck we're visiting today that actually lives right by the pier." She walks down the boardwalk and I follow. "He makes his chorizo every day from scratch. His wife taught him the recipe forty years ago in Guadalajara, and he's never changed it. Not once. He says–"

But where a taco truck should stand, there's only a gleaming silver vehicle with "LA's Best Lobster Rolls" in a hip retro font.

Her brow furrows. "This can't be right."

Madge hurries up.

"Aarti, I'm so sorry, I mean to tell you," she says. "We tried to track him down, but–"

It hits her.

"How long?" Aarti's still staring at the brand-new truck.

"We called his old number but it was disconnected–"

"How long?"

"The lobster guy took over Don's usual spot six months ago, he came highly recommended."

"Six months." Aarti laughs, but there's no humor in it. "I haven't been to see him in six months."

The lobster truck owner, oblivious to the tension, waves at

our cameras. "Want to try the special? We're famous on Gramsta!"

I see her TV training kick in again–the smile appearing like armor, professional courtesy overriding personal heartbreak.

She orders one roll to split. When she takes a bite, her expression shifts. "Goddammit."

"Good?"

"Incredible. I hate it." She passes it to me. "Twenty years. Don Chente was in Santa Monica for twenty years. He let me practice my Spanish crowd work on his customers at three in the morning. Drunk people wanting tacos, and this teenage kid trying out jokes in eighth-grade-level Spanish." Her voice cracks slightly. "They were the kindest audience I ever had."

"I'm sorry, Aarti."

"All the people who worked all day and night, who fed me, who kept me safe–they're disappearing. Priced out. Replaced by..." she waves at the lobster roll, "artisanal butter and tripled rent."

"Cut," Madge calls softly.

As the crew scatters, Aarti turns to me. "Want to know something pathetic?"

I nod.

"I kept a map. Every person who fed me when I was starting out. Every truck, every auntie, every late-night counter. I thought when I made it, I'd go back. Pay them back somehow." She laughs bitterly. "But I was so busy making it, I forgot to check if they'd still be there."

"You're honoring them now," I point out. "By telling their stories."

"Am I? Or am I just another opportunist with a TV show, mining my community for content?"

"Hey." I wait until she looks at me. "You're not mining anything. You're remembering. There's a difference."

She studies my face for a moment, then puffs out her cheeks in an exhale. "How do you do that?"

"What?"

"Make me feel like less of a fraud."

Before I can answer, Madge is calling us back to base camp, and the moment passes. But as we walk back, Aarti links her pinky with mine, just for a second, so quick our onlookers wouldn't possibly catch it.

"Thank you," she murmurs.

I can tell she means it.

✳ standup ideas ✳

Growing up in LA is pretty different than what my parents were used to culturally. Like yesterday, we met a girl named Krispin, with a K, who has three moms. It was crazy, I was like... I can't even handle one.

Can you imagine? Three moms to tell you to eat vegetables, three moms to tell you to go to bed, three moms to relentlessly nag you about your future and rant about 'why, beta, why you keep trying to do this comedy thing! you're smart girl, use your brain!'

CHAPTER 23

AARTI

"BETA, you know Dr. Agarwal and Baba play pickleball together and I've been up all night!"

My eyes are barely open and it's still dark outside when I answer the *emergency* call on my cell.

"Maa, slow down," I say, trying to wrap my head around the words she just said.

"*Diti*, beta. Dr. Agarwal said she is missing school. What's going on over there? Are you not feeding her?"

I roll over onto my back and pinch between my brows. Of course five in the morning is the correct time for my mother to address her concerns over my younger sister, and of course *I'm* the one she calls about it.

Over the years, I've had ample practice for these sorts of calls from Maa. I remember the first one–I was out of the house for the first time, living on my own (with several roommates, of course) in a dingy Hollywood apartment. I stumbled home with my fellow comedy nerds after a rager of a house party. The sun was cresting the horizon and I was gonna vom at literally any moment. My phone rang, a call from my mom, and I was immediately snapped from my boozy stupor. I was poised to hear the worst of it: my mom was in a car accident, Uncle Arjun had an oil fryer mishap, my dad was locked in Astavakrasana pose and couldn't be unwound.

But no. No.

"I can't find Diti! She is missing!" my mom cried.

Because I'm the coolest, most trustworthy older sister in the world, Diti had texted me the night before that she was sneaking out of the house to sleep over with a friend. She had been grounded for a less-than-stellar report card, but couldn't miss her best friend's sister's cousin's birthday party *for the world*.

I distinctly remember rolling my eyes and telling her to be back before our parents would notice. *Obviously, Aarti,* she had texted back.

Yet there I was, far outside of my normal cognitive capabilities, trying to put the puzzle pieces together. I remember looking down at my Chucks as I shuffled away from my pack of friends.

"She must be on a walk?" I told my mom, squinting into the sunrise.

"A *walk?!* At five a.m.? Come now, beta, don't be *absurd*," she said, as if, on the other hand, *me* being awake at this hour was totally reasonable.

I forced some lie about how Diti told me she was trying out for cross country in the fall and was practicing with early morning runs, immediately texting her to a) get her ass back home and b) corroborate my story. She was thrilled–this lie would provide her with an endless excuse to sneak out of the house, and she could simply "not make the team" come fall.

Little did I know, this one lie would spiral into a lifetime of covering for my little sister, call after call, from high school through college, and now on into med school.

"She had a cold, Maa," I say, pulling yet another lie out of my barely conscious ass. "She's good as new and heading back today."

After a few minutes of reassuring my mother, I hang up and close my eyes, only to be assaulted with the blaring sound of my alarm clock.

I trill my lips, attempting to rid myself of the negative energy already injecting itself into my day, and heave myself from bed to Diti's room. I gently knock and push open the door, only to find her gone. Shocker. I check my messages to find a misspelled text from the wee hours of the morning. She'd obviously been out partying. I send her an irritated response that she better be back in class today or else, then pop in an espresso pod, searching for a sweet, sweet bean release.

Turns out, there aren't enough espresso shots in the world to lift the dark cloud hanging over my head this morning. It's not just covering for my sister–lord knows I'd be in a bad mood most days if that was enough to set the tone for my life. No, it's the way my groggy wake-up call and ensuing lies send me spiraling straight into thoughts of the last few days.

The cat café. The way Noa sat there sneezing through her allergies just to keep me company. The food truck shoot. How I grabbed her pinky without thinking, that tiny touch sending electricity through my whole body.

I need to stop this. Stop wanting Noa Hart like she's oxygen and I'm drowning.

I convince myself I should be relieved the crew is visiting the Jen & Mary's flavor lab for a behind-the-scenes shoot today. I won't be the center of attention for once–I just have to be quippy and ask a few questions to drive the segment along. Right now, any respite from having to divulge my deepest sense memories is highly welcome.

I walk into the main entrance of Jen & Mary's and am greeted with the delicious scents of half-baked brownies and freshly pressed waffle cones, exactly what you would expect from the ice cream mecca. A teeny woman hobbles toward us on a cane and I put the pieces together that this is Noa's boss, Stella. She greets me with her free hand.

"So nice to have you and the team, Aarti," Stella says. "I take it Noa has been…?" She trails off and I realize I'm supposed to fill in the blank with some sort of impromptu performance assessment.

"Excellent. Decisive. Creamy?"

Jesus.

Stella nods as if that was an acceptable response, then leads us back to the labs. She scans her badge and pushes the door open, leading me down a long flight of stairs. I see Noa, standing behind a work bench in her lab coat and safety glasses, making a hairnet look like the cutest fashion accessory I've ever seen.

Noa walks over to distribute the safety glasses to me and the crew, her fingers grazing mine as she hands them over. The shy smile she gives me is so genuine, so warm, that I have to look away.

"Thank you," I say, voice clipped and professional once again.

Her smile drops.

"I'm thrilled to have you all on *my* stage for today," she addresses the group, trying to recover her composure. "Please keep your protective gear on at all times and defer to our Commander-ess in Chief, Stella Wexler." Her dry-humored boss doesn't even blink at the moniker as she takes Noa's place in front of everyone.

Admittedly, Stella is a scene stealer. From the industrial-sized mixers to the indoor herb garden, she Vanna Whites our crew on a tour of every piece of equipment in the lab. I focus every ounce of my energy on channeling the most engaged, peppy, inquisitive version of myself–the exact opposite of how I feel inside–and everyone but Noa seems to be buying it.

Eventually, Madge calls cut, and Stella grasps her cane with both hands like she's about to do a vaudeville shuffle.

"Who'd like to raid the flavor testing room during our lunch break?" she pitches.

My crew of beefy, gluttonous dudes can hardly contain their excitement as they skip toward the door behind her.

As they file out, I feel fingers wrap around my elbow.

"Come with me," Noa says firmly, steering me toward a side door.

"Noa, I don't think–"

But resisting will cause a scene, so I let her pull me into what appears to be a walk-in freezer, the door closing behind us with a click.

"I don't want to talk right now," I say, the cold air hitting my face. "I just can't."

I reach for the handle to escape confrontation. It doesn't budge.

"Oh, come on." I yank harder. "Open this, please." I point to her badge, assuming she can wield her power to let me free.

"That's... not supposed to happen," Noa says, genuine alarm in her voice. "They fixed the door a month ago."

"You mean we're... stuck?"

"I–I mean–this wasn't my intention, I swear."

The accusation flies out before I can stop it. "This is all your fault."

"*My* fault? How was I supposed to know the door would break?"

I bang on the thick steel. The sound barely travels.

"They'll realize we're missing soon. They have to."

I pull out my phone and, miracle of miracles, I have one bar of service. I fire off a text to Madge:

911 locked in freezer send help!!

The message sits there, the progress bar barely moving.

"Great. We're going to die in here." I move as far from Noa as the small space allows.

After a moment of silence, Noa straightens, crossing her arms.

"You're being *weird*," she says.

"Duh."

"Why?"

"I don't know, Noa."

"Yeah, you do," she presses.

"I don't–"

"You *do*–"

"I don't know how to act around you!" The words explode out. "You make me want to do crazy things like grab your pinky for comfort without even thinking about the cameras, which, thankfully, were off!"

"Sorry for having comforting pinkies?" She throws her hands up, exasperated.

"That's not–you know that's not what I mean."

"Do I? Because you've been treating me like I have the plague all morning. Professional to the point of robotic. 'Thank you,'" she mimics my cold tone from earlier. "Like we're strangers."

"We *are* strangers!" I snap. "We've known each other for what, a week?"

"A week and a *half*–"

"Big difference."

"–where you almost kissed me!"

"That was a mistake!"

The hurt that flashes across her face makes me want to take it back, but I barrel on, desperate to create distance.

"This whole thing is a mistake. I should have never agreed to these segments."

"Oh, so now I'm ruining your show?" Her voice rises. "I'm

just trying to do my job, which you make impossible when you run hot and cold like some broken thermostat!"

"Maybe if you weren't so–" I gesture wildly at her.

"So *what?* Myself? So unwilling to pretend there's nothing between us?"

"So PRESENT!" The word tears out of me. "You're everywhere. In my head. Making me think about things I can't think about. Making me want things I can't have."

We're both shivering now, the message to Madge still crawling through the singular bar of service.

"That's not my fault," Noa says, quieter now but still defensive. "I didn't ask for this either."

"You grabbed my elbow. You pulled me in here."

"Because I wanted to clear the air! How was I supposed to know we'd get trapped?"

"Everything with you is a trap," I mutter, moving to the farthest corner of the freezer.

"What's that supposed to mean?"

"Nothing. Forget it."

"No, say it. Say whatever cruel thing you need to say to make yourself feel better about being a coward."

"*Coward?*"

"What else do you call someone who hides beneath some silly characters instead of being themselves? Who's so scared of their own feelings they'd rather freeze to death in the corner than admit they're human?"

The fight drains out of me all at once. I slide down the wall, bury my face in my hands. I'm so tired. Tired of fighting this. Tired of hurting her. Tired of pretending I don't wake up thinking about her laugh.

The floor beside me creaks as she sits. Then warmth–not much in this freezer, but more than nothing–as she leans her body against mine.

"I'm sorry," she says quietly. "I shouldn't have called you a coward."

"No," I lift my head, turn to look at her. "I am. I'm sorry. For being hot and cold. For being mean. For being too scared to–"

We're looking at each other now, really looking. Her face is so close I can see ice crystals forming on her lashes. Without thinking, I reach up to brush them away. She catches my hand, holds it against her cheek.

"Your hands are freezing," she whispers.

"Everything's freezing."

"Not everything," she says, and then she's cupping my face with both hands, and I'm leaning in, and the cold disappears entirely as our lips finally meet.

This kiss is nothing like our almost-kiss at Aiden's. That was tentative, careful. This is desperate, tension breaking like a dam. I pull her closer, needing her warmth, needing her, just needing. She makes a small sound against my mouth that sends heat through my whole body despite the freezing temperature.

"We should–" she starts.

"Don't," I say against her lips. "Please don't become the logical one right now."

Then we're kissing again, deeper this time, my hands tangling in her hair, her body pressing against mine like she's trying to share every degree of warmth she has.

Despite the glacial temperature, her lips are hot against mine. Her warm tongue slips into my mouth and I bring her closer, ripping off her hairnet so I can dive my fingers into her perfect curls. I pull away for only a moment to make sure this is real, this is really happening, and then allow our lips to crash back together. I can taste her smile, her longing for me like I've been longing for her. My hands make their way inside her lab coat and up her sumptuous curves. I feel her shiver at my touch, but not because she's cold. Her head tips back and a small moan escapes her lips as I bring mine to her neck and pull her closer toward me, wrapping her legs around my core.

She tilts her head back up and looks into my eyes as I massage her scalp with a deep lusty grasp.

"We might freeze to death in here," she breathes into my forearm.

"At least we'll die happy."

I dive back into her, first kissing her rosy cheeks, then her tender neck, down to her chest. I pick her up and lay her back on the icy floor. She arches her back and I place my hands around her head, hair spilling out around her face. I stare into her eyes with a newfound desire, but instead of going in for the kiss, I catch her off guard and slip a chilly hand beneath her shirt, twisting her nipple between my cold fingers. She gasps and I watch, a devilish grin curling onto my face. Nothing is better than catching your audience off guard, and, boy, do I have her now.

Even in the cold, I feel the warmth for her between my legs grow. I grab her hips and pull her into me, as close as I can get us between our layers of clothing. I let a growl slip from between my lips and just as I'm about to live out my dreams on Noa Hart...

The door clicks open.

THE DOOR CLICKS open and suddenly we're two magnets with reversed polarity, repelling to opposite sides of the freezer with physics-defying speed. My back hits the shelving so hard that several pints of experimental cacao-Earl Grey tumble to the floor.

"There you are!" Stella hobbles in, followed by the entire crew. "We've been looking everywhere for–" She stops, taking in the scene: Aarti smoothing down her shirt, me frantically trying to tuck the curls back under my hairnet, both of us pink-cheeked and breathing like we've just run sprints.

Marcus the Sound Guy's eyebrows climb all the way toward his receding hairline.

"So cold!" I blurt.

The entire crew stares, puzzled by my exclamation.

Aarti tries to save me. "We were locked in. We're freezing."

Madge claps her hands with theatrical urgency.

"Glad you're not dead! Let's get you some blankets from the medic." She herds everyone toward the door and shoots Aarti a look. "We need to get the workstation footage before we lose the afternoon schedule. Noa, you'll give us the grand tour of your lab setup?"

My legs feel like jelly as I lead everyone to my station, hyper-aware of Aarti trailing behind with the others. We kissed. We actually, finally *kissed*. And it was even better than all my fantasies combined. My lips still tingle from the cold and the heat of her mouth, and I have to grip the edge of my workbench to steady myself.

"So, um, this is where the magic happens."

Aarti chokes. Okay, poor word choice, but I forge ahead despite my whole body buzzing with the secret knowledge that the magic has actually relocated to the freezer.

"I've been working on synthesizing Aarti's sensory memories from our shoots–"

"Noa has an incredibly unique process. Tell us," Stella prompts, always quick to sense I'm flailing. "How do you translate experience into flavor?"

I pick up a small jar of pale orange cubes from my station, hands only slightly trembling.

"Take the sound shoot. Aarti's upbringing as a first-gen Indian kid in LA oscillated between memorizing Tupac on the school bus and Bollywood dances at parties, so I decided to start with a flavor that could meld two worlds together."

I pass out my handmade candies to the crew, knowing that in mere seconds I'll have to navigate the minefield of giving one to Aarti, too. "I began with the most SoCal note I could find, sunburst orange, then folded in marigold essence, classic in Indian sweets. After the climbing shoot, I spun that combo into crystallized rock candy for texture. Our Taste shoot revealed that basically all of her go-to food trucks led with heat, so I dusted the candy with Tajín and chaat masala until it hit that perfect sweet-spicy snap."

I hand Stella a cube, then turn to face the inevitable. I quickly drop a sample into Aarti's outstretched palm, avoiding contact in order to prevent any city-wide electrical outages. I watch as she pops it into her mouth, hoping to catch a glimpse of her reaction. Her eyes widen as the candy melts on her tongue. *Her tongue…*

I shake my head in an attempt to clear it like it's an Etch-a-Sketch. *Get. It. Together.*

"It's incredible," Aarti says, and when I look up, she's staring at me with such intensity that I completely lose my train of thought. "When did you even find the time?"

"I… um…"

She tilts her head slightly, the ghost of a smile playing at her lips. The same lips that were just on mine, that were just–

"What about the Sight shoot, when you scanned every-thing?" Madge disrupts my whimsy.

"I'm holding onto that one for last. The final look is the most fungible aspect of the whole process, although I did get some textural ideas from that outing, too."

Aarti holds her hand out again and my brain glitches, at first thinking she wants to hold mine, before I realize she's requesting another sample.

"Right! Yes." I knock over a beaker on my way to offer her more candy. "Sorry! That was just… sugar water."

Aarti steps closer, ostensibly to examine the equipment, and I catch her scent–that nutty perfume mixed with something else now, something that makes my stomach flutter. *Would that I could infuse an ice cream with her pheromones…*

"How do you decide which memories are the most… deli-cious?" Aarti asks, her voice perfectly professional, but her eyes doing something else entirely.

"I…" My brain malfunctions. She's looking at me like she wants to devour me, right here in front of everyone, and I'm supposed to explain flavor chemistry? "I look for the moments that feel most essential to who my… subject… is. The subject's identity."

"Mmm," she hums. "You're really talented, Noa."

Aaaand I have to grip the counter again.

The next twenty minutes are torture. Every question she asks, every intrigued noise she makes, sends electricity through my body. I stumble through explanations of extraction methods and emulsification techniques while she watches me with those dark eyes, occasionally biting her lip in a way that she *must* know is going to make me spontaneously combust.

Finally, mercifully, Madge calls wrap and steers Aarti and me toward a waiting van.

"Great work today, you two," she says, and I swear there's a knowing glint in her eye. "The car will take you back to CBT."

We slide into the backseat, and the second the door closes, Aarti turns to me.

"I–"

She's interrupted by three other crew members hoisting their bags into the pass van. We sit in silence beside each other, knees knocking with each bump of the road, neither of us resisting the current drawing us together. Somehow, no one else in the vehicle takes notice of the gravitational anomaly occurring in the backseat. Maybe we can exist peacefully on our own little planet after all.

We walk through the CBT doors and are greeted by Claire.

"Dailies time!" Claire trills, turning toward the elevator.

"Dailies?" I ask Aarti.

"The unedited footage from set." She looks to Claire. "But hopefully a little edited by the time my eyes get to it?"

"Of course," she smiles.

We hop out of the elevator to a floor I've yet to see. It's a long dark hallway lined with closed doors.

"Spooky," I mumble.

"Editing bays," Aarti tells me. "Where the movie magic happens."

Claire guides us through a heavy door which thuds shut

behind us. A woman with thick bluelight glasses sits in front of a computer screen.

"Hey, y'all, take a seat." We sit in the row of folding chairs behind her. "I'm Sheena. Usually the shorts editor, but so excited about this segment!" She extends her hand toward me.

"I'm Noa."

She nods politely, but as soon as my giant face appears on the screen above us, I realize she probably already knew that.

At first, watching the *assembly edits,* as Sheena calls them, isn't so bad. The banter from our LA driving shoot feels fun and natural, and even our awkwardness on the portable scanner day plays like a deliberate bit with how Sheena spliced it together.

Footage of the rock climbing shoot is when my stomach drops. Seeing all of myself on screen, squished into that harness, falling extremely short of any athletic prowess, is not something I was prepared for. I haven't been on camera being active like that since my early teenage track days, recording myself for scouts. My now-adult body has me reeling. Does my ass really look like that in shorts? My boobs are *ginormous,* like two additional boulders on camera. Mere hours ago, Aarti was worshipping my body and I'd never felt more like a goddess. I feel a pit of shame in my stomach at how easily my self-confidence can be shaken.

"What do you think?" Sheena turns to face us and I realize I've just zoned out through the remaining footage. I'm pretty sure it's not my opinion that matters, so I stay quiet.

"You're so quick," Aarti tells Sheena with genuine appreciation. "I'll make some notes and send them over?"

"Sounds good!"

Sheena waves us out and I feel like my feet are sinking through the floor. Aarti gives me a long look.

"What'd *you* think?" she asks.

"Honestly? It was… weird." I try to brighten my tone. "But um, that's, like, a me problem!?"

A look of concern spreads across her face.

"We don't have to use any footage that makes you uncomfortable," she reassures me.

"Thanks, yeah, no, I mean… I don't want to be difficult," I fumble as she pushes the down arrow for the elevator.

Aarti's brow furrows, but before she can press me, the door dings open and Gretchen Gordon appears, tablet in hand like it's superglued on.

"Ladies," she says. "Just who I wanted to see."

We step in and the doors close.

"Sheena sent me the dailies," Gretchen continues, finally gracing us with eye contact. "Your chemistry is… compelling."

"Thank you," Aarti manages, her voice impressively steady. "We're committed to making this collaboration work."

"I can see that." Gretchen's lips twitch. "I'm eager to see how Dr. Hart channels all this *raw material* into a pint."

"Absolutely," I squeak. "I think it's all about–"

"Excellent." She cuts me off. "*Variety* called. Their cover story fell through–that Hadid cousin was caught sellin' white-label Shein as couture–and I told them you two would make the perfect replacement."

The elevator feels airless.

"The cover?" Aarti's voice pitches up slightly.

"The cover. Shootin' tomorrow." Gretchen prepares her exit. "Diane will send the details. Try not to look like a deer in headlights when the flash goes off, Dr. Hart."

She slips through the hardly-open elevator doors with her typical abruptness, leaving us in stunned silence.

"Holy shit," Aarti breathes excitedly. "This is huge. A seal of approval from Gretchen!"

She beams at me and I conjure a weak smile in return.

"Hooray," I muster as we exit the elevator into the parking lot, desperately darting my eyes around to remember where I parked Ringo so I can make a speedy escape before I break down.

I'm so disappointed in myself right now. Today should be ending on a high note–we finally kissed, Aarti loves our footage, and Gretchen's newfound support is yielding what's clearly a huge PR win for the show. Yet all I can do is selfishly spiral over my dumb, embarrassing insecurities, which are reaching peak intensity at the prospect of shooting a magazine cover tomorrow with no time to fix everything that's wrong with me.

The moment I spot my car, I speedwalk toward it.

"Hey," Aarti catches my arm. "What's going on? Want to take a walk? We could–"

"No." The word comes out harsher than I intend. "I need to go home. Today's just been... a lot."

I see the flash of hurt in her eyes before she masks it. "Noa, talk to me. Was it the freezer? Should I not have–"

"No, god, no, it's not–it's not obvious?"

She shakes her head innocently. I laugh, but it sounds hysterical even to my ears.

"*I'm* going to be on the cover of *Variety*. Me. A weirdo ice cream PhD who looks like I'm being held at gunpoint in my driver's license photo."

"You're not–"

"I am, I'm weird, Aarti. I make weird ice cream and wear weird clothes and I have zero control over my hair." I gesture at my frizz. "I have dessert every day, and you can tell when you see me in a climbing harness. I'm not a covergirl. I'm not what people want to see. I'm going to make you look bad. You should just do the shoot by yourself."

"Noa–"

My voice cracks. The tears I've been holding back prick at my eyes.

"I'm not built for this," I whisper. "You're like this toned, leggy, confident Indian Barbie and I'm just... me."

"Hey." Aarti steps closer, but I back toward my car.

"I need to go," I manage, fumbling for my keys. The first tear escapes and I turn away, mortified. "I need to go home. I'll… see you in the morning."

"*Hey.*" Her voice is firm enough to turn me back around. I peek up into her eyes, which are big and kind and filled with concern. "Please don't leave like this. Whatever's going through your head, I can handle it, okay? Don't run away right now."

She brushes a tear from my cheek, and I shiver at her touch. She looks around the empty lot to check that we're alone. There's no one in sight, but she sighs nevertheless.

"Will you come back up to the editing bays with me? Just us, no Sheena. We can talk in one of the rooms, total privacy."

I nod shakily, unable to refuse her when she looks so pained on my behalf.

She leads me back through the lobby, past the security guard who barely glances up from his crossword. We make our way back to the editing bay and Aarti beeps us into one of the other rooms.

"Sit," she says softly, gesturing to a worn couch.

I perch on the edge, still ready to bolt. She settles beside me, close but not touching.

"Talk to me," she says. "Not about the magazine or the cameras or any of that. When do you feel most like yourself? Most… real?"

The question catches me off guard. "I dunno…"

She tucks one leg under herself. "When are you the most confident version of yourself?"

I think about deflecting, making a joke, but her expression stops me. She's not asking to fix me or reassure me. She genuinely wants to know.

"In the lab," I admit. "When I'm creating flavors, experimenting with temperatures and textures. When it's just me and the ice cream and no one watching."

"Why?"

"Because I know what I'm doing there. I'm good at it. Really good at it." The words come easier now. "No one can tell me I'm wrong about how marigold extract pairs with orange blossom, or that my curls are too much, or that my body is–" I stop, swallowing hard.

"Your body is what?" Her voice is gentle but insistent.

"Wrong. Too much. Not enough. Both somehow." I laugh bitterly. "The camera adds ten pounds, sure, but it also adds every insecurity I've literally ever had. Seeing myself on screen today..."

"Noa." She shifts closer, and I can feel the heat from her body. "Can I tell you what I saw?"

I nod, not trusting my voice.

"I saw someone brilliant. Passionate. The way you explained your process, how your whole face lit up when you talked about the candy..." She reaches out, fingers ghosting over my hand. "I couldn't stop watching you."

"That's different–"

"Is it?" She leans closer. "When you're in your element, when you forget to be self-conscious, you're magnetic. And your body?" Her voice drops. "Noa, do you have any idea what you do to me?"

Heat floods through me. "Aarti..."

"In that harness during the touch shoot. The way your shorts fit. How you moved when you finally started climbing." She's close enough now that I can feel her breath on my cheek. "I had to remember we were surrounded by cameras because all I wanted was to..."

"What?" My voice is husky. "What did you want?"

Instead of answering, she cups my face, thumbs stroking over my cheekbones. "You're beautiful. Every single part of you. And tomorrow, I'm going to make sure you see it too."

"How?"

"Trust me?"

Looking into her eyes, I realize I do. Completely.

"Yes," I breathe.

"I could also... show you right now."

I nod, not sure if she means what I think she means, but hoping for it all the same.

Aarti leans into me, her nose brushing my cheek. Her lips hover at the corner of mine, waiting for me to meet them. I close my eyes...

"Wait," she whispers.

She pulls back and goes to the computer, pulling up a music app. The speakers flood with the sounds of Fiona Apple. "Slow Like Honey."

I swoon. If this isn't sexy-time music, I don't know what is.

She walks to the dimmer by the door, adjusting it.

"The light has to be just right," she says, admiring me on the couch. "Too bright, kills the mood. Too dark... I can't see the show."

She nods as she perfects the lighting, then walks back to me, slowly, taking me in like a painting, inspecting every inch.

She tilts my chin up to her. "My screening this week was all clean."

"Mine, too. The last one, I mean," I say, hardly believing it's happening.

And finally, *finally*, her lips meet mine.

This kiss is different from the freezer. Slower, deeper, like she's trying to prove something with her mouth that words can't convey. I melt into her, letting her guide me back against the couch cushions as she swings one leg over me to straddle my hips.

"Let me show you," she murmurs against my lips. "Let me show you how beautiful you are."

Aarti wastes no time. Her fingers work the buttons of my blouse with practiced ease while she trails soft, deliberate kisses down the column of my neck, each one sending heat spiraling through me.

"Noa Hart," she murmurs against my skin as she takes in my retro balconette bra. Her fingertips trace the delicate trim on top, just above my nipples. "You've had me completely fooled."

She hooks a finger beneath the underwire, teasing the underside of my breast. "Walking around looking so innocent when you're wearing something like this underneath."

She tugs down the left cup and takes my nipple between her lips, tongue flicking against the sensitive peak. The sensation shoots straight through me and I can't hold back the moan that escapes. I clap a hand over my mouth to muffle the noise, but she immediately reaches up to take it away.

"You can be as loud as you want here. These walls are soundproof."

The wicked promise in her voice makes me shiver, and this time I let my moan fill the air between us.

"Mmm, much better," she praises, looking up at me through her dark lashes, sultry eyes holding mine captive. Her tongue returns to my nipple, teasing it in slow, deliberate circles.

She sits back for a moment to unhook the front closure on my bra, freeing my breasts with a contented sigh. She palms them, her thumbs rubbing across my taut nipples.

"So perfect."

I wantonly press my tits back up toward her, silently begging to have her mouth back on me. She obliges, alternating between gentle suction and warm strokes of her tongue.

My hips are already writhing beneath her. She quirks a smile at my desperation.

"Are you ready for more?"

All I can do is nod, eyes half-lidded with lust. "Please," I breathe.

Her lips trail down my stomach as her fingers pop the button of my khakis.

"These fucking low-rise pants," she mutters, nipping at my hip bone. "Your perfect ass teasing me as you flounced around that lab like I wasn't dying to lick you right there in the freezer."

"L-lick me?" I stutter hazily, warmth pooling between my legs in an instant.

"You'd like that, huh?" Aarti slides my pants the rest of the way off, laughing under her breath when she sees my MONDAY thong. "Oh, sweet Noa. I hate to break it to you, but... today's Wednesday."

Before I can feel embarrassed, she's pulling the offending underwear down my legs, too, exposing my pussy with an admiring gaze. "Much, *much* better. Besides," she says, settling between my thighs, "time is a construct."

Nothing could have prepared me for the first touch of her tongue. She starts soft, exploratory–kissing the crease of my thigh, working her way inward with a patience that's both torturous and perfect. When she finally reaches my center, she takes a tentative lick, all the way from my dripping entrance up to my swollen, sensitive clit.

"Ahhh," I groan, unable to hold it in.

Aarti looks up at me, the flat of her tongue extended across my pussy, eyes swirling with hunger. She trains her gaze on me as she begins to lap, slowly at first, then quicker, the tantalizing, wet, rhythmic sound making my entire body buzz with elec-tricity.

My hips writhe in her grasp, and she uses her strong arms to press my ass into the couch, holding me steady as she devours me, licking and sucking and diligently mapping my pleasure. She takes her time learning what makes my breath hitch, what makes my body arch up toward her mouth of its own accord.

Each sound I make seems to encourage her, and she responds by shifting slightly, adjusting her angle until finally, digging her tongue deep inside of me, she finds the spot that makes my thighs shake around her head.

"Mmm," she hums, the vibration of her voice adding another layer of sensation.

"Oh god–" The words tear from my throat as she thrusts her tongue deeper and deeper.

"Good girl," she says, barely taking her mouth off of me. She sucks and licks and, just as I'm nearing climax–

"I want to watch you come," she says, and like the lesbian superhero she is, Aarti removes her own pants in one swift movement and flips me from my back to atop her thigh. She looks up at me, pulling at my mouth with her thumb.

"Much better. Now." She leans back into the couch, a smug smile painting her lips. "Come for me, Noa."

She's unlocked something in me, wild and uninhibited, so I don't even question what's next. I grind on her thigh as she holds down my hips, making each thrust hit *just* right. She moves one hand to cup my tits, bouncing wildly before her. And then, oh my god, *then...* she bites her lip as she stares up into my eyes with an expression of pure *want*. No. *Need*.

I unravel on top of her. She pulls my shaking body closer to hers and I breathe in that same scent, now mixed with all of me.

She unwraps her arms from around me and I fall dramatically onto the couch.

"I really hope no one else has any dailies to watch here," I laugh.

"No," she says, tracing her finger down my stomach. With the other hand, she taps her temple. "But fortunately, I've got some mind-dailies I'm going to have to go over tonight."

She kisses me again, and I can tell we're both about to clock some serious overtime.

FLAVOR SYNERGY AND ANTAGONISM IN COMPLEX ICE CREAM SYSTEMS: MAPPING TASTE INTERACTIONS AND VOLATILE COMPOUND BEHAVIOR IN FROZEN DAIRY MATRICES

A dissertation submitted in partial satisfaction of the requirements for the degree

Doctor of Philosophy

in

Ice Cream Sciences

by

Noa J. Hart

2022

Dissertation Committee:

Dr. Angela D. Rowan, Chair
 Department of Integrative Biology & Physiology

Dr. Catarina Torres-White
 Department of Geography

Dr. Michiko Ngai
 Department of Chemistry & Biochemistry

Dr. Thomas C. Candy
 Department of Electrical & Computer Engineering

University of California, Los Angeles

Los Angeles, California

EVEN THOUGH I need my beauty rest for the photoshoot, I can barely sleep. Every time I close my eyes, I'm back in that freezer or the editing bay, having my way with Noa–her lips on mine, her body arching beneath me, the little gasps she made when I touched her. I can still taste her, still feel the involuntary squeeze of her thighs as they wrapped around me.

Despite last night's breakthrough, I worry Noa's anxiety will resurface for today's photoshoot. It's one thing to feel beautiful and wanted in the dark with just your lover. It's another to face cameras and stylists, poking and prodding at every flaw. It's something else entirely to digest that millions of people will judge you on the cover of the biggest entertainment magazine of all time.

I arrive at the studio early, wanting to be there when Noa walks in. The hair and makeup team is already prepping as the photographer tests lights on stand-ins.

"Aarti Nair!" Casey Chen, celebrity fashion photographer, saunters over, all swagger and confidence in ripped jeans and a tank that shows off impressive arms. Her pink wolfcut is tied back in a bandana, revealing the dimples that, at one point or another, have made every lesbian in LA weak. Luckily, I've managed to avoid her charms. "Been too long, babe."

"Casey, nice to see you," I nod.

"Haven't seen you since that wild night at the Chateau." She leans in conspiratorially. "How is Brigitte, by the way? Still breaking hearts across the greater Los Angeles area or... have you decided to lock it down?"

"We're just friends," I say, looking around. "Let's keep it professional."

"Since when are you professional?" She laughs.

I don't fold, and she raises her hands in mock surrender. "Alright, alright. All business. Where's your ice cream girl?"

The way she says it–dismissive, minimizing–makes my blood boil. But before I can respond, I hear footsteps in the hall.

Noa appears in the doorway, and my heart does that stupid fluttery thing it likes to do in her presence. She's wearing a bubblegum-pink cardigan, curls pulled back in a messy bun, and she looks determined. Until she sees Casey.

Her jaw promptly drops and Casey's brows go higher than the Hollywood sign.

"Noa Hart. *You're* the ice cream girl?"

Noa turns to me, still unable to speak, her eyes pleading for me to do something. What exactly? I'm not entirely sure. But whatever it is, I'll do it.

Casey's gaze ping-pongs between us, and like a lesbian Sherlock Holmes, I see the exact moment she puts it together. That Noa and I...

"Well, well," she murmurs. "This should be *fun*. Like old times." She gives Noa a wink. *Weird.*

"Let's check out wardrobe options," I say, dragging Noa toward the racks.

"What's going on?" I whisper once we're alone.

"Casey–that's–*Casey*," she says, panic rising in her voice. "We... It was..."

"You don't need to say another word."

LA is big, but the lesbian community within it? Not so much. From what I know about Casey Chen, she's done quite the number on people in our circles. She's a classic love-bomber–tells women how special they are, leads them on, then dumps them the moment she's onto the next... if they're lucky. Given that Noa looks like she's seen a ghost, I'm guessing she got the Casey Deluxe.

"Be right back," I assure Noa.

I cross the room to speak to Casey. "Can I talk to you for a sec?"

She shrugs, following me to the corner of the room.

"Loosen up, Nair," she says, giving my shoulder a slight shove. "I can't have you this stiff when we're about to take some hot photos of you and your new–"

"So glad we got to reconnect, but this isn't gonna work."

Her eyebrows shoot up. "Excuse me?"

"We're going for something different than your usual style. You understand?"

"You can't be serious." She laughs, but there's an edge to it now. "Does the network know you're dismissing their photographer? Does Gretchen? She requested me specifically."

"I'm sure she did." I pull out my phone, texting Madge:

> Sending Casey home. Need to get someone else ASAP.

"This is about her, isn't it?" Casey's voice drops. "Noa can handle it. She's a big girl. Unless she's like... still in love with me."

My fists clench and Casey must see something flicker in my face because she steps back, hands raised. "Fine. Your funeral." She packs her camera and leaves.

My phone buzzes.

"You didn't have to do that." Noa appears beside me.

"It is not a problem," I assure her, and her tight shoulders drop a smidge.

"She just–" Noa begins.

"You don't have to say anything," I tell her. "I want you to feel good."

A half hour later, the door to the dressing rooms bursts open and Claire appears. "Your new photographers are here! They're… um… parking?"

We follow her to the window, where a giant rainbow-painted truck is attempting to parallel park across three spaces.

"What is *that*?" Noa asks, and I'm relieved to hear wonder instead of anxiety.

"That," I grin, "is exactly what we need right now."

We make our way down to the parking lot to greet the crew of The Photo Truck. A brunette with a septum ring hops out and waves.

"I'm Emma," she says, extending her hand. "I'll be your photographer today."

The back of the truck rolls open and another short-statured human fumbles out.

"Ohmigod, Aarti Nair, I am a *huge* fan!"

"That's Max," Emma says. "Technically they have no reason to be here other than they love you."

"Cool with me, as long as we get good photos for *Variety*."

"Wait, *Variety*?" Max shouts. "Jo is gonna lose her–I mean, Emma is a consummate professional and will absolutely get you what you need. For *Variety*."

Max hides a giddy squeal as they turn on their heel and head to the truck. "Follow me!"

We hop into the back and it's just as magical as the exterior.

"Wow," Noa marvels, taking in the space, filled to the brim with costumes, props, and every piece of photography equipment imaginable. "What *is* this place?!"

Max and Emma beam.

"The truck is all about feeling comfortable and yourself. And channeling that into amazing photographs, of course!" Max says, already pulling out options. "Let's play!"

The next two hours are pure joy. Max tosses us outfit after outfit–Noa in a flowy sundress, me in a sharp suit, Noa in an over-the-top tuxedo, me in the fluffiest dress I've ever donned. I take every opportunity when Max and Emma's backs are turned to let Noa know I'm delighting in how her curves fill out each look.

"Wait, wait!" Max produces a collection of fake mustaches. "These are from our last wedding shoot."

Soon we're posing with handlebar mustaches, monocles, feather boas. Emma snaps away, occasionally calling out directions but mostly just capturing our natural interactions.

"The chemistry between you two!" Emma says, reviewing shots from the tethered capture. "Makes sense you're doing this segment."

Noa blushes.

"Oh oh oh!" Emma exclaims. "I'm having an idea! We have this prop from last month..." She disappears into the front of the truck, emerging with what appears to be a human-sized martini glass. "Alcohol campaign. But what if...?"

Max is already bouncing. "Oooh!! Aarti's a sundae!"

"And Noa's the scientist creating me?" I add.

Max dives back into the costume rack. "Wait, wait, I have the PERFECT thing!" They emerge with a vintage silk cream-colored corset bodysuit, dyed with chestnut swirls that look like chocolate syrup. "Willy Wonka burlesque promo."

I hold it up–it's gorgeous but far more revealing than anything I've worn on camera before.

Minutes later, I'm folded into the massive glass, legs dangling over the side, the corset doing its job a little too well. Every breath threatens to spill me over the push-up cups.

"Here," Max brings Noa a sexier-than-it-is-accurate lab coat and an array of giant food props I can only imagine were accumulated from the aforementioned Willy Wonka shoot–cherries, a whipped cream can, sprinkles, and merino wool that functions surprisingly well as moldable scoops of ice cream. "Go forth and create your masterpiece!"

Noa falls into her element, circling me, arranging clouds of wool around my body, strategically placing each sprinkle. Her concentration is admirable, save for when I catch her eyes lingering on where the chocolate swirls curl up into my cleavage. She looks up, realizing I caught her peeking, and blushes an adorable shade that nearly matches the massive cherry she just grabbed.

"Um," she quickly covers, "This could–"

I glance down at my breasts bursting out of the bodysuit. "Maybe that cherry can be my fig leaf? Give me a little coverage?"

She smiles, grateful for the save. "That's what I was gonna say."

"Love it!" Emma says.

Noa leans in to hand me the cherry and trips over a gaff-taped lighting cord, nearly wiping out. The foam prop is her saving grace, stopping her fall as the basketball-sized cherry squishes against my decolletage.

"Oh my god, I'm so sorry!" Noa gasps. The cherry is compressed between us, and she's pinning me in the glass with her body.

"It's fine, just–" I try to shift, which only makes the corset situation more precarious. The movement causes Noa to lose her balance again, her free hand landing on the rim of the glass right by my hip for support.

We lock eyes and the absurdity of it all hits us both at once.

A giggle escapes me. Then Noa snorts–so loudly she surprises herself–which makes me laugh harder.

We're both gone, collapsed into hysteria. For a split second, Noa's forehead drops to rest against mine as we shake with laughter, the cherry still ridiculously sandwiched between us. She pulls back just enough to look at me, both of us teary-eyed and breathless, and for a moment everything else falls away. It's just us, sharing the most perfectly ridiculous moment.

Emma's camera clicks, but we barely notice. "Don't move! That's it, that's the shot!"

Max squeals. "Y'all are gonna break the internet!"

By the time we wrap, Noa's glowing. The anxiety from this morning has melted away, replaced by something lighter, freer.

"Thank you," she says to Max and Emma. "You made me feel so at home."

Emma shrugs. "You two made my job easy."

"Yeah, you were incredible," I tell her. "You always are."

Max tries to hide a smile at Emma, and something in their eyes tells me they know their fair share about co-worker relationships.

"We'll have these processed tonight and send them to Gretchen by tomorrow," Emma tells me as I hop off the truck.

I give Noa my hand to assist her on the step down. "Great. We'll dry-clean these outfits and get them back to you," I shout up to Max.

"Oh, don't even worry about it," they say. "All of it was from that thrift store on La Brea. $1 Sundays, baby!"

"You two are truly magical."

Max grins and closes up the truck. We wave them off as they drive onto Hollywood Boulevard and into the night.

The lot is empty aside from our two cars, and neither of us seems to want to leave quite yet.

"What do you say we go take some of this makeup off?"

I buzz us back in with my keycard. Everyone but the security guard has gone home. We quietly make our way to the dressing rooms, both of us silently fizzing with leftover glee from the shoot. The automatic lights turn on and Noa faces me.

"We should probably change," Noa says, but she doesn't move.

"We probably should," I agree, stepping closer.

The air between us crackles. She's looking at me the way she did in the editing bay, all want and need, and I can't stop myself. I back her against the vanity, a rogue lipstick slowly rolling off the tabletop before it clatters to the ground. Neither of us follow it, eyes locked.

"Aarti," she breathes.

"Tell me to stop," I murmur, my hands bracketing her hips.

"Don't."

"Don't what?"

"Don't stop."

I kiss her like I've been dying to since yesterday–deep and desperate and claiming. She melts against me and I lift her onto the vanity, stepping between her legs.

"The door," she gasps as I kiss down her throat.

I reach behind her to twist the lock, then return my attention to the spot where her neck meets her shoulder that makes her whimper.

"You're so beautiful," I tell her between kisses. "So fucking beautiful. When are you going to believe me?"

She pulls me back up to her mouth instead of answering, and I lose myself in her–the taste of her sticky cherry lipstick, the little sounds she makes when I touch her in just the right spot.

In a shocking turn of events, I can't get enough of Noa Hart. So I break my own rules. I invite her over to my place for the first time.

She says yes.

AARTI CLICKS OPEN the door of her condo and I follow her in. For whatever reason, I assumed she would live in some sleek, minimalist-modern box, but this place is nothing of the sort. It's a charming Old Hollywood building bordering Hancock Park, where the stucco and wrought iron from the exterior beautifully match the arches, ornate decorative tiles, and exposed beams of the interior.

"Diti, you home?" she calls out. Silence. She turns to me. "Want anything to drink?"

"Water would be nice."

She pads to the kitchen, returning with two glasses. There's something about watching her in her private space, a place almost no one else gets to witness, that makes my pulse quicken. *Up Extra Late with Aarti Nair: audience of one.*

"Do you want to…?" She nods toward her bedroom, voice dropping slightly. "Just in case Diti comes home."

I follow her into her bedroom, immediately drawn to the massive floor-to-ceiling arched window that opens onto a vine-covered balcony.

"Wow." The lights of the city shimmer in the distance, and I can tell that in daylight, the Hollywood sign must be visible from here.

"The view will never get old." Her arms circle my waist from behind, chin settling on my shoulder. "How are you feeling?" she murmurs against my ear. "Do you need anything?"

I turn my head to catch her eyes, struck by how genuinely she's asking. "I'm perfect," I tell her, meaning it completely.

"Good."

She kisses me from behind, soft and lingering. Her hands find the hem of my T-shirt dress and follow the curves of my body as the fabric rises.

When I try to turn around, she guides me back to face the window.

"Enjoy the view," she whispers, voice carrying a hint of command that sends heat straight through me. Her lips find my neck as her hands map my skin beneath the dress.

I'm beginning to understand something fundamental about Aarti–how much pleasure she takes in my pleasure, how she seems to come alive when she's focused entirely on me.

I let my head fall back against her shoulder as her hand slides down the front of my panties. The first touch of her fingers against my wetness makes me gasp, and she hums approvingly, using the slickness of my arousal to circle my clit in perfect, maddening strokes.

"Aarti… " I breathe her name. I want to tell her how incredible this feels, how right, but I can barely form coherent thoughts as her palm presses against me and her fingers find exactly the right spot inside. My legs begin to shake and she holds me steady, supporting my weight effortlessly.

"Come here," she murmurs, guiding me to her California King. When I move to sit, she turns me around once more, hands gentle but insistent as she guides me to bend over the plush comforter.

She leans down, her body a warm line across my back. "I

want you like this," she whispers against my ear. "Is that what you want, too?"

The question, asked so softly, so carefully, sends fire racing through my veins. "Yes," I manage. "Please, yes."

I feel her smile against my shoulder before she straightens, lifting my dress off and letting it fall away. Cool air hits my skin as she slides my panties down my legs, and when I glance back, she's kneeling behind me, taking me in with appreciation.

Her palm connects with my ass in a playful spank before she leans forward to press kisses along the back of my thigh. "God, you're beautiful," she murmurs against my skin. "I want to taste every inch of you."

"Please," I whisper, and I hear her soft laugh at my eagerness.

Her hands spread me open and then her mouth is on my pussy, tongue working in slow, deliberate strokes that make my spine arch. Every lick sends shockwaves through me, and when I moan for more, she responds immediately, her tongue slipping inside me.

I stretch forward, gripping the comforter as I rock back against her mouth, chasing the sensation. But as incredible as this feels–

"Can I… will you…?" I attempt.

"Words, Noa."

"Will you get on the bed?" I manage to ask, voice rough with need. "Please."

She pulls away and turns me around, capturing my mouth in a deep kiss that lets me taste myself on her lips. The intimacy of it makes me dizzy.

"How do you want me?" she asks, and the genuine question in her voice, the way she's willing to give me whatever I need, makes my heart stutter.

"Lay back," I instruct.

She settles against the pillows and pulls her camisole over

her head, revealing she's braless underneath. Her perfect breasts culminate in perky erect nipples that have my mouth watering. I slide her pants down over her hips, then her silk boyshorts.

I smile, satisfied. Finally, we're both fully naked together.

I lean over her and suck her tits into my mouth. They're smaller than mine, like generous scoops of ice cream–the ideal size for me to devour whole. She groans and it's the sweetest sound I've ever heard. My pussy pulses, even wetter. Aarti's hand slides down to touch me again, and I hear her sharp breath when she discovers how aroused I am.

"Get up here," she demands, hands circling my ass and pulling my dripping pussy over her face.

The view from up here–her dark hair spread across the pillow, eyes bright with desire–is almost too much.

"Yes." She breathes me in. "Good girl."

She pulls me onto her face, her tongue finding my center. She controls my movement, setting a rhythm that has me crying out, one hand braced against the headboard while the other tangles in her hair. The city lights blur beyond the window as my pleasure builds and builds, radiating outward from where her mouth works magic.

The orgasm hits like a wave, starting deep in my core and spreading through every nerve ending until I'm shaking above her, her name falling from my lips like a prayer. I rock against her mouth until the last tremor subsides, then collapse beside her, boneless and breathless.

"I could do that forever," she says, pulling me close, pressing soft kisses to my temple. "Watching you fall apart like that."

I curl into her side, still catching my breath. As the waves of pleasure subside, my hunger for her builds in me.

"My turn," I whisper against her neck, pressing a kiss there that makes her shiver. "I need to touch you."

The vulnerability in her eyes, mixed with desire, makes my

heart race. She nods, and I begin my own exploration, trailing kisses across her collarbone.

"You're incredible," I exhale, letting my hand trail down her body, watching as she arches into my touch.

My fingers reach her wetness and she gasps, hips lifting toward me instinctively. She's so ready, so responsive to every caress. I start slow, learning what makes those beautiful sounds spill from her lips.

"Noa," she breathes, her hands twisting in the sheets on either side of her wriggling hips.

I love the way she says my name like that–desperate, needy. I increase the pressure of my fingers, until I find a rhythm that makes her whole body tense with pleasure.

"That's it," I whisper, watching her face as I work her toward the edge. "Let me take care of you."

She's close–I can tell by the way her breathing changes, how her thighs squeeze around my hand. I lean down to capture her lips in a deep kiss just as she comes apart beneath me, her body arching as waves of pleasure wash over her.

I hold her through it, fingers gentle now as she rides out every aftershock, until she's pulling me up to collapse against her chest.

"That was…" she starts, then trails off with a contented sigh.

"Perfect," I finish for her, settling into her arms as we both catch our breath.

Outside the window, the city continues to twinkle, but in here, wrapped up in each other, it feels like we're the only two people in the world.

I tiptoe out of Aarti's apartment the next morning and fire up Ringo with a grin I can't wipe off my face. Not even the Tesla driver who flips me off for going the speed limit can dampen my mood. I just smile and wave, singing *have the day you deserve, sir!*

I park on the street, skipping as I make my way to my apartment, whistling Fiona far too cheerfully and completely off-key. I unlock the door and–*jumpscare*–am greeted by the demonic grin of my twin knitting a giant carabiner plushie on the couch.

"Noa," he nods at me.

"I should have never given you keys," I groan, dropping my purse to the floor.

"But alas, you did." He stands, circling me like a hawk. "Where might you have been this morning?" His eyes narrow.

"I, uh–went to get–"

"DON'T you lie to me Noa Jacqueline!" he cries. "Twin telepathy!!!" He points to his temples as if he's reading my mind.

"Fucking *fine*," I start, then immediately stop myself. "Actually, no. You know what? No." I cross my arms. "I don't owe you an explanation for where I spend my nights."

"Oh, come on."

"I'm serious, Aiden. Just because we're twins doesn't mean I have to report my every move to you." I'm deflecting hard and we both know it, but I can't help myself. The whole thing with Aarti still feels too new, too fragile, like if I say it out loud it might evaporate.

His theatrical energy deflates a little, and he settles back onto the couch. "Okay, look." His voice drops to a more genuine tone. "I'm not gonna force it out of you, alright? That's not... that's not what this is."

I eye him suspiciously. "Since when are you not nosy?"

"I'm always nosy. But I'm not cruel." He runs a hand through his hair–the same unconscious gesture I have. "Here's the thing, Noa. I have eyes. And a brain. And two feet that walked into a very suspicious vibe in *my own backhouse* several nights ago."

My stomach drops.

"So if you wanna keep pretending I don't know, we can

totally do that," he continues. "But you should know that I know. And I think I know that you know that I know." He pauses. "You know?"

I stare at him for a long moment, my resolve crumbling. Of course he knows. He's always been able to read me better than anyone, even when I desperately don't want to be read.

"This is ridiculous," I mutter.

"Is it?" He tilts his head. "Because right now you look like someone who spent the night getting thoroughly–"

"Okay!" I throw my hands up in defeat. "Jesus Christ, fine. Yes. Okay? Are you happy? You can't say a word to *anyone*."

"That you're fucking Aarti Nair?"

"Aiden!"

"WHERE'S THE LIE!!!?" he shouts dramatically, his serious moment officially over.

I collapse onto the couch and bury my face in my hands. "There isn't one."

"I fucking knew it." He bounces like he just won the lottery.

"You're impossible."

"I'm right." He settles in next to me, propping his chin on his knuckles with delight. "Now tell me everything."

I tell him from the beginning about the dumpster, the rising tension between me and Aarti, the night we saved Diti, the BFI freezer. How we started off at odds and suddenly that, well... yeah, turned into hot, hot sex. That *absolutely no one* can know about.

"Firstly, may I say that I love this for you," he squeals. "And B, my lips are sealed..." He trails off and gives me a loaded look.

"Say it," I sigh.

"What's the long-term plan here if she can't be out?"

"No further questions at this time, your honor," I plead.

He squints his eyes, not thrilled about it, but resigned. "Case dismissed." He bangs my vintage candle holder on the table like a gavel. "For now."

AFTER NOA LEAVES MY PLACE, I slip on some sweats and open my bedroom door, expecting Diti to pounce. *You little minx! Who was that? What kind of fuckgirl activities are you getting up to now?*

But all I find is her, passed out on the couch, hand in a bowl of now-congealed macaroni and cheese. I grab a towel from the kitchen and dampen it. The cheese is so deeply caked beneath her nails, I can't help my snort–half-amusement, half-second-hand embarrassment. She stirs and I remove the last remnants of white cheddar.

"Deets, it's eleven," I whisper. She grimaces and groans, curling into herself. "Let's go."

But she refuses to move.

This used to be funny. I used to not mind hiding her antics from our parents. But something about this moment strikes a chord in me that rings *this is not normal.*

But who am I to say what *normal* is? My life surely isn't normal by any stretch. I get paid entirely too much money to do weird things with my body on television, not to mention I'm presently having hot and totally boundaryless sex with my co-worker who I first met while in a dumpster.

I tuck her under a fluffy decorative blanket and decide we'll talk tomorrow.

My phone *pings*–an email with today's callsheet. At the top, right under the weather report, my parents' address is listed. A nervous energy shoots up my core.

Today, during our Scent shoot, Noa will be meeting my parents.

I have never done things conventionally, and today certainly won't be the day that starts.

I pull up to my parents' house an hour before the rest of the cast and crew are scheduled to show up. Maa opens the door draped in her favorite sari, an ocean-blue silk one she saves for special occasions.

"I finally get to be a star on television just like you!" she exclaims, beckoning me inside. "Help me make chai."

Helping her make chai entails me perching on a stool at the counter, while Maa bustles around the kitchen making us tea and telling me all the latest gossip from her book club while I ask follow-up questions at appointed intervals. I suppose it's not so different from what I'll soon be doing on stage every night from behind my legacy desk, and perhaps it's why I'm so good at it.

She finally settles across from me, pouring steaming chai into two mugs and sliding one in front of me.

"You spoke to Diti?" she asks, and there it is–that tone. The one that says *tell me what I want to hear, not what's true.* "Everything is okay now, yes?"

I've spent my whole life giving her the answers she wants. *Yes, Maa, school is great. Yes, Maa, comedy is just a hobby. Yes, Maa, I'll find a nice accountant soon.*

I can't do it anymore.

"Maa," I set down my cup, meeting her eyes. "Something's not right with Diti. I really think she…"

"What are you saying?" Her voice is soft but quick–I can hear the fear underneath.

The doorbell rings before I can answer.

"That must be Magenta!" Maa says, already standing, moving away from the conversation she doesn't want to have.

When she opens the door, it's not Madge, but Noa, holding a bouquet of marigolds and looking adorably nervous in a floral sundress that makes my heart skip a beat.

"Mrs. Nair?" Noa offers the flowers with a shy smile. "I'm Noa. Thank you so much for having me in your home."

Maa's entire demeanor shifts. "Oh! Such beautiful flowers! And look at you, what a pretty dress! Please, call me Gita!" She ushers Noa inside, shooting me a look that clearly says *why didn't you tell me she was so lovely?*

"Aarti, show her the house while I finish cleaning in here," Maa commands, retreating to the kitchen. "The cameras will find every speck of dust."

I know what she's doing–using Noa as a buffer, a distraction from the conversation about Diti she desperately does not want to have. But I don't entirely mind her suggestion, either. I look at Noa.

"House tour?" I offer.

"Lead the way."

I show her the living room with its shrine to Ganesh, the wall of family photos documenting every academic achievement of my sister's and a singular photo of when my parents came to see a *Midnight Live* show and didn't even make it halfway through before they left, nearly asleep. We climb the stairs, and I pause outside my teenage bedroom.

"Fair warning," I say, hand on the doorknob. "It's extremely 2008 in here."

The room is exactly as I left it–Bollywood posters competing for wall space with Sarah Silverman and Margaret Cho, my debate trophies gathering dust on shelves that also hold my stash of OG *Vice* magazines stolen from a UCLA dumpster.

"Wow," Noa says. "You were actually a kid once."

"Guilty as charged," I laugh. I watch her explore, trying not to think about how close we are to my dinky twin-size bed and how easy it would be to get horizontal right about now.

Noa turns to me, something tender in her expression. "Thank you for showing me your inner sanctum."

"There's one more thing," I say impulsively. I open my closet door.

She follows me into the walk-in closet, past the kurti my mom still hopes I'll wear to family functions, past the stack of comedy show flyers I've promised myself I'd eventually scrapbook.

"You're a bit of a packrat, huh–"

I press Noa against the back wall, between my old school uniforms and the jumpsuit I wore to my first open mic, and kiss her like I've been dying to since she walked through the door.

She makes a soft sound of surprise before melting into me, hands coming up to tangle in my hair.

"I missed you," I smile.

"It's literally been four hours," she laughs.

"Four hours too long." I lean in again, ready to melt into each other like we did last night… and this morning.

"Your mom?!" she whispers.

"Is busy downstairs," I murmur against her neck. "And this closet is very metaphorically appropriate."

Noa pulls back, her expression tense. "I, uh, need to tell you something."

The way she says it makes my stomach drop, but I nod for her to continue.

"I kinda got caught this morning… by Aiden." Her words tumble out. "I had to tell him. I mean, he suspected ever since that night at his place with Diti, so I wasn't really telling him anything he didn't already know, but–" She takes a shaky breath. "I'm sorry. I know this complicates things for you, and I tried to deflect but he's my twin and he's annoyingly perceptive and–"

"Hey." I reach up to cup her face, thumb stroking across her cheekbone. "Breathe."

She does, but I can still see the worry there, the way she's bracing for me to pull away or get upset. And honestly? A big part of me wants to. The familiar panic starts to creep up my spine–another person who knows, another variable I can't control, another potential way this all falls apart.

But then I look at Noa, at how scared she is of disappointing me.

"Do you trust him?" I ask.

"With my life," she says without hesitation.

I take a breath, let it out slowly. She trusts her brother, and I trust her judgment.

"Okay," I say.

"Okay?" The relief in her voice is immediate, but there's still a lingering uncertainty.

"Okay." I lean my forehead against hers. "Now what were we doing?"

She pulls me in for a kiss that has me forgetting about nosy brothers entirely.

We kiss until the smell of frying oil forces us apart–a smoke signal that assistance is required and if it is not received voluntarily, Maa will come searching.

We stumble back downstairs, hopefully not looking too disheveled, to find the kitchen transformed into organized chaos. Madge and the crew have arrived, setting up lights while Maa bustles around with tiny china bowls of syrupy gulab jamun, pressing the warm treats into everyone's hands as she welcomes them into the family home.

Dad, finally back from work at the university, observes from across the room, hands folded in his chair. It's the most worn piece of furniture that he refuses to let go of. As a child, I enjoyed chasing Diti around our old house in a backbend while making throaty demon growls, once causing her to spill an entire styrofoam cup of chaas across the already faded corduroy. To this day, you can still see the chartreuse Pollockian mess, forever memorialized in the light fabric. "I held you in this chair when you were one day old," Dad always says when I offer to buy him a new seat. "You cannot replace those kinds of memories."

I grab Noa's hand and lead her over to my dad. He clocks the grasp and I let go.

"Dad, this is Noa, my... ice cream scientist."

"So nice to meet you," she says, offering a handshake.

Dad, always calm amongst the chaos, takes her hand with both of his. "You as well, Noa. How are you doing with all of this?"

"Me? Oh, it's... I'm all right. It's a lot. But I'm good." She shoots me a glance.

"Hmm. Yes, it is a lot, isn't it?" He leans back into his chair. "You two must always remember to take care of yourselves first, before all of that." He waves his hand at the hustle and bustle of the kitchen.

Noa nods, thoughtful.

"Tell that to my paycheck," I finger-gun him. I want to talk with him about what Rosa told us during the Taste shoot, that he always knew I was sneaking out and performing, but I can't risk breaking down into tears during another segment. I'll save it for later, in classic Nair family fashion.

Maa beckons us over and we make our way back to the kitchen. Madge gives me a nod as she listens to Syd pitch coverage of the scene. Noa, Maa, and I get mic'd up as Maa mutters to herself.

"*This* is how you make a proper samosa!" she says under her breath. Noa and I exchange a glance, trying not to giggle at the lines Maa has clearly written and assigned to herself.

"All right everyone, we're ready to roll," Madge says. Sound and camera speed, and Syd calls action.

"Noa, welcome to our home. You're going to learn to make proper samosas," Maa says, sounding surprisingly unrehearsed. "But first, you can't make a samosa without a visit to the garden."

For the next hour, Maa is in her element. She tours us around the small herb garden in the backyard, plucking some of her favorites as we go. She picks cilantro and mint, rubbing them between her fingers and offering us a sniff.

"Now over here, these I am very proud of," she says, guiding us to a patch of dirt with small greens protruding from the soil. She pulls a few, revealing potatoes and ginger.

Noa takes a deep breath. "So earthy. Fresh ingredients from your own garden really do make a difference."

We return inside and Maa takes Noa through her spice collection, allowing her to smell each one individually. She shows Noa the precise way to fold the samosa dough, the exact temperature for the oil, which aromatics to add when. I've seen her teach cousins and family friends before, but watching her guide Noa's hands feels different—the way she nods approvingly when Noa asks thoughtful questions, taking time with each answer.

"See how Noa listens?" Maa boasts to the cameras. "This one knows food is about patience."

"Maa, she's literally a food scientist."

"*Diti* knows patience. Noa and Diti would make the best samosas," she says to herself, plating the batch.

A pang of guilt strikes me again as I take a nibble of the savory pastry. *Diti should be here.*

"You were right, these smell *incredible*," Noa says to me, then catches the slight falter in my expression.

Behind the counter, out of sight of the cameras, Noa's pinky finger wraps around mine with a little squeeze. I look down at my samosa, feigning interest in the filling. Really, I'm trying to contain my emotions, knowing that, despite the absolute chaos that is my life, I have Noa, my little umbrella to shelter me from the storm.

Before Noa leaves, Maa hands her a small, delicately wrapped bouquet–fresh curry, fenugreek, and mint leaves bound together with cinnamon sticks and fennel, their mingled fragrance already escaping the tender bundle.

"This is going straight to the flavor lab," she beams, and I picture what it would be like to see Noa and Maa collaborate on more dishes. To have her here, part of our world, for good.

TASTE NOTES:

Pineapple

Ube!!! the purple

Cheesey pupusa texture

pinky pinky pinky

SCENT NOTES:

fresh curry, fenugreek, mint leaves,

cinnamon sticks, fennel,

ohmygodijustmetherparents

"WE DON'T HAVE to do this if you don't want to," Aarti hedges on speakerphone. I'm already setting out ice cream samples for Aiden, inspired by the herb bouquet her mom gave me earlier–I couldn't resist experimenting with them right away. "It's only two days. But I totally get it if that's not how you want to spend your weekend."

"Um." I hesitate. A whirlwind trip with Aarti to New York City, a place I've never been but always dreamt of visiting. All expenses paid by CBT... emphasis on *expense*. The studio would be covering our first class tickets, rooms at the swankiest NYC hotel, meals *wherever we want*. Sounds like a fantasy, except being chauffeured everywhere and wined and dined comes with a catch: Aarti and I have to go on *live national television*. Pre-taping our segment has already required immense compromise of my natural instinct to live out my career in a basement lab, but a morning show broadcast in real-time is a whole 'nother echelon.

Aiden prods at my side and waves the belt of his rainbow marijuana kimono like a lasso.

"You HAVE to go!" he stage-whispers.

"*You're* not the one who has to go on *live TV*," I snip, covering the phone mic with my hand.

"Noa, don't be a pussy! This is your *Pretty Woman* mome!"

"Pussies are strong! And do you even remember what that *classically LA* movie was about?!" I shoot back under my breath.

"What was that?" Aarti asks.

"Nothing, I, um–"

"Look, I know the whole 'live' thing can be intimidating, but... I've got you," she says. Aiden coos, making the little Gen Z heart with his fingers. I flip him off. "I did it for years on *Midnight Live*. And the hosts are there to guide things along if we get stuck."

I appreciate her use of 'we' as if we're equally likely to make fools of ourselves.

I chew on my nail, weighing the pros and cons. Everything with Aarti: major, *major* pro. Making ice cream on TV for the world to see: a Neapolitan swirl of pro, con, and neutral, depending on whether I can remember how to do my job under hot stage lights with a live audience. And speaking of the live audience...

They'll have to wheel you off stage and cut to commercial! It'll be soooo embarrassing!

"Ugh." I collapse into a dining room chair.

"Is... Jerky McGee in the room with us right now?" Aarti asks.

Aiden scoffs. "Aarti knows about Jerky McGee?!"

"Yes and I'd like you to tell him to fuck off, please, because this conversation is between me and Noa," she says.

"Me and you," I repeat back, glaring at Aiden. He raises his hands in defeat.

"I don't want to force you into this. I can do the morning show on my own, even if Gretchen is putting the pressure on both of us. But..." Aarti sighs. "Save for the times we have to be on camera... New York is pretty special. It's easier to be anony-mous there, too."

I hear the parts she's not saying: *New York is special* to me. *We can be anonymous there.*

I look at Aiden for help, but I don't know why I'd expect anything resembling neutrality from my overzealous twin.

"Jesus fuck, she'll go!" he shouts at the phone.

"Aiden!"

"Will you? I promise I'll be with you every step of the way," Aarti can't mask the excitement in her voice. For all her probable annoyance at Aiden being our peanut gallery on this call, she's quickly come on board now that they've formed an alliance. *Sigh.*

"Fine," I say. They both cheer. "But if I have an aneurysm on live television, I blame both of you."

The next morning, a sleek black SUV pulls up outside my apartment. Travel pillow wrapped around my neck like a boa constrictor, I stumble down the stairs with my carry-on. The driver, dressed in a full three-piece suit despite the LA heat, sprints to assist me.

"Thank you," I pant, regaining my balance.

"My pleasure," he says in a delectable French accent. "My name is Henri."

"Noa." I reach for Henri's hand and he tries to mask his confused expression. I realize mid-handshake that greeting a chauffeur this way is probably not typical of his clientele. *Off to a great start, bumpkin!*

Aiden, who insisted on seeing me off, waves from the apartment door. "Go spend that CBT money, henny!"

I heave one last exasperated wave and climb into the backseat. The interior temperature is a perfect seventy-two degrees with individually adjustable AC, and I'm surrounded by snacks of both the sweet and savory persuasion. My stomach growls. Aarti told me to eat light this morning, so Aiden insisted we have what he calls 'LA girl breakfast'–a spirulina Moon Juice concoction that's completely unfilling and even harder to stuff down than his unsolicited advice.

"Is this extra?" I ask, holding up a bag of Gardetto's.

"For you, Noa, everything is free," Henri smiles in the rearview.

I can get used to this.

After the most luxurious drive to LAX ever, I brush the pretzel dust off of me and head through security, already feeling 2% less dread than when I woke up this morning. There's a lot to be said for a doting Parisian chauffeur and free snacks.

I meet Aarti at our gate. She's in baggy sweats, a Dodgers cap, and sunglasses even though she's inside.

"Too bright in here for you?" I tease.

"Hate getting photographed at the airport. LAX is prime hunting grounds for tourists trying to snag a spotted-in-the-wild Gramsta shot before they leave. Paps, too."

Duh, Hart.

Aarti must see my face fall because she quickly follows up with, "Don't be freaked out. It's not that bad... yet."

Her final caveat does nothing to make me feel better, but I brighten my face with a smile anyway and push down that familiar dread about what Aarti's public life means for whatever this is between us.

I glance around. "Where's Madge?"

"It's just us," she smiles.

"Just us," I grin back.

We grab a bite in the lounge, which turns out to be the reason Aarti told me to eat a light breakfast. I don't mention my car snacks, deciding that foods consumed in a vehicle simply don't count. I load up my plate with caviar and wagyu beef sliders that would be impossible to regret even if I'd eaten a turducken this morning. We sit down beside each other in big massage chairs.

"Maybe we don't even have to get on the plane?" I ask her as I wiggle about in my chair, mother of pearl spoon in hand.

Aarti snorts. "I'll bring you back to this lounge anytime, princess."

I buzz with warmth, due to more than the vibrations of the massage chair.

On the plane, our cushy first class seats are in the front row. When the stewardess takes my drink order, I ask for champagne. I'm a princess today, after all.

Aarti and I cheers and the effervescent bubbles immediately tickle my nose as I take a sip.

"This is incredible," I sigh into my seat.

"I'm glad you're having a good time," she smiles at me. "I've got some work to do but–"

"Don't worry, I can keep myself entertained." I flash her the Solitaire app on my phone.

Over the course of the flight, I spy on what she's up to. Before her is a run-of-show document for Season One, Episode One of *Up Late! with Aarti Nair*. She's got a segment called One Star Reviews where celebrities read their terrible movie reviews to camera. Another where she challenges her first interview guest to a rap battle. And of course, her opening monologue. She chews her cheek as she writes and rewrites.

"What?" She catches me staring.

"Oh, just wondering how someone can be so cool and smart and talented, is all."

She rolls her eyes, but grabs my pinky with her free hand as I drift off to sleep.

The drive to our hotel is even better than my drive to the airport. Aarti narrates landmarks to me as I take it all in. When we cross the Queensboro bridge and Manhattan appears before us in all her skyscraping glory, excitement bubbles up in my throat. I'm struck by the fact that while I've never been here, New York is already familiar, etched into my mind's eye by its depictions in the romcoms Aiden and I binge, in the novels I devoured as a kid.

I imagine twenty-three-year-old Aarti stepping off the plane from LA, arriving in this city already knowing she was destined to be a star. I peek at her beside me. She has a wistful look on her face and I wonder if she's reminiscing about the same thing.

It's hard to picture Aarti ever being young or naïve. She's got this ease and confidence about her that make it seem like she was always fully fledged, arriving in the delivery room as an infant with a pen tucked behind her ear and a list of demands. I laugh at the thought and she smiles back at me without questioning what's so funny. I like that. She lets me exist in my Noa-world sometimes, and doesn't make me feel weird for my inner life, the scramble of my thoughts that are often hard to broadcast outwardly.

We pull up to the St. Augustine, a towering hotel with an elaborate limestone facade.

The driver unloads our luggage in the lobby and we head to check-in, where the woman behind the desk bestows us with steamy towels for our hands.

"Thank you, Ms. Nair," she says. "We'll bring your bags to your rooms if you'd like to go explore the city?"

We take our key cards and step into the crisp fall air.

"What are you feeling for dinner?" Aarti asks.

"I'll go wherever you take me." I can tell she likes that.

"I'm gonna need a suggestion from the audience here," she laughs. "Give me something to work with."

I ponder. "Hmm. Something… classically New York."

"I've got just the place."

After a few blocks, we come to a deli that looks straight out of 1950, the line of patrons snaking down the sidewalk.

"Don't worry, it moves fast," she assures me.

"Fine with me, I've got nowhere to be."

"Actually…" she tries to contain her smile. "I've got a surprise for us later."

After throwing out enough guesses to get us to the front of the line, Aarti orders for both of us. When the sandwiches arrive–towering pastrami monuments–she turns to me.

"Let's find a seat and stuff our faces. We've gotta fuel ourselves enough to stay up past midnight."

My face lights up. *Is she saying what I think she's saying?*

"Well, well, well, look who's a real fan now," Aarti chuckles.

Half an hour later, we're stuffed full of fresh rye, pastrami, and pickles. We set out on our much-needed walk uptown to Rocke-feller Plaza. Aarti grabs my hand, hurrying me along in a tight jaywalk, but doesn't let go. I stare down at our hands then back at her.

She shrugs. "One of the reasons I love New York is because no one cares here. They all mind their own business, too busy to give a fuck about some D-list celebrity who may or may not be gay."

"It's a place where you can be yourself," I observe. "Feel normal?"

"Where I can partake in one of my favorite hobbies–crying on the subway in broad daylight–and no one blinks an eye."

"That sounds… kinda depressing?"

"We'll try it someday, you'll see."

My heart flutters. *Someday.*

Midnight Live is better than I could have imagined. Aarti gives me a tour behind the scenes, and I can tell from the looks we get that this is a privileged experience reserved only for a former cast member and her plus-one.

I get to see the writers' rooms and am able to point out the editing bays like a real pro, though they're slightly less sexy than CBT's, if I do say so myself. On the tenth floor, there's a small museum of famous characters and their costumes, including Aarti's King Louis. I get to meet the current cast, plus the head honcho himself, Larry Michelson.

"I knew you'd be big-time someday, kid," he says to Aarti with a pat on the back. "While you're here, think you could step in for the cold open?"

I watch from the front row as Aarti performs like it's second nature, reading her singular line of "That's an awful lot of blood, Mr. President," from the cue cards. When she returns to sit by me, our knees press together in the dark until curtain call, when she hops back onstage to a standing ovation.

We make it out of the theater well past one a.m., wandering hand-in-hand back to our hotel.

"Sorry I got a bit social back there," she says.

"No!" I gasp. "That was–this whole night was an incredible experience. Thanks for sharing your old stomping grounds with me."

She smiles and, right there, for all of Manhattan to see, plants a kiss on my lips. I feel the blush tinge my face. As we pull apart, I glance around–she's right about this city, there's not a soul looking at us.

"More where that came from," she promises.

We arrive back at the hotel, our rooms across the hall from one another.

She leans against her door. "It really is more for show, the two rooms of it all..."

I can't hide the smile on my face as I take her outstretched hand.

Aarti's opulent suite feels like stepping into another era. The marble bathroom alone is larger than my entire apartment, housing a clawfoot tub with corner seats that could easily fit three lumberjacks (a valid form of measurement when you're from the Pacific Northwest) and a crystal chandelier casting kaleidoscopic shadows across the coffered ceiling.

"This is ridiculous," I breathe, running my fingers along the gold-veined marble.

"Ridiculously perfect," Aarti amends, already turning the ornate brass faucets. Steam rises as the tub fills, and she adds a generous pour from one of the complimentary bath oils. The scent of bergamot and sandalwood fills the air.

How lucky am I? I marvel. This comedy queen whose flawless smile graces billboards all over the city, who gets standing ovations just for showing up. And here she is, running a bath for *us*, and–my-oh-my–slipping her blouse over her head.

I step forward to help her pull the silky button-down off, revealing a lacy lavender bra. I unhook the clasp while staring up into her twinkling eyes. When I set her perky tits free, my breath hitches and I lean in to suck first one nipple, then the other, feeling them pebble on my tongue.

While I kiss and tease her breasts, she unbuttons her pants and slides them off. I pause my ministrations only to rapidly undress myself, taking in her matching lavender thong with... what is that? I get on my knees in front of her and confirm my suspicions. The darker purple on her panties is her arousal seeping through, summoning me like a siren's call.

"What are you–ah..." she trails off as I run the flat of my tongue over the damp lace, teasing out my first taste of her, struggling to pace myself.

Everything I've ever learned about developing one's palate is about being methodical, experiencing new flavors slowly so as to pick up on the subtleties and nuances. But right now, it's truly a feat of self-denial that I'm not devouring her with abandon. Even through the fabric, I wish I could bottle the honey and peach and orange blossom of Aarti Nair and taste it on everything, cover myself in her scent, always and forever.

My hands trace the waistband of her thong until they find their way around the plumpness of her ass, squeezing her cheeks as I straighten my tongue and use it to shove her panties aside, exposing her dripping pussy at long last.

Her fingers wrap in my curls with intensifying urgency as my mouth suctions over her swollen clit.

Slow, slow, slow. I have to keep checking myself. I want to tantalize her. As much as I want to take it fast, I want her as urgent as possible. I want to leave an impression.

So I pull my mouth back, releasing the suction entirely. She wiggles her hips, pushing her pussy closer to me with a sexy little groan of frustration.

I answer her with a firm kiss planted over her lush wet opening, helping myself to another taste of her exquisite jus before pulling away once more, sneaking a peek up at her. She meets my gaze with a playful pout, but her glazed eyes and blown pupils tell me my edging is not all that bad. Which gives me an idea.

I pull the plug on the tub for thirty seconds, letting a few inches of water drain as Aarti looks on, confused but too dazed to interrupt.

Then I jut my chin. "Go sit?" Yes, even my commands in bed are questions. I've never claimed to be a top, just a bottom eager to devour and tantalize and claim.

Aarti nods at my request and climbs into the steaming bath, lowering herself onto the raised corner seat. *Perfect.* Her pussy is exposed while her spread legs relax underwater. I climb in after her, kneeling in the tub, unable to hide my fleeting wince at the hard ceramic. Her brows furrow and she reaches to grab a folded towel.

"Knees," she states plainly. I take the towel and tuck it

beneath me in the water, breathing a sigh of relief at the cushioning.

"Where were we?" I tease her. She huffs and toys with her perfect nipples, putting on a show.

I click my tongue at her brashness, but my playful admonishment doesn't hold much weight as I lose all self-control again and dive into her pussy with the ferocity I've been attempting to restrain. And thank god I do, because as I push my tongue into her tight tunnel and nuzzle her pulsing clit with my nose, she starts moaning at a brand new octave. Suddenly, there's nothing I want to chase more than the desperation and unbiddenness of her cries.

I can tell she's getting close when her hands abandon her nipples and return to tug on my curls with urgency. Her hips dance of their own accord, and she's saying my name over and over again like an incantation to bridge the final gap between her arousal and its crescendo.

"Noa Noa Noa NOA!" she chants, legs and hands and fingers twisting and twitching until a grand shudder overtakes her entire body and the sweetest culmination of every flavor I've tasted from her tonight arrives on my tongue.

And suddenly, without stimulation from anything but my own thighs pressing together, I'm cumming too, unable to maintain the suction of my mouth catching her final drops as I moan into her thigh.

As soon as she realizes what's happening, she strokes my head as I shake and groan against her, still kneeling.

When my quakes subside, I look up at her sheepishly. "I didn't realize..."

Aarti scoffs in kindly disbelief. "Don't you *dare* apologize for cumming hands-free while giving me the most mind-blowing orgasm of my entire life. That was... that was insanely hot. Is that... does that happen a lot?"

I shake my head hazily. "I... never in my life," I admit.

"Well, alright then." Aarti's mouth quirks with a hint of pride. "Get up here, please."

I scoot between her knees and she wraps her hands around my face and kisses me deep and long, her tongue exploring my mouth, tasting herself on me. We stay like that for a while, time slipping by unnoticed as our tongues dance, making out like teenagers in a backseat, no further agenda but to stay this close for as long as possible.

Eventually, we pull apart, breathless. We hop into the shower and take turns washing each other's hair, Aarti turning my wet curls into a sudsy mountain, while I turn her long locks into a bona fide George Washington. Bundled up in the hotel's waffle-knit robes, we settle in to watch *Mean Girls*, curled against each other. For a moment, I believe this is our life. Our real life that will go on and on even after we return home to LA.

"I feel like Regina and Cady are into each other," I posit as the cafeteria scene plays out. "Is that crazy?"

Aarti snorts. "I mean yeah, textbook pre-gay-awakening female frenemyship canon event."

"Did you ever have one?" I ask. I turn to face Aarti, and notice her brow is furrowed. "Oh, we don't have to–"

"Her name was Evie." She exhales. "Truly a cliché. I was totally and completely in love with my best friend when we were thirteen."

"Did she… like you back?"

"Incredibly, yes," she says, quiet. "We'd been… figuring things out together. Practice-kissing that turned into real kissing. Holding hands at sleepovers. It was… lovely."

"My middle school homoerotic friendship started dating a boy who put glue all over his hands during math class just to prove to she didn't feel the same way about me–you're lucky," I tell her.

Aarti shakes her head. "Dunno if I'd say that."

I tuck a silky lock of hair behind her ear. "What happened?"

"Evie was my original fan. She dragged me to my first open mic even though I was terrified."

I smile. "How did it go?"

"I did okay, got some laughs. She was in the front row, cackling at every joke." Aarti's voice gets softer. "But as we were leaving the venue, this drunk guy followed us out. Evie was a baby butch even back then–pixie cut, basketball shorts. He started yelling at us, calling us dykes, telling us to try a real man."

I trace the beauty marks on her shoulder.

"Evie grabbed my hand, you know? Stared him down, this barely five-foot tall middle schooler glaring up at a six-something ogre with a beer belly." She takes a shaky breath. "He started screaming, 'I knew it! Couple of little lezzies!' And I just…"

Aarti's eyes go distant.

"You don't have to finish," I reassure her, but she shakes her head.

"No, I want to. I–I panicked. I dropped Evie's hand and stepped a foot away from her and told him we weren't *lezzies*, we were just friends."

"Oh, Aart."

She rubs her temples. "Evie looked like I'd slapped her. I'll never forget the hurt in her eyes. We took the bus home in silence, she wouldn't speak to me. She never really did again."

"You were a kid, Aarti. You were scared."

"I saw how easy it was to compromise myself in the name of appeasing people that hated me. I was a coward. And I've been one ever since."

I want to tell her she's wrong, that survival isn't cowardice, that the world failed her, not the other way around. But I also can't dismiss the pain in her voice, the weight she's carried all these years. I search for the right words that don't exist.

Aarti glances at my face, reading my struggle, and I watch her walls come back up in an instant.

"Wow," she says with a forced laugh, rolling onto her back. "Heavy much, Nair? You don't need to respond to that." She rolls her eyes. "God, I'm such a buzzkill. Here we are in this beautiful room and I'm trauma-dumping about middle school."

"Aarti, no–"

But she's shifting to face me with a practiced smile.

"Our call time is four thirty," she whispers, her arm wrapping around my shoulder. "What do you say we pull an all-nighter? Do some more of this?" She brushes her hand on the inside of my thigh and I'm already wet despite my mind reeling from her story. "Never let this night end?"

I climb on top of her and bring her face to mine, understanding this is how she needs to cope right now. "We are in the city that never sleeps, after all."

NOA and I roll up to CBT Studios New York looking like we actually slept–which, *yeah*, I made sure that didn't happen. NYC's got us buzzing like we're twenty-somethings with endless nights of boozing and partying ahead of us.

Or maybe it's just that we're fucking like twenty-somethings and that's what keeps you glowing. I wouldn't know from experience; my city days were absent of love affairs unless you count my love affair with what the *Midnight Live* writers called Fifteen Hour Energy.

I don't watch many morning shows–not enough fart jokes or cursing for my taste–but *Wake Up Call with Karin and Malik* has a reputation for being the best. The hosts are genuinely cool, in their late thirties rather than the usual Medicare-eligible crowd you see on other networks. Magenta has assured me that this is fluff for elder millennials casually watching while their Nespresso brews–no hard-hitting questions, no manufactured drama. *Relax and be yourselves*, Magenta told me. We'll be ourselves within reason, and that's the best I can ask for.

"Last looks!" the assistant director calls as we step onto the stage. A crowd of early-rising tourists cheer outside the window with signs that say "WE LOVE YOU AARTI!" and "WILL YOU MARRY ME AARTI?!"

"Well? What do you say?" Noa asks, pointing to the man holding the sign.

"Hmm…" I feign, the makeup artist powdering me one final time. "Not my type."

"Aarti! It's so good to finally meet you!" Karin–a woman whose style, voice, and mannerisms have been so carefully calibrated by committee that she could plausibly belong to any demographic focus group–greets us with a firm handshake. "And Noa. Did you have a hand in *Rocky Road to Justice?* My fridge is absolutely stacked with that flavor."

"That one was all Jen and Mary," she smiles. "They're flavor geniuses in their own right."

"Oh, I have so many questions. Let's save it for the screen." She winks and motions us over to a sleek white leather couch. Across from our seat sits the biggest man I've probably ever seen in person–and my show's grips are beefcakes.

"This is Malik "The Tank" Williams, your other host for today."

I shake his hand, a surprisingly softer grip than Karin's.

"Pleasure!" He shoots us a smile straight out of a Crest commercial.

"I'll have to have you two on my show soon," I say, still blinded by his teeth.

"We'd *love* that," Karin coos.

"But until then, you're *our* guests," Malik says. "Take a seat, take a seat!"

I look over at Noa to see if these tried-and-true morning people have drained the life from her yet, but she's all smiles. I give her a nudge with my elbow as we sit.

"Feeling okay?"

"Better than okay."

"Can we have you two sit closer?" a camera operator asks. "Better for my shot."

"No problem!" I say, scooting toward Noa.

"So," Karin says, "Nothing too complicated today, we're just going to ask you about the show, how you met, make a little ice cream, and then do the big reveal!"

"The big–what?" Noa asks.

"Your *Variety* cover. The network sent it over this morning for us to announce," Malik says.

"Oh." I look to Noa. "We, uh, didn't know that would be ready today."

"It is, and we'll all be seeing it together for the first time, live on air!" Karin says.

Noa's face pales and I pat her hand.

"We got this," I whisper. And I mean it.

The assistant director calls from offstage. "We're back from break in three… two…"

"Welcome back! Our next guests are fresh from LA to promote the return of legendary talk show, *Up Late* with a brand-new host and a brand-new, positively *delicious* segment sidekick! Please welcome Aarti Nair and Noa Hart!"

On the monitors, I see the camera cut to me as the growing crowd outside cheers.

"Thanks for having us," I wave.

"Aarti," Malik says. "We used to have you as a resident of our city when you were a staple over on *Midnight Live!* How is it being back in town?"

"I always love being in New York. It's the only city where being ignored is a form of respect."

Malik laughs. "Too true, too true! And what have you been up to while you're here?"

"We got to see all my *Midnight Live* friends last night. It was a great show."

"Just like old times, how fun!" Karin chirps.

This is softball, just like Madge promised.

"Now, Ms. Hart–" Malik begins.

"*Dr.* Hart," I chime in. Noa blushes.

"Thank you, Aarti! Dr. Hart... You're an ice cream scientist at Jen & Mary's. Can you tell us how in the world you got involved with *Up Late?* We've been told the story is a hoot and a half."

"Well, my involvement wasn't planned, I can tell you that much," Noa begins. She paints our disastrous CBT meeting with colorful details and plenty of self-deprecation, charming our hosts with an ease that fills me with a bubbling pride I can barely contain.

We go to break, and when we come back, Noa captivates the hosts once again with her quick and dirty ice cream workshop.

"For those of you who want to try this at home," she cautions, "don't let your nitrogen canister explode and cause the fire alarms to go off on a *very* expensive set."

"And they say *you're* the physical comedian, Aarti!" Malik laughs.

I shrug. "Noa can definitely hold her own."

"We'll be right back with one more surprise from–honestly– my new favorite guests!" Karin says, hands covered in ice cream batter.

"And we're out. Thirty seconds!" the AD says. "Great work, you two. One more segment and then you're wrapped."

I look to Noa, a small dollop of whipped cream in her curls.

"Ready?" I ask, cleaning the ringlet.

"I think so," she says, taking a deep breath. "Been okay so far, I think?"

"You're incredible," I assure her.

We sit back on our couch as the crew clears out the ice cream station. The camera guy doesn't have to remind us to sit closer this time as I give her pinky one last squeeze.

"And we're back in three... two..."

"Now, before we let our two wonderful guests go, we've got an exciting development. You two are about to be on the cover of *Variety*," Malik says. "And we have the cover reveal right here on *Wake Up Call!*"

We all turn to face a giant screen on the other side of the studio.

The *Variety* cover fades in, and there we are in high resolution. It's me as a sexy human sundae, that giant cherry the only thing between Noa's hands and my barely-contained cleavage. Our gazes are locked, captured in that breathless moment after our foreheads touched. The joy between us is unguarded, genuine. The headline curves around Noa's silhouette: AARTI NAIR POPS HER LATE-NIGHT CHERRY! I try not to laugh at the boldness of the title.

Karin marvels at the photo. "*Wow*. Who took this?"

"The Photo Truck," I tell her. "I believe they have a truck in the city, too."

"I know who I'm getting to take our next headshots!" She soft-punches Malik.

"This isn't just the photographer," Malik says, staring at the photo. "Making ice cream involves chemistry, but you two have *chemistry!*"

"Thank you," I say, trying not to totally blow our cover. "Make sure to tune in next week to watch my signature flavor unfold on the show!"

"It was so lovely having you two," Karin says, hardly able to take her eyes off our picture. "We'll be right back!"

The camera slowly, slowly, *fucking slowly* fades out from the photo.

"And… we're out. Nice work everyone!"

The makeup artist hands us face wipes.

"You two are going to be everywhere after this!" she gushes. "Can't wait to tune in."

And with that, we grab our bags and catch our flight back to LA with everything going exactly to plan.

AS SOON AS we hop off our plane at LAX, I realize the dreams and cardigans are but a Pop 100 fairytale. When I turn my phone on, I've got eighty-three texts, an entirely overwhelming amount for my current melty sundae of a brain. I ignore them–which I immediately realize is a mistake. We step into the terminal and are swarmed by camera flashes and people yelling.

"Aarti!" I yell, losing her in the crowd of what I'm quickly realizing are paparazzi.

"Noa! Noa! Right here, Noa!" a photographer yells. "How long has this been going on between you and Aarti?"

"Did nepotism get you the job?" another asks, holding a tiny mic to my face.

"No–I–what?!"

I tuck my head down and shove my way through the mob, hoping that Aarti has figured out her own exit strategy. I make it to the pickup curb and am relieved to find Henri waiting there. He leaps out to open the car door and take my bag.

"Let's get you out of here, Dr. Hart."

Great, even Henri watched this morning's interview.

"How did those paparazzi get in the airport?" I ask, watching some stragglers take photos of the car as we leave.

"Zey, how you say? Buy super cheap ticket and pretend to take flight."

I pull out my phone to confirm Aarti made it to her car. Blue dots appear for a moment, then nothing. My stomach knots but I tell myself she's probably still juggling the logistics of her escape from the LAX mob.

I check Aiden's texts while I wait for Aarti to respond. Shoulda known–his make up at least half of the eighty-three. One is a link to the *Variety* website. I tap it, and the homepage loads. There we are–Aarti being served up like the dessert she is, and me, gay panic and admiration etched clear as day upon my features.

I scroll down, reading the comments, and my stomach drops.

Queerbait = clickbait.

Why can't women work together without playing into a male fantasy to market themselves?

Didn't think pieces teach us anything about this with that Gossip Girl *shoot?*

My pulse quickens. I scroll faster.

Instead of my deepest fear of people analyzing my body, somehow, this is worse. People are analyzing our body *language*, the way we're looking at each other. They're adding our cover shoot to carousels of vamped-up femme costars fake kissing to promote their latest network procedural. They comment on our closeness on the interview couch, how Aarti defended my degree, and how I couldn't stop blushing at her every word.

What did Max say? That we were gonna break the internet? That was a tame way to put it.

I press a button to raise the privacy partition before I dial Aiden in a panic.

"Okay, deep breaths," he starts the moment he picks up. "I'm looking at the same posts you are."

"It's bad, right? Tell me it's not as bad as I think it is."

"Listen, the internet has the attention span of a goldfish," he says. "Remember when people were convinced that K-pop star had been replaced with a double? That lasted like three days before everyone moved on to arguing about whether hot dogs were sandwiches."

"One, they're definitely not sandwiches. Two, that doppelganger conspiracy *boosted* ticket sales," I groan. "Aarti could lose her show over this."

"Or," Aiden counters, "maybe it's the buzz her show needs. People are invested! Most of the comments are supportive. The homophobic trolls are getting ratioed to hell."

"You don't understand the network pressure she's under–"

"Maybe not, but I understand you, Nono," he interrupts delicately. "And I can tell you're catastrophizing right now. Has Aarti said anything to you? Has the network released a statement?"

"No, but–"

"Come eat spooey with me here before you decide the world is ending. Someone will post a controversial ranking of pasta shapes and everyone will forget about this by tomorrow."

As Aiden rambles about a new art show he's planning, I finally take one of the deep breaths he wisely suggested. I put him on speakerphone so I can see if there's been any word from Aarti yet. *Nada.* I refresh Gramsta to see if a social media savior has ranked linguine above bucatini yet, but my stomach drops instead.

"Oh no."

The first video that pops up has 2.3 million views. It's a green screen reaction to the photoshoot. The woman commenting is breathtaking, all cheekbones and bronzed tan, with *Brigitte Blanchette* in her bio alongside a blue check.

"Who is Brigitte Blanchette?" I ask, not sure I actually want to know the answer.

"Holy shit, *the* Brigitte Blanchette? Did she post, too?" I hear

Aiden tapping on his phone, finding the answer. "Okay, honey, you're in the zeitgeist!"

I scoff, seeing as I've just told him the zeitgeist is *not* where I want to be.

He covers. "And like I said, the zeitgeist moves fast!"

But now I'm barely listening to my twin because Brigitte is speaking directly to the camera:

"Okay, so everyone's asking me about the *Variety* shoot and whether it's queerbaiting. Here's my take–how do we ever really know if it's queerbaiting when we're talking about individuals? Like, we can't see into someone's heart or bedroom, right? But what I will say is that using queer aesthetics for clicks when you're not actually about that life? Not cute. Especially when there are actual queer people in entertainment fighting for visibility."

The video cuts to another featured shot of me and Aarti laughing, clearly in our own world, as Brigitte reappears above us.

"But hey, maybe they're just really good friends who happen to look like they're desperately in love. We've all been there." She winks at the camera. "Anyway, stan authentic representation. Peace." She blows a kiss.

The comments are actively exploding, including people asking for *my* Gramsta handle. Thank goodness I've never been anything but a lurker with an incognito username.

I watch in real time as the likes flood in. *100K, 200K, 500K.* The share count climbs.

"This can't be good," I whisper.

IT SHOULD BE impossible to sit amongst the bonsai at my favorite section of the Huntington Gardens and feel anything but tranquil. But here I am, hunched on the handmade wooden bench, baseball cap pulled low, sunglasses on despite the shade, trying to become invisible.

My phone has been off since yesterday afternoon when #Gaarti started trending and I made the mistake of watching Brigitte's viral response video. Her comments section was a battlefield between people calling us queerbaiters and others insisting they can see the truth in our eyes.

I know there are complex emotions underlying Brigitte's commentary. She knows there's truth in what others are merely speculating on, and I'm sure seeing me beaming like a love-struck teenager at another woman on a magazine cover stings. I certainly didn't help matters by ghosting her the minute things with Noa began to flicker into something real. But the worst part? I can't even claim her hot take is wrong. I may not have stepped into that photoshoot with the intention of broadcasting queer-coded longing while refusing to claim it out loud–but that's exactly what happened, intent be damned.

Speaking of queer longing, the other reason my phone has

been off is so I don't have to see the climbing number of texts and calls from Noa. I'm acutely aware that talking to her will veer me into burn-it-all-down instincts so unreasonable and irresponsible my career may never recover. It's not fair to make her responsible for a decision like that when all of this has already been incredibly unfair to her.

Someone taps me on the shoulder and I nearly send a fist to their face.

Instead, I take a deep breath to deal with the stranger. "As I'm sure you know, I've already had enough photos for the week."

"Trust me. I get it."

I look up to see Madge.

"How the hell did you find me?"

"When you didn't show for the house band rehearsal this morning, I had to use my emergency Aarti tracker," she says, settling beside me on the bench.

"Your what now?"

She holds up her phone, showing me a map dotted with locations. "Every place you've been known to run off to." She tucks the phone away. "The paparazzi still camped outside your building tipped me off that you weren't gonna be found there."

"There are paparazzi at my building?" I had my driver take me to a hotel last night so I haven't been home yet. I didn't want to be findable, but I flinch thinking of Diti, alone, dealing with their prying eyes.

"Six of them when I drove by. They got some choice shots of your neighbor in an open bathrobe walking his Pomeranian."

Cringing, I sink lower on the bench, aware that the next thing out of my mouth is going to change everything. "I can explain," I say softly.

"You don't have to explain anything to me, Aarti."

I caution a glance at her. "Don't I?"

She shakes her head. "I mean, you can say anything to me. I'm safe. You can trust me. But..." she trails off.

I swallow hard. I've been avoiding this conversation with Madge for years, and yet–

"Have you always known?"

She shrugs, eyes averting to the Japanese maple before us. "For a while, I suspected. The way you'd edit pronouns out of stories. How you'd light up around certain women. But we had an unspoken agreement–I'd never push, you'd never have to lie to me directly."

"Why didn't you ever say anything?"

"It wasn't mine to say. And honestly? Part of my job is protecting you, including from conversations you aren't ready to have."

"Fuck." I bury my face in my hands, overwhelmed by the odd combination of relief at Madge's steadiness and dread over the uncertainty of basically everything else. "I wanted this gig. I wanted this so bad, *too* bad, that I sacrificed everything I am for it. And now I'm paying. Probably with my entire idiotic career."

"If your career is idiotic, it's the smartest idiotic thing I've ever had the privilege to produce." Madge rests a hand on my back and I peer through my fingers at her. "Can I be real with you for a second?"

I crack a tiny smile at the preposterous notion of Madge ever holding herself back around me. Although, with this latest epiphany, apparently she has untold restraint that I've never given her credit for. "By all means."

"I get why this feels massive to you. But from a producer standpoint? This could blow over by Tuesday. You haven't actually been outed. It's an ambiguous photo that's been released into a universe of AO3 fanfic writers and shippers who see chemistry between any two people who make eye contact." She pauses. "If we don't add gasoline to this fire, it could just as easily burn itself out."

"But what about Gretchen? And CBT? Aren't they furious?" My network overlords are the other reason I've been keeping my phone off, not ready to face the music.

Madge shakes her head. "I called Diane this morning to get the temperature on the C-suite buzz and she said Gretchen's on the links today. No one else seems worried either, especially not the younger assistants who are aware of the chatter. They're used to these mini-non-scandals on an hourly basis. And I fear the actual executives are all dinosaurs when it comes to online discourse."

"Can you tell all that to the adrenaline coursing through my veins at warp speed?"

"Aart, this is what the internet does. You know as well as anyone–look at KurtaGate last month."

Perhaps my adrenaline catches up to what Madge has been trying to tell me, because suddenly, horrifyingly, I'm sobbing. Ugly, shoulder-quaking sobs that I try desperately to muffle with my hands.

I'm certain Madge has never seen me cry. I'm certain I could count on one hand the number of people who ever have.

Without hesitation, she pulls me into her arms, rubbing circles on my back as I completely fall apart.

"I'm so sorry," she whispers. "I'm sorry the world made you feel like you had to hide. I'm sorry the industry is so fucked up that being yourself feels like career suicide. I'm sorry for all of it."

I cry harder, years of control dissolving in the shelter of her embrace. She holds me, murmuring reassurances while I soak her vintage band tee with tears and snot.

Finally, when the sobs subside to hiccups, I pull back. "I'm sorry, I don't–I never–"

"Don't you dare apologize for being human." She pulls tissues from her bag–of course she has tissues. "You've been carrying this alone for so long."

I wipe my face, knowing I look destroyed. "I don't know what to tell Noa… I'm paralyzed."

"You don't have to figure it all out today, but she deserves something, even if it's just 'I need time to think.'"

I nod, looking around at the meticulously maintained bonsai, these tiny trees that have been shaped and controlled their entire lives to fit someone else's vision of beauty.

"Can I just… sit here for a few more hours? Before I turn my phone back on and face everything?"

"Take all the time you need. I'll run interference with Gretchen. If anything does come up, I'll tell her you're taking a personal day." Madge squeezes my shoulder as she stands. "But again, Head Girlboss in Charge won't care about you today unless you're a par 4 or whatever."

"Madge?"

She turns back.

"Thank you. For knowing. For not making me say it before I was ready. For finding me here."

She gives me a soft smile. "That's what I do. Even when you're trying really hard not to be found."

After she leaves, I sit among the bonsai and wonder what would happen if one of them was allowed to grow wild.

AARTI HASN'T TAKEN a single one of my calls the past two days. I can't say I'm shocked. Whether it's crisis management in her own head or with the actual network, or maybe both... I feel ill-equipped to know what I can do right now to help her. Despite my helplessness, all I want right now is to talk to Aarti, for us to find some reassurance in each other. Instead, I'm sitting on the couch in Aiden's living room, where I also slept last night, absentmindedly coloring in a picture of Anna Delvey in his Vibrant Scammers coloring book.

"Stop moping and get in the car," Aiden commands, jangling his keys. "We're going on an adventure."

"I'm not moping."

"You're positively catatonic." He grabs my arm. "Come on. Felix gave me the all-clear to scavenge his property. I need your muscles."

Forty minutes later, we're winding through Topanga Canyon in Aiden's ancient van, windows down, the smell of sage and sun-baked earth filling the car. The recent fires left their mark here–blackened tree skeletons reaching their arms toward the sky, the underbrush eerily sparse.

"Here," Aiden says, pulling off onto a dirt road. "We can take anything from the back acre."

We park and he hands me work gloves. The property stretches before us, a patchwork of devastation and new growth. Tiny green shoots push through ash-darkened soil, nature's stubborn insistence on renewal.

"What exactly are we looking for?" I ask, following him.

"Burnt wood." He kneels beside a twisted piece of manzanita, running his fingers along its charred curves. "I'm making wind chimes for my next group show. *Destruction Sounds.* Repurposed objects damaged by fire."

Of course, in my deepest moment of despair, my twin brings me here to do physical labor.

We work in companionable silence for a while, filling his canvas bags with meticulously selected pieces.

"So," Aiden says eventually, because he can never let me process in peace. "You want to talk about your pattern?"

"What pattern?"

He gives me a look. "Noa, you've been prematurely putting your entire, beautiful heart in undeserving partners' hands since freshman year of college. Remember Tandy? You were already rearranging your schedule to accommodate her pre-med courses during *orientation.*"

"She was gonna be really busy! It would've been hard to see each other–"

"And Aaron? You pet-sat his ferret for literal months after only a week of dating."

"It was only *one* month. Plus Roger Ferreter was cute!"

"He ate my earbuds!" He picks up a piece of blackened oak, examining it. "And what about Carrie?"

I sigh.

"You let her borrow your car for ages when hers broke down–*while she was still dating someone else.*"

"I was biking a lot back then! My car was just sitting there... also I didn't know she was dating that guy until later."

Aiden fixes me with a capital-L Look.

I chuck a piece of wood into the bag harder than necessary. "Okay, so I have a tendency to give my all. Is that a bad thing?"

"Yes. And you're doing it again." He straightens, fixing me with his knowing twin-stare. "Giving Aarti your whole heart before you even know if she can hold it."

"I know that," I protest, kicking at a stump. "I'm trying to protect my heart here. But also..." I trail off, then force myself to continue. "How am I supposed to live my life if I don't let myself try to love?"

Aiden freezes mid-reach for a twisted branch. "*Love*?"

"I mean, the possibility of it." I can feel my face heating. "I don't know."

"Oh, god." He drops the branch entirely. "You're so far gone."

"Shut up."

"No, seriously. *Love*? We're talking about *love* now?" He's way more upset than he was about the Roger Ferreter incident. "With the closeted comedian who's currently ghosting you because a supermodel and a bunch of internet forums implied you're gay together?"

"When you put it like that–"

"It sounds insane? Because it is?" But his voice is gentler now. "Nono, I don't want to see you get hurt again."

"I can take care of myself, Aid, promise."

He's quiet for a little while, a rarity for Aiden. Then he says: "You have endless empathy for others, but when it comes to standing up for what *you* deserve, you're willing to compromise every time."

His words pierce me somewhere deep and uncomfortable and raw. I can't tell whether the lump in my throat is impending nausea or tears, but I manage to swallow it down either way.

"Let's just find these sticks, okay?" I manage.

He doesn't press me further.

We continue collecting wood until the long shadows of the afternoon sun stretch into an early canyon dusk.

By the time we load everything into his car, I'm covered in ash and my heart feels just as charred.

Back at Aiden's place, he drops the wood in his studio before emerging with an armful of clothes.

"Come on," he says. "We're going out. Velvet Tongue, dancing, forgetting about complicated women for a few hours."

"Aiden, I don't think–"

"Nope. No thinking. Only sequins." He holds up a sparkly corset I'm pretty sure he's worn for a drag night or twelve, then rummages around and pulls out a maroon leather skirt. "Trust your big brother."

"We are literally twins."

"But I have so much more testosterone. Chop, chop."

I let him dress me up because resistance is futile when Aiden's in caretaker mode. He finishes my eye makeup–bi pride colors blended to the gods–and we're headed out the door when he throws his hands up in exasperation.

"Fuck!" he screeches.

"What happened?"

"*You* happened, my darling devil of a sister. You stole my Polaroid camera!"

I furrow my brow. "I didn't even know you *had* a Polaroid camera."

"Whatever, I left it at your place weeks ago. We gotta grab it on the way. I told Danya I'd snap cool pics for her Soundcloud profile."

On the drive to mine, Aiden chatters away about Danya's set tonight and the who's who of attendees. My mind strays to Aarti. How she's doing. What she's feeling. Does she cry over stuff like this? Or does she not let it crack her tough exterior?

Maybe she's just doing damage control and I'm last on the need-to-know list. Which would be a really big bummer considering we're partners in all of this... Partners.

Barf.

Needless to say, my mind is somewhere else entirely, and I don't know how I'm going to even slightly enjoy myself when my stomach is churning harder than the twenty-quart industrial gelato maker at work.

"Spiral, much?" Aiden whips me out of my–*fine*–spiral.

"Let's just get your friggin' camera," I say, stepping out of the car.

Aiden stops me dead in my tracks. I look down at his arm, halting me from walking any further. And then I look up.

Aarti stands on my apartment doorstep on the second floor, hand raised, about to knock. She looks exhausted–hair messy, no makeup, donning athleisure for possibly the first time in her life.

"Hey," Aiden calls after a beat, entirely too casual for the circumstances.

Aarti spins around, leaning over the railing to wave awkwardly down at us. "Hi."

Aiden glances between us. "I'll, uh, see you later maybe." He squeezes my shoulder as he gets back in his car. "Or not. Whatever."

And then it's just us. Me, standing on the dirty curb. Her, waiting by my front door.

Move your legs, ding dong!

I snap myself out of it and bound up the stairs to Aarti.

"Hi," I greet her, fumbling with my keys.

"Hi," she repeats.

I open the door. She walks in slowly, like she's not sure she's welcome. She doesn't speak for a long moment, just stands in the living room looking lost.

I lean against the far wall, unsure of what I'm meant to do.

"This is my place," I say, nervous. "Wait, how did you know my address?"

"Madge knows everything about everyone," she sighs. "Producers."

I nod, fighting every instinct to fill the silence.

But she breaks it. "Madge knows about me."

I look at her in shock. "*Knows* knows?"

Aarti nods. "I owe you an apology. Apologies, plural. I've been completely freaking out–"

"You don't say," I quip, instantly regretting my glibness. I can't help trying to lighten the mood, anything to turn Aarti's brightness up a notch. Thankfully she doesn't seem bothered by my attempt.

"Madge doesn't think things are as bad as they feel in here." She taps her head. "Apparently Gretchen hasn't said a word."

I try to decipher the disparity between what she's saying and the downtroddenness of her demeanor. "That's... all of that is good, right?"

Aarti shrugs. "I guess it is. I don't even know what I'm doing here. We live to see another day, but in the long run, I'm ruining your life, dragging you into this horrible fishbowl of secrecy and lies and hiding–"

I cross the room in three strides and silence her with a kiss. Not gentle, not tentative.

She makes a surprised sound against my mouth, then melts into me.

"You can drag me anywhere you please," I murmur against her lips. "I insist."

CHAPTER 33
AARTI

I SCOOP Noa up around my hips and carry her blindly toward what I assume must be the bedroom, but we end up in her kitchen instead

"Where are we going exactly?" she laughs.

"Not here," I say, though honestly, anywhere with her sounds ideal right now. I spin us around, catching glimpses of her well-stocked spice rack and Post-it-covered cookbooks. Part of me wants to stop and ask her about everything–her favorite recipes, the collection of salt and pepper shakers sitting on the ledge above her stove, what her preferred coffee brewing method is–all the little details that make up her world.

But there's definitely a bedroom we need to find right now.

I carry her toward what looks like a hallway, and that's when I see it hanging in the doorway above us.

"A pull-up bar?" I stare at the apparatus, genuinely surprised.

"You seem shocked," Noa says, amusement dancing in her voice.

"Just didn't picture you as a pull-up bar kind of girl, I guess."

Without warning, she reaches up and grabs the handles, her thighs tightening around my hips as she adjusts her grip. The sensation makes my knees nearly buckle.

"Isn't it obvious this is where I got these guns?" She flexes slightly, and I have to pull her closer before I completely lose my composure.

With her face now level with mine, I can see the intricate makeup she'd applied for her night out with Aiden–the way her hazel eyes pop against the indigo and magenta eyeshadow. She could be anywhere tonight, but she's here with me, and the thought makes something warm unfurl in my chest.

With her weight supported by the bar, I slide one hand to cup her ass while the other traces up her arm, feeling the soft dusting of hair raise under my touch.

"Your guns…" I murmur, biting my lip as her breath hitches in response. The sound sends electricity straight through my core. "…are absolutely perfect."

Her thighs squeeze me even tighter. "Don't you want to see my party trick?"

I'm nodding before I even consciously register the question.

Like something out of Cirque du Soleil, she flips her grip and tucks her legs up and over the bar. She's hanging upside down in front of me, cheeks flushing pink from the rush of blood.

"You've done this before," I say, smiling down at her inverted face.

"Usually just to think through problems, never to–"

I silence her with a hand between her thighs, and she gasps, the sound making my pulse spike.

"Never to… what?" I tease, pressing a soft kiss just above her knee.

The maroon leather of her skirt rides up as she spreads her legs wider, and I can't resist tugging at the fabric with my teeth until it slides down, revealing simple black lace underneath.

When I brush my thumb over her panties, I can feel how wet she already is.

"Fuck, Aarti," she breathes.

I pull the lace aside and the sight of her, glistening and ready, sets my nerves on fire. I wrap my arm around her, supporting her weight as I lean forward and take my first taste.

Her abs contract and she lets out the most adorable squeal of pleasure, making me smile against her skin. But one taste isn't enough.

I grip her inner thighs, opening her further for me, and properly dive in. My tongue works over her wetness as her whole body trembles. I can feel every shiver run through her core.

"You okay down there, Spider-Woman?" I ask between strokes of my tongue.

"Mmm-hmm," is all she manages, which makes me grin before I return to circling her swollen clit, alternating between gentle suction and firm pressure.

When I dip my tongue inside her, she squirms beautifully.

"Just like that," she pants. "Don't stop."

I follow her instructions exactly, and soon she's coming undone, her whole body shaking as I hold her steady, making sure she doesn't have to worry about anything except the waves of pleasure washing over her.

As her trembling subsides, I give her one final, lingering lick before carefully supporting her shoulders and lowering her to the kitchen floor.

Her flushed face turns to me, eyes bright and dazed. "It's official," she pants. "The Thinking Bar is no longer designated for thinking."

I capture her mouth in a deep kiss. "Maybe we should rename it... the Lightning Rod?"

"Very apt," she agrees, and then her hands are sliding down into my waistband, making me gasp as she easily slips two fingers inside me.

"God, you're so wet," she murmurs, biting her lower lip in that way that makes me shudder. "All from taking care of me?"

Her fingers find my G-spot with devastating precision,

stroking slowly but firmly before sliding out, leaving me aching for more.

"Patience," she says with a wicked smile, circling my clit instead.

"Patience was never my strong suit," I murmur against her lips, grinding down onto her fingers. "But I'll show you what is."

I pull her sequined shirt over her head, tossing it somewhere behind me because I need to see her, need her skin under my mouth. Her breasts spill over her bra and I can't be bothered to remove it properly. I tug the cups down and take her nipple between my teeth while continuing to rock against her fingers.

She props herself up on her elbows to watch me, head falling back as I work my way up her neck to whisper in her ear.

"I want all of you."

The look she gives me is pure hunger. "Yes."

We manage to get the rest of our clothes off between kisses and desperate touches, giggling when her skirt gets tangled around her ankles and I nearly trip getting out of my sweats.

Noa lowers herself on top of where I'm sitting on the linoleum, her legs straddling my thigh, the slick of her entrance sliding across me, her knee pressing against my pussy.

All of my consciousness is focused entirely on that molten point where we grind together, her skin catching on mine with a friction that sends sparks ricocheting through my pelvis. Her breath hitches against my collarbone, each exhale a soft puff that makes my nipples tighten against her chest.

Her fingers dig into my hips, blunt nails leaving crescents in my flesh as I arch up, meeting her downward thrusts with a desperate, fluid roll. The rhythm is instinct now–a primal, wet glide that draws gasps from us both. She trembles, thighs clamping as if trying to fuse us deeper. I feel the flutter low in her belly against mine, the precursor to release tightening her body like a coiled spring.

"Aarti," she chokes out. Her gaze locks onto mine. The intimacy is terrifying, exhilarating: no artifice, just skin and sweat and the sound of flesh against flesh, echoing in the tiny kitchen.

I press my forehead to hers, our noses brushing, the air between us thick with shared exertion. The pressure builds like a storm surge–deep, inevitable, tightening my abdomen until my muscles quiver uncontrollably. Her slickness coats my thigh, hot and impossibly slippery. My clit grinds into her knee at the same time. She gasps my name again and I feel the first tremor ripple through her–a sudden clenching deep inside her hips.

Her cry shatters the air as the tension snaps. Her back arches with a thrash, thighs locking around me like iron bands. Each throb of her shuddering climax is a hot, liquid pulse against my skin that pushes me over the edge, triggering my own release. My orgasm crashes over me, forcing a groan from my throat as my hips stutter against hers. We cling through the aftershocks, trembling against each other. Her breath fans across my neck.

She collapses onto me, face in my hair, breathing deep. Outside, a car horn blares, a reminder that beyond these walls, there's somehow a world oblivious to the universe we've just dissolved into.

I wake up in Noa's bed, and for a split second between sleep and waking, I drift in the breezy haze of Noa's scent, the soft cloud of her comforter, her warm hand slipped into mine. But alas, nature calls.

On my stroll back from the bathroom, I catch a glimpse of something on the coffee table. I grab it and return to the room.

Noa stirs in bed, the sheet perfectly draped over her curves. She sits up on her elbow, a literal recreation of a Renaissance painting. I lean on the doorway and drink her in.

"Say 'I'm gorgeous.'" I bring my new-found Polaroid up to my eye and snap a photo.

"Thank god that thing doesn't save photos to the cloud–it's Aiden's."

"Well, thank you, Aiden," I say as Noa's form begins to take shape on film. I climb back on top of her in bed and give her a kiss. "I'll be saving this for later."

The harsh buzz of my phone jolts us from our reverie and I fumble to answer.

"Madge?"

Noa sits up instantly and I put the phone on speaker.

"Gretchen wants to see you."

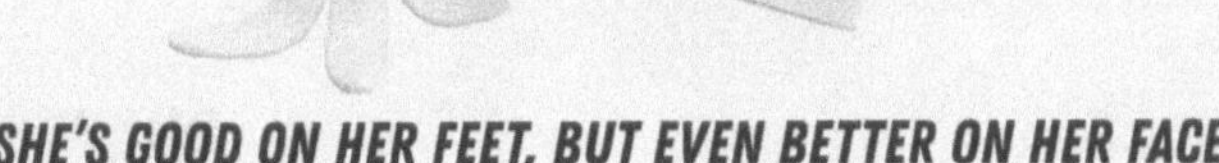

SHE'S GOOD ON HER FEET, BUT EVEN BETTER ON HER FACE

AARTI NAIR'S
FACE FIRST
TOUR

"DELICIOUSLY
FUNNY"
-THE GUARDIAN

"LAUGHED SO HARD
I THREW UP"
-THE TIMES

MORE DATES ADDED!

August 11 Boston
August 12 Manhattan
August 13 Brooklyn
August 14 Jersey City
August 18 Philadelphia
August 19 Baltimore
August 20 D.C.
August 21 Atlanta

August 25 Nashville
August 26 Memphis
August 27. Austin
August 28 St. Louis
September 1 Detroit
September 2 Chicago
September 3 Portland
September 4 Los Angeles

CHAPTER 34

AARTI

THE ELEVATOR CLIMBS to Gretchen's floor in oppressive silence, punctuated only by electronic chimes and Madge tapping her foot on the floor until I catch her eye.

"Sorry." She stops and attempts a reassuring smile. "Don't worry."

Don't worry. I want to laugh at the absurdity of her suggestion, but I can't even muster that degree of levity right now. I sweated out every last ounce of reassurance Madge soothed me with yesterday on the car ride over. I feel like I'm being led to my execution. At least the iced matcha she brought me will make a decent last meal.

When the doors finally open, Diane is waiting like my very own Crypt-Keeper.

"Ms. Gordon is ready for you," she says, pointing me down that endless hallway. I give Madge one last nod and head to the gallows.

Gretchen stands behind her desk, tablet in hand, tapping her blood-red nails on the tempered glass.

"Aarti." As usual, she doesn't look up, making her expression impossible to read.

"Gretchen." My voice is hoarse. I take a sip of matcha and

choke it down, which yields a glance from her. *Nope, still unreadable.*

"Sit," she commands.

I sit.

"I assume you've seen the online response to your *Variety* cover," she begins, and my stomach plummets. *Here it comes.*

"Brilliant work."

Gretchen actually smiles. It's unsettling, to say the least. "The engagement numbers are through the roof. Do you know how hard it is to trend organically these days? At least that's what the social kids tell me." She taps around on her tablet and it's hard to believe she's actually accomplishing anything with the erratic patter.

"So you're not… upset about the speculation?" I venture.

"About the *Variety* cover? No, course not," she says.

Relief floods through me so fast I feel dizzy. *We're not getting fired. We're not–*

"But this?"

Gretchen opens a manila envelope and pushes a glossy 8x10 print toward me like she's straight out of *CSI*. The photo is dark and pixelated, but unmistakable: me kissing Noa on the moonlit streets of New York City.

My jaw drops.

"Two beautiful women who aren't afraid to ham it up for the male gaze in an entertainment rag? We can milk that. Happens every day. But this?" She glares at the print. "This is a story that divides our audience. A story that already cost me a pretty penny to stifle. This is 'CBT doubles down on bein' divisive.' This is '*Up Late* chooses to trade one political controversy for another.'"

The nerves electrifying my pulse have rapidly transmuted into something I never expected to harness in the presence of Gretchen Gordon: *rage*. Of course I've known this entire time what the stakes of coming out are. But hearing her spout bigoted potential headlines comfortably to my face ignites a fury that has been bottled up and suppressed within me for far too long.

"Political? Please, Gretchen, explain to me how who I kiss in my private life is political." My voice is still shaky, but the steady anger underpinning it gets her to fully meet my gaze for once.

For better or worse, she doesn't seem all that fazed by my outrage. But she stares back as she replies, "Oh, darlin', you know the answer to that already. It's not a question of if it *should* be a political statement. It *is* a political statement because the bigots that hate us have made it so."

I'm gearing up to tear into her, when her words catch up to my brain. "You–what do you mean *us?*"

Gretchen slides open her desk drawer and takes out a small picture frame. She pulls the little stand out and faces it toward me. It's a photo of a younger Gretchen, her eyes as soft as I've ever seen them, smiling on the steps of the LA County Court-house with her arms around a dark-haired woman I don't recognize.

"That was twelve years ago when it became legal here in California. We had a commitment ceremony in the mid-90s," she turns the photo around and studies it fondly. "This is Laura."

My head is spinning. "I–I had no idea."

"Precisely." Gretchen places the picture back inside her desk and leans forward in her leather chair. "Aarti, I have gotten to where I am because I have not dragged my personal life into my job. Sure, things have gotten better since I started in this indus-try. But we have not reached a place in society where coming out of the closet yields a neutral response. And I'm just an execu-tive. As long as I don't wave it in anyone's face, I can go home every night to my wife and be as lesbian as Emily Dickinson."

I feel ill. I have the urge to sprint for the hills like Noa, but my legs are too shaky to even stand.

"But you," she continues, "you are the face of a talk show. People recognize you from their TV screens, lobbin' softball questions to their favorite Marvel Chrises every night. For as long as you host *Up Late*, and I do hope it's a long time, there are very few boundaries you can maintain between your personal life and your job."

"What am I supposed to do?" I ask, hating how quickly my righteous anger dissipated into full-body dread.

"You cover your damn tracks. I don't care if it's three a.m. on the side of Route 66 with not a soul for miles, you do not so much as hold hands with a woman outside the safety of your own home with the blinds drawn." She squints at me. "Or you walk away right now. You disappoint your fans. You get a black mark next to your name in Hollywood for tankin' a massive show that employs hundreds of hardworkin' people with mouths to feed one week before it goes to air. You figure out how to live with yourself with all that on your conscience."

"It's not fair," I say feebly, pointlessly.

Gretchen nods. "No it ain't. But that's showbiz, baby. I'll see you and Noa at the premiere on Monday."

The descent is even worse than the climb. This elevator has become my express route to hell. I stumble out, shell-shocked, and find Madge waiting for me.

"Well?" she asks.

All I can manage is a shake of my head.

"Are you okay? We're not fired, right?"

I look at her, only one thought swirling in my mind.

"I need to talk to Noa."

I PARK Ringo Carr in Aarti's guest spot and loop too many Trader Joe's bags around my forearms. The second I got her text inviting me over, I tore through my recipe box and landed on pierogi. She didn't mention a plan for dinner, so I'm hoping it's not presumptuous to show up with groceries. From what I've seen, Aarti rarely cooks for herself. And however the meeting with Gretchen went, I'm a firm believer that homemade dumplings filled with cheesy potatoes will be the answer.

I knock on her door with my foot and as soon as she opens it, my firm belief in fried Polish food falters. She looks beyond depleted.

I let the bags fall from my arms and wrap her in a long hug.

"What is all this?" she asks from within my embrace.

"I'm making you pierogies," I mumble into her chest, not ready to let go. I hear the little huff of laughter she lets out, long arms giving me an extra squeeze before she steps back.

"You're incredible, Noa. Way, way too incredible."

The way she says it makes me uneasy.

She scoops up half the grocery bags and I grab the rest, following her into the kitchen where she takes a seat at the counter.

"Uh, what does 'way too incredible' entail? Is that just, like, a terrifying new way of complimenting someone?" I ask as I begin unpacking ingredients to give my anxious hands something to focus on.

She chuckles but it's halfhearted and sad. "No. I'm sorry for how that came out. You are incredible. I'm just feeling... very inadequate in comparison."

I shake my head. "What happened? Talk to me."

I get to work mixing the pierogi dough as Aarti relays the events of her meeting, from the whiplash of her enthusiasm about our *Variety* cover to the paparazzi shot from New York to the bomb-drop about Gretchen's sexuality.

"She has a *wife*?" I exclaim.

Aarti massages her temples. "I know. Quite the third-act twist."

"Okay, so Gretch quashed the picture of us kissing, and she's not mad about the photoshoot, so maybe we just count this all as a close call and thank our lucky Hollywood Boulevard stars that TMZ didn't get to that photo first?"

Aarti shakes her head. "No, Noa. This isn't just a close call we get to write off."

I pause my kneading, dough sticky on my fingers. "What do you mean?"

"Gretchen made it clear that everything changes now. Before, there was this concept of... caution, I guess." She laughs bitterly. "Now it's a mandate. No holding pinkies out of frame. No taking you to my favorite restaurants and bumping knees under the table. No being my date to events as 'friends'. Just kissing in this condo with the curtains drawn."

"Okay! That's totally fine. I mean, who needs restaurants when you're with a food scientist?" I laugh, rolling the dough with perhaps more vigor than necessary. "And sunlight is overrated. We can buy sun lamps and board up the windows for all I care!"

Aarti stares at me. "Noa–"

"No, seriously, I'm easy. A night like tonight, making you pierogies, holding hands without an audience, without worrying about other people. That's all I need," I reassure her.

She watches me work, expression unreadable. "You don't have to be easy, Noa."

"Oh, I'm not, don't you worry. But for this, I am," I insist, giving her hand a squeeze with my doughy one. "We'll make it work. We have each other."

Aarti gives me a smile for the first time tonight.

We spend the next hour preparing the pierogies together. I teach her how to stuff and seal them, and we move around one another in her kitchen with ease, as if we've always made dinner together.

By the time we're sitting at her table with plates full of golden-brown dumplings topped with sour cream and chives, she seems marginally cheered.

"These are transcendent," she says, and I can tell she means it.

"My babcia's recipe," I tell her. "She always said pierogies could fix anything."

"Smart woman."

We eat in comfortable silence, and for a moment I can almost pretend everything is normal. That we're just two people sharing a meal, not two people negotiating the terms of our confinement.

When we're both stuffed and groaning from carb overload, I see Aarti stifle a yawn.

"I should go," I say, standing to clear our plates. "You need to sleep all this off, and I need to get up early to work on the flavor."

Aarti walks me to her front door. I pull it open, then turn

back for a goodnight kiss. She pulls me back in, away from prying eyes, and pushes the door shut. She presses me against it, kissing me like she's trying to make up for every kiss we won't be able to have in public. Her hands frame my face, fingers tangling in my curls, and when we finally break apart, we're both breathing hard.

"Goodnight," she whispers against my lips.

"Goodnight."

She reaches around me for the handle, opens the door just enough for me to slip through, and then I'm in the hallway, door locked behind me.

CHAPTER 36

AARTI

NOA LEFT after filling my kitchen with the scent of caramelized onions and my heart with a lead weight. She tried so hard to reassure me, to make everything seem manageable–*we'll make it work, I'll make it work, we'll have each other*–but her words only made the knot in my chest tighten.

Much like sneaking an extra samosa when my mother's back was turned as a kid, I've once again bitten off more than I can chew because of something so tempting, so fulfilling, so delicious, that all reason and logic flew out the window.

My mouth is full, and I've been caught red-handed. Do I swallow it all down and lie? Or do I spit out that damn good samosa?

From inside my room, I hear movement in the kitchen and peel myself up out of my carb coma to investigate.

Diti, not partying her night away for once, is rummaging through the freezer.

"Just in time for ice cream sundaes!" she calls out brightly.

I attempt a smile, but it's weak. "I think I've had enough ice cream for my entire life."

"Oh, come on," she pouts. "You look like someone kicked your puppy. Sundaes fix everything."

"Or complicate them," I mutter, sinking into the couch.

Diti studies me closely, spoon suspended mid-air.

"Is this about your mysterious girlfriend of late?"

"She's not my–" I say reflexively, then deflate. "I don't know what she is right now. Everything's... fucked."

"Good fucked or bad fucked?"

I gesture helplessly at my general state of being. "The worst kind. The kind where someone amazing is willing to make themselves smaller for you."

Diti finishes assembling her bowl of chocolate syrup with a side of ice cream and joins me on the couch, her familiar touch on my back loosening the emotions I've been stuffing down all day.

"Talk to me, Aart. I know I haven't been around much lately, but I'm here."

So I do. I spill everything about my mysterious not-girl-friend: our dumpster diving meet-cute. Gretchen's ultimatum. Tonight's dinner and Noa's devastating eagerness to accept a life lived entirely in the shadows.

"She was ready to give up restaurants and sunlight and being seen in public," I finish miserably. "She'd rather hide forever than lose me."

"And that's... bad?" Diti asks.

"It's heartbreaking! She's this brilliant, funny, gorgeous woman who lights up every room she enters, and she's ready to become invisible for me. How is that not the saddest thing you've ever heard?"

Diti is quiet for a moment, considering. "You know what I think? I think you're projecting."

I blink. "Excuse me?"

"You've been hiding parts of yourself your whole life, Aart. Maybe seeing Noa willingly do the same is forcing you to confront how much you hate doing it yourself."

The observation hits like a slap.

"Hey," she nudges me. "I'm great at keeping secrets. I can help you two navigate this. Cover for you, provide alibis, whatever you need."

Her words should be comforting, but they land like a stone in my stomach. *Great at keeping secrets.* The Nair family motto.

"Aarti, you haven't picked the easiest path in life, but that doesn't mean you don't deserve to be happy."

"At the expense of Noa's happiness, though?"

My sister shifts to face me fully. "From where I'm sitting, it sounds like she's choosing to fight for you."

"But what are we supposed to do? Pretend we're roommates until I retire from the show at seventy-five?!"

"With the way things are going, our generation probably won't be able to retire until one hundred and seventy-five."

"You're not helping," I whine.

"What if... you don't need to worry about all of it right now?" she tries. "What if you don't have to think as far out as when you're geriatric, and you just enjoy it for what it is right now, in the moment? Obviously Noa cares about you and is willing to make sacrifices, so what if you just... accept them?"

Could it all really be that simple?

Diti looks at me for a long moment, then reaches over and flicks my forehead.

"Ow! What was that for?"

"You should just enjoy the fact that you're stupidly in love for the first time in your life."

Despite everything, I crack a smile. "Stupidly in love?"

"Ridiculously. Embarrassingly. I've never seen you like this before, and honestly? It's kind of beautiful."

I roll my eyes. "Whatever."

"So... what are you going to do?"

I shake my head, not believing what I'm about to say. "I guess I'm going to listen to my little sister for once?"

"Can I get that in writing?"

"Don't let it go to your head."

But it's too late. She's up and twirling herself back into the kitchen.

"I'm gonna make you a sundae that restores your faith in ice cream!"

If only restoring faith in *myself* was as easy as a few scoops and some chocolate sauce.

AARTI'S BEEN SWEPT into a whirlwind of rehearsals, lighting tests, and last-minute rewrites for Monday's premiere. Which means I've had three long days to disappear into my lab work and ignore the complicated emotions swirling in my gut since Wednesday's pierogi dinner.

It's Saturday morning at the BFI but I've been here since the late hours of Friday night, unable to sleep. Just me, the chicken scratch in my notebook, and the impossible task of distilling Aarti Nair into thirty-two ounces of frozen perfection.

Spread across my workstation like evidence in a crime scene are all the elements I've extracted from our weeks together:

The cherry ribbons Stella originally conceived–bright, grabby, an allusion to her cultural impact on *Midnight Live*, their stability improved with the addition of aged balsamic, oxidized much like the rust of her childhood schoolyard.

Orange blossom and marigold essence crystallized into yellow-flecked rock candy–her Los Angeles roots tangled with her Indian heritage, expressing the tactility of her climbing and the crunchy beats of the West Coast rap that soundtracked her first-gen upbringing.

A matcha syrup infused with fenugreek leaves from her

mother's garden–the caffeine that fuels her tireless work ethic, made bittersweet by her family's expectations.

Lavender and ube sprinkles–the scent of Arjun's patio blended with the pure sugar of the food truck owners and bus drivers who watched over her when she was young.

I line everything up, rearranging and pairing various combinations, trying to solve a puzzle where every piece feels essential.

This is different from my usual process. Normally, I'm just chasing the best version of a flavor, no limitations other than the usual constraints of upholding the Jen & Mary's brand. But here, every choice is about so much more than flavor. I'm deciding which parts of Aarti the world gets to taste and which parts stay hidden.

The truth is, I don't want to get rid of any of it.

The thought arrives with such clarity it makes me gasp. I love every contradictory, complicated piece of her. The way she can command a room and then curl into my arms like she needs protecting. The sharp wit that cuts and the tenderness that heals. The performer and the person underneath.

I love her.

Love.

The word sits heavy in my chest, undeniable and terrifying. When did it shift from attraction to... *this?* This bone-deep certainty that she's it for me?

And suddenly, I see it. The vision arrives fully formed, like when you've been staring at one of those Magic Eye pictures and the image suddenly snaps into focus.

I grab clean containers, working with the fervor of divine inspiration, and it all comes together.

A rich mango kulfi base, free of the basil and saffron that complicated my previous mango experiments. At its center, a swirl of all four elements lined up at my workstation, contained and concealed within the mango so that only the dense orange cream is visible when the pint is first opened.

It takes twelve attempts to get the viscosity right, to ensure each aspect maintains its integrity while swirling together into something that makes my heart race. When I finally nail it, when I dig my spoon into the center and see that perfect rainbow spiral, I actually laugh out loud.

Then immediately want to cry.

Because this is it. This is Aarti. Every hidden piece, every beautiful complicated truth about her, frozen in time with sugar and cream.

And it can never, ever leave this room.

The euphoria of creation crashes into cold reality. I've made the most perfect flavor that will never see the inside of a grocery store. A love letter that has to stay sealed.

I label it simply: *Sweet Talk*. Because isn't that what we've been doing? Sweet-talking the world into believing we're just colleagues with good chemistry?

With shaking hands, I set the pint aside, return to my workstation and pull out my notebook. Turning to a dog-eared page, I locate the safer recipe I sketched out weeks ago, before Aarti and I really got to know each other–a facsimile of who I thought she was and what I thought her audience would want. Building off of Stella's cherry ribbons as well, but beyond that, purely rooted in aesthetic and taste cohesion. A brown butter base accented with a chai spice blend and midnight snacking elements. Pretzel swirls, caramel chunks, chocolate-covered espresso beans.

I work mechanically on this version, and it comes together quickly, which normally would please me, but instead leaves me feeling empty.

It's delicious. It'll sell. It says nothing real.

I have a name for this one, too, one that's cutesy and superficial and broad. I scrawl *Aarti After Midnight* on the lid.

"You're here early. Or late, depending on perspective."

I jump, nearly dropping my spoon. Stella stands in the doorway, looking oddly casual in jeans and a Stanford sweatshirt instead of her usual lab coat armor.

"Couldn't sleep," I manage.

"Hm. Me either," she admits. "I'm used to everything happening on my timeline in ice cream-land, but my ankle is determined to teach me a new lesson."

I think it's the most honest thing she's ever shared with me.

She crosses to my station, her cane tapping a steady rhythm. "May I?"

I slide the safe pint toward her.

She tastes it methodically, letting it melt on her tongue before speaking.

"Brown butter, nice choice. The pretzel provides textural interest without being gimmicky." She nods. "The network will love it. Safe but sophisticated. Well done, Hart. I'm impressed."

There it is. The approval I've been seeking from my boss for oh-so-long.

"Great," I say, moving to store both pints, desperate to get the rainbow one out of sight.

But Stella is eagle-eyed. "What else are you working on? Another mold-breaking monstrosity from home?"

"Oh, that's nothing–"

But she's already reaching for it. She pops the lid, her eyebrows raising slightly at the kulfi. She scrapes a small spoonful off the surface and looks at me, confused.

"Delicious, but where's that Noa twist? Even the chai in that brown butter was unusual, if not toned down for your normal speed."

"Dig deeper," I tell her.

She does, and the spoon reemerges with the mango kulfi on top of the red-orange-green-purple swirl beneath it.

Stella takes a bite and closes her eyes.

When she reopens them, they're twinkling.

"*This* is extraordinary. Why aren't you submitting this one?"

The words stick in my throat. "It's not... Aarti hasn't approved it."

"Ah." She sets down the spoon carefully. "She hasn't or she won't?"

Stella has always been perceptive–you have to be, to taste the intricacies of a flavor as both a chef and a scientist.

"I can't totally explain it," I say, hesitant, "without sharing information that's not mine to tell."

Her brows scrunch together and she closes one eye as she inspects the ice cream again. "I suppose the swirl isn't particularly subtle."

My only answer is silence.

Stella pops the lid back on the pint. "You're talented, Noa. You have real vision. Don't make the mistake of overthinking your cherry ribbons and forget to watch your step."

Stella heads to her office and closes the door behind her.

SWEET TALK RECIPE

1. Crystallize rock candy
2. Cool cherry ribbons
3. Whisk matcha syrup
4. Make ube sprinkles
5. Churn kulfi base
6. Layer kulfi. Create center swirl. Top with remaining kulfi.
7. Freeze (minimum four hours)
8. Try not to cry as you eat the entire pint alone.

CHAPTER 38

AARTI

AFTER HOURS in hair and makeup, a glammed-up Diti pulls at the ends of my sequined purple bowtie and gives me a satisfied nod. She steps to the side and I see myself in the mirror for the first time today, clad in head-to-toe purple in my silk suit, face beat to the gods. In less than an hour, I'll be standing near Noa on the red carpet for the premiere at a plausibly deniable distance for coworkers. I've decided I'm okay with it. Like Diti said, it's just for now.

I get a text letting me know our SUV is downstairs.

"You ready?" Diti asks, nudging me with her elbow.

I admire myself one last time in the mirror and push all of the uncomfortable feelings in my gut aside. This is it. This is the moment I've prepared my whole life for. It's finally here.

"Ready," I grin.

Diti adjusts her dark blue sari as our car pulls up to Hollywood Boulevard.

"How do I look? Anything in my teeth?" she asks, baring her entire mouth for me to inspect.

"Shouldn't I be the one worried about that?" I laugh.

"Mom and Dad are right in front of us! Eeeee!" she squeals. "Can you believe it's really happening?"

She gives my hand a squeeze and as I look out the window, I spot Aiden in a white tux paired with a frilly rainbow blouse, and next to him… Noa stands in a light blue chiffon dress with an array of colorful butterflies fanning down its length. She looks perfectly in place, like a red carpet is exactly where she belongs. I want nothing more than to stand close to her, to hold her, to kiss her in front of all the flashing cameras for the world to see.

A girl can dream, right?

Ahead of us, my parents are ushered from their car and out to the step and repeat. Maa looks around at the photographers and shoots them a showy grin.

"Think they'll be proud of me now?" I ask Diti, who turns to me.

"Aart, they've always been proud of you."

The back door of the SUV opens and I step out to yells of "Aarti! Aarti, here!" from the photographers lining the carpet. I pop out my right hip and stick a thumb in my pocket, flashing my best smize. A handler approaches, escorting Noa into my shot, and our eyes meet as we see each other for the first time in days. She looks even more beautiful up close.

I lean in and whisper, "You look incredible," pulling away fast enough that no one would suspect I was uttering sweet nothings. Photographers yell our names and for the first time, I actually feel like Diti was right, like maybe we can successfully lead these double lives, as long as we're together.

We walk down the carpet toward entertainment correspondent Ryan Delaney, whose megawatt smile and slicked-back hair scream *I peaked as prom king*.

"Aarti Nair! The woman of the hour!" He thrusts the mic at us. "And Dr. Noa Hart! You two have been setting the internet on fire with that *Variety* cover."

"Thank you so much, Ryan," I say, slipping into my media-trained voice.

"The chemistry between you two is just..." he makes a 'chef's kiss' gesture. "Electric! Can you comment on the controversy that's arisen accusing you of queerbaiting?"

I feel Noa tense beside me, but I barrel forward, heeding Gretchen's warnings.

"You know, Ryan, I think what people are responding to is the genuine connection between two women who respect each other's talents," I say, throwing a megawatt smile in Noa's direction. "When you put passionate people who care about their craft in the same room, that energy is going to translate on screen. We're great friends, and we can't wait for folks to watch the segment. Right, Noa?"

Noa manages a tight smile. "Right."

"Break a leg tonight, Aarti!"

"Thanks so much, Ryan," I say, already moving on.

"I need to go," Noa mutters as soon as we're out of earshot.

"Where are you–?"

The same handler from earlier escorts my family to me. I lose sight of Noa in the crowd as my parents pull me in for a hug.

My dad gives me a peck on the cheek.

"Beta, this is... this is all for you!" he beams.

"I could get used to this!" Maa grins from ear to ear. "Now show me how you pose with your hips like this." She juts her hip forward, imitating my go-to red carpet pose.

I sneak a look at Diti and she shoots me a told-ya-so gleam.

My phone buzzes with a text from Uncle Arjun. He's sent a selfie of him and Benny and dozens of their friends, all gathered in their living room wearing *Midnight Live* and Face First Tour merch. They're hosting a massive watch party at their home, and while I'm touched by the support, a part of me wishes the two of them were standing here with my parents right now, all together as a family.

After a few more snaps and interviews, Madge waves me over from the sidelines. Her tie matches her bright green hair, but she's otherwise sleek in a head-to-toe black suit. I join her at the other end of the red carpet, wrapping my arm around her waist and posing.

"Thank you, Madge. I couldn't have done this without you."

"There's literally no one else I'd ever want to make this happen for." She gives me a smile but tucks in her lips like she has something else to say.

"You good?" I ask, all the cameras still flashing our way.

"Yeah, it's Noa, actually," she says.

I turn to face her, suddenly unconcerned with the cameras.

"She, uh, didn't want to take any more photos. Said she needed to drop something in the office."

My desire to stay on the carpet a second longer vanishes. I give Madge a nod and wave to the cameras before I duck into the CBT building.

The ground floor is buzzing with audience members standing in line to be let in. They jump up and down at the sight of me. While I'm used to being recognized, this is a whole new ballgame. I give them a quick wave and a "see ya soon!" then head toward the production wing.

Our offices are the quietest they've been in months with all of the show commotion culminating outside. I peek my head into the writers' room–nothing–and head down the hall to my office. I almost don't see her, crouched down to the height of the mini fridge behind my desk.

"Noa?"

She stands quickly, closing the fridge door. "I thought you'd still be taking photos."

"Madge said you left." I step closer, noting her rigid posture. "What's going on?"

"I needed to drop something off before I go." Her voice is flat, controlled.

"Are you not staying?"

She finally looks at me directly, and I see tears threatening to spill. "I can't do this, Aarti."

"Do what?"

"This." She gestures between us. "Stand next to you to smile and pretend like we're just two friends who respect each other's talents."

Hearing my words quoted back to me stings.

"Noa, you know that's not the truth. If I could, I would shout it from the rooftops how crazy I am about you."

A tear tracks down her cheek. "You *could*, but you won't."

"I would lose everything."

She shakes her head sadly. "And if I stay, I'll lose myself."

I think back to Noa rolling out dumpling dough in my kitchen, ready to forgo the luxury of natural light in order for us to be together. "I don't want you to lose yourself. I really, really do not want that. But the other night, you—"

Her smile is bitter. "I know. And I'm sorry. That's what I do, that's what I've always done, and I'm making this decision now because I need to change the way I live my life. I've always been so ready to give up my sovereignty, my fulfillment, my needs, if it meant I could be loved." The tears spill over in a cascade now. "But if I don't start loving myself, I'm never going to break that pattern."

The pain is almost too much for me to bear. I want to double over, fall to the ground, beat my fists into the earth.

Noa looks at me, mascara smudged around her hazel eyes. "I hope you like your ice cream. And I hope your show goes really well and that people love our segment. And I hope you find your happiness."

"You're just walking away? On the biggest night of my life?"

I hate how accusatory and biting I sound, when inside I've never felt more guilt-ridden and helpless.

"I'm walking away *because* it's the biggest night of your life," she says. "Because you deserve to have your moment without me complicating it. And because I deserve..." She pauses, gathering herself. "I deserve to be with someone who isn't afraid to love me out loud."

The words hit like physical blows.

"I'm not afraid to love you–"

"You're afraid of what it will mean for you. And I get it. But you were right. I can't–" her voice breaks. "I can't make myself small to keep your fears at bay."

She moves toward the door, and I want to stop her, want to say something that will fix this, but what can I offer? I have no right to push back and I don't even want to. I love her. Why would I try to change her mind?

She pauses in the doorframe. "You're beautiful, Aarti. The world deserves to know all of you. There's another life out there waiting for you if you're brave enough to go find it."

Then Noa brushes past me, to Aiden who's appeared down the hall. He throws me a sad smile, and then they're gone, leaving me alone in my office, in my sequined suit, about to host the biggest show of my career with a heart that's shattered.

My opener starts in fifteen minutes. I need to get downstairs, need to fix my face, need to be the version of Aarti Nair that everyone expects.

But all I can think about is the version of me that Noa sees– the one that's apparently too beautiful, too true, for the world not to experience.

The one I'm about to lock away for good.

I'M HANGING from the bar in my kitchen that took a short-lived turn as a Lightning Rod. *You and me both, buddy, but it's back to reality.* Tears pour, and from my inverted position, they roll down my forehead and into my hairline, which feels way more pathetic than crying right-side up.

Aiden dropped me off at my place after we left CBT, running to the store for 'supplies.' Entering my apartment, with tears blurring my vision, every cell inside me was screaming to turn around, go straight to Aarti's and wait outside her door until she came home. To tell her I was rash, that it was all a big mistake, and can we just go back to what we had, even if it's not ideal, even if I'm compromising myself for love like I always do?

But I'm not going to do that anymore, even if this first step feels like torching every instinct I have. When I walked away from track for Aiden, I left behind everything I'd worked for because I couldn't bear to see him hurting. I've never regretted that choice, not once, but it was the beginning of a lifetime of prioritizing everything other than myself, over and over and over again.

And what has that gotten me? A string of exes who mistreated me, yet I'm still proudly on decent terms with?

Sharing my sunny disposition with road ragers who've never deserved an ounce of my good energy? The best pint of ice cream I've ever crafted, relegated to the back of Aarti's office fridge behind her stash of emergency kombucha, never to be shared with the world?

Keys jangle in my front door, and I hear Aiden's voice before I see him.

"Noa Jacqueline, I have returned with fresh spooey!"

He rounds the corner into the kitchen and stops short at the sight of me dangling like a sad, glittery bat.

"Oh, honey."

"I can't get down," I hiccup, face hot from the emotion and the blood rushing to it. "I'm too sad to safely d-dismount."

He wordlessly positions himself beneath me and guides my legs down until I'm sitting on the kitchen floor, a mess of chiffon and runny mascara. He gives me a hug.

"I know it was the right thing to do, so why does it feel like I just set myself on fire?"

Aiden is quiet for a long moment, braiding a section of my curls while I lean against his shoulder.

"You know," he finally says, "knowing I was trans and actually deciding to medically transition were two completely different things in my life."

I look up at him, surprised by the shift.

"Like, I knew who I was. I'd known for years. But the actual choice to transition–to live visibly, to deal with the medical stuff, the social backlash, the extended family drama–that didn't always feel rewarding or perfectly fulfilling moment to moment."

He tugs gently on the braid he's made. "There was pain. Shame. So much second-guessing, especially when people made comments or I had to explain myself to strangers or insurance companies or TSA agents. Sometimes I'd think, wouldn't it be easier to just... not? To keep hiding?"

"But you didn't."

"No. Because even when it was hard, even when it hurt, it was still the truth. And living the truth is better than living a lie."

I wipe my nose on my dress.

"You made a choice tonight to protect yourself," Aiden continues. "To refuse to be someone's secret. That's brave as hell, Noa, and I'm so proud of you. You're also allowed to feel terrible."

"I just… I love her. And I know she loves me too, in her way. What if I'm throwing away something real because I'm being too proud? Too demanding?"

"Or," Aiden says gently, "what if you're finally demanding what you deserve? What if you're refusing to shrink yourself to fit someone else's requirements?"

We sit in silence for a while, my breathing slowly returning to normal.

"It's okay to feel uncomfortable with making new types of decisions for yourself," he adds. "You've spent most of your life taking care of other people. Choosing yourself is the brave thing to do. Even when it sucks."

"Will you stay tonight?" I ask.

"Obviously."

I lean my full weight against him, grateful to have someone to carry this heaviness with me.

CHAPTER 40
AARTI

THE SHOW ITSELF WAS A BLUR. I stood on stage. My guests were great, whoever they were. People laughed. Applauded. Stood on their feet for me, even. Pats on the back as I walked off. Everything recorded. Sent to air.

You did it, Aarti, you won the room. You won America!

The after-party is even more of a fever dream. The swanky nightclub pulses with music so loud I can feel it in my chest, but it's nothing compared to the ache that's taken up residence there since Noa walked out of my office.

I'm on autopilot, my TV persona cranked up to eleven. I air-kiss executives, pose for photos with writers, laugh at jokes I don't really hear. The sequined purple suit that felt so powerful an hour ago now just feels itchy and over-the-top.

"There she is!" A surprisingly ebullient Gretchen appears with a martini, pressing it into my hand. "The woman of the hour! Phenomenal show, Aarti. Just phenomenal."

"Thank you so much," I hear myself say, the words automatic. "Couldn't have done it without the team."

She launches into something about ratings projections and demographic reach, but all I can think about is Noa crouched by my mini fridge, tears streaming down her face.

"…quarterly earnings will be through the roof," Gretchen is saying. I nod, smile, take a sip of gin that burns all the way down.

The writers have commandeered a VIP booth, and I can see them from across the room. Syd's Burger King shirt has been replaced with an actual button-down for once. Rohan's attempting to teach Freya some elaborate hand gesture that's probably from an anime. They're celebrating, as they should be. We did it. We saved the show.

So why does victory taste like ash in my mouth?

I excuse myself and weave through the crowd. Everyone wants to stop me, congratulate me, take a selfie. I oblige them all because that's what I do. That's who I am. The consummate professional. The one who never lets them see her sweat.

Madge is having what looks like an intense conversation with Claire by the bar. Well, Claire's doing most of the talking, gesturing animatedly while Madge watches on, completely oblivious to her traumatized talent spiraling thirty feet away.

I slip into the bathroom and pull out my phone. Three missed calls from my mom, probably wanting to gush about the show on her way home. Too many congratulations texts to count.

And nothing from Noa.

I try Diti, desperate to hear a familiar voice, someone who knows me without the suit and the cameras. It rings and rings before going to voicemail. Of course. It's a Monday night and my premiere was just a pre-game for her continued weekend antics. She's probably at some med school rager, doing keg stands with future surgeons.

"Diti, it's me," I say to her voicemail, my voice cracking. "I just… I need… never mind. Have fun tonight."

I hang up and stare at myself in the bathroom mirror. My makeup is still flawless–whatever wizardry they used, it's apparently heartbreak-proof. But my eyes look hollow, like someone dimmed the lights inside.

The bathroom door swings open and two influencers stumble in, giggling.

"Oh my god, Aarti Nair!" one of them squeals. "Can we get a pic?"

"Of course!" The smile snaps back into place like a rubber band. *Click. Post. Tag. Repeat.*

Back in the main room, the music shifts to something with a heavier bass, and the dance floor erupts. Bodies press together, moving as one mass of celebration and sweat and success. This should be my moment. Everything I've worked for since I was thirteen years old, and all I can think about is Noa at the *Variety* shoot, throwing her head back in laughter as she placed whipped cream atop my head. Noa bringing me a damp washcloth to dab Diti's forehead the night we rescued her from the bar. Noa and the way she looked at me, first a quick glance, then falling deep into my gaze, in the freezer right before our lips met.

I can't do this.

I duck behind a group of tipsy PAs and make my way to the exit. The security guard barely glances up as I push through the door into the cool night air.

The street is packed with the usual Hollywood crowd–beautiful people in beautiful clothes pretending their lives are as perfect as their Gramsta feeds. One of the studio's town cars idles at the curb, waiting to take me home. All I have to do is walk over, slide onto the leather seat, let myself be delivered back to my empty condo.

Instead, I turn left and I walk.

Even my Louboutins aren't made for this, but I don't care. I need to move, need to feel something other than the crushing weight of success that tastes like failure.

Two blocks down, I spot the bus stop. The 4, on its way back from Santa Monica. The same route I used to take to and from the beach when I needed to clear my head after bombing at The Laugh Track.

A woman waiting at the stop does a double-take when she sees me.

"Hey! You're–"

"Just trying to get home," I say quietly.

Miraculously, she just nods, understanding something in my voice, and goes back to scrolling her phone.

When the bus arrives, I dig in my clutch for exact change before giving up and bribing the driver with a crisp twenty. He doesn't recognize me, thank god, just scoffs at the giant bill and then begrudgingly beckons me to board. I find a seat in the back, and sway with the familiar rhythm of stops and starts.

A teenage boy across from me writes in a notebook, probably homework, maybe poetry. He reminds me of myself at that age, scribbling jokes on any available surface, convinced that if I could just find the right words, I could make the world make sense.

The bus lurches to a stop at Fairfax. More people get on–a tired-looking nurse, a couple speaking Portuguese, a guy with a battered guitar. Real people living real lives, none of them knowing that the woman in the ridiculous purple suit is supposed to be having the best night of her life.

My phone buzzes. A notification that #UpLateWithAarti is trending. I switch to airplane mode.

The city rolls by outside the window: taco trucks I've frequented, basement comedy clubs where I've bombed and killed and bombed again, the thousand little landmarks of a life built in public.

I used to love this view.

Now it's just a reminder that no matter how far I travel, I'm still carrying myself with me. Still the girl who learned to hide in her performances and praise so early she never learned how to stop.

By the time I get off the bus, my feet are screaming and my heart feels like it's been put through the industrial mixer in Noa's lab. I limp the last block to my building.

My place is dark, silent.

I don't turn on the lights. Just stand in my living room in my stupid expensive suit, in my stupid expensive condo, with my stupid expensive success, and let myself feel the full weight of what I've lost.

I DRAG MYSELF TO WORK, the emotional hangover of last night a dark cloud over me. For better or worse, no one else seems to notice amidst all the fanfare.

A giant banner reads "CONGRATS NOA!" and everyone–tens more people than on a typical Tuesday–claps for me. I walk through the crowd, face red and puffy, throwing out little nods of appreciation.

"I'd love to get a sneak preview of that flavor!"

"It's gonna be so good!"

"Did you see you and Aarti are trending?!"

I plaster on a smile until I can force my way through to my safe place.

The BFI is cold and quiet. I lean against the door and close my eyes. My phone *buzz buzz buzz*es in my pocket and I hastily turn it off. All morning I've been receiving calls and texts, congratulating me, telling me how fun the first segment was. It's overwhelming, and I wonder how much more attention Aarti is receiving. How much more she's having to pretend to be someone else.

"You're late," Stella says, walking out of her office. But when I meet her eyes, I see she's giving me that classic Stella smirk.

"I sent a sample of your work to Jen and Mary," she says slyly.

This stops me in my tracks. Jen and Mary have become such symbols of change that they hardly have anything to do with the ice cream approval process anymore. They trust in Stella so deeply that they allow her to make those calls. Having them taste test is...

"Wow," I mutter. "Thank you."

It's difficult to be sincere at this moment, but I am. Jen and Mary are my heroes in more ways than just ice cream, and it's an honor for them to even try my work.

"They want to see you. In their office... Now."

My eyes grow wide. "Jen and–*now?*"

She smiles. "Now."

In the lobby, I press the UP button and the elevator doors open. I walk in and feel like I'm in the Upside Down–my entire world has changed and I have no idea what to do about it all besides breathe and bawl and maybe laugh at the fact that I've gotten everything I've ever wanted and I've finally, *finally* stood up for myself, yet here I am crying in an elevator on my way up to live my dreams despite everything feeling so entirely fucking *wrong.*

Ding. The elevator opens and I'm welcomed onto the top floor of Jen & Mary's for the first time. The vibes match those of the lobby, but the windows overlooking East Hollywood capture another level of awe. I walk down the open hallway, lined with photos of the founders, but these are less iconic and more... personal. Jen and Mary on their rescue dog farm. Jen and Mary with a positive pregnancy test. Jen and Mary surrounded by their grown children on a family vacation to Harmony Springs.

I stop in front of the final photo. It's old, maybe the oldest photo of the two of them. Jen cranks a vintage ice cream mixer while Mary tries to sneak a taste. The feeling of new love emanates from the image and I let another tear fall.

"That was our first date," a voice says from behind me. I turn and it's Mary Hinklebohm, in the flesh. I attempt to form words but either she knows I'm incapacitated by her presence or she's got a busy schedule to attend to. Probably both. "Come in, Noa."

Mary guides me into her office, the bright daylight flooding in. A slobbery mess of a mutt hobbles over to me from her bed and plants her face between my palms for chin scritches, which I oblige.

"That's Mrs. Pierogi. We came to town to rescue her and bring her back home to Wisconsin."

"I love pierogies," I say, reminiscing about making them with Aarti just a few nights ago.

I turn to face the desk and Jen sits behind it, a walker to her left. I've never seen her with that before, so it must be new.

Mary gives Jen a quick kiss on the temple and they sit behind their custom mahogany dual desk.

"Please, Noa, take a seat."

I give Mrs. Pierogi a boop on the nose before sitting, and she waddles back to her bed like it's business as usual.

"She seems comfortable already," I say, still nervous to be so casually chatting with my heroes.

"You'd never know she was chained up near Skid Row with no water or shade mere hours ago," Jen sighs. "Dogs can be so very forgiving of us humans."

I nod, not sure how to hold a conversation with these legends.

"So, Noa," Mary begins. "We got to try your new flavor for *Up Late*. Incredible work."

"Reminded us of our early ice cream days," Jen says. "Classic even though its flavor profile is deeply complex."

"Thank you," I say, trying to maintain a normal breathing pattern.

"It was great, but... the other one was even better."

I freeze. *The other one?*

Mary pulls out the test pint with *Sweet Talk* scribbled in my handwriting on the side.

She removes the reading glasses from her gray curls and turns the pint in her hand. "Mango kulfi with a rainbow swirl center." She pops the lid and grabs a spoon from her desk drawer. She dips into the middle and twists, revealing the beautiful core I worked so tirelessly on.

Jen steeples her fingers. "You can tell you put so much of yourself into it," she says.

Yeah, my literal tears.

"It's... complex," she continues. "Certainly not like anything I've had before."

Mary takes the giant spoonful of rainbow swirl and savors it with an *mmmmmm*. "And it is quite possibly the best thing I've ever put in my mouth."

Jen takes a spoonful for herself. "Stella didn't share the details, but we understand you had to make a complicated decision to set this flavor aside to appease the client. We really value that discretion."

"But!" Mary adds, "We'd also like to recognize you for the genius work of this pint in particular, and your contributions over the years, which Stella has sung praises of."

"That is why," Jen grabs Mary's hand, "we feel secure in our choice to take time away from the business. We're promoting Stella and we need someone to take her place."

They look at me hopefully.

"...Me?" I ask.

"We'd love for you to accept the position of Chief Flavor Officer, Noa," Mary says. "There's no one else we–or Stella– would want to fill her shoes. And of course you'll keep working together, but you'll run the lab."

"Custom flavors for a range of clientele–big events, activists, all kinds of artists and celebrities." Jen beams.

"You've proven you have what it takes to really shine in a role like this."

What have I proven about myself? That I know how to prioritize marketability over honesty? That I'll always be a yes-woman to everyone but me?

"If you accept, of course," Mary gives me a cheeky grin. Because why wouldn't I accept? I'd be crazy not to accept.

"Thank you," I muster. "I really appreciate the offer…"

Jen and Mary exchange a glance. "…But?"

I clear my throat. Time to speak from the heart, sweet talk be damned.

THREE MONTHS LATER.

CHAPTER 42
AARTI

"THE RATINGS ARE TANKING AGAIN!" Madge spits at me.

In fairness, I did ask her to "spit it out" but didn't expect her to do it so literally. I haven't seen her this stressed since launching the show, and while I find it unfortunate, I can hardly say I'm surprised. The original viewers stuck around for a few weeks, hoping to see more of the chemistry that came with the Noa segments, but eventually tuned out when they realized she wasn't coming back. The flood of Gramsta comments made it clear that at least some of the audience preferred the scandal of me queerbaiting to me just being straight and boring. Even the novelty of the signature ice cream has worn off and Jen & Mary's decided to make it a "Special Edition"–a.k.a it's not selling–despite good reviews.

Part of me wonders if Noa had any say in the ice cream's cancellation. I doubt it, but I can't help looping her into my thoughts these days however I can.

I lean back in my office chair and casually wipe the spittle from my face, but Madge doesn't notice anyway because old habits die hard, and she's pacing the fuck out of the office.

"Madge," I say, trying to grab her attention.

"Gretchen is right, we should've gotten her under a longer contract," she grumbles, and I shoot her a look. "Sorry, I know that's not helping."

She collapses into a chair. "All right, let's wipe our brains and start fresh. What can we do to bring the audience back?"

"Be funny again," I say, equal parts sarcastic and the most serious I've ever been in my whole life.

She chides me with her big doe eyes. "You will never not be funny, Aarti."

"Tell that to the comments section," I shrug. "It's late. I'll figure something out. Go home and take a load off."

She's unsure, but I stand and force her out with me.

When I get home, I am alone. Diti has been even more absent than usual and I can't stifle the feeling that I'm a failure in every avenue of my life. I abandoned her for my work, and now I can't say I've succeeded at either my goal of helping my sister get it together *or* having a hit show. I'm bombing at my job, my career, my romantic life, my family life... Sometimes I just wish someone would give me a report card with big red-circled Fs so I could at least have a memento to document the downfall of my existence.

I sink deep into the couch and check my Gramsta. On my home page is a post of Brigitte with her new girlfriend, which I like. I'm genuinely happy for her, and maybe–obviously–envious that she found someone who stayed. I keep scrolling, passing a post from The Laugh Track about a comedy storytelling event. I go back and read. Tonight. Nine p.m.

It takes everything to pull myself out of the upholstery and get ready to go back out of the house, but I know if anything will make me feel better, it's a good old-fashioned comedy show.

. . .

"Soda water, please," I say to the bartender who doesn't recognize me. He shoots me an annoyed look until I place a ten-dollar tip by my free drink.

I pull up my hood and sit at an empty table behind the back row of seats. I stir my little black straw until the baby-faced host hops onstage.

"Welcome out to The Laugh Track, everybody!" he shouts to a smattering of applause. "That's a Tuesday for ya," he laughs. "All right, we have a great show for you tonight, please welcome to the stage…"

And for an hour, I get to return to being Little Aarti. I get to hear hilarious stories from comedians of all kinds, and for the first time in a long time, not feel the pressure to be funny.

Until the host comes back out.

"Thank you, thank you! Now I did see that we have a legendary guest in the house tonight. Someone who is one of my personal comedy heroes, who inspired me to be here on this stage today…" He uses a hand to shield his eyes from the spotlight and the crowd murmurs. *What A-lister shows up to a Tuesday night crowd?*

"There she is! Aarti Nair, everyone!"

Aw, fuck.

Everyone in the crowd turns to me. I sink into my seat with a little wave.

"We know you've got some stories to tell, and we'd be honored if you could share a little something with us. Whaddya say?"

The small but sure audience claps and whoops, and now, I have no choice.

Pulling my hoodie off, I walk up to the stage and take the mic.

"Thank you, man who is now my mortal enemy," I half-joke. "My name is Aarti Nair, some of you probably know me from being on TV."

That gets a whoop.

"I'm glad someone is still watching. Based on my ratings, it's literally one person. Mom, you can stop clearing your browser history—I know it's you."

The audience laughs and I feel myself begin to loosen up. I pace the small stage, feeling the eyes of the intimate crowd, no cue cards or teleprompters or producers in sight.

"This is less of a story, more of a random question: has anyone here ever gotten everything they ever wanted?"

A few hands go up.

"Cool, cool... Did it fucking *suck?*"

Some claps and laughter.

"Glad it's not just me. Because I'm living the dream right now. I got the job I've wanted since I was thirteen years old. The job half of you probably want, too."

I get another laugh.

"Everyone is like 'you've got it so good, I wish I was you!' You don't. I promise," I breathe into the mic. "Sure, I eat LA's most expensive takeout on my overpriced white sofa—because I can afford infinite Tide Pens—but you know what's happening while I'm doing that? I'm hate-watching my own TV show. My internal monologue is like *Inside Out*, but it's all anxiety and they're debating whether I'm too much of everything or not enough of anything."

The crowd likes that one.

"My predecessor, Guy Morrison—remember him? He used to say that comedy comes from truth. The deeper you dig, the funnier it gets." I shake my head. "Guy got fired for telling too much truth. So I thought, well, I'll just tell the committee-approved truths. But truth by omission has never been a thing."

Staring into the tiny audience makes me nostalgic for the period of my life where I did this every night of the week.

"When I was a teenager, I would sneak out to perform here. Three buses each way to tell jokes to seven people who were literally just too drunk to leave. And I was happy. You know why? Because when I bombed, at least it was my truth failing. Now, I'm noted to death by the network like, 'don't mention existential dread, it tested poorly in Ohio.' Glad you're so happy that the rest of us can't even bitch about it, *Ohio*."

I look around the intimate space.

"But tonight? In this room that definitely violates several fire codes? You twelve people aren't here for the focus-grouped version. You're here for the truth. And I think, finally, so am I. So thanks for reminding me that bombing as yourself beats killing as someone else."

I grin.

"I'm Aarti Nair, and this is the most honest I've been in months. Thank you and goodnight!"

Before I can set the mic back in its stand, the crowd is on its feet, and I'm on a high that I haven't felt since the last time I kissed Noa Hart.

WHEN I WAS old enough to read, Dad gifted me Mom's childhood collection of leather-bound, gilt-edged fairytales and folklore. I pored over those books, tracing the arcs of princesses and ugly ducklings, searching for spaces to slip myself into their stories, hoping their happy endings might one day find me, too. More than anything, I dreamt of a fairy godmother–a kindly witch-woman who would see me, instantly knowing which enchanted spell or pumpkin-on-wheels to conjure to help me fulfill my destiny.

Over the years, I learned why fairy godmothers who materialize from thin air to solve problems exist strictly in the realm of fantasy. In real life, the reins of fate rest squarely in your hands. You become your own whimsical wish-granter. I've certainly tried–after all, earning a PhD in ice cream science is pretty whimsical. Yet, despite my best efforts, I've realized there's nothing passive about conjuring your magic. Wishes demand work.

Which is why, three months ago, I turned down a pair of glass slippers that didn't fit me, and walked away from Jen & Mary's job offer in favor of chasing my dreams. What I didn't expect was that, in true fairytale fashion, this protagonist's sacrifice would yield its own reward. My lesbian activist ice-cream-visionary fairy godmothers accepted my resignation on one condition: that I take their severance package, which came with a letter of intent to invest in my next venture–my very own ice cream truck.

I've spent twelve weeks outfitting a vehicle, applying for permits, developing my menu, and enlisting Aiden's help with designing a logo and painting the outside of my converted Chevy step van with a sprawling cursive *SPLIT HAPPENS*.

I can't deny that launching a business from scratch has also given me a productive outlet to pour my focus into–a convenient excuse to ignore certain nationally broadcast, billboard-on-the-Boulevard-sized distractions.

I've done my best to tune out the hype surrounding Aarti's show and the ice cream launch. Jen and Mary mentioned a few weeks back that *Aarti After Midnight* was being relegated to a limited edition, soon to be pulled from the shelves, but I held myself back from questioning the implications. It's not my job to worry about Aarti anymore, and I did my best to inform my fairy godmothers as much. They didn't ask for details, just shared a knowing look, and haven't offered any updates since.

Today, I'm hunched over a table in Aiden's backyard, gluing hand-written menus to pretty handmade-paper backings while he puts the finishing touches on the truck's mural–a vivid explosion of fruit mid-split, their juicy insides spiraling into colorful swirls.

When Jen and Mary invested in my venture, they insisted I define my philosophy.

"What does your ice cream stand for?" they pressed, approaching my fledgling business with the same intentionality that built their empire around activism and social justice.

The answer came to me instantly, though I'd voiced it only

once before, tipsy at Arjun's restaurant, passionately ranting about the tyranny of banana splits.

Split Happens isn't just a playful pun; it's the core belief I've been striving to embody since everything happened with Aarti. Life splits us open in unexpected ways, exposing our messy, complicated centers. When that happens, we deserve something sweet, something that celebrates the beauty of being cracked open, of being different, richer, and more complex beneath the surface. Besides, bananas have monopolized the split game for far too long. Why not mangoes crowned with coconut sorbet, or poached pears nestled lovingly between scoops of cardamom-honey ice cream?

"Pass me the coral," Aiden calls from his perch on a ladder.

I walk over and hand him the paint, admiring how the mural is coming together.

"You spiraling about tonight?" he asks, dabbing coral into a papaya's flesh.

Tonight. My stomach does a little flip.

"I'm not spiraling."

"You're doing that thing where you subconsciously organize things by size." He gestures with his brush toward my supplies for the menu, lined up in psychotic size-progression on the table.

"Maybe a little spiraling," I admit.

Tonight is Aiden's collective art show, *Destruction Sounds,* and it's also my soft opening of Split Happens. His wind chimes made from fire-scorched Topanga wood will hang alongside other artists' work exploring destruction and renewal. I've been trying to convince myself that my ice cream truck parked outside signifies another form of rising from the ashes, even though it also kinda makes bile rise from my stomach.

Aiden climbs down and pulls me into a paint-smeared hug. "Terror means you care. Tonight's gonna be incredible."

. . .

By seven p.m., the gallery space in Silver Lake is thrumming with energy. Aiden's wind chimes clink out an ethereal soundtrack as people move about. I'm stationed in my truck, wearing the apron Aiden embroidered with "Dr. Split" in rainbow thread.

I've got three flavors debuting this evening: Split Personality (a brown butter base with caramelized banana slices and miso served over a flambeed plantain), Mango Unchained (a halved mango topped with coconut sticky-rice ice cream and toasted sesame seeds), and Pear Pressure (poached pear filled with brown butter caramel ice cream and crushed honeycomb brittle).

The first few customers are Aiden's friends, offering enthusiastic support, but soon strangers are lining up as well.

"Oh my god, Pear Pressure PLEASE!?" A woman with paint under her fingernails exclaims.

I serve up the concoction and her eyes close on the first taste.

"Holy shit," she breathes. "This is art."

For the first time in three months, I feel fully present. Not thinking about Aarti, not replaying our last conversation, not wondering if I made the right choice. Just here, serving ice cream I created from my whole heart to people who appreciate it for exactly what it is.

The line grows. I'm in a rhythm now, scooping, splitting, drizzling house-made sauces, explaining flavor profiles to curious customers. The crowd is queer LA scene kid central: a guy with a graffitied mandolin slung over his shoulder, two girls hyperfocused on adding piercings to each other's Labubus, a drag queen reciting e.e. cummings aloud to no one in particular. Hair every color imaginable–blue, purple, pink, even a brilliant shade of green approaching the counter...

Hold on.

Make that an *achingly* familiar shade of green.
My heart drops into my stomach.

offerings

Split Personality
brown butter base with caramelized banana slices
and miso served over a flambeed plantain   **$9**

Mango Unchained
halved mango topped with coconut sticky-rice ice
cream and toasted sesame seeds   **$9**

Pear Pressure
poached pear filled with brown butter caramel ice
cream and crushed honeycomb brittle   **$9**

CHAPTER 44
AARTI

THE HIGH OF my Tuesday night storytelling event fades fast. I'm pulled right back into the falling empire that is *Up Late,* and that quick hit of confidence is but a fleeting boost.

After Friday's taping, I park my car in front of my parents' place. Diti and Arjun's cars are already lined up in the drive, and through the window, I see them all at the dinner table.

I walk through the door and am greeted by Maa.

"We've been waiting for you, beta!"

"Got here as soon as I could, Maa."

I find my seat and give Diti a polite nod from across the table. I haven't seen her in days, but here we are, once again, pretending like everything is totally normal.

Arjun gives my shoulder a squeeze and I lean into his hand.

"How're you?" I ask. I've seen him a couple times since the spectacular blow-up with Noa, so he knows the whole story.

"I'm good," he says, smiling smaller than I can tell he would like to. Last time we spoke, he told me that he and Benny were getting married, and I can still hardly contain my excitement. "How about you?"

"Oh, you know."

I look over at Dad and get his usual quiet wink and a nod. Maa returns with a dish of piping hot naan.

"Dig in!" she says.

We all gladly load up our plates as Maa addresses us one by one.

"How's school, Diti?"

"Great," she says, coolly.

"And the restaurant, Arjun?"

"Just swell."

"How is the show, Aarti?"

"Fine."

A silence falls over the table, partly because everyone is chowing down but mostly because no one at this table except probably Maa can talk without chancing the slip of a deep dark secret. I listen to the clanking of silverware on plates and it's as if they're banging directly into my skull. Usually, I'm the queen of the avoidant dinner chat, but for some reason I can't slip into the typical ease of being a big fat fucking phony.

In fact, it's pissing me off more than any family dinner we've had before. Diti is on the biggest downward spiral of her life, I'm reeling from heartbreak, Arjun is *getting married* for chrissakes, and all of us are just sitting here, nibbling away at our vindaloo as if we don't have these massive life-altering realities outside of this table.

"You know what," I clear my throat. "It's actually not fine. It's very not fine." I wipe my mouth with my napkin and feel everyone's heads turn to me.

Maa raises her brows in surprise, surely because everything is always *fine*. "Why not, beta?"

I neatly place the cloth back into my lap and for a split second wonder if I'm actually going to go there.

Fuck it.

"Because I feel like my whole life is a lie. I went to a comedy show this week and put on an impromptu performance and it was the best thing I've done in over a year, because you know what? I was telling the truth for once."

I catch a glimpse of Diti, whose cheeks pinken with worry. Arjun stares down at his plate, forking around some grains of rice he's not actually trying to eat. Mom and Dad stare at me with their full attention. So I power forward.

"That one little show felt so freeing and fulfilling and *real*, and you know what I did with that? Nothing. Nothing at all! I went back to my normal routine of hiding in plain sight. Hiding from my writers, my producers, my audience, my family."

"What are you hiding from us?" Dad asks, concern growing on his face.

Diti gives me a small shake of her head from across the table. But what is there left to lose?

"I'm gay."

Arjun drops his fork with a clatter. Maa looks to Diti, then Dad. Then me.

"I mean..." she says. "We... assumed."

Arjun chokes. Diti's eyes go wide. Dad shrugs.

"But you always said you wanted me to settle down with some accountant?"

"Beta, women can be accountants, too."

And then I laugh.

I laugh and laugh and laugh and realize that everyone else has joined in with me. I take a sip of water to calm down, but then Arjun steps in.

"I'm gay, too."

"We *definitely* knew that."

And we're all laughing again. Hysterical, wheezing, cathartic laughter.

When it dies down, I ask the question that's been gnawing at my gut. "And... you're okay with it?"

"Aarti," Dad shakes his head. "We love you and Arjun no matter."

"What about me?" Diti pipes up.

"Now if you're gay, I will be shocked," Maa says.

"No, but... I am an alcoholic."

This time, there's no laughter. Diti's eyes are turned down, but with my own, I urge her to look at me.

"I've been, uh, not in a good place these past few months," she says. "Aarti has been hiding it for me and I don't want to make her do that anymore."

My heart breaks for Diti. I've wanted nothing more than for her to admit she had a problem, but as soon as she does, I want to wrap it back up and put it away for no one else to see.

"But the good news is," she finally looks at me, "I've been going to AA. I'm getting help, and I'm trying to be better. I'll be one month sober next week."

"That is very admirable, Diti," Arjun says.

"It is," Dad agrees.

Maa's eyes well with tears and she nods in agreement. "We love you, Diti."

"I love you, too."

The rest of our meal is looser than ever before, like finally being honest has unlocked a previously unfathomable level of familial camaraderie. Arjun announces his engagement and regales all of us with his and Benny's uproarious wedding planning saga. Maa invites her brother to bring his fiancé to dinner the following week, and everyone leaves with smiles broader than I've ever seen at the conclusion of a Nair dinner.

I squeeze Diti before getting into the car. "Proud of you."

"I couldn't have done it without you," she says. "Any of it."

I give her one last hug before I slide into the driver's seat, heaving a sigh of relief. In no world could I have expected tonight to go the way it did, but everything about it felt so good. So *right*.

Noa's words echo in my head. *There's another life out there waiting for you if you're brave enough to go find it.*

CHAPTER 45
AARTI

"A LIVE SHOW, HM?" Gretchen interlaces her fingers.

"A return to my roots, to that electricity that only generates when the audience knows you're speaking to them in real time," I pitch.

Gretchen leans back in her expensive leather chair. "It could be a fun gimmick to bring viewers back. But we need them to stick around past the gimmick."

"Don't worry, they will." I look at Madge and she nods along with me.

"Well, as I told Tom Hooper when he signed on to direct *Cats,* it's fine to embarrass yourself but just don't embarrass me." Gretchen pulls a fidget spinner out of her desk and gives it three twirls, then slides it back in the drawer. "He embarrassed a lot more people than himself and I will *never* get over it. *Capiche?*"

Madge and I nod even more vigorously.

We hustle out of Gretchen's office and down the hall, trying to contain our excitement.

"Phase one, done," Madge says as we enter the elevator. "Now, we plan."

. . .

For the next week, Madge, the writers, and I spend every spare moment planning the special *Up Late! Live* episode. The theme comes to me during one of our late-night mind-melds: *Unfiltered.* A celebration of people whose careers depend on their ability to think on their feet, to connect authentically with their audiences without a script or safety net.

The guest list kicks off with Brigitte Blanchette and her new girlfriend Mila, who just founded a non-profit using their runway modeling expertise to empower young women with confidence and financial literacy. Then there's Ava Garcia-Greene, the founder and ex-CEO of Gramsta who now runs The Photo Truck nationwide, whose career as an entrepreneur has hinged multiple times on her ability to talk her way out of sticky live interviews. Carmela Clauson, the Paralympic swimmer who saved the life of one of her teammates who had a medical episode in the water during a competition. Orville Madison, the trans jazz pianist whose keyboard improvisations will also soundtrack the entire live show.

"This is brilliant," Freya says, reviewing our guest list late one night in the writers' room. "They're all boundary pushers in their own way."

Madge catches my eye. She knows what I know–that every single person on this list also happens to share something else in common. But the beauty is, that's not why they're here. They're here because they're fucking brilliant at what they do.

We structure the show around improvised segments that play to each guest's strengths. Brigitte and Mila will do a fashion challenge where audience members suggest ridiculous scenarios and they have to "walk" them. Ava will crowdsource a silly startup concept from the audience and then pitch it back to viewers as if they're angel investors.

"And you?" Madge asks me quietly after Freya and the other writers have left. "When's your big moment?"

I've been thinking about it constantly.

"I'll know when it's time," I tell her. "Sometimes the best moments are the ones you don't plan."

I'm not sure if I believe myself, but I need Madge not to question me for now, and thankfully, she doesn't.

The Friday of the live show arrives faster than expected. I'm in my dressing room, hands shaking as I adjust my pantsuit.

Madge pops her head in. "Twenty minutes to showtime. You good?"

"I might not do it," I blurt out.

She steps inside, closing the door behind her. "You don't have to. The show is already going to be incredible."

"I know." My voice is barely a whisper. "But if I don't do it now, when will I?"

She squeezes my shoulder. "I'll support you no matter what. And I'll do my part to ensure the cameras keep rolling."

After she leaves, I pace my dressing room like a caged animal. My throat is dry, my palms are sweating, and I need something to ground me. Kombucha. My emergency kombucha stash will help.

I scurry back to my office and yank open the mini fridge, shoving aside bottles to reach the ginger-turmeric in the back. But my hand hits something else. A small pint container, frost-covered and forgotten.

My heart stops.

Noa must have left it there.

With trembling hands, I pry open the lid. The surface has a layer of teeny ice crystals atop it, the hallmark of being left in the freezer too long, but I grab a spoon from my desk drawer and take a bite.

The taste is familiar and nostalgic, a rich mango kulfi that's impossibly smooth and creamy. But as I dig in deeper, my spoon reveals something that makes me gasp. A swirling rainbow core.

It's the flag. My flag. Our flag.

I take another spoonful, then another, tears streaming down my face as I power through brain-freeze.

I turn the container, and on the side in Noa's dainty scribble is the name: *Sweet Talk*.

The tears flow even more. It's like Noa is here, delivering the punch herself.

That's what we were doing, wasn't it? Sweet-talking the network. Sweet-talking the world. Sweet-talking ourselves into believing we could work. And we couldn't. We didn't.

"Five minutes!" Claire calls through the door.

I dry my eyes, find a stray powder puff to address the mishap that is now my face, and ready myself.

The live show is electric from the moment I step onstage to give my opening monologue and introduce the Unfiltered theme. The audience is with me for every joke, every improvised moment, every unscripted interaction with our guests. Brigitte and Mila have the crowd screaming with their "these pants need a belt" runway walk. Ava formally announces a ludicrous new Passive Aggressive Weather app without breaking once.

I'm in my element, fueled by the sugar rush of my pre-show indulgence as well as the life-affirming panic of knowing I'm back on live television with only a three-second delay. The stage lights blind me as always, transforming the audience into an anonymous sea of laughter, which makes performing easier.

Madge stands in the wings, the only person I ever glance at while onstage, ready with her encouraging thumbs-up. Tonight is going well. I could quit while I'm ahead, but there's an urgency in the pit of my stomach thrusting me head-on into the scariest promise I've ever made to myself.

As we near the end of the show, I gather all the guests back onstage.

"Tonight has been about being unfiltered," I say, my heart hammering. "About showing up as yourself, no script, no safety net."

The audience quiets, sensing a shift.

"And I realize I've been asking my guests tonight to do something I haven't been brave enough to do myself." I take a breath. "I've been hiding behind scripts my whole life. Even when I'm improvising, I'm still playing a version of myself that feels safe, that I committed to playing long ago, for a thousand reasons that used to make so much sense to me."

Brigitte catches my eye from her spot on the couch. She knows. In fact, as my eyes travel across the stage, I suspect they all know, or at least have some inkling of what's coming. And their faces are telling me: *it's okay*.

I walk to center stage, hopeful that no one can see how badly my legs are shaking, and stare into the void of the crowd, wishing for the first time that I could actually see their faces, too. But since I can't, I just gaze into the abyss and try to conjure the face of the one person I wish was there.

"A few months ago, we launched my ice cream, *Aarti After Midnight*, with the legendary Jen & Mary's. Millions of you tuned in to watch Dr. Noa Hart work her magic during those first weeks of *Up Late*, witnessing her extraordinary gift for translating sensory snapshots of my life into a pint that represented who I am. But the ice cream we released? It was delicious, but it wasn't the real one. It wasn't the real me."

There's a wave of murmurs in the audience.

My throat tightens.

I stare out into the black. "Noa stopped herself from submitting her true masterpiece because it revealed parts of myself that I wasn't ready to own publicly. It had a secret: beneath the surface lay a symbolic swirl. Hidden, but there. Waiting for someone brave enough to dig deep.

"I don't know if you'll ever taste Noa's true creation, but I couldn't go another night without sharing my unfiltered self. Because she taught me that telling your truth doesn't have to be bitter. It can be the sweetest thing you've ever tried. So here goes."

The studio is suddenly so quiet I can hear my heartbeat in my ears. *Am I really doing this?*

I startle as a comforting hand lands on my back. I turn to see Brigitte, eyes glassy, a warm smile on her usually sardonic face. She gives me a nod, as if to say *go on, I'll be standing right beside you.* I hear the creaking of the couch as my other guests stand up and link arms on either side of me in a show of quiet solidarity.

"My name is Aarti Nair. I'm the first woman to host *Up Late.* I'm also the first Indian-American. People have been calling me a diversity hire, so I figured, why not give them their money's worth?"

The audience chuckles hesitantly. I clear my throat.

"I'm all of those things, and as of right now, I am also *Up Late*'s first openly gay host."

The audience gasps. I nod as tears pool in my eyes.

"I've been so afraid of being too much. Too brown, too female, too queer. But you know what? I am all of those things. And, frankly, pretending I'm not has been as exhausting as the mental gymnastics required to explain why I own fifty flannel shirts despite never having been camping."

Thank goddess, they laugh. Truly laugh. The weight lifts more with each passing moment, and I feel like I'm exactly where I need to be.

"The truth is, I'm rich and complex and sweet and surprising, with a rainbow heart I'm done hiding."

There's a collective thrum as people stand and clap.

I look to the wings for reassurance from Madge, only to find her back turned, in deep conversation with one of the lighting techs. Before I can question why she's checked out at the biggest moment of my career, a spotlight blazes to life in the audience, illuminating the one person I hoped against hope would be out there listening.

FOR ALL THE segments we filmed months ago, this is my first time in the bright-white pillar of a studio spotlight. I know I should feel nervous with the millions of eyes of a live national television broadcast upon me. But right now, there is only one deep brown gaze that matters, anchoring me as I slowly stand up, clutching the ridiculous bouquet of ice cream scoops that Aiden helped me cobble together after Madge reached out.

When Madge appeared at my order window that night at the soft opening, I didn't know what the interaction would be like. But the second I popped out of the truck, she pulled me into a fierce hug, complimented my new business with her hallmark enthusiasm, and bought one of each split. We didn't talk about Aarti or the premiere or anything beyond ice cream and art, but there was a knowing in her eyes, an acknowledgment of all the things we weren't saying. I figured that would be it. A nice moment of closure with someone who'd been peripheral to my heartbreak.

When she called two days ago, I almost didn't answer.

"Noa, I have something to ask you," she said without preamble. "Aarti's doing something big on Friday's live show. Really big. And I think… I think she'd want you there. Not that she knows I'm calling. She doesn't. But afterward, maybe you two could meet privately? Talk?"

My heart did gymnastics in my chest. "What's she doing?"

"I can't say. But it's–well, I'm pretty sure it's what you wanted. What you both needed."

I gripped my phone tighter. "Can I… can I be in the audience instead? If she's doing what I think she's doing, I want to be there. Not hiding backstage."

Madge was quiet for a long moment. "She might see you."

"Good."

Talking to Madge, it finally clicked: the night of the premiere I'd chosen myself, and that had been right–yet I'd misread Aarti's refusal to come out as a verdict on my value. Her hesitation was never about whether I was worth the risk; it was about whether she could withstand the quake her honesty would unleash, whether the world would still want every brilliant, complicated inch of her once it knew.

Coming out isn't a gift you hand to someone else; it's a truth you claim for yourself. Now, hearing she was ready to claim hers, I knew one more thing for sure. I'd be damned if I'd let her do it alone.

Now, watching her on that stage with shaky legs and her chin up, declaring her truth to millions, I've never been prouder of anyone in my entire life.

Aarti's eyes find mine across the distance, questioning, vulnerable. I nod, already moving toward the aisle. The crowd parts as I set down the clattering bouquet and make my way to the stage.

As I climb the steps, Aarti reaches for my hand. The moment our fingers touch, that familiar electricity ignites between us. She turns to the audience, raising our hands together.

"Ladies and gentletheys," her voice wavers with emotion, "Dr. Noa Hart. The genius who saw me before I could see myself. And who I–I had no idea she was here tonight."

The audience erupts in applause. Aarti guides me onstage, trying to untangle all of her competing emotions, live, on broadcast television. I'm impressed by her all over again.

"Wow. I can't believe you're here," she says to me, but also to everyone. "Noa Hart. She's perfect, except she's allergic to cats which is obviously a lesbian dealbreaker."

The audience laughs, and somehow, through it all, Aarti still manages to shoot me a soul-melting wink.

I clear my throat. "I'm not sure what avenues we'll need to explore to release *Sweet Talk* to the world." I turn to the audience. "Her signature rainbow swirl, of course." I turn back to Aarti. "But I've got two fairy godmothers in Jen and Mary who can probably help us navigate that. They've already helped me start my own truck."

"Truck?"

"Of the ice cream persuasion."

"No way?" Aarti lights up.

"'Split Happens'," I grin.

She laughs that full-body laugh I've missed so desperately. Then her expression softens. "You're responsible in so many ways for tonight. Do you want to say a few words to close us out?"

I turn to face the audience, still gripping Aarti's hand, which she squeezes back.

"The last time I was on this stage, I impaled myself on a diorama of LA's public transit system and exploded a canister of nitrogen."

Laughter rings out across the studio.

"But even concussed and bleeding on that seven-hundred-thousand-dollar backdrop," I continue, "I couldn't help but feel I was in exactly the right place. Sometimes you have to break everything apart to see what's at the center."

I turn back to Aarti. We communicate everything in a single

look–forgiveness, understanding, hope… permission. We both nod, ever so slightly.

"And for the record," I say, looking directly into her eyes, "I love you and your rainbow heart."

The audience explodes. But I barely hear them because Aarti pulls me close, and we're kissing on live television–not the tentative kiss of new love but the certain kiss of two people who've found their way back to each other.

"I love you, too, Noa Hart," she murmurs into my ear.

When we finally break apart, both of us crying and laughing, Aarti turns to Camera A with that mischievous grin I fell in love with.

"That's it for tonight. And possibly my entire career! Sorry to Gretchen Gordon, but… I guess that's showbiz?" she winks. "Thank you everyone!"

The credits roll, the audience is on their feet, and I'm exactly where I belong: standing beside the woman I love who makes life infinitely sweeter.

EPILOGUE
NOA

"LIVE IN FIVE!" I hear Madge call over a grip's walkie backstage.

"Can I get you anything?" Claire asks, scurrying up to me.

"Claire, you're not a PA anymore, you don't have to take care of me."

She grins. "I know, but we're forever trauma-bonded, *Hart*."

It's true: the beginnings of *Up Late! with Aarti Nair* were, erm, humbling for me, but things have gotten oh-so-much better. When Aarti came out live on air, we were in a lavender haze of adoration… for the two-point-five seconds until the lights went down and she had to face the wrath of Gretchen. Shockingly, the head woman in charge doesn't appreciate it when you go behind her back to stage a big gay bomb drop in real time on her network. Aarti and Madge took it in stride, though; they knew what they were doing was risky.

And it paid off.

Despite Gretchen blowing a gasket, the internet rejoiced. Gaartis were redeemed. Aarti's bravery was celebrated and cheered on. People who never watched late night started tuning in in droves. Jen & Mary's released the *real* Aarti flavor and made a massive donation in our name to The Comedy Closet, an

LGBTQ+ non-profit helping queer comedians pursue their dreams. Even Claire got promoted to Madge's assistant producer. And with the highest ratings in *Up Late* history, Aarti Nair became untouchable.

My Aarti Nair.

So here I stand, one year into the show that made my favorite person a household name, ready to celebrate her and her accomplishments.

As the warmup artist cracks their final joke on stage, said favorite person bursts through the backstage doors, along with her entourage of makeup artists and writers and assistants.

"Well, don't you look very important." I drink her in as she rocks the finely tailored rainbow pinstripe suit we chose with Aiden's assistance.

"This *is* my show after all," she smirks.

"Two minutes til live!" Madge shouts again.

"Nervous about another live show?"

The last one had been a roaring success, but Gretchen was hesitant to let them put on another one for obvious reasons. After a year on air with the highest ratings of a late night show on any network, she finally gave in.

"I'm never nervous with you around." She gives me a sweet, deep kiss. I still feel butterflies.

"Keep it in your pants," Madge says, making her way backstage. "You ready?"

Aarti looks at me. "Are *you* ready?"

"I'm just here for the ice cream," I say. While I've made some appearances over the last several months, Aarti wanted me to come on and let the audience try my new *Up Late*-inspired flavor, only available at Split Happens: *Butter Late Than Never*. "Which… where is my cart?"

Since I can't take my ice cream truck everywhere, I invested in a cute little cart that does the job for indoor events like these. But it seems to have wandered off with a PA.

"Here it is!" Claire interjects. "Just needed to polish it off for the camera!"

I give Aarti a look but she shrugs.

"All right team, we're live in thirty seconds," Madge says into her walkie. "I'll be in the sound booth if you need anything." She gives Aarti a wink and a nudge, then bounces off.

"You're gonna kill it!" I say giving her one last kiss.

"I know," she smiles.

Madge counts down over the walkie. "In three... two..."

With one last look at me, Aarti jogs out onto the stage to greet her audience.

"Hello and welcome to our second ever live episode of *Up Late! with Aarti Nair!*"

The audience whoops and claps.

"I'm your host Aarti Nair and we're going to do things a little differently tonight."

I raise an eyebrow at Claire. *Are they trying to pull another fast one on Gretchen?*

Claire nods back to Aarti on stage.

And she's looking right at *me*.

"Noa? Will you come on out here? Bring your ice cream," she says.

I look around in confusion–this was *not* the run-of-show I was given–but am ultimately pushed out on stage by Claire and greeted with applause.

"You all remember Noa. She's here to tell you about her latest treat. Noa?"

"Um, yeah..." I say, shooting Aarti a look, but she has zero reaction, only that aggravatingly beautiful smile on her lips. "I'm going to share a very special flavor with you all tonight called–" I open my ice cream cart.

But the ice cream is gone.

I panic and look to Aarti.

"What?" she asks.

I point wordlessly into my cart.

"Maybe look a little harder?" she says.

I roll my eyes and mock her, leaning down into my cart when I see–

"Wh–what?"

Sitting at the bottom of what once was a tub of ice cream is a small, navy box. When I look up, I no longer see Aarti.

Because she's on one knee.

"Noa Jacqueline Hart," Aarti begins, grabbing my hands. "This show brought you into my life, and I am forever grateful for that. Do me the honor of not embarrassing me in front of literal millions of people and tell me... will you marry me?"

I gasp and turn to the audience, noticing for the first time that the front row is stacked with the A-listers of my life: Aiden, my dad, Aarti's family. Even Stella is there, tears in her eyes.

I look back to Aarti who's patiently awaiting my response.

"Duh!" I cry out.

Aarti stands and twirls me around as our family fills the stage.

"Don't forget..." She leans down and picks up the box, opening it to reveal a shimmering yellow diamond ring. "I know we talked about picking one together so if you don't like it–"

"I love it. And I love you." We kiss and the applause is thunderous.

"I feel bamboozled. I can't believe you'd do this to me, Madge!" I point to the sound booth. "Are we even live?"

"Oh, yup, definitely. Which reminds me." Aarti turns to the camera. "We've gotta take a break, but we'll be right back with the new Dr. Noa Nair and me, forever bragging that I bagged a doctor!"

The ON AIR sign turns off and I still can't figure out if what just happened was real.

"We're back in one minute, people!" Madge says, running to

the stage, ripping her headset off. "I'm so happy for you two." She squeezes us both.

Aiden taps me on the shoulder and I spin around to hug him.

"I knew you were being weird, I knew it!" I tell him.

"It's very difficult to add radar blockers to twin telepathy, but I tried my darnedest. Now *please* tell me that absolute monster of a rock wasn't mined by children in the Congo?"

Aarti puts her hand on her heart. "Made in a lab, swear."

"Good girl," he nods in approval.

Diti jumps onto Aarti's back. "You did it!!!!"

She turns around to hug her sister. "Thanks for all your help."

"You, too," Diti says seriously, and I can tell she means for all the support Aarti has given her over this past year of staying sober.

"Proud of you, Nono," my dad says. I give him the tightest hug I've ever hugged.

"Love you forever and ever, Dad," I say into his shoulder.

"All right, everybody, back to your seats," Madge shoos them all off. "We're back in three... two..."

"Dr. Noa Nair, huh?" I ask Aarti as the cameras turn back to us. "That sounds *really* good to me."

I give her another kiss for the whole world to see.

You're invited! Let's celebrate our love.

14 December 2027 at 3pm
rancho del cielo
malibu, ca

dinner and (lots of)
dancing to follow

ACKNOWLEDGMENTS

Thank you to everyone who has come along for the Smokeshow journey. Our second book is just the tip of our queer entertainment iceberg; we have so much in store that we can't wait to share with the world!

To our families: thank you for everything. Sari and Richard, your support and belief in what we are doing has been unparalleled. Dick and Rhonda, for being real life sitcom inspo and for always being willing to take Ella back in if her career implodes. Ramona, for always being the first to buy our book, but more importantly, for your Tennis Channel login. Forever beholden to you. ¡Vamos!

Michael: once again, we'd *love* to thank you, but you're simply too distracting.

Jim!!! Our business dad. Your belief in us has permanently bolstered our belief in ourselves. You are the method that grounds our madness. We are endlessly indebted to you.

Wynnie and Murray, our furever besties: your tolerance of one another despite your ongoing marital dispute is nothing short of inspiring. Thank you for maintaining your poise during this very public separation.

Menitha: you legend. Thank you for reading the whole damn thing and mapping out the timeline—you saved us from countless continuity errors and mild public shame. You rule, and we can't wait to watch you take over the world.

Morgan Lee Miller, thank you for telling us hot model sex comes first. You were right.

To Nana, whose writing desk in Maine saw the birth of so many scenes, thank you.

And finally, to you, the reader: thank you for making it to the end. We hope you laughed. We hope you swooned. We hope you finished this book with your heart a little fuller than when you started (and maybe a craving for ice cream).

ABOUT THE AUTHORS

Smokeshow co-founders Rena Sapon-White and Ella Schaefer met by pure cosmic accident while developing made-for-TV romcoms. United in their mission to tell queer stories with heart, humor, and hijinks, they're also passionate about environmental causes, animal rescue, the healing power of comedy, and sapphic pop.

Their debut novel, *The Christmas Pic*, hit the top 10 in Amazon's Lesbian Fiction and won the 2024 Lesfic Bard Award for Best New Author. They're currently developing film, TV, stage, and podcast projects–so follow them on social media to stay in the loop!

Thanks for reading!

If you enjoyed this book, please rate and review on
Amazon and Goodreads!

Join our mailing list and shop merch on our website
www.smokeshow-entertainment.com.

Follow us on
Instagram: @smokeshow.press
TikTok: @sm0kesh0w.press

For an extra scene, strap in and scan the QR code below. ;)